VELIKOVSKY DESERVES TO BE RECONSIDERED!

"The latest dispatches from the front lines of physics and astronomy leave no doubt that some rewriting of the rules is in order," says **Kirkus Reviews.** "For example, Venus turns out to be a very hot planet that rotates backwards in relation to its sister planets; the earth has a magnetosphere: Jupiter is a source of radio waves; and remnant magnetism has been found in moon rocks . . . all matters predicted by Immanuel Velikovsky 25 years ago on the basis of his analysis of ancient myths and texts and his knowledge of geology and astronomy."

"**VELIKOVSKY RECONSIDERED,** a round-up of 29 articles culled from the quarterly **Pensée,** provides an exciting introduction to the controversies surrounding Immanuel Velikovsky," agrees **Publishers Weekly,** that "should reawaken interest in his bold speculations." "Great fun" is the **Birmingham News'** opinion, calling it "a courageous book, relentless in its factuality . . . you must cheer its prevailing rebelliousness."

Pensée was the magazine of the Student Academic Freedom Forum. Its publisher and chief editor respectively were David N. Talbott and Stephen L. Talbott. The magazine was published in Portland, Oregon, which is also the home of the Talbott brothers.

VELIKOVSKY RECONSIDERED

by the
Editors of *Pensée*

Editor: Stephen L. Talbott
Associate Editors:
Lewis M. Greenberg
Ralph E. Juergens
William Mullen
C. J. Ransom
Lynn E. Rose

WARNER BOOKS

A Warner Communications Company

PREFACE

COLLISIONS AND UPHEAVALS

A Fragmentary Scenario Based on Velikovsky's
Worlds in Collision and *Earth in Upheaval*

Immanuel Velikovsky manifests a strong distaste for summaries and popularizations of his books. In the past, many erroneous criticisms of his work have been based upon such popularizations, the critics never having studied his books. And indeed these books, detailed in their arguments and exhaustive in their documentation, do not easily lend themselves to summarization.

Nevertheless, in embarking on a project designed to give the fullest possible coverage of all aspects of Velikovsky's work, the editors of Pensée *felt it desirable to reacquaint readers with the flow of events described in his revolutionary reconstruction of recent solar-system history. The evidence, amassed in* Worlds in Collision *and* Earth in Upheaval, *is not presented here, and to those who have not read these works the events must necessarily appear fanciful and insupportable. This difficulty can be remedied, of course, only by direct reference to the scholarly, evidential texts of Velikovsky himself.*

The following brief sketch was prepared entirely without Velikovsky's help. The serious student and scholar should resort to a careful and intensive reading of Worlds in Collision *and* Earth in Upheaval.

Global cataclysms fundamentally altered the face of our planet more than once in historical times. The terrestrial axis shifted. Earth fled from its established orbit. The magnetic poles reversed.

In great convulsions, the seas emptied onto continents, the planet's crust folded, and volcanos erupted into mountain chains. Lava flows up to a mile thick spilled out over vast areas of the Earth's surface. Climates changed suddenly, ice settling over lush vegetation, while green meadows and forests were transformed into deserts.

In a few awful moments, civilizations collapsed. Species were exterminated in continental sweeps of mud, rock, and sea. Tidal waves crushed even the largest beasts, tossing their bones into tangled heaps in the valleys and rock fissures, preserved beneath mountains of sediment. The mammoths of Siberia were instantly frozen and buried.

Surviving generations recorded these events by every means available: in myths and legends, temples and monuments to the planetary gods, precise charts of the heavens, sacrificial rites, astrological canons, detailed records of planetary movements, and tragic lamentations amid fallen cities and destroyed institutions.

"ALL IS RUIN"

Aware of a link between the circuit of heavenly bodies and the catastrophic ruin of previous generations, the ancients ceaselessly watched the planetary movements. Their traditions recalled that when old epochs dissolved, the new "Age," or "Sun," was marked by different celestial paths. Astronomers and seers diligently watched for any change which might augur approaching destruction and the end of an age.

Prior to the second millennium B.C., ancient Hindu records spoke of four visible planets, excluding Venus. Babylonians, meticulous in their observations, likewise failed to report Venus.

But long before 1500 B.C., Jupiter, for centuries chief among the deities, shattered the serenity of the skies. A brilliant, fiery object, expelled from that planet, entered upon a long elliptical orbit around the Sun. The feared god Jupiter had given birth to the comet and protoplanet Venus.

Terrified, men watched the "bright torch of heaven" as it traversed its elongated orbit, menacing the Earth.

Venus, a Chinese astronomical text recalls, spanned the heavens, rivaling the Sun in brightness. "The brilliant light of Venus," records an ancient rabbinical source, "blazes from one end of the cosmos to the other."

The fears of the star watchers were justified. As Venus arched away from one perihelion passage during the middle of the second millennium B.C. (ca. −1450), the Earth approached this intruder, entering first the outer reaches of its cometary tail. A rusty ferruginous dust filtered down upon the globe, imparting a bloody hue to land and sea. The fine pigment chafed human skin, and men were overcome by sickness. Those who sought to drink could not. Rivers stank from the rotting carcasses of fish, and men dug desperately for water uncontaminated by the alien dust. "Plague is throughout the land. Blood is everywhere," bewailed the Egyptian Ipuwer. "Men shrink from tasting, human beings thirst after water. . . . That is our water! That is our happiness! What shall we do in respect thereof? All is ruin."

As recalled by the Babylonians, the blood of the celestial monster Tiamat poured out over the world.

But as the Earth's path carried it ever more deeply into the comet's tail, the rain of particles grew steadily more coarse and perilous. Soon a great hail of gravel pelted the Earth. ". . . there was hail, and fire mingled with the hail, very grievous, such as there was none like it in all the land of Egypt since it became a nation." So recorded the author of *Exodus*.

Fleeing from the torrent of meteorites, men abandoned their livestock to the holocaust. Fields of grain which fed great cities perished. Cried Ipuwer, "No fruits, no herbs are found. That has perished which yesterday was seen. The land is left to its weariness like the cutting of flax." These things happened, say the Mexican *Annals of Cuauhtitlan,* when the sky "rained, not water, but fire, and red-hot stones."

As our planet plunged still deeper into the comet's tail, hydrocarbon gases enveloped the Earth, exploding in bursts of fire in the sky. Unignited trains of petroleum poured onto the planet, sinking into the surface and floating on the seas. From Siberia to the Caucasus to the Arabian desert, great spills of naphtha burned for years, their billows of smoke lending a dark shroud for human despair.

Our planet was pursuing a near-collision course with the massive comet's head.

Suddenly, caught in an invisible grip, the Earth rocked violently; its axis tilted. In a single convulsed moment, cities were laid waste, great buildings of stone leveled, and populations decimated.

"The towns are destroyed. Upper Egypt has become waste. . . . All is ruin. . . . The residence is overturned in a minute." Around the world, oceans rushed over mountains and poured into continental basins. Rivers flowed upward. Islands sank into the sea. Displaced strata crashed together, while the shifting Earth generated a global hurricane which destroyed forests and swept away the dwellings of men.

In China, the Emperor Yahou spoke of waters which "overtopped the great heights, threatening the heavens with their floods." Decades of labor were required to drain the valleys of the mainland. Arabia was transformed into a desert by the same paroxysms which may have dropped the legendary Atlantis beneath the ocean west of Gibraltar.

With dulled senses, survivors lay in a trance for days, choking in the smoky air.

The tilting axis left a portion of the world in protracted darkness, another in extended day. From the Americas to Europe to the Middle East, records tell of darkness persisting for several days. On the edge of the darkness, the peoples of Iran witnessed a threefold night and a threefold day. Chinese sources speak of a holocaust during which the Sun did not set for many days and the land was aflame. Peoples and nations everywhere, uprooted by disaster, wandered from their homelands.

CELESTIAL DRAGON

Led by Moses, the Israelites fled the devastation which brought Egypt's Middle Kingdom to an end. As they rushed toward the Sea of Passage, the glistening comet, in form like a dragon's head, shone through the tempest of dust and smoke. The night sky glowed brightly as the comet's head and its writhing, serpentine tail exchanged gigantic electrical bolts.

The great battle between the fiery comet's head and the column of smoke—between a light god and a leviathan serpent—was memorialized in primary myths around the Earth. Babylonians told of Marduk striking the dragon Tiamat with bolts of fire. The Egyptians saw Isis and Set in deadly combat. The Hindus described Vishnu battling the "crooked serpent." Zeus, in the account of Apollodorus, struggled with the coiled viper Typhon.

The fugitive Israelites, having reached Pi-ha-khiroth, at the edge of the Red Sea, were pursued by the Pharaoh Taoui-Thom (Typhon). The great sea lay divided before the slave people, its waters lifted by the movement of the Earth and the pull of the comet. Crossing the dry sea bottom, the Israelites escaped from Egypt.

As the comet made its closest approach to Earth, Taoui-Thom moved his armies into the sea bed. But even before the entire band of Israelites had crossed to the far side, a giant electrical bolt flew between the two planets. Instantly, the waters collapsed. The Pharaoh, his soldiers and chariots, and those Israelites who still remained between the divided waters were cast furiously into the air and consumed in a seething whirlpool.

The battle in the sky raged for weeks. A column of smoke by day, a pillar of fire by night, Venus meted destruction to nations large and small. To the Israelites, however, it was an instrument of national salvation.

Through a series of close approaches, the comet's tail, a dreadful shadow of death, cinctured the Earth, wreathing the planet in a thick, gloomy haze that lasted for many years. And so, in darkness, a historical age ended.

Possibly, the human race would have become extinct, but for a mysterious, life-giving substance precipitated in the heavy atmosphere—the nourishing "manna" and "ambrosia" described in the ancient records of all peoples. It fell with the morning dew, a sweet, yellowish hoarfrost. It was edible. The ambrosial carbohydrates, possibly derived from Venus' hydrocarbons through bacterial action, filled the atmosphere with a sweet fragrance. Streams flowed with "milk and honey." When heated, this "bread of heaven" dissolved, but when cooled, it precipitated into grains which could be preserved for long periods or ground between stones. Its presence allowed man and beast to survive.

In the new age the Sun rose in the east, where formerly it set. The quarters of the world were displaced. Seasons no longer came in their proper times. "The winter is come as summer, the months are reversed, and the hours are disordered," reads an Egyptian papyrus. The Chinese Emperor Yahou sent scholars throughout the land to locate north, east, west, and south and draw up a new calendar. Numerous records tell of the Earth "turning over." An Egyptian inscription from before the tumult says that the Sun "riseth in the west."

While men attempted to determine the times and seasons, Venus continued on its threatening course around the Sun. Under Joshua, the Israelites had entered the Promised Land, and again Venus drew near. It was while the Canaanites fled from before the hand of Joshua in the valley of Beth-horon—some fifty years after the Exodus —that the daughter of Jupiter unleashed her fury a second time. "The Lord cast down great stones from heaven upon them unto Azekah, and they died." The terrestrial axis tilted. Once more, the Earth quaked fiercely. Cities burned and fell to the ground. Above Beth-horon, the Sun stood still for hours. On the other side of the Earth, chroniclers recorded a prolonged night, lit only by the burning landscape. This occurred, Mexican records report, about fifty years after an earlier destruction.

As in its first encounter with the young comet, the Earth's surface was torn with great rifts and clefts, and hurricanes scoured the land. Strata pressed against strata, rising thunderously into mountains or engulfing cities. But the Earth and some of its inhabitants survived.

Anticipating renewed devastation following another fifty-year period, nations bowed down before the great fire goddess. With bloody orgies and incantations, they enjoined the dreaded queen of the heavens to remain far removed from the human abode. "How long wilt thou tarry, O lady of heaven and earth?" inquired the Babylonians. "We sacrifice unto Tistrya," declared a priest in Iran, "the bright and glorious star, whose rising is watched by the chiefs of deep understanding."

In both hemispheres, men fixed their gaze anxiously on the comet as, for centuries, it continued its circuit, crossing the orbits of both Earth and Mars. Before the middle of the eighth century B.C., astrologers observed dramatic irregularities in its wanderings. Viewed from Babylonia, Venus rose, disappeared in the west for over nine months, then reappeared in the east. Dipping below the eastern horizon, it was not seen again for over two months, until it shone in the west. The following year, Venus vanished in the west for eleven days before reappearing in the east.

But this time it was Mars, not Earth, that endured a cosmic jolt. Passing by the smaller orb, Venus pulled Mars off its orbit, sending it on a path that endangered the Earth. A new agent of destruction was born in the unstable solar system.

This occurred in the days of Uzziah, King of Jerusalem. (Lucian, the *Bamboo Books* of China, the Hindu *Surya-Siddhanta*, the Aztec Huitzilopochtli epos, the Indo-Iranian *Bundahish*, etc., describe the reordering of Mars's and Venus' orbits.) Aware of the baleful meaning of irregular celestial motions, the prophet Amos, echoed by other observers of the sky, warned of new cosmic upheavals. Events soon vindicated the pessimistic seers.

As Mars drew near, the Earth reeled on its hinges. West of Jerusalem, half a mountain split off and fell eastward; flaming seraphim leaped skyward. Men were tossed into streets filled with debris and mutilated bodies. Buildings crumbled, and the Earth opened up.

These cataclysms were associated with the founding of Rome (placed by Fabius Pictor at 747 B.C.) and with the death of Rome's legendary founder, Romulus. "Both the poles shook," Ovid relates, "and Atlas shifted the burden of the sky. . . . The sun vanished and rising clouds obscured the heaven. . . ." Mars, the lord of war, became the national god of Rome.

Much smaller than Earth, Mars could not equal Venus in destructive power. But again the Earth altered its course around the Sun. The old calendar, with 360-day years and 30-day months, became outdated. Emperors and kings directed their astrologers to develop a new calendar.

BATTLE OF THE GODS

Mars and Venus now competed for the allegiance of men. Tribes moved from their homelands, confronting new enemies while petitioning Mars or Venus for a swift victory. Cities and temples were dedicated to the two planetary gods who determined the fate of nations.

The era of conflict between Mars and Earth continued until 687 (or possibly 686) B.C. Hebrew prophets after 747 B.C. cried apocalyptically of upheavals yet to come. Reminding the Israelites of their passage out of Egypt, they declared that once more the whole Earth would quake, the Moon turn to blood, the Sun darken, and the Earth be consumed in blood, fire, and pillars of smoke.

The catastrophe, as Mars hurtled past the Earth, came in the year 721 B.C., on the day Jerusalem's King Ahaz was buried. Under the influence of Mar's passage, the Earth's axis tilted and the poles shifted. Earth's orbit swung wider, lengthening the year.

Israelites observed the Sun hastening by several hours to a premature setting. Thereafter, the solar disk made its way across the sky 10 degrees farther to the south.

Seneca records that on the Argive plain, in Greece, the early sunset came amid great upheaval. The tyrant Thyestes beckoned the entire universe to dissolve. The Great Bear dipped below the horizon. In the days which followed, states Seneca, "The Zodiac, which, making passage through the sacred stars, crosses the zones obliquely, guide and sign-bearer for the slow-moving years, falling itself, shall see the fallen constellations."

Once a peaceful, barely noticed planet, but now the "king of battle," Mars was still not finished with his work of destruction. In 687 B.C., a powerful Assyrian army led by Sennacherib marched toward Judah. On the evening of March 23, the first night of the Hebrew Passover, when Sennacherib and his army camped close to Jerusalem, Mars made a last, fateful approach to the Earth.

A great thunderbolt—a "blast from heaven"—charred the soldiers' bodies, leaving their garments intact. The dead numbered 185,000. Ashurbanipal, Sennacherib's grandson, later recalled "the perfect warrior" Mars, "the lord of the storm, who brings defeat."

The same night, March 23, 687 B.C., in China, the *Bamboo Books* reveal, a disturbance of the planets caused them to go "out of their courses. In the night, stars fell like rain. The Earth shook." Romans would celebrate the occasion: "The most important role in the (Roman) cult of Mars appears to be played by the festival of *Tubilustrium* on the twenty-third day of March."

The Sun retreated by several hours. In certain longitudes the solar disk, which had just risen, returned below the horizon. In others, the setting Sun retraced its course, rising in the sky. The Hebrews witnessed the prolonged night of Sennacherib's destruction.

The Sun's retreat, due to a 10 degree tilt of the Earth's axis, corrected the axis shift of 721 B.C. "So the sun returned ten degrees, by which degrees it was gone down," reads Isaiah 38.8.

From one continent to another, men, oppressed with terror, watched Mars battle Venus in the sky, speed fiercely toward the Earth bringing blasts of fire, retreat, and engage Venus once more. Perhaps the most startling literary account of this *theomachy*, or battle of gods, is contained in Homer's *Iliad*. (Velikovsky's revised chronology places Homer later than 747 B.C.) As the Greeks besieged Troy, Athena (Venus) "would utter her loud cry. And over against her spouted Ares [Mars], dread as a dark whirlwind. . . . All the roots of many-founted Ida were shaken, and all her peaks." The river "rushed with surging flood" and "The fair streams seethed and boiled."

Mars was thrown out of the ring; Venus emerged a tame planet pursuing a near-circular orbit between Mercury and Earth. Where once it ranged high to the zenith, now it became the morning and evening star, never retreating more than 48° from the Sun. Isaiah, who had witnessed the planet's destructive power, sang of its disgrace: "How are thou fallen from heaven, O Lucifer, son of morning! How art thou cut down to the ground, which didst weaken the nations! For thou hast said in thine heart, I will ascend into heaven, I will exalt my throne above the stars of God."

CONTENTS

INTRODUCTION

This collection of papers from the pages of *Pensée** is but a sampling of an ongoing and expanding discussion triggered a quarter of a century ago by the publication of Immanuel Velikovsky's *Worlds in Collision*. As the Preface to this book recalls, the dominant celestial character and immediate cause of all the turmoil in the inner solar system during the near millennium of history reconstructed in Velikovsky's book was Venus—a planet now orbiting the Sun on the most nearly circular path in the entire system of planets and clearly a threat to no other body. Could this beautiful object in our skies be the same as that which Velikovsky describes as one of antiquity's most feared gods?

When *Worlds in Collision* first appeared, the attribution of such a violent recent history to a planet widely regarded as essentially another Earth seemed perverse in the extreme. From what was then known of Venus, many astronomers felt justified in describing it as the Earth's sister planet. Of course, as might be expected for an alien world, Venus presented a few puzzles: Its surface lay hidden from earthly view beneath a perennially impenetrable cloud cover; its quarter phases (disk half-

---

* *Pensée* magazine, an organ of the Student Academic Freedom Forum (P. O. Box 414, Portland, Ore. 97207), published ten issues during 1972–74 under the title "Immanuel Velikovsky Reconsidered." The papers assembled here are selected from the first several issues of that series, and are intended to serve as an introduction to one historical phase of the discussion of Velikovsky's work.

illuminated) occurred typically too soon or too late to agree with the schedules worked out by astronomers; its atmosphere seemed to contain three hundred times as much carbon dioxide as the Earth's; and there were known to be several further points of obvious difference from the Earth. But even so, twentieth-century astronomers frequently pointed to Venus as the most logical place to search for extraterrestrial life.

"Of all the planets, Venus is most like the earth. It is the one which comes nearest to us, excepting our moon and some of the little bodies called 'asteroids' or minor planets. Eight-tenths as massive, more highly reflecting, and two-thirds as far from the sun as the earth, Venus seems more fit on many accounts than any other of the planets to support life similar to ours." (C. G. Abbot, *The Earth and the Stars* [New York: Van Nostrand, 1925], p. 72.)

But then along came Velikovsky, arguing that Venus was born from Jupiter in a violent event less than ten thousand years ago, that it rampaged through the inner solar system as a comet for an unspecified length of time, that it finally (ca. -1500) came into conflict with the Earth on at least two occasions, that it proceeded to eject Mars from its orbit so that Mars began to menace the Earth, and that Venus thereafter settled into its present orbit, neatly and safely positioned between the orbits of Mercury and Earth. More than one reviewer of *Worlds in Collision* suggested that Velikovsky's impact on the science of astronomy was every bit as calamitous as the events he attributed to the injection of Venus into the inner solar system.

On the basis of his historical researches, however, Velikovsky was quite prepared to stake his work to a large extent on its implications for astronomy, and more particularly for newcomer Venus itself.

THE HEAT OF VENUS

A puzzling observation of the 1920s was that the dark hemisphere of Venus seemed to radiate as much heat as the sunlit hemisphere. In *Worlds in Collision*, Velikovsky called attention to this matter and to the single explanation offered up to that time: Venus must rotate fast enough to keep its nights too short for significant cooling to take place. This was permissible speculation, since the dense clouds of the planet prevent direct observation of its surface, and its period of rotation was therefore unknown. But spectrographic evidence acquired about the same time as the thermal findings seemed to rule out a short period of rotation; there was no detectable shifting of spectral lines at the limbs of the planetary disk, as would be the case if one limb were moving toward and the other away from the Earth due to rapid rotation. Right up to the publication of Velikovsky's book, the conflicting thermal and spectroscopic evidence constituted a scientific mystery.

"In reality," however, wrote Velikovsky, "there is no conflict between the two methods of physical observation. The night side of Venus radiates heat because Venus is hot. . . . Venus experienced in quick succession its birth and expulsion under violent conditions; an existence as a comet on an ellipse which approached the sun closely; two encounters with the earth accompanied by discharges of potentials between these two bodies and with a thermal effect caused by conversion of momentum into heat; a number of contacts with Mars, and probably also with Jupiter. Since all this happened between the third and first millennia before the present era, the core of the planet Venus must still be hot." (*Worlds in Collision,* "The Thermal Balance of Venus.")

As it turned out, this was one of the earliest of Velikovsky's advance claims to be verified by independent research and, possibly for that very reason, it has been one of the most disparaged of his many successful predictions.

In the *Irish Astronomical Journal* for June 1956, astronomer Ernst Öpik reported that "Pettit and Nicholson [the astronomers who discovered the thermal excess of the dark side of Venus] have recently revised their radiometric observations [which initially pegged the dark-side temperature at −25° C], made between 1923 and 1928 at Mount Wilson. They arrive at a temperature of 240° K or −33° C for the *dark* side and −38° C for the *sunlit* side." Notice that Pettit and Nicholson's results give a dark-side temperature actually higher than that of the daylight hemisphere, as emphasized by Öpik's use of italics.

Ironically, just about the time Öpik's report was being circulated, radio astronomers were announcing that Venus has a temperature "higher than boiling water" (New York *Times,* June 5, 1956). Of course, the radio emissions, presumably from deeper in the atmosphere than the infrared emissions detected by Pettit and Nicholson, did not invalidate the figures cited by Öpik. The point is, however, that just when temperature estimates for Venus based on one set of observations were being revised downward, the first evidence that Venus is really a very hot place was coming to light.

Nearly two decades have passed since radio astronomers turned up the first indications of Venus' extraordinary surface temperature, and the fact has become so familiar as to be treated in rather cavalier fashion by a new generation of astronomers. But it is important to recall that this finding was contrary to the expectations of everyone except Velikovsky.

Remarks made at the time establish this beyond doubt. For example, in discussing the history of radio astronomy in *Physics Today* for April 1961, Frank D. Drake of the National Radio Astronomy Observatory wrote: "One of the earliest surprises was the unexpectedly strong radio emission from the planet Venus . . . very much greater —about three times more—than had been expected. . . . We would have expected a temperature only slightly greater than that of the earth, whereas the actual temperature is several hundred degrees above the boiling point of water. . . ."

And Cornell Mayer of the U. S. Naval Research Laboratory commented in *Scientific American* for May 1961: "The radio emission of Venus . . . [is] consistent with a temperature of almost 600 degrees [F]. . . . The temperature is much higher than anyone would have predicted. . . ."

Mayer emphasized that the radio measurements up to that time (1961) gave "the temperature mainly of the dark side of Venus." But it was not long before a similarly high temperature for the sunlit side was demonstrated. In *Nature* for September 1, 1962, Drake reported observations of the planet near superior conjunction that indicated surface temperatures upward of 600° K and therefore "there is little surface temperature difference btween the illuminated and dark hemispheres of Venus."

During the 1960s, successive studies of the temperature of Venus merely compounded the problem; nearly every new estimate raised the temperature. Even on the basis of some of the earlier estimates near 600° K, R. B. Owen pointed out (NASA Technical Note D-2527, 1965) that "since the melting points of aluminum, lead, tin, magnesium, zinc, and bismuth might be reached, pools of molten surface material could cover much of the [surface of Venus]." And today the favored figure is 750° K.

Velikovsky's detractors have displayed a penchant for arguing that his term, "hot," is not quantitative enough to warrant recognition of his claim as a valid prediction. An early instance of this appears in an article by astronomer Donald H. Menzel, then director of Harvard College Observatory, on "The Debate over Velikovsky" (*Harper's* magazine, December 1963): "As to the 'high temperature' of Venus, 'hot' is only a relative term. For example, liquid air is hot, relative to liquid helium; the sun's surface is cold, relative to the star Sirius, and so on. Hence, to see what Velikovsky implied by 'hot' we turn to his own work, *Worlds in Collision,* last chapter. Here he refers to actual astronomical observations of the infrared radiation from Venus, which showed that the dark side of Venus was just as hot as the sunlit side. The measured temperatures were comfortably warm, not 800° F."

Menzel obscures the issue by stating, incompletely, one fact too many (if one concedes it a fact that −25° C is a comfortably "warm" temperature). The infrared radiation from Venus indeed indicates temperatures in the neighborhood of −25° C (or −38° C)—but for the tops of the clouds, not for the body of the planet; the actual temperatures inferred are thus entirely irrelevant, and by mentioning them Menzel sidesteps the whole point of Velikovsky's argument. The point is that if the planet rotates slowly, as the spectroscopic evidence indicates, then the relative constancy of the cloud-top temperatures from sunlit to dark-side hemispheres implies that the heat source maintaining those temperatures is not the Sun, but is, instead, the "hot" body concealed within the clouds.

Menzel is quite correct in suggesting that one ought to turn to Velikovsky's work to see what he means by "hot." And in this context, the term "hot" would appear to be as quantitative as the data behind it would bear. Indeed, had Velikovsky offered some precise estimate of the temperature of Venus, he would surely have been criticized for drawing a conclusion far too specific for the nature of his data.

From any objective point of view, Velikovsky's entire treatment of the history of Venus makes abundantly clear what he had in mind. His sources describe the planet (or protoplanet) as incandescent only a few thousand years ago, rivaling the Sun in brightness. In the very paragraph where he states that "Venus must still be hot" he lists his reasons for drawing this conclusion: a violent birth, close approaches to the Sun; and encounters with Earth, Mars, and "probably Jupiter" in which electrical discharges took place and in which kinetic energy was converted to heat. In another connection, also in *Worlds in Collision* ("The Gases of Venus"), he writes: "On the basis of this research, I assume that Venus must be rich in petroleum gases. If and as long as Venus is too hot for the liquefaction of petroleum, the hydrocarbons will circulate in gaseous form." Volatilities of many common hydrocarbons are such that, at atmospheric pressure on Earth, temperatures in the hundreds of degrees Fahrenheit are required to "boil" them; on Venus, where the atmospheric pressure at the surface is nearly a hundred times that on Earth, distillation temperatures would be correspondingly higher.

THE GREENHOUSE THEORY

As early as 1940, at least one astronomer considered the possibility that the surface of Venus might be uncomfortably hot. Rupert Wildt of Yale University Observatory suggested (*Astrophysical Journal,* 91, 266) that the carbon dioxide known to be abundant in the planet's atmosphere might trap solar radiation—admit light in the visible part of the spectrum, but inhibit the escape of infrared rays emitted by light-heated surfaces—and thus generate higher temperatures than would otherwise be expected, by a "greenhouse effect." Wildt predicted a surface temperature of 135° C (275° F).

This is obviously not the kind of temperature Velikovsky had in mind when he wrote *Worlds in Collision,* nor is it anything like the actual surface temperature of Venus measured by Soviet landers in recent years. And Wildt's moderately high temperature was not even accepted by many astronomers at the time, for it was thought to be much *too high.* Cornell Mayer, in his *Scientific American* article on "The Temperatures of the Planets," (May 1961), cites Kuiper's estimate of 170° F (77° C) as the maximum possible due to the greenhouse effect on Venus.

In the late 1950s and early 1960s, as it gradually but unmistakably became apparent that Venus is actually much hotter than even Wildt had imagined, the greenhouse theory was resurrected and modified in various attempts to account for the phenomenon in non-Velikovskian terms. An "enhanced" greenhouse effect was proposed by Carl Sagan in 1960 (*Astrophysical Journal,* 65, 352), and a decade later a "runaway" greenhouse effect was suggested by S. I. Rasool and C. de Bergh (*Nature,* 226 [1970], 1037).

Both these proposals depend upon reinforcement of the carbon-dioxide effect by additional entrapment of heat by water vapor not known, but simply postulated, to be present in the lower atmosphere.

Sagan, in his recent book, *The Cosmic Connection* (1973), defends his hypothesis and states unequivocally that Venus is heated by the greenhouse mechanism, and that both carbon dioxide and water are available to do the job (p. 51). No less self-assured was his statement on the same subject at the AAAS symposium on "Velikovsky's Challenge to Science" (1974): "The atmosphere [of Venus] has a surface pressure about 90 times that of the Earth and is composed primarily of carbon dioxide. The large abundance of carbon dioxide, plus the smaller quantities of water vapor which have been detected on Venus, are adequate to heat the surface to the observed temperature via the greenhouse effect. The Venera 8 descent module, the first spacecraft to land on the illuminated hemisphere of Venus, found it light at the surface, and the Soviet experimenters concluded that the amount of light reaching the surface and the atmosphere constitution were together adequate to drive the required radiative-convection greenhouse. Velikovsky is certainly mistaken when he says 'light does not penetrate the cloud cover' and is probably mistaken when he says 'greenhouse effect could not explain so high a temperature.' "

But how convincing are the Venera 8 findings? The craft landed at a point on Venus where the Sun at the moment was only about six degrees above the horizon. The investigators assumed that the very dim light detected there was indeed sunlight—not, for example, light from the glowing surface, reflected back from the unbroken cloud deck overhead—and that therefore the average illumination on the sunlit hemisphere must be about five times the measured illumination. On the basis of this fivefold amplification of their actual findings they conclude that the greenhouse mechanism is feasible (cf. M. Ya. Marov *et al., Icarus,* 20 [1973], 407–21).

The Venera 8 results are questioned on other grounds too. A. A. Lacis and J. E. Hansen of Goddard Institute for Space Studies find them so ambiguous as to leave many important questions unanswered, and in particular those most pertinent to the greenhouse hypothesis (*Science,* 184 [31 May 1974], 979–82).

So sunlight may or may not penetrate to the surface of Venus. If it actually does, what of the water vapor that the greenhouse model requires to do the major part of the job in trapping thermal radiation and raising the surface temperature?

After an intensive microwave study of Venus, M. A. Janssen and several colleagues at the Radio Astronomy Laboratory of the University of California at Berkeley report (*Science,* 179 [9 March 1973], 994), that they find "no evidence of water vapor in the lower atmosphere of Venus." They add that "it remains to be shown that a 'greenhouse' mechanism can be supported with the present constraints on the water vapor content."

Clearly, two of the most important postulates of the greenhouse model—sunlight of consequence reaching the surface of Venus, and water vapor in the atmosphere—remain very much in doubt, in spite of Sagan's confident assertions to the contrary. And there is another matter, seldom mentioned by the greenhouse proponents, that is just as vexing to their hypothesis.

If the Sun is the ultimate source of the heat of Venus, the input of energy must always be confined to the sunlit hemisphere. Since Venus is now known to rotate very slowly, so that a night on that planet is as long as fifty-eight Earth days, it is reasonable to expect, as I. I. Shapiro has pointed out (*Science*, 159 [8 March 1967], 1124), "larger temperature differentials between day and night" on Venus than on Earth. Even if it is assumed that heat generated on the sunlit hemisphere is convected and conducted to the dark side of the planet, something less than 100-per-cent efficiency must also be assumed, and the dark side should therefore be observably cooler than the sunlit side.

We have already noted that Pettit and Nicholson, observing infrared radiation from near the top of the cloud deck, actually found the dark hemisphere at a higher temperature than the illuminated hemisphere. We have also seen that Drake's early radio studies indicated essentially equal day and night temperatures for the surface. However, later radio investigations at various wavelengths turned up less-definitive results and seemed to hold out a measure of hope for the greenhouse theory.

In 1967 and 1968, at the suggestion of Sagan, David Morrison, then connected with Harvard College Observatory and Smithsonian Astrophysical Observatory, undertook to settle this issue with intensive observations of Venus' radio emission at various phases of illumination. After "more than 100 hours of observing time," he reported (*Science*, 163 [21 February 1969], 815–17), that he could find no phase effect. He offered excuses for his findings by suggesting that the emissions he monitored, at a wavelength of 1.95 centimeters, "must originate

27

primarily in the lower atmosphere and not in the sub-surface of the planet," as he had initially supposed when he selected that wavelength. On this basis, he termed his findings "not surprising" and concluded his report with the wry suggestion that "it is still possible to expect a phase effect at wavelengths longer than 5 cm, where, according to recent atmospheric models . . . , the radiation arises primarily in the subsurface of Venus rather in the atmosphere."

In the years since Morrison's report was published, however, no such phase effect has yet been observed, and the greenhouse theory rests in limbo on this score, too. Nevertheless, in 1974 Morrison spoke at the McMaster University symposium on "Velikovsky and the Recent History of the Solar System" and insisted: "Those who have made recent quantitative studies of the mechanism for producing such high temperatures [on Venus] are virtually all in agreement that the high infrared opacity of the atmosphere provides the explanation (the 'greenhouse effect')."

The entire premise of a "runaway greenhouse" has been severely challenged by British astronomer V. A. Firsoff (*Astronomy and Space,* Vol. 2 [1973] No. 3): "Increasing the mass of the atmosphere may intensify the greenhouse effect, but it must also reduce the proportion of solar energy reaching the surface, while the total of the available energy must be distributed over a larger mass and volume. Indeed, if the atmosphere of Venus amounts to 75 air-masses, . . . the amount of solar energy per unit mass of this atmosphere will be about 0.01 of that available on the Earth. Such an atmosphere would be strictly comparable to our seas and remain stone-cold, *unless the internal heat of Venus were able to keep it at temperatures corresponding to the brightness temperatures derived from the microwave emission* [emphasis added]."

VELIKOVSKY'S HOT VENUS

Though Firsoff is in no sense a supporter of Velikovsky (and indeed prefers to deny the evidence that Venus is hot, since he assumes Venus to be as old as the solar system and therefore just *cannot* still retain natal heat), his comment is entirely pertinent. If the surface of Venus is as hot as the microwave emission implies (and this seems beyond any doubt on the basis of the Venera 7 and Venera 8 temperature measurements), then it must be because the internal heat of Venus is able to keep it that way. We are left with Velikovsky's thesis as the only explanation that accords not only with observational facts but with physical theory as well.

In his 1961 review of "Radio Emission from the Planets" (*Physics Today,* April 1961), Drake argued that "sources of internal heating will not produce an enhanced surface temperature simply because the conductivity of the atmosphere itself is very high compared with any conductivity we can imagine for the outer portions of the planetary body, and would carry away heat conducted to the surface too quickly to allow significant rise in surface temperature." This argument is probably generally valid, although several years later it was proposed (G. T. Davidson and A. D. Anderson, *Science,* 156 [1967], 1729) that Venus' high temperature could be due to a high rate of conduction of heat from interior sources. It is important to notice, however, that these writers all speak of heat that is *produced*—e.g., through radioactivity—and not of heat that is *residual,* having been deposited by external causes and events.

This is not to say that two kinds of "heat" are at issue. The point is that in Velikovsky's view Venus is a heat reservoir that was filled with heat, so to speak, only a few thousand years ago. Presumably, this heat is continually conducted to the surface from below, and from there it is continually conducted into the atmosphere and ultimately dissipated into the interplanetary medium. But the process has been going on for so short a time that Venus' surface, even though it must be cooling as the supply of internal heat dwindles, is still at a temperature in the neighborhood of 750° K. (See Velikovsky's paper "Is Venus' Heat Decreasing?" in Part V of this volume.)

A recent discovery concerning Venus lends further, if indirect, support to the idea that the Earth's "sister" planet is much hotter on the inside than could conceivably be the case if it were billions of years old. In 1973, the radar mapping team at Jet Propulsion Laboratory made headlines with the announcement that the surface of Venus is cratered. All the craters observed, however, were peculiarly shallow; one, about a hundred miles in diameter, was observed to be only about one quarter of a mile deep. In the total area of observation—about the size of Alaska—a dozen large craters were identified, but the total geographical relief observed amounted to "no more than about 3,300 feet," according to Richard M. Goldstein, head of the mapping team (*Science News,* 104 [August 4, 1973], 72–73).

At the news conference at which the JPL team's findings were first announced, Harold Masursky of the U. S. Geological Survey suggested that the shallow craters could well indicate that Venus is still hot enough internally to have only a thin crust—a crust too weak to support high crater rims.

Still more recently, Mariner 10 relayed to Earth suggestive evidence in a similar vein: Venus is *extraordinarily round.* ". . . Venus is shaped far more like the classic globe than is the earth, which is flattened by its spinning. . . . If [Venus] ever did rotate more rapidly, either that was when the planet was still a plastic, molten mass, or else Venus is a much less rigid body than the earth, capable of returning to its more spherical shape as it slows down" (*Science News,* 105 [February 16, 1974], 100–1).

Thus the figure as well as the surface features of Venus, to the extent those features are known, support the idea that the planet is extremely hot on the inside, and that this is the explanation for its high surface temperature.

On balance, Velikovsky's history of Venus seems much more concordant with the known facts about the heat of Venus than any rival explanation that has yet been put forward. What his view lacks in quantitative terms, it more than makes up for by leaving no single item of observable evidence to be explained away by some entirely unrelated hypothesis.

We have gone into this matter of the heat of Venus in considerable detail here because it illustrates not only the apparent pertinence of Velikovsky's thesis to a phenomenon he predicted long before it was discovered, but also the extremes to which his opponents still go to deny him recognition for his achievements. In the pages of this book, the reader will encounter many similar incidents—and some illuminating discussion of issues still unresolved—all of which must inevitably raise the question: Why is it that whenever Velikovsky's ideas appear vindicated on one count or another, establishment scientists find it expedient to resort to every sort of *ad hoc* theorizing rather than concede that the available evidence lends credence to those ideas?

The editors of *Pensée* have no satisfactory answer to this question to offer here. What we do offer is a record of the discussion to date of certain aspects of Velikovsky's work and the reception it has received at the hands of scientists.

Ralph E. Juergens
1974

PART I

The full story of the reception of Velikovsky's revolutionary world view will one day surely fill many volumes in the telling. Some of the salient features of this strange story were revealed in 1963, when the *American Behavioral Scientist* devoted an entire issue (September) to a review of, and commentary on, the disturbing events of the first dozen or so years following the appearance of *Worlds in Collision*. That bare-bones account was partially updated in 1966, when the same material was amplified and published as a book, *The Velikovsky Affair*. The April 1967 issue of the *Yale Scientific Magazine*—another special issue devoted entirely to Velikovsky—further documented the story of scientific misbehavior then still unfolding. *Pensée* took up the cause of seeking fair play for Velikovsky in 1972 and still pursues that goal. Unfortunately, although the quality of the debate has shown some improvement in recent years, it is fair to say that the scientific community as a whole has not yet accorded Velikovsky the hearing he deserves. The efforts of certain spokesmen to discredit this heretic, coupled with *de facto* censorship by others, constitutes a depressing chapter in the history of science.

The papers that follow here throw further light on some of the earlier events in this shameful story and, to a limited extent, bring it further up to date.

A concise review of what happened in the years covered by the *American Behavioral Scientist*'s special issue is provided by David Stove. His paper, "The Scientific Mafia," was delivered before the Aristotelian Society of Sydney, Australia, in 1967. It was first published that same year (September 7) in *Honi Soit,* a campus publication of Sydney University. It was not revised for *Pensée* or for the present volume, so the reader should keep in mind its date.

Stove, a native Australian, is senior lecturer in the Department of Philosophy at Sydney University. He is the author of a recent book, *Probability and Hume's Inductive Skepticism* (Oxford University Press).

In "The Censorship of Velikovsky's Interdisciplinary Synthesis," Lynn E. Rose analyzes arguments raised against Velikovsky by his critics: He disregards boundaries that have traditionally set various fields of inquiry apart and invades sciences for which he carries no credentials; he dares to suggest the presence of physical forces not taken into account in conventional celestial mechanics and he challenges uniformitarian notions that deny the solar system a natural history. Rose stresses the fallacies in such arguments and suggests that Velikovsky's historical reconstructions do not require us to abandon anything science has truly "learned" (as distinguished from things assumed and presumed).

Dr. Rose, professor of philosophy at the State University of New York at Buffalo, teaches courses in the history and philosophy of science and is the author of several books. He has instituted a course of study devoted entirely to Velikovsky's *Worlds in Collision.*

"Shapley, Velikovsky, and the Scientific Spirit" is an adaptation of a much longer manuscript by Horace M. Kallen, who was among the first public figures in academia to speak out for fair treatment of Velikovsky. In this paper, Kallen recalls his efforts in this cause, and particularly his exchanges with Harlow Shapley, the late "dean" of American astronomers and former director of Harvard College Observatory. He also calls attention to evidence indicating that Shapley never veered from his initial, snap judgment of Velikovsky—a verdict based on secondhand summaries of Velikovsky's works and a very few minutes of conversation with Velikovsky himself.

Kallen sternly rebukes Shapley, his long-time friend, for this conduct and declares that "the record for integrity is entirely in favor of Velikovsky." And he urges Velikovsky, as Albert Einstein also did, to savor the story of his reception by orthodoxy for its amusing side.

Professor Kallen was a co-founder of the New School for Social Research in New York City and was chairman of its graduate faculty for many years. He was named by William James to edit that writer's unfinished book, and he became the literary executor of Benjamin Paul Blood. His own books on philosophical, religious, and sociological subjects number more than twenty and include *Art and Freedom* (two volumes), *The Liberal Spirit, The Education of Free Men,* and *Liberty, Laughter, and Tears*. At the time of the present writing, Kallen was professor emeritus of philosophy and research professor in social philosophy at the New School.

Since this article was written, Harlow Shapley has passed on, and now Horace Kallen, too, is gone. He died February 16, 1974, at the age of ninety-one. Only a few months earlier, he had published his last book, *Creativity, Imagination, Logic: Meditations for the Eleventh Hour,* in which he made yet another plea for objectivity and open-mindedness concerning heretical ideas like those of Velikovsky.

The concluding document in this part, Velikovsky's "H. H. Hess and My Memoranda," illustrates the rapport and open-mindedness that is possible between two scientists who, though they often fail to agree even on the most basic assumptions in the fields they discuss, respect one another's point of view. Velikovsky gives a full accounting of Hess's background, credentials, and status as a scientist—information that it is unnecessary to repeat here.

Pensée's publication of Velikovsky's various memoranda written at the request of Hess gave most readers their first opportunity to study these documents, which demonstrate Velikovsky's close attention to developments throughout the first decade of the space age and provide valuable additional insight into the thinking that underlies many of his already substantiated advance claims.

THE SCIENTIFIC MAFIA

David Stove

The story of Velikovsky's theory, its reception, and its subsequent confirmations, constitutes one of the most fascinating chapters in the entire history of thought; and it is one which is still unfolding. This paper can be no more than a sketch of a sketch of it. Those who wish to know more can best begin by reading *The Velikovsky Affair,* edited by A. de Grazia (New Hyde Park, N.Y.: University Books, 1966).

A book called *Worlds in Collision* was published in the U.S.A. in 1950. According to its author, Venus as a planet is only some thirty-five hundred years old. The protoplanet, in effect an enormous comet, had originated, at some earlier time, by disruption from Jupiter. It moved for centuries on a very eccentric orbit, and about 1500 B.C. made its two closest approaches to the Earth. During the eighth and seventh centuries B.C., the comet Venus repeatedly approached Mars, and Mars in turn menaced our planet. Only after all these encounters did Venus finally lose its last cometary characteristics and settle down to its present, planetary behavior. The effects of these encounters, especially the earlier ones, on the Earth, are portrayed as truly catastrophic. Oceans were displaced, continents drowned, mountains built and demolished, organic populations extinguished, civilizations overwhelmed, the diurnal motion interrupted, the month and year lengthened, the axis of rotation changed, et cetera.

The author was one Immanuel Velikovsky, a Russian Jew born in 1895. He graduated in medicine in Moscow in 1921, and after various other occupations and places of residence he was to be found practicing psychoanalysis in Tel Aviv in the thirties. A book he projected on Freud's heroes was the unlikely germ of all his later work, for it led him to think about Moses and the Exodus. Now, the Bible portrays the Exodus as taking place amid a series of extraordinary natural disasters; and especially when Velikovsky found an Egyptian document which seemed to refer to the same events, he began to wonder whether the disasters might not have been real.

NATURAL CATASTROPHISM

Ten years later, *Worlds in Collision* presented his evidence, accumulated from testimony, tradition, legend, and religions the world over, for the story of the birth of Venus as a planet after a period in which earth, sea, and sky were convulsed. The next few years saw the publication of his *Earth in Upheaval,* which assembles geological, paleontological, and archaeological evidence for the same theory; and of *Ages in Chaos,* Velikovsky's revised chronology of Egyptian history (which he needs to shorten by five hundred years).

It does not need an expert in the history of geology to recognize in Velikovsky's theory a revival of eighteenth-century catastrophism. It differs from most earlier catastrophisms, however, in not attributing catastrophes to a supernatural agent; in attributing them to an *extraterrestrial* agent; and in supposing catastrophes to have occurred in historical times. There have been other theories, in this century, of catastrophes due to a natural extra-terrestrial agent. But I am sure that no catastrophism has ever been developed with so much ingenuity and comprehensivenes as by Velikovsky. The range of subjects on which his theory has led him to novel suggestions is really almost incredible: from the chemistry of Mars's atmosphere to the original of the "plumed serpent" of Mexican mythology; from the nature of manna to the cause of (the ending of) the quaternary ice age; from the origin of species to the identity of the Queen of Sheba; and so on, forever.

Worlds in Collision quickly became a best seller. Such a book has, of course, enormous appeal to what I call the "anti-fluoride belt" in modern societies. But it also quickly became the target of nearly universal abuse and derision. The Dallas *News* thought it was a Russian propaganda ploy. The *Daily Worker* saw in its popularity a sure sign of the dying days of bourgeois society. Well, one doesn't expect a great deal from the Dallas *News;* or anything at all from a Communist newspaper. But what of that mighty intellect J. B. S. Haldane in Britain? He thought that the book was an attempt by the U.S. warmongers to soften us up for the atomic war they were preparing to launch!

The professional scientists' campaign against *Worlds in Collision* began well before the book appeared. Harlow Shapley, probably the best-known American astronomer alive today, led an energetic attempt to stop the publisher, Macmillan, from publishing the book. He arranged for denunciations of the book, still before its appearance, by an astronomer, a geologist, and an archaeologist, in a learned journal. None of them had read the book. When it did appear, denunciatory reviews were arranged, again, in several instances, by professors who boasted of never having read the book.

Velikovsky was rigorously excluded from access to learned journals for his replies. Then Shapley and others really got busy on the old-boy circuit. They forced the sacking of the senior editor of Macmillan responsible for accepting the Velikovsky manuscript. (He had been with the firm twenty-five years.) They forced the sacking of the director of the famous Hayden Planetarium in New York, because he proposed to take Velikovsky seriously enough to mount a display about the theory.

Then Macmillan representatives all over the country began to report that science professors in the universities were refusing to see them. Macmillan finally caved in, and prevailed on Velikovsky to let them transfer their best-selling property to a competitor, Doubleday, which, as it has no textbook division, is not susceptible to professorial blackmail.

The process thus begun did not stop. In 1964, the *Bulletin of the Atomic Scientists*—that famous organ of the kind of scientific conscience of which the late Robert Oppenheimer was the most adored representative—hired an ignorant journalist to deride Velikovsky on his Egyptological expertise and other matters equally atomic. But Velikovsky could not get space for a reply.

All this belongs on the level of what the Russians call "administrative measures." What of the intellectual level? Well, a great many "refutations" of Velikovsky's theory have appeared in print, some by very famous people, such as Donald Menzel at Harvard, and Cecilia Payne-Gaposchkin, also of Harvard, the author of the well-known astronomical textbook. I cannot enter into any details of them here. Some of them are chiefly remarkable for dishonesty or incompetence. They misquote the text they are critizicing. They willfully misrepresent the theory Velikovsky advanced. And they are replete with errors of fact and theory.

But they are now of only historical interest, for they aimed to prove too much, far too much: that a theory of this *kind* is impossible. Whereas it would, I am sure, now be generally admitted that a story like the one Velikovsky told cannot be excluded on grounds of its conflict with any deeply entrenched law or theory; for there is no such conflict. The theory is a local, historical one, and has to be assessed as such.

What, then, of the positive evidence *for* the theory?

As to the evidence assembled in Velikovsky's books—well, you must read them, and see for yourself what you think that great mass of evidence is worth. For my part, the books convinced me of two things: that a thesis of extraterrestrial catastrophes in historical times is at least a distinctly live option; and that in historical times Venus has done . . . something peculiar, at any rate.

But I must mention some of the more startling pieces of evidence that have come to light since Velikovsky published.

According to Velikovsky, there were tremendous electrical discharges between the earth and the giant comet, and between the comet's head and tail. This, among other things, led him to ascribe an altogether novel importance to electrical and magnetic forces in the solar system. You must remember that this was in 1950—i.e., before the dawn of the space age; these were the good old days when inertia and gravitation were still thought to be equal to every task (plus only a little help from the sun's light-pressure, to blow comet tails the right way).

Well, the whole trend of discovery since then has of course been Velikovsky's way. He did not actually predict the Van Allen belts, but he said that the earth must have a magnetosphere much stronger, and extending much farther into space, than anyone else believed possible. He did predict that Jupiter would be found to be a radio source, long before the astonished radio astronomers found it so. And there is much more like that.

According to Velikovsky, there were all over the world, as folklore alleges, rains of burning pitch. This, among other things, led him to assert in 1950 that the clouds of Venus must be very rich in petroleum gas. All contemporary knowledge of the chemistry of the planet's clouds was flatly against it. Yet it has turned out to be so. If you think this is a bit creepy, you have heard nothing yet.

According to Velikovsky in 1950, Venus must still be very hot, because of the circumstances of its recent birth and subsequent career. The astronomers had long "known" that it was cool, and, as late as 1959, accepted estimates of its temperature such as 59 degrees centigrade were still being revised slightly *downward*. Yet it has turned out that the planet has a surface temperature around 800 degrees Fahrenheit.

This would be hard enough to reconcile with any "uniformitarian" theory which requires a common origin for all the planets. But worse was to come. For Mariner 2 put it beyond doubt that the rotation of Venus is retrograde—that is, while it revolves in the same direction as that in which all the other planets both revolve and rotate, it rotates in the contrary sense! No doubt, *ad hoc* amendments will be tried to fit this fact into conventional theories of the origin of the planets (just as desperate *ad hoc* amendments to a "greenhouse" theory are still being made to account for the temperature); but *this* one will test their ingenuity, that is certain.

Of things that have come to light since the De Grazia book was published, two deserve mention, however briefly. First, the fantastically turbulent and hot state of Jupiter—the enormous explosions it suffers, the changes in its speed of rotation, and a surface temperature perhaps around 1,000 degrees F. (Remember your astronomical textbooks, and all that ice, miles thick, on Jupiter? We all "knew," ages ago, how cold and dead Jupiter is.) Second, what appears to be a vestige of an earlier gravitational "lock" of the Earth on Venus: for Venus is found to turn the same face to us at each inferior conjunction! (For references on these two matters, see *Yale Scientific Magazine, 41* [April 1967]).

Well, this is how things are going. The process of silently "borrowing" Velikovsky's ideas began as soon as he first published; but as can easily be imagined, with everything going his way this industry has become enormous. (One distinguished archaeological career has been made out of a single paragraph in *Worlds in Collision*.) But still no power on earth, apparently, is strong enough to oblige a single professional scientist to give Velikovsky the smallest footnote acknowledgment in a learned publication. The stony silence continues perfectly unbroken.

There are certain observations I want to make which are quite independent of the question whether Velikovsky's theory is true.

First, on the reception of the theory, and the light this throws on the intellectual and moral quality of contemporary science and contemporary life.

Consider how different the reception of Velikovsky's work would have been if it had been Christian fundamentalism, say, or fashionable French metaphysical anthropology. Or psychoanalysis; suppose Velikovsky had interpreted the folklore of catastrophe as distortions of infantile or intrauterine experience. Of course it would have gone down smooth as silk! You could get degrees in it by now. Think about that.

Consider, again, how different the reception would have been if Velikovsky had produced a work of *literature*. Who can imagine science professors conspiring to suppress an *avant-garde* play or novel, however vicious or insane its contents? Far from it, they would be scandalized by any such attempt at censorship, and would rally to the author's aid. You think about that! C. P. Snow was wildly wrong here: scientists have not succumbed less than the rest, but if anything more, to the aesthetic propaganda of the present century. The treatment accorded to Velikovsky is one of the pleasant fringe benefits we get from fifty years of popular preaching in praise of art.

But it is on professional science itself that the case throws the most revealing light. We all grizzle about specialization, professionalization, departmental empire building, et cetera. But unless and until you read the details of this case, you can have no idea of the pitiless ferocity or the organizational muscle that organized science can display. Talk about the "military-industrial" complex! We need a Wright Mills to begin to do justice to *this* almost unacknowledged locus of power in modern society. The great Italian probability theorist De Finetti, speaking in 1964 about Velikovsky's case, compared the scientific complex to a "despotic and irresponsible Mafia."

Second, some brief observations arising from the theory itself but still independent of its truth.

One is this, that if anything *remotely like* Velikovsky's theory is true, what vistas it opens up for the whole study of religion, and of the fear of the skies in general! (Though Velikovsky himself never says a word about this.)

Another is this. If anything remotely like Velikovsky's theory is true, the whole range of humanistic studies, classics, history, archaeology, psychology, anthropology take on an entirely new interest, through being brought into living connection with astronomy and the earth sciences. The eighteenth century convinced men that old books—the Bible, et cetera—were "literature." Thereupon mankind quite properly lost interest in them. Now, however, it becomes possible to regard them as something else; and suddenly old books are important again.

Finally, thanks to the degree of success that Velikovsky's theory has *already* had, even if it has no more, we can begin to see in perspective the character of the world-wide view which has just died but into which everyone here was born. The solar system as a gigantic clock, the parts of which are separated by perfectly clean space, and among which only gravitation and inertia operate; with all the planets originating together, and subject thereafter to no disastrous mutual interference whatever.

This is the world view which Newton bequeathed almost singlehanded to the following centuries. It is the world view of the French Academy, which until 1803 continued to classify all stories of the fall of meteorites from the sky with astrology and superstition. It is the world view of the conventional historians of astronomy, who confidently compute the time and path of eclipses thousands of years ago, down to the second and the inch—for all the world as though they were Laplacian calculators.

DISRUPTED HEAVENS

As Livio Stecchini points out in the De Grazia volume,

it is a neo-Aristotelian world view. It sets a gulf between the heavens, where all is perfect order and perpetual peace; and this lower world of ours, where disorder and strife are not unknown. It furnished the basis on which the eighteenth century could set aside revelation, put all its money on the argument from design, and proclaim the religion of reason and nature. Alas for the Voltaires! What they insisted on taking for a demonstrated consequence of Newtonian laws—the stability of the solar system—was something agonizingly different for Newton himself: namely, an absolutely essential premise for the argument from design, yet one for which he could never find adequate support. Hence, *inter alia,* his terrible falling out with his former protégé, Whiston, who ascribed the Noachian deluge to the close approach of a huge comet!

Anyway, that's all over now. The neo-Aristotelian age of Newton died as the space age came in. We can even date its demise specifically to 1962, when Mariner 2 confirmed the retrograde rotation of Venus. The new air is wonderfully exhilarating; but also chilling. Of course, the Copernican new air was dreadfully chilling in its time. But then, when Newton had completed the Copernican revolution, the earth, although it was no longer still and no longer at the center, had received a great compensating advantage: *it was safe.* Now that's gone too.

THE CENSORSHIP OF VELIKOVSKY'S INTERDISCIPLINARY SYNTHESIS

Lynn E. Rose

I

What may we expect of an empirical theory before we judge it successful? The criteria are three: 1) the overall logical simplicity or economy of the theory in comparison with other theories, 2) the extent to which statements deducible from the theory turn out to be true, and 3) the absence of any statements deducible from the theory which turn out definitely to be false.

Velikovsky's theory (1950) of global catastrophes, the more recent of which occurred within historical times, is by now a near-classic case of a successful empirical hypothesis, namely, it was accompanied by an extensive collection of evidence that seemed to lend it considerable plausibility; it provided a simple, yet comprehensive set of premises around which to organize and to understand a vast range of previously disconnected phenomena; the theory was eminently open to testing, since it entailed a number of important consequences not yet verified, and many of these were incompatible with rival theories; and finally, succeeding years witnessed the verification of a great many of those consequences and the disconfirmation of none. By all the usual canons of sound methodology the theory should now be accepted as a successful one, that is, one that may be regarded as very probably true.

Nearly all bold theories that were on the right track

have encountered initial opposition irrelevant to the canons of acceptance listed above. Scientists often reveal elaborate and sometimes inflexible views about the traits a theory must have merely in order to be proposed for examination; usually, these traits have nothing to do with the traits that theories are expected to have in order to be judged successful.

The theory proposed by Velikovsky in 1950 led to the expression of a number of such views about prior requirements. On May 20, 1950, in a letter of protest and threat written to the Macmillan Company, Dean B. McLaughlin, Professor of Astronomy at the University of Michigan, wrote:

"The claim of universal efficacy or universal knowledge is the unmistakable mark of the quack. No man can today be an expert even in the whole of geology or the whole of astronomy. There is specialization within specialties. I do not mean that we are ignorant of all fields but our own; I do mean that we are not equipped to do highly technical original research in more than several distinct specialties for each scientist. But no man today can hope to correct the mistakes in any more than a small subfield of science. And yet Velikovsky claims to be able to dispute the basic principles of several sciences! These are indeed delusions of grandeur!"

Four paragraphs later, McLaughlin reveals that:

"No, I have not read the book."

One notes in passing that this self-confessed ignorance of the contents of *Worlds in Collision* does not prevent McLaughlin from protesting the Macmillan Company's

"promulgation of such *lies*,—yes, *lies*, as are contained in wholesale lots in *Worlds in Collision*."

But McLaughlin's principal objection seems to be directed both at the interdisciplinary character of Velikovsky's investigations and at the boldness of his conclusions. It is interesting that what McLaughlin sees as grounds for objection are in other quarters seen as grounds for

46

admiration. Thus, Professor Horace M. Kallen, then Dean of the Graduate Faculty of the New School for Social Research, wrote to Velikovsky on May 21, 1946:

> "The vigor of the scientific imagination that you show, the boldness of your construction and the range of your inquiry and information fill me with admiration."

Range and boldness, then, are the points at issue, and it is true that Velikovsky's investigations have led him into many different fields of learning. It is also true that the conclusions to which his theory leads are in conflict with some of the more popular *theories* in those fields. But his theory is not in conflict with any clear-cut *facts* unearthed by other disciplines, and claims to the contrary have never been substantiated. Whether it is true that "no man can today be an expert" in several fields at once depends upon what is meant by "expert." If it means "able to hold his own in debate with specialists from many fields for more than a quarter of a century," then it appears that Velikovsky himself is an exception to McLaughlin's rule. And on the chance that there *are* occasional exceptions to that rule, we would do well not to censor in advance any suggestion that happens to cut across disciplinary boundaries.

Unlike universities, the world around us is not neatly divided into departments and specialties. If each specialty restricts itself to its own selected subject matter, with no serious regard for the relevance of other specialties and with no real effort toward synthesis, what chance is there that the mere summation of isolated special theories will be anything more than a disconnected jumble of progress reports that cries out for synthesis into a unified, coherent theory that has some real chance of truly representing the unity and integration of the operations of nature? Indeed, many students of scientific methodology have concluded that *only* an interdisciplinary approach, seeking one coherent theory to describe our one universe, has much prospect of turning out to be true.

An important consequence of the present disciplinary isolation has been the continuing preference for theories that are uniformitarian. Uniformitarianism is the thesis that only the processes that we see operating today could have operated in earlier periods of history; this rules out any of the sudden, global catastrophes of the sort described by Velikovsky. What seems to have happened is that each discipline has borrowed unchallenged the uniformitarian conclusions of each of the other disciplines, and has assumed that those other disciplines have encountered no serious indications of catastrophism. Each discipline is left with the impression that only in *that* discipline are there any data that might suggest a catastrophic model rather than a uniformitarian model. These unwanted data are then either ignored or else forced into a uniformitarian framework they do not really fit. The strain is tolerated so as not to conflict with the uniformitarianism of the other disciplines.

Thus, each isolated discipline tends to borrow only the uniformitarian *conclusions* of the other disciplines, and to remain unaware of the catastrophic *data* that are hidden away as skeletons in the closets of all the disciplines. Velikovsky has removed those skeletons from the various closets and has been rattling them loudly for all to hear. His suggestion is that when one looks at all of the evidence, without restricting oneself to the limited number of "facts" usually considered by one group of specialists, it becomes possible to make a strong case for catastrophism. This interdisciplinary foundation of his arguments is one of the principal reasons for both their novelty and their cogency.

Giordano Bruno long ago pointed out that what the "facts" are will be determined in large part by the observer's *intenzioni*, the whole "set" that he brings to his work. Sometimes these disciplinary "sets" are so influential in our methodology that we decide in advance what ramifications will ensue even from "facts" whose nature is not yet known! And so NASA was able to announce, prior to any moon landing, that the findings of such expeditions would shed further light on the creation of the solar system some billions of years ago, when, as everyone (except Velikovsky) knows, the moon's features were being formed. Here it would seem that each investigator works on his own specialized assignment, and has no responsibility for the overall theory, since it has not been included as part of his assignment; and yet the overall theory, that general uniformitarian picture, serves as an unquestioned backdrop for his activity, and is so influential that it even predetermines the character of a new, unexplored world.

We have seen that the viewpoint expressed by McLaughlin rejects in advance any interdisciplinary reforms that would transgress the boundaries of the separate specialties; and that it rejects Velikovsky's theory in particular both because of the degree of boldness in Velikovsky's constructions and because of the number of areas in which that boldness is expressed. Anyone who is led to challenge the basic conclusions of several different disciplines is said to be suffering from delusions of grandeur; any kind of universality in such enterprises is seen as "the unmistakable mark of the quack." But is it not possible that there are some people whose range and capacities exceed the disciplinary boundaries? Is it not possible that some of the basic conclusions of a number of disciplines do need to be challenged? Has there ever been a time in history when all of the basic conclusions of all of the various disciplines were beyond any need of re-examination?

Discoveries in the years since 1950 have forced extensive revision of astronomy texts in order to correct the misinformation they contained about the temperatures of the planets, the role of electricity and magnetism in astronomical phenomena, the wanderings of the Earth's axis, et cetera. On the other hand, no major claim made by Velikovsky in *Worlds in Collision* in 1950 has had to be retracted, though a great many of the claims that he did make and that were at the time considered by others to be false are known to be true.

Velikovsky's own theory illustrated the danger of rejecting a theory in advance because it is interdisciplinary and daring. This policy, if successfully applied, would have led us to discard just about the only theory of the solar system and of ancient history that has *not* had to be drastically revised during the past two decades.

II

Despite the success of Velikovsky's theory, one continues to hear objections of the same sort that were advanced when the theory was first proposed. Perhaps the most frequently expressed objection is that Velikovsky's theory violates the laws of "celestial mechanics," that it overthrows Newton's theory of gravitation, that it is dynamically impossible. Usually this attitude is traceable to a merely hearsay grasp of what Velikovsky has written. One of the earliest statements of this objection was made in a letter to Horace Kallen, on May 27, 1946, by Harlow Shapley, then Director of the Harvard College Observatory:

"Dr. Velikovsky's claim that there have been changes in the structure of the solar system during historical times has implications which apparently he has not thought through; or perhaps was unable to convey to me in our brief conversation. If in historical times there have been these changes in the structure of the solar system, in spite of the fact that our celestial mechanics has been for scores of years able to specify without question the positions and motions of the members of the planetary system for many millennia fore and aft, then the laws of Newton are false. The laws of mechanics which have worked to keep airplanes afloat, to operate the tides, to handle the myriads of problems of everyday life, are fallacious. But they have been tested completely and thoroughly. In other words, if Dr. Velikovsky is right, the rest of us are crazy."

(All that Shapley knew of Velikovsky's work at the time of this letter was the latter's claim that the present order of the solar system was stabilized only in historical times —not billions of years ago. Later [1950], it transpired that Velikovsky claimed the participation not only of gravitation and inertia but also of electromagnetic fields and forces in celestial mechanics, even if only as minor factors; in catastrophic conditions and at close distances these ignored forces could become dominant.)

The general motions of the bodies in the solar system at present conform very closely to Newton's gravitational formulas. But there are numerous phenomena that are not explained, such as the origin and movements of solar spots, the paths followed by solar prominences, certain librations of the Moon, the variations in the planets' periods of rotation, some of the orbital perturbations of the exterior planets, the capture of particles by the Van Allen belts, et cetera. And it has certainly not been established that even the large-scale motions of the planets have *always* been primarily in accord with celestial mechanics built on gravitation and inertia alone.

The history of the solar system is but one branch of natural history, and if historical data conflict with astronomical theories, it is strange that history should have to be rewritten to conform to these theories! Indeed, it is the historical material itself, together with corroborating evidence from other fields, that led Velikovsky to conclude that space is not empty, but is swept by particles and permeated with electromagnetic fields, and that when planets are in close approach they are greatly affected by electromagnetic interrelations, so that their subsequent paths are not determined solely by gravitational fields.

As a matter of fact, in *Worlds in Collision* Velikovsky has not only denied that gravity plays a role in determining the motions of astronomical objects, but has also shown, in the epilogue, how the historical events could have happened in the frame of the celestial mechanics in which gravitation and inertia are the only forces in action. Yet he admitted that in "searching for the causes of the great upheavals of the past and in considering their effects [he] became skeptical of the . . . celestial mechanics based on the theory of gravitation" in which "electricity and magnetism play no role." In his admiration of Newton, Velikovsky likes to stress that on the last page of the *Principia* Newton prophetically wrote of electricity —very little explored in his time—as a force that will need to be reckoned with in future studies.

Shapley assumes that to deny gravity the *sole* role in astronomy is to deny gravity *any* role in astronomy. But in all sorts of familiar situations on Earth we see gravitational attraction outweighed by other factors. The laws of gravitation are not then wrong; they are simply seen for what they are: descriptions of *one* of the factors that determine the actual motions of objects. The Newtonian laws need not on this account be revised; what does need to be revised is the unjustified belief that gravitational laws are the sole factor determining astronomical events.

Shapley begs the question by assuming that the planetary motions have been successfully calculated "for many millennia fore and aft." The only way to check these calculations is to wait several millennia and see, or to check them against the testimony of history, a procedure that Shapley has ruled out of court in advance.

Shapley continued to insist that if Velikovsky is right, then *everything* we have learned about the operation of gravity is wrong. When *Worlds in Collision* was finally about to be published, Shapley wrote a threatening letter to Macmillan (on January 25, 1950) and reiterated "that if the earth could be stopped in such a short space of time it would overthrow all that Isaac Newton had done."

The history of science will inevitably record, even if Velikovsky should somehow turn out to be mistaken, that Shapley and his colleagues made a snap decision about Velikovsky. That decision will be seen as based far less on evidence and argument than on various untenable prejudices.

SHAPLEY, VELIKOVSKY, AND THE SCIENTIFIC SPIRIT

Horace M. Kallen

One day late in March 1970, Dr. Immanuel Velikovsky called me on the telephone from Princeton. Among other things, he mentioned that in April it would be twenty years since the publication of the first of his controversial books and that the assault on his personal integrity based on disbelief in the conceptions which the books expound had not ceased. I asked for concrete facts. He named Harlow Shapley, quondam professor of astronomy at Harvard, now emeritus.

Because I expressed surprise and shock, Dr. Velikovsky offered to send me copies of correspondence between Shapley and Albert Burgstahler, professor of chemistry at the University of Kansas, exchanged in 1967; and between Shapley and a girl student at Bay Village High School, Ohio, exchanged in March 1969. To Burgstahler, Shapley wrote: ". . . I find little happiness in reading or thinking about Velikovsky. He seems to be one of our most erudite charlatans." To Burgstahler's request for proof of his statement, Shapley failed to reply. His reply to Miss Lindeman's question was: "All professional astronomers consider Velikovsky a fraud. Can't you find a reputable subject for your research paper?"

Shapley's recent comments on Velikovsky, false on their face, seem to me variations of a persistent libel begun over twenty years ago, practically with the libeler's first contact with Velikovsky. It happens that I had a part in furthering the contact, and I cannot help feeling chagrin and disgust over its unbelievable consequences.

To Dr. Velikovsky, disagreement regarding facts and theories was integral to the scientific enterprise; he expected his views to be met with dissent; constructing them as working hypotheses, he hoped that others in the field might help him to get them tested by observation and experiment. He did not expect that *soi-disant* scientists would, without reading and reflection, blacken his reputation and libel his character because of his scholarly views.

For, as in practically no other vocation, the relations between those who engage in any one of the sciences are presumed to exemplify the principles of equal liberty and equal safety in the cooperative competition and the competitive co-operation on which its achievements depend. But this presumption seems more a compensation in idea for the facts of scientific behavior than a description of science seen "like it is."

By and large, scientists, however they begin, work at their vocations as organization men, serving the vested interests of their establishment and defending the diverse doxies on which they rely in their personal rivalries for place, power, and prestige. Via these rivalries, scientific "truth" becomes a function of the "success" which the establishment awards. Alternatives which challenge such sanctioned "truths" get condemned without examination as "unscientific heresies, mad inventions, dishonest fabrications." Their proponents get denounced as crackpots, charlatans, or frauds. And this is what the establishment has done to Velikovsky and his reconstructions of astronomical processes and human events.

On the record, Harlow Shapley was the initiator and instigator of this exemplification of scientific fair play. The Ureys, the Whipples, the Payne-Gaposchkins, the McLaughlins and the rest but followed his strange, unpredictable lead.

Reading the exchanges between the emeritus Harvard astronomer, the Kansas chemist, and the Ohio high school girl, I began to feel that I may well have made a mistake in trusting time and the authentic scientific spirit to dissipate the Shapley infection. Maybe only court action would stop Shapley and clear Velikovsky's name and fame. I hope still, however, that telling the story "like it is," at least in terms of my part in it, will help toward a purer air.

I myself had been acquainted with Shapley from my days at Harvard and had come to regard him as a true believer in the method of science, with a concern to popularize the knowledge which it brings. Dr. Velikovski came into my orbit soon after his arrival in the United States, by way of an introduction from Judge Morris Rothenberg, a leader in Jewish affairs.

Velikovsky had only seen Shapley's name in the papers in connection with libertarian causes. Having read that Shapley was to be the principal attraction at a college forum luncheon which the magazine *Mademoiselle* was holding in New York on April 13, 1946, Velikovsky sought him out. He told Shapley that, as a result of six years of research, he had come to believe that there were changes in the constitution of the solar system. He now had written down his findings, drawn from mankind's ancient records, from geological treatises, and the like, and asked that Shapley might be good enough to read his manuscript and, if he thought the data sufficient, to advise about having "one or two uncomplicated spectroscopic analyses" made.

"It will be interesting a year from now to hear from you as to whether or not the reputation of the Macmillan Company is damaged by the publication of *Worlds in Collision*. . . . Naturally you can see that I am interested in your experiment. And frankly, unless you can assure me that you have done things like this frequently in the past without damage, the publication must cut me off from the Macmillan Company."

Harlow Shapley in a letter (January 25, 1950) to James Putnam of the Macmillan Company.

"The claim that Dr. Velikovsky's book is being suppressed is nothing but a publicity promotion stunt. . . . Several attempts have been made to link such a move to stop the book's publication to some organization or to the Harvard Observatory. This idea is absolutely false."

Harlow Shapley in a statement to the Harvard Crimson, *printed in the* Crimson *on September 25, 1950.*

Shapley demurred; he was very busy—but if someone he knew were to read the manuscript first and recommend it, he would read it too. And the spectroscopic analysis might be made either by him or his colleague Professor Whipple of the Harvard Observatory.

Among the tasters mentioned to protect Shapley from intellectual poisoning, I was one, and Shapley agreed that if I read Velikovsky's manuscript first and recommended it, he too would read it. After canvassing another nominee, Velikovsky brought his work to me. Meanwhile,

55

Shapley had withdrawn his offer to make those spectroscopic analyses, because what Velikovsky had written him in a brief letter about the atmosphere of the planets did not justify an examination of his claims. On May 23, at Velikovsky's request, I wrote Shapley, expressing the hope that he would make the proffered analyses.

Concerning Velikovsky's manuscript, I wrote: "I have just finished reading it. From the side of the history of ideas and social relations, it seems to me that he has built up a serious theory deserving of the careful attention of scholars—theory and facts showing a kind of scientific imagination which on the whole has been unusual in our times. If his theory should prove valid, not only astronomy but history and a good many of the anthropological and social sciences would need to be reconsidered both for their content and explanation. If it should not prove to be valid, it would still be one of those great guesses which occur far too infrequently in the history of human thought.

"I am myself so impressed by what Dr. Velikovsky has had to say and the way in which he has established his hypothesis that I feel as eager as he to have it undergo the crucial test which the spectroscopic analyses he suggests would be."

To which Shapley replied on May 27: "The sensational claims of Dr. Immanuel Velikovsky fail to interest as much as they should, notwithstanding his exceedingly pleasing personality and evident sincerity, because his conclusions were pretty obviously based on incompetent data"—this a peculiar comment on a book he hadn't read to one who had read it.

He continued with the argument that the notion of changes in the constitution of the solar system in historical times flies in the face of the successful record of celestial mechanics and their role in man's work. "The laws of mechanics . . . have been tested competently and thoroughly . . . if Dr. Velikovsky is right, the rest of us are crazy. And seriously, this may be the case. It is, however, improbable." He concluded by saying that the Harvard Observatory wasn't equipped to make the spectroscopic analyses and recommended that Velikovsky get in touch with Walter Adams of Mount Wilson Observatory or Rupert Wildt at the McCormick Observatory. These recommendations I sent to Velikovsky.

Meanwhile, the latter had the usual luck of an original mind with publishers. Eight turned his book down as unprofitable—because of its many footnotes. But Macmillan saw its commercial as well as its intellectual promise, and in May 1947 gave him a small advance on an option for a contract against royalties from publication. The manuscript had been read for them by several readers, among them Gordon Atwater, then curator of the Hayden Planetarium of the American Museum of Natural History, who thought it might serve as a scenario for another starry show among those he was staging.

With publication by Macmillan in prospect, Velikovsky kept checking and rechecking *Worlds in Collision*. On March 18, 1949, *Harper's* magazine, having learned from James Putnam, the Macmillan editor in charge of *Worlds in Collision*, about its challenging content, asked permission to have one of its editors, Eric Larrabee, do a couple of articles summarizing the book. Velikovsky hesitated a long time, but finally gave permission—in September or October of that year. Larrabee's report appeared in *Harper's* in January 1950. An editorial comment declared: "No one who has read Mr. Larrabee's article can never again read the Old Testament prophets with the same piety or same blind skepticism that he felt before."

The intent is carried by the word *blind*. It is rendered vitally expressive when one realizes that before the end of this same January, 1950, Harlow Shapley had entered upon his inquisition against the Velikovsky heresy and in defense of the establishment's true faith that our scientific and industrial salvation—with its ever-identical solar system changeless through time—rests on celestial mechanics hallowed through the past three centuries. He wrote Macmillan a subtly worded letter.

He had, he told them in his letter of January 18, heard rumors that they were *not* going to publish Velikovsky's *Worlds in Collision*. This was a great relief to him. He had talked about the book with a few scientists, including President Conant of Harvard. All were astonished that a house famous for its scientific publications was carelessly venturing into the Black Arts. Velikovsky's theory that the Sun stood still was the most arrant nonsense of his, Shapley's, experience. That the Earth still exists is proof that the Sun couldn't have stood still in historical times.

". . . Oddly enough, in its anti-scientific account of the book, *Newsweek* has unwittingly done the Doubleday Company a considerable amount of harm. They have made public the high success of the spontaneous boycott of the Macmillan Company by scientifically minded people. . . . In any case, since I believe that the Blakiston Company is owned by the Doubleday Company, which controls its policies as well as the distribution of its books, I am now then a fellow author of the Doubleday Company along with Velikovsky. My natural inclination, were it possible, is to take *Earth, Moon and Planets* off the market and find a publisher who is not associated with one who has such a lacuna in its publication ethics. This is not possible, however, so the next best that I can do is to turn over future royalty checks to the Boston Community Fund and to let *Earth, Moon and Planets* die of senescence. In other words, there will be no revision of *Earth, Moon and Planets* forthcoming so long as Doubleday owns Blakiston, controls its policies and publishes *Worlds in Collision*."

Fred Whipple, Shapley's successor as director of the Harvard Observatory, in a letter (June 30, 1950) to Eunice Stevens, associate editor, the Blakiston Company.

"With regard to Mr. Velikovsky's *Worlds in Collision* there is no change in my attitude or in the situation since the book was first released nearly a decade [sic] ago. There is no truth to allegations that I sought to dissuade the Doubleday Company from publishing this book or any other book. . . ."

Fred Whipple in a letter (July 2, 1970) to Clark Whelton of The Village Voice.

James Putnam, for Macmillan, replied on January 24 that they were not publishing the book as a "scientific publication" but as the statement of a theory that scholars of the various fields of science on which the theory draws should know about. He enclosed a summary of Velikovsky's biography and offered to send Shapley a copy of the book as soon as it was issued—probably in March.

To which Shapley replied on January 25 that Velikovsky's celestial mechanics is "complete nonsense"; that I (Kallen) had introduced Velikovsky to him; that the two had met in some New York hotel where Velikovsky had sought Shapley's endorsement of his theory; that Shapley had looked around to see if Velikovsky had a keeper with him; that he had tried to explain to Velikovsky that if he were right, science was wrong, life on Earth would have been wrecked, and that they couldn't possibly have had this interview in a New York hotel. So, likewise, if Macmillan was right, it is the millions not agreeing with Velikovsky who need keepers, inasmuch as they refuse to abandon what is known of nature and her laws "in the interest of exegesis." Macmillan must prove that they have already published like works "without damage," else publishing Velikovsky must cut him, Shapley, off from the Macmillan Company. In view of the biographical note on Velikovsky, it "is quite possible that only this *Worlds in Collision* episode is intellectually fraudulent."

The threat implicit in the Shapley letter scared the head of Macmillan, George Brett. The book was already on the press. On February 1, Brett wrote the champion of science words of gratitude for "waving a red flag" and promised that he would have the book rechecked by three new readers. Velikovsky was advised that two said *Publish,* one said *Don't.*

Meanwhile, the article in *Harper's* had started winds of controversy among geologists, archaeologists, and others who could not possibly have read Velikovsky's yet unpublished *Worlds in Collision.* Significantly, one instrument of inquisition was *Science News Letter,* which reported its president, Harlow Shapley, as saying on behalf of his fellow astronomers that Velikovsky's theory was "rubbish and nonsense." For at least one of these he could surely speak. This was a Dr. Cecilia Payne-Gaposchkin, a member of his staff who, although the book had not yet been published and she could not have read it, composed an attack on Velikovsky. This was first very widely distributed in mimeograph and then published in the now defunct *Reporter*. I am told that Shapley sent out a number of these mimeographs in person, including one to the editor of the New York *Post*, Ted Thackrey.

Dr. Payne-Gaposchkin gagged especially at the suggestion that "the sun stood still" might be a report of an actual occurrence. Her argument that this was impossible was Shapleyism garnished with some Payne-Gaposchkinisms, astronomical, geological, and other. It is this astronomer's broadside which President Shapley's *Science News Letter* reprinted and praised as a "detailed scientific answer to Dr. Velikovsky's theory," still some time before his book was available in print. After it was on sale, Dr. Payne-Gaposchkin, taken to task by Larrabee, wrote the *Reporter* that now she had read it but hadn't changed her mind.

Meanwhile, editor Thackrey had left the New York *Post* to start the New York *Daily Compass*. He and Shapley seem to have been political kinsmen, close enough to call each other by their given names. Thackrey had republished the *Harper's* article in the *Compass*, whereupon Shapley wrote him privately in late February 1950, enclosing the prepublication mimeograph of the Payne-Gaposchkin confection from the *Reporter*. He suggested that the *Compass* might like to republish "this comment from an American astronomer of the highest standing." Velikovsky, he added, had asked him to endorse his work so that he could get it published, and Shapley had pointed out how wrong Velikovsky was, since if he were right, "All that Isaac Newton ever did was wrong."

To this, editor Thackrey replied on March 7, 1950. He wrote that Shapley's letter had so shocked him that he had had to cool off before answering it as frankly as a worthwhile friendship requires. He took sharp exception to Shapley's "wholly unwarranted and unfounded" characterization of Dr. Velikovsky and reminded his friend how he, Thackrey, had defended Shapley when his political views had led to "nearly as unwarranted" an assault" upon his own integrity.

Thackrey himself had come to know Velikovsky as "a man of unusual integrity and scholarship, whose painstaking approach to scientific theory is at least a match for your own." Shapley, Thackrey wrote, was engaged "in a totally unscientific and viciously emotional attack" on Velikovsky and his work, pressing Macmillan not to publish it without ever once having taken the trouble to examine it or even glance at the research with which it had been accomplished. Shapley, Thackrey charged, was campaigning to destroy a man whom he did not know and to damn a theory he obviously knew nothing about. His course of action was "both morally and criminally libelous." As for the article Shapley had had Dr. Payne-Gaposchkin prepare, it was an attack on a book the latter had not read, attributing to Velikovsky statements he had never made in order to quarrel with them as if he had made them.

"Can we afford to have 'freedom of the press' when it permits such obvious rubbish to be widely advertised as of real importance? . . . Can we afford 'freedom of the press' when it can vitiate education, as this book can? Can we preserve democracy when education in true scientific principles . . . can be nullified by the promulgation of such *lies*,—yes, *lies*, as are contained in wholesale lots in *Worlds in Collision*? . . . Any astronomer or geologist or physicist could have pronounced it trash of the first order. Its geological errors are so absurd that even I, an astronomer, can identify them at a glance! . . . No, I have not read the book. . . . And I do not intend to waste my time reading it. . . ."

Dean B. McLaughlin, late professor of astronomy, University of Michigan, in a letter (May 20, 1950) to G. P. Brett, Jr., president of the Macmillan Company.

"Velikovsky is a tragedy. He has misguided people like you in great numbers, and my advice is to shut the book and never look at it again in your lifetime."

Harold C. Urey, professor of chemistry, University of California (San Diego), in a letter (March 7, 1969) to Katherine Lindeman.

Dr. Urey, on his own admission, has not read Velikovsky's books.—the editors.

To this, on March 8, 1950, Shapley made a "confidential" reply. He was, he wrote, keeping silent on Velikovsky. He had written hotly *only* to Thackrey, but all kinds of authorities were agreeing with his views. He did concede that no protest against the publication of Velikovsky's book should be made to Macmillan by the Council of the American Astronomical Society, because "such action would give greater publicity to Velikovsky's contributions." But for Macmillan to publish the book would be to "throw doubt" on how they evaluate "other manuscripts on which we want to depend." In a postscript, he recalled his letters to me back in 1946 and asked if Velikovsky had reached Adams at the Mount Wilson Observatory or Wildt at Yale. It seems a curious tangency that might intrigue a psychoanalyst.

Thackrey's response to this was dated April 10. He again charged that Shapley was working to prevent Macmillan from publishing Velikovsky; that he had written the publisher two letters "so sizzling that your letter to me might seem tepid by comparison." But he, Thackrey, had read the book while Shapley and Payne-Gaposchkin had written about it without reading it.

To this, Shapley responded on June 6. In the interval, Macmillan had broken with Velikovsky, even though *Worlds in Collision*, published April 3, had become the number one best seller on the national charts. Shapley's letter to Thackrey took note of this success in sales, for which he consoled himself with the remark that he had not yet met a scientist of any sort who took *Worlds in Collision* seriously, while many are "unrestrained in their condemnation of the once reputable publisher."

The Shapleyist proscription of Velikovsky and his revolutionary astronomical concepts extended to all who, even though doubting or questioning the concepts, did take them seriously. One such was Gordon Atwater, fellow of the Royal Astronomical Society and curator of the planetarium and chairman of the department of astronomy at New York's Museum of Natural History, who had read the manuscript for Macmillan. Although Atwater was skeptical of many of Velikovsky's findings, and doubted that Venus could have been ejected from Jupiter, he took the records of world-wide catastrophes in historical times to be evidential. He was dismissed from both his positions with the museum the night before *This Week* published his review of *Worlds in Collision*, in which he urged open-mindedness toward the book.

James Putnam, for twenty-five years with Macmillan and the editor who made the contract with Velikovsky, was immediately dismissed from that establishment. Latham, the editor-in-chief, left the firm later. In *My Life in Publishing* (1965) he tells of his feeling of shame at Brett's surrender.

Velikovsky himself was, of course, again and again refused space and place to defend his theories against both honest and malicious errors regarding them. And in the *Harvard Crimson,* Shapley declared over his signature that it was "absolutely false" that he or the Harvard Observatory had any connection with attempts to suppress the book's publication.

Meanwhile, unintended verifications of Velikovsky's theses began to come from unexpected sources. Mariner probes of Mars, Venus, and the Moon, as reported by NASA, provided evidence of the sort that Shapley had

---

Albert Einstein, having received from Dr. Velikovsky a copy of Ages in Chaos *as a birthday gift, wrote the following letter one month before his death. (Reprinted by permission.)*

17.III.55.

Dear Mr. and Mrs. Velikovsky!

At the occasion of this inauspicious birthday, you have presented me once more with the fruits of an almost eruptive productivity. I look forward with pleasure to reading the historical book that does not bring into danger the toes of my guild. How it stands with the toes of the other faculty, I do not know as yet. I think of the touching prayer: "Holy St. Florian, spare my house, put fire to others!"

I have already read carefully the first volume of the memoirs to "Worlds in Collision" and have supplied it with a few marginal notes in pencil that can easily be erased. I admire your dramatic talent and also the art and the straightforwardness of Thackeray [Thackrey], who has compelled the roaring astronomical lion [Shapley] to pull in a little his royal tail, yet not showing enough respect for the truth. Also, I would feel happy if you could savor the whole episode for its humorous side.

Unimaginable letter debts and unread manuscripts that were sent in, force me to be brief. Many thanks to both of you and friendly wishes.

Your
A. Einstein

---

first offered and then said he hadn't the equipment to seek. A scientist here and a scientist there was impressed by the confirming happenstances, and like geologist Hess and physicist Bargmann of Princeton and astronomer Motz of Columbia, urged that in view of these confirmations, Velikovsky's other conclusions should be re-examined without prejudice.

To this I should add that Albert Einstein, who often saw Velikovsky in Princeton, had read and re-read his work, and continued as firmly pro-Newton as Shapley, but with the open mind of the authentic scientist. A few days before his untimely death, in 1955, he offered (after learning that, as Velikovsky had predicted, radio noises from Jupiter were unexpectedly recorded) to help arrange other experimental tests which Velikovsky sought.

Einstein had, I am told, urged Velikovsky to get the story of his proscription by Shapley et al. fully on record, and Velikovsky had written an account himself, for Einstein to read, which the latter did. "Ich möchte glücklich sein," he wrote Velikovsky in a letter of comment on March 17, 1955, "wenn auch Sie die ganze Episode von der drolligen Seite geniessen könnten." ("It would make me happy if you could savor the entire episode from its amusing side." This is a stance I had been recommending to Velikovsky for a long time, understandably without effect to date.

Despite the excommunication of his theories by the Shapleyites, curiosity about their nature, origin, and evidential grounds spreads and diversifies as the new instruments disclose new data which may confirm or refute. When I urged Velikovsky to disregard the libelous attacks upon his personal integrity, this is what I believed was likely to happen. The new tools, bringing in hitherto inaccessible evidence which would either confirm his conceptions or cause him to abandon them for others, would render his vindication as a man of science "objective," that is, independent of solely personal appraisals.

As between Shapley and Velikovsky, the record for integrity is entirely in favor of Velikovsky.

H. H. HESS AND MY MEMORANDA*

Immanuel Velikovsky

On August 25, 1969, Professor Harry Hammond Hess died of a heart attack while presiding over a meeting (convened at Woods Hole, Massachusetts) of the Space Science Board of the National Academy of Sciences. The board had the task of overseeing the activities of the National Aeronautics and Space Administration, with its multibillion-dollar spending. At the Woods Hole meeting, Hess had intended to discuss the role of thermoluminescence (TL) tests in the lunar programs, an issue I had discussed with him.

When I moved from Manhattan to Princeton, in the early summer of 1952, I became steeped in library work for *Earth in Upheaval*, and the library of Guyot Hall (Princeton's geology department) was a place I frequented. Already known for my *Worlds in Collision* and the discussion it provoked, I caused some curiosity among the numerous faculty members of the department. I do not remember my first contact with Hess, but from our first meeting something in both of us attracted each other.

Hess was the chairman of the department. Once when I mentioned the Vening Meinesz submarine expedition for gravitational measurements in the Caribbean in the 1930s, during which, paradoxically, a positive anomaly was regularly detected, and the greater it was the deeper was the sea, or the less mass there was, Hess surprised me by telling me that he participated in that expedition.

Another highlight of his career took place during World War II. In command of a naval vessel in the Pacific with certain exploratory assignments, he utilized the opportunity to explore the bottom of the ocean in a certain area. Under the water he discovered flat-topped mountains, which he named "guyots," honoring the late Princeton professor of geology, Arnold Henry Guyot (1807–84).

By the end of the war, Hess was retired from active duty with the rank of rear admiral. In the university, he taught mineralogy and crystallography, but marine geology remained his favored subject.

In November 1955, *Earth in Upheaval* was published. Soon it was made required reading in paleontology under Professor van Houten at Princeton—along with an antidote: Loren Eiseley's *The Firmament of Time*. Hess several times during those years gave me the opportunity to address the faculty and graduate students of his department. Since from 1953 (when I spoke before the Graduate College Forum of Princeton University) to 1963 practically no college or university or scientific society extended to me an invitation to speak, those appearances at the behest of Hess meant much to me.

He gave me his published paper on guyots. Upon reading it, I wrote a rather merciless criticism of his idea that the accumulation of a sediment caused the submergence of the sea bottom and with it the submergence of the flat-topped guyots. In his response he showed graciousness.

By mid-1956, preparations for the International Geophysical Year were gaining momentum. On December 5, 1956, I gave to Hess a memo describing briefly several projects for inclusion in the IGY. (The International Geophysical Year, due to start July 1, 1957, would continue until the end of 1958.) There was not yet a Space Science Board, so I gave the memo to Hess in his capacity as chairman of the geology department. Hess sent the memo to Dr. Joseph Kaplan, one of the scientific organizers of the Year. The answer came from Edward O. Hulburt, another scientist in charge of the program, and it was addressed to the "chairman of the department of physics" at Princeton. The first of the suggested projects—to investigate the Earth's magnetic field above the ionosphere —had been, according to Hulburt, considered by the planning committee. (In my Forum Lecture [October 14, 1953] I had already claimed the existence of a magnetosphere above the ionosphere—the lecture was printed as a supplement to *Earth in Upheaval*.)

Three months after the beginning of the IGY, the Russians startled the world by launching the first Sputnik (October 4, 1957), opening the space age. I was then on a visit to Israel, my second since I came to the States in July 1939.

Although Hulburt referred to the plan of measuring the strength of the magnetic field above the ionosphere as considered for the program, the fact is that the discovery of the Van Allen belts, the main achievement of IGY, was not anticipated or considered: when no charged particles were registered at a certain altitude, Van Allen, of the University of Iowa, was startled, but one of his co-workers suggested that possibly the recording apparatus was jammed by too many charged particles; the apparatus was modified, and the belts were discovered. At the beginning, they were featured in the form of two halves of a doughnut; only much later was it recognized that the half on the anti-solar side is stretched far out. But in my memo, as also in the Forum Lecture, I visualized a magnetosphere reaching as far as the lunar orbit.

Another claim made in my Forum Lecture of 1953— namely, that Jupiter could be a source of radio signals —had already been confirmed, in the spring of 1955. I never came out with "claims confirmed" until I read in the New York *Times* that nobody ever thought of Jupiter as a source of radio noises before they were discovered by chance. I turned to Lloyd Motz, Columbia University astronomer, and V. Bargmann, Princeton University physicist, both of whom were entrusted by me with the script of my Forum Lecture soon after its delivery. They wrote a joint letter to *Science,* which published it in the

December 21, 1962, issue, concurrent with the yearly convention of the American Association for the Advancement of Science, publisher of *Science*. It almost coincided with the first reports of Mariner 2, which had passed its rendezvous with Venus a week earlier, on December 14. The high temperature of Venus was confirmed.

This last announcement was made by Dr. Homer Newell for NASA in February 1963. The presence of hydrocarbons in the clouds surrounding Venus was also announced as confirmed—this on the basis of the work of Dr. L. D. Kaplan (Jet Propulsion Laboratory): only compounds containing the radical CH (polymerized) could lend to the 15-mile-thick cloud the same properties at the $-25°$ F temperature at the top of the cloud and at the $+200°$ F temperature at the bottom of the cloud, separated by forty-five kilometers of lower atmosphere from the sizzlingly hot ground surface of the planet.

I wrote an article, "Venus—A Youthful Planet," and sent it to the editor of *Science*. I found it back in my mailbox less than forty-eight hours later, returned unread.

I discussed the case with Hess, and he decided to offer it for publication in the American Philosophical Society *Proceedings*. As a member of the society, he was entitled to sponsor a paper by a non-member. The paper was submitted, and its fate was related by *Yale Scientific Magazine* (April 1967, p. 8):

"The paper was discussed at the editorial board meeting of the Society and caused prolonged and emotional deliberations, with the Board split between those favoring the publication and those opposed to it. For several months a decision could not be reached . . . the decision was made, in order to safeguard the very existence of the Board, to delegate the decision on the article to three members of the society, not members of the Board. Their names were not disclosed but on January 20, 1964, Dr. George W. Corner, Executive Officer of the Society and the editor of the *Proceedings,* informed Dr. Hess that the decision had been made to reject the article.

"Subsequently it was also rejected by the *Bulletin of Atomic Scientists*. In that magazine in April, 1964, an abusive article was published by a Mr. Howard Margolis, attacking Velikovsky and his work. The editor of the *Bulletin*, Dr. Eugene Rabinowitch, in a letter to Professor Alfred de Grazia, editor of the *American Behavioral Scientist*, offered Velikovsky an opportunity to reply with an article 'not more abusive' than that of Margolis, or, instead, to have some of his views presented in the *Bulletin* by some scientist of repute. Then Professor H. Hess submitted the article "Venus—A Youthful Planet," to Dr. Rabinowitch. The latter returned it with the statement that he did not read Velikovsky's book, nor the article."

In July 1963, *Harper's* printed an article by Eric Larrabee calling for an "agonizing reappraisal" of my work. Menzel, of Harvard College Observatory, who not so long previously had revoked his earlier estimate of Venus' temperature as much too high, now wrote in *Harper's* (December 1963) that "hot" is a relative term and liquid helium is hot in relation to liquid hydrogen. As to my claim concerning the magnetosphere, Menzel argued that since I claimed that the magnetosphere reaches as far as the lunar orbit, I made a wrong prediction. The magnetosphere, he said, does not reach more than a few terrestrial radii, whereas the Moon is sixty terrestrial radii distant.

Hess was adversely impressed by the attitude of the scientific community toward me and my work; still subscribing to the accepted uniformitarian doctrine, he had sympathy for my independent stand. He wrote a letter that was intended for public record and which Doubleday incorporated in its "Report on the Velikovsky Controversy," printed in the New York *Times* Book Review (August 2, 1964).

While a debate was going on in several issues of *Harper's*, the Australian physicist/cosmologist V. A. Bailey joined the fracas and accused Menzel of pre-space-age thinking.

Hess, now president of the American Geological Society and chairman of the Space Science Board, suggested that I put together a program for space investigation. I responded without delay; the memo of September 1963 resulted (see below).

About that time, De Grazia published a special issue of the *American Behavioral Scientist* dealing with the reception of my work. When he came to see me, Hess came too.

Once or twice, I asked Hess to organize a panel of members of various faculties of Princeton University that would investigate what was right and what was wrong in my theory and what was proper or improper in the attitude of my critics. Before he decided whether to follow this course (perhaps, expecting a negative attitude by faculty members, he tarried), an initiative came from Dr. Franklin Murphy, at that time chancellor of the University of California at Los Angeles. He asked UCLA's geophysicist Professor Louis Slichter to organize a committee for the same kind of inquiry I had proposed to Hess. Murphy's initiative, however, foundered, and the story needs to be told separately. It embraced the period from January to November 1964.

In January 1965, Hess took the initiative to organize the Cosmos and Chronos Study and Discussion Group, and he placed in the *Bulletin* of the university an announcement of the first open discussion. Originally, we planned a debate on evolution based on the uniformitarian principle versus evolution based mainly on cataclysmic events. My opponent was to have been the Princeton professor of biology Colin Pittendrigh. There was a mutual respect between us (earlier, he had visited me and also inscribed to me a biology text which he had coauthored with G. G. Simpson, my early antagonist), but Pittendrigh insisted that the problem of extinction in the animal kingdom should not be a part of the debate. I could not see how the two parts of the evolutionary problem—the evolution of new species and the extinction of the old—could be separated in a meaningful debate. It appeared that the friendly relations between us were in jeopardy. Hess, without fanfare, offered to be my opponent.

The debate took place in the auditorium of Guyot Hall and fared well. Next, Professor Lloyd Motz came from Columbia University to debate me on astronomical subjects. The third open debate was between me and philosopher Walter Kaufmann of the Princeton faculty. Other study groups spontaneously organized themselves on various campuses. The story of the first four or five years of Cosmos and Chronos and what changes in the structure of the organization I had to demand is a story by itself.

In the fall of 1966 I spoke in the new auditorium of the Wilson School of Princeton University under the aegis of the Princeton chapter of the American Institute of Aeronautics and Astronautics. The lecture was described by Walter Sullivan, science editor of the New York *Times,* in his column of October 2, 1966. As he described it, he first visited Hess to find out whether Velikovsky is a person of integrity. Hess assured him of my complete integrity and added something about my memory, ascribing to me more than I deserve.

An unusual memory was actually one of Hess's own characteristics. Things spoken or letters read were remembered by him years later. Once, when I exhorted him to reread a chapter in *Earth in Upheaval,* he replied that he knew the book by heart. His many very large tables that served him as desks were covered with stacks of papers, but it seemed that he could always find the necessary document; he was helped by a devoted secretary, Mrs. Knapp, who, it seems, also relied on his memory.

Despite his heavy schedule (he never stopped teaching crystallography), Hess was available for many a demand on his time. I remember the case of an uneducated but dedicated man who, living in Michigan, collected many rocks, obviously burned, and wrote me regularly of his belief that one of the Great Lakes was scooped by an asteroid impact. He mailed me, at intervals, boxes with stones. I sent some of them to a scientist at the University of Pittsburgh whom I knew, and brought some others to Hess. The former did not answer; the latter took a few of them to investigate their possible meteoritic nature.

Hess ascribed the reversal of the rocks' magnetic orientation to a spontaneous process in the minerals, as he had claimed in debate with me at my occasional lectures at the geology department. But when he finally realized that such spontaneous reversals could not occur simultaneously in rocks of various composition, he volunteered to tell me that he was wrong.

When, years after my first memo, of December 5, 1956, he read or heard a paper concerning the reversal of the direction of winding in fossil vines and shells from both Southern and Northern hemispheres, he was pleased to let me know that the claims the IGY would not investigate were confirmed by independent research.

In 1967, I gave him a memorandum on radioactivity hazards for astronauts in several localized areas of the Moon and Mars, results of interplanetary discharges. Dr. Homer Newell of NASA sent the memo to scientists on the staff who he thought would be the ones to consider the subject. By that time, Hess and I started to call one another by first names.

In 1968, Hess was named by the Italian Government and Academy of Sciences the recipient of a major prize (in monetary value, approaching the Nobel prize) for his old work on the guyots. Despite all the distinctions he received, he remained a quiet and humble man. I never heard him speak in a loud voice. He did not pull or push and, which was unusual in the academic atmosphere of the time, he was sought out for his fairness.

Not long before his death, he purchased a new home. Until then, he had lived in a university house on Fitzrandolph Street. The house, built with its gables like a chalet, had been occupied by Woodrow Wilson when he was president of Princeton University. At one of my rare visits, Hess drew my attention to the bookcases built at Wilson's behest.

The last and possibly the most exciting event was quickly approaching. Hess, usually shy of publicity, made himself available to the press to state his belief that water in quantity would be found under the lunar surface. I remember how he showed me a winding rill or rift photographed on the Moon and wished me to agree with him that it was caused by running water. I discussed with him my views, namely that the Moon was once showered by water of the universal deluge, but that all of it or almost all of it dissociated before the later cosmic

73

catastrophes. The face of the Moon we see was formed in those later catastrophes.

On May 19, I wrote down a few of my advance claims concerning the Moon and handed it to Hess's research assistant, who strongly supported the view that large water reservoirs lay under the Moon's surface. Hess said to me, "This time you will be wrong." Until then, closely following my record, he found that all my expectations ("predictions") turned out to be true. Once, on our way from Guyot Hall to our respective homes, he ascribed my record to intuition. When I asked which of my claims does not follow from my thesis, he replied, "Noises from Jupiter." He was right, but only to the extent that I have not yet published the story of the earlier cataclysms, promised in the final chapter of *Worlds in Collision*.

The events surrounding the first manned landing on the Moon had a dramatic urgency, and they, too, need to be recorded separately. My two telephone conversations in which I tried to obtain Hess's support for thermoluminescence tests of lunar core extracts, as also envisioned in my article in the New York *Times* on the evening of the first lunar manned landing, can be read in the correspondence.

I saw Hess once more—he was with his secretaries and assistants, preparing for the Woods Hole meeting; he was not in a cheerful mood—that morning the news came that hydrocarbons (petroleum derivatives) were discovered on the Moon, but no water yet, (Now, almost three years later, signs of the one-time presence of water have been detected.) He was, it appeared to me, gloomy.

About half a year later, he had suffered a heart attack. He had always been a chain smoker. The load of work, the excitement of the last few weeks, and possibly a discouragement, but quite probably his premonition that he would not be able to witness the entire lunar program of many landings, must have weighed heavily on him.

On the morning of August 26, 1969, I picked up a newspaper at the Princeton Junction railway station and saw Hess's friendly face on a page carrying a eulogy.

The day the university arranged a memorial service in its chapel, I was delivering a lecture to the faculty of the Ocean County College. I spoke of Hess.

On October 21, exactly three months after the first landing on the Moon, at my initiative, the geophysical department (the new name for the geology department), together with the Cosmos and Chronos Study Group, arranged a memorial lecture at the auditorium of Guyot Hall. The opening part of my lecture, "From Sputnik to Apollo XI," was dedicated to Hess.

In Hess's passing I lost the only member of the scientific elite who demanded a fair treatment for me and my work. When in November the assistant to the president of the university came to see me, I spoke of Hess and could not hide the tears in my eyes. For the rest of 1969, I felt depressed.

Of people who were prominent in their fields and who, since the beginning of my work and through the years showed me more than casual interest and sympathy, I name Robert Pfeiffer, orientalist and biblical scholar (died 1958); Horace M. Kallen, philosopher and educator; Walter S. Adams, astronomer (died 1956); Albert Einstein (died 1955); and Harry Hess, who died in his sixty-fourth year, three years ago. Kallen alone of all of them is alive, having these days reached the venerable age of ninety, still active as writer and lecturer, with time having dimmed none of his mental abilities. [Horace Kallen died early in 1974—Ed.]

They were few, but each of them was great as a human being.

Editors' Note: All memoranda and letters published here remain in their original form, without editorial change.

DECEMBER 5, 1956

Dear Professor Hess:

I have read with vivid interest your paper on the guyots in the Pacific: I will continue here to think aloud. The size of the guyots is no argument against their volcanic nature. The truncated upper surface of a guyot nine miles wide is larger than the widest known crater on earth, yet certainly smaller than Mauna Loa in cross-section measured half way from the bottom of the ocean. I would not shrink even from thinking of them as gigantic mesas: some of the shapes in your drawings have this form. A great volcanic activity took place in the Pacific at an early age. Large stretches of lava in its bottom (Pettersson), and large quantities of ashes indicate this. The moon with its large craters and dried seas of lava comes into mind (without agreeing with the theory of the origin of the moon from the bed of the Pacific).

Your idea of the guyots being islands submerged ca. 500 fathoms (3,000 feet) is well supported by the findings of M. Ewing in the Atlantic (sand beaches submerged 3 miles, or 15,000 feet).

The explanation of *isostatic* subsidence of the oceanic floor weighed with accruing sediment requires enormous amounts of this sediment and, I ask myself, whether the figures would hold this portion of the theory. You assume that the oceanic area would decrease because of submergence of the bottom loaded with the sediment and prisms of it along continental margins. Would not the oceanic area increase in such circumstances? The submergence would be more than compensated by the accrued sediment and the displaced water would encroach on the coasts.

I am not familiar with the calculations concerning loads in relation to isostatic subsidence. I assume that a layer of ten feet of sediment would not lower the bottom by the same amount of ten feet, and probably not even by a single one. An earth crust that is neither elastic (resilient) nor rigid, but only plastic, with magma underneath exerting only a minimal opposition to the pressure from above, would submerge a foot for a foot of load of the specific weight 2.5 (if the ocean does not change its horizontal area). Therefore 2,000 feet of sediment since pre-Cambrian time (Kuenen's figure) appear to me not enough to account for the rise of the sea level relative to the upper surface of the guyots by ca. 3,000 feet (p. 296).

Also the land on the bottom of the Atlantic Ocean

cannot be accounted for by isostatic movement; Ewing found very thin layers of sediment where he expected hundreds or thousands of feet deposited. All of which indicates that some other causes lifted the crust in some places and depressed it in others.

I offer here those thoughts for whatever they are worth. Since 1947, when your paper was written, you may have thought of the guyots in the light of certain facts made known by Pettersson's expedition. I assume that his finds support your ideas of volcanic origin and submergence of these formations discovered by you in 1942.

I accompany this letter with a list including seven questions which I would like to see included in the program of the International Geophysical Year. I shall be grateful to you if you will consent to offer their inclusion in the program (a carbon copy is for your files). Should you wish first to discuss them with me, please give me a ring.

I liked the friendly atmosphere last Friday when I spoke in Guyot Hall.

Very sincerely,
(signed) Im. Velikovsky

DECEMBER 5, 1956

Tests and Measurements Proposed for Inclusion in the Program of the International Geophysical Year. Immanuel Velikovsky

1. Measurement of the strength of the terrestrial magnetic field above the upper layers of the ionosphere. It is accepted that the terrestrial magnetic field—about one-quarter of a Gauss at the surface of the earth—decreases with the distance from the ground; yet the possibility should not be discounted that the magnetic field above the ionosphere is stronger than at the earth's surface.

2. An investigation as to whether the unexplained lunar librations or rocking movements, in latitude and longitude coincide with the revolutions of the terrestrial magnetic poles around the geographical poles.

3. An inquiry into the magnetic orientation of the lavas

77

erupted in the middle of the second millennium before the present era (e.g. in Thera-Santorin) may establish the recentness of the reversal of the magnetic field of the earth.

4. An analysis of the magnetic inclination (dip) in the clay of the pottery of the Old and Middle Kingdoms in Egypt may disclose substantial shifts, actually reversals of the magnetic field of the earth; similar tests could also be performed on various neolithic pottery.

5. An investigation of the direction of the spirals of fossil snail shells and of the windings of fossil vines which are now usually clockwise in one hemisphere and counter-clockwise in the other, may reveal, with the help of radio-carbon analysis, the time of changes or reversals in the direction of the rotation of the earth.

6. Measurement of the gravitational constant within a Faraday cage with varying distances between the attracting bodies in order to exclude the influence of the atmospheric electricity on the obtained results, and thus to verify the inverse square law.

7. Tests in comparing the velocity of fall—and of the acceleration constant—of charged and neutral bodies.

JANUARY 2, 1957

Dear Dr. Velikovsky:

Your comments on guyots are acute. You have put your finger on most of the deficiencies of my hypothesis as it stood in 1946. Perhaps you would like some further explanation. When written Kuenen's earlier estimate of the thickness of oceanic sediments agreed very closely to my needed 3000 ft. of submergence since the Protero-zoic. Now the thickness has been reduced to $\frac{1}{5}$ of the old estimate and the age of beginning of submergence also decreased to about $\frac{1}{5}$. So I was off by a factor of 25. A more recent reprint which I am enclosing repairs the damage.

One km. of sediment on the ocean floor would cause sea level to rise one km. relative to some point on the original floor. The bottom would sink isostatically by

.4 km. To get 1 km. of sediment on the sea floor means eroding 2.3 km. from the continents on the average. This looks as though the continents would be flooded but they rise most of the 2.3 km. isostatically and repeated mountain building thickens the crust about enough to leave sea level vs continent level relatively in the same place it was when the process started.

Ewing's sand at 15000 ft. is now largely explained by him as the result of turbidity currents rather than submergence.

With regard to paleomagnetism, Runcorn is very convincing but he completely neglects a most important phenomenon, that is self reversal which some iron minerals are known to go through dependent on composition and rate of cooling. Some or all reversals may be due to this phenomenon. Runcorn will lecture on his views in Guyot [Hall, Princeton] January 11th.

I will pass your ideas on to Dr. Kaplan in the IGY organization. I take a rather gloomy view of IGY and doubt if anything of much interest will come of it. Fifty six million dollars will produce a lot of scurrying back and forth to the South Pole and an indigestible mass of random observations on everything. Scientific discoveries and ideas are produced by the intuition, creativeness and genius of a man. Dollars of themselves don't produce this, any more than they could be expected to produce another Mona Lisa. This is something which I believe you can readily understand.

I would like to thank you for coming to talk to us. The students were most appreciative.

Sincerely,
(signed) H. H. Hess

JANUARY 18, 1957

The Chairman
Department of Physics
Princeton University

Dear Sir,

A copy of a document is enclosed "Tests and Measurements Proposed for Inclusion in the Program of the International Geophysical Year," dated "Princeton, Dec. 5, 1956," and with the words "From Velikovsky via H. H. Hess" written at the end.

This document was handed to me for comment after passing through so many hands that its origin is completely obscure to me.

With reference to paragraph 1, the measurement of the strength of the terrestrial magnetic field above the upper layers of the ionosphere is in the U.S. IGY program. At present five rockets are assigned to the experiment, and the third earth girdling satellite will carry magnetic equipment.

With reference to paragraph 2, a study of lunar librations with geomagnetic pole movements is not included in the IGY program, but may possibly be done later after the IGY magnetic data are available.

The other paragraphs 3 to 7 give suggested experiments which are not included in the U.S. IGY program. These experiments, except 6 & 7, are concerned with micro-magnetic analysis. Such experiments and ideas were quite familiar to our Panel on Geomagnetism, and as I recall were discussed to a considerable extent. We decided that they could be done by individual investigators, and did not require international cooperation. Therefore, they did not fall readily into the general character of work which was considered appropriate to IGY programs.

Yours very truly,
(signed) Edward O. Hulburt
Senior Scientist, USNC-IGY,
also Chairman, USNC Technical
Panel on Geomagnetism

MARCH 15, 1963

Dear Velikovsky:

We are philosophically miles apart because basically we do not accept each other's form of reasoning—logic. I am of course quite convinced of your sincerity and I also admire the vast fund of information which you have painstakingly acquired over the years.

I am not about to be converted to your form of reasoning though it certainly has had successes. You have after all predicted that Jupiter would be a source of radio noise, that Venus would have a high surface temperature, that the sun and bodies of the solar system would have large electrical charges and several other such predictions. Some of these predictions were said to be impossible when you made them. All of them were predicted long before proof that they were correct came to hand. Conversely I do not know of any specific prediction you made that has since been proven to be false. I suspect the merit lies in that you have a good basic background in the natural sciences and you are quite uninhibited by the prejudices and probability taboos which confine the thinking of most of us.

Whether you are right or wrong I believe you deserve a fair hearing.

Kindest regards,
(signed) H. H. Hess

SEPTEMBER 11, 1963

Dear Professor Hess:

At our conference the day before yesterday I had the impression that you would welcome some suggestions on my part to the program of space investigation. Readily I have prepared a memorandum of four pages which I submit to you in your capacity as Chairman of the Space Board of the National Academy of Sciences. I have not elaborated on the reasons that make me in some selections, at least, follow an unexpected line of thought. In those tests where a condition or a fact is looked for, its finding, depending on the case, is anticipated as not impossible, probable, or even certain. All these experiments and tests spring from a common concept, basic to my theory of the structure of the universe and of its recent past. Should your Board wish oral or written explanations, I would gladly accept such invitation.

Would you also think it proper to submit the proposals contained in my memorandum to wider circles for possible criticism or for a start in exploring the problems it raises and would you consider to offer the memorandum as a paper for an early publication in the Proceedings of the National Academy of Sciences? With such idea in my view, I enclose my "Propositions for Inclusion in the Program of Space Probes for the rest of 1963 and the following years" accompanied by a carbon copy of it.

You will find here also a xerox copy of the recent letter by Prof. V. A. Bailey of the University of Sydney. Hardly any addition to the staff of NASA could be of equal importance.

Cordially yours,
(signed) Im. Velikovsky

SEPTEMBER 11, 1963

Propositions for Inclusion in the Program of Space Probes for the Rest of 1963 and for the Following Years. Prepared by Immanuel Velikovsky, Princeton, N.J., and Submitted to H. H. Hess, Chairman, Space Board, National Academy of Sciences, Washington, D.C.

I. Magnetosphere

A. mapping of the intensity of the magnetic field of the magnetosphere.

B. measuring the reach of the magnetosphere on the day and night sides.

C. testing as to the over-all excess of positive or negative particles in the magnetosphere layers, and generally as to the positive or negative charge or neutral state of the globe with its ionosphere and magnetosphere.

D. synchronization observations as to the travel of the magnetic poles of the earth around the geographical poles (diurnal) and the daily latitudinal and longitudinal lunar librations.

II. Mercury

A. the cause of the precession of the perihelion should

be re-examined in the light of the presence of a magnetic field of solar origin and solar plasma through which Mercury plows. An artificial satellite with a perihelion close to the sun could be tracked as to the precession of its perihelion.

III. Venus

A. high-altitude spectral analysis of the ashen light for hydrocarbons and organic compounds (especially carbohydrates).

B. temperatures of the dayside and nightside and of the terminator compared; the phenomenon of a highest temperature at the terminator and the lowest on the dayside can be verified by testing (radiometric) from the ground and from a balloon.

C. the temperature of the clouds measured at three year intervals; it is conceivable that a slow drop of the temperature of the Cytherian cloud surface will be observed.

D. the phenomenon of Venus (a planet with a weak magnetic field) shielding the Earth, at conjunctions, from protons of solar origin, should be evaluated as to a probable net charge of the planet.

IV. Mars

A. spectra analysis of the polar caps is possible at the time when they are melting and evaporating seasonally. Chances are that they are composed of the same organic molecules as the envelope of Venus.

B. in space probes and by balloon spectroscopy Martian atmosphere should be investigated with the intent of detecting the presence of neon and argon.

V. Jupiter

A. precise calculations should be made as to the effect of the magnetic field permeating the solar system on the motions of the planet which is surrounded by a magnetosphere of [a radiating intensity], presumably, 10^{14} times that of the terrestrial magnetosphere. This is basic to the impending re-evaluation of electromagnetic effects in celestial mechanics.

B. the retrograde satellites of Jupiter should be compared as to their charges with the direct satellites. Experiments should be performed with positively and negatively charged metallic drop solutions revolving in a magnetic field.

C. spectroscopic analysis of the red spot should be performed as to the presence of iron and sulphur vapors, especially over the periods of conjunction with Saturn.

VI. Saturn

A. tests should be devised for detection of low energy cosmic rays emanating from Saturn, especially during the weeks before and after a conjunction of Earth-Jupiter-Saturn.

B. with Doppler effect data at hand, the velocity of revolution of the Saturnian rings, possibly in excess of the velocity of the axial rotation of the planet, should be plotted.

C. chlorine should be looked for in the Saturnian spectrum of absorption.

VII. Uranus

A. the polar magnetic intensity of Uranus, at the time when its axis points towards the earth, should be measured (Zeeman effect).

VIII. Pluto

A. the charge of this planet in relation to its mass is presumably very high, which would explain its perturbing power. Calculations should be made of the potential difference needed to account for the unaccounted perturbations of Uranus and Neptune.

IX. Sun

A. solar net charge should be made the object of intense investigation. Solar plasma winds should be tested as to the presence of electrons, besides protons, and to the direction of their flow (drift), whether sunward.

B. experiments should be devised to enlarge our knowledge of the behavior of very hot, charged, rotating bodies in a room of very rarefied atmosphere, close in temperature to absolute zero; of the magnetic field created; of the behavior of cold, or of graded temperature, bodies (conductors) suspended (in a planetarium fashion) at various distances from the larger central hot body.

C. the solar system should be investigated as to the existence of magnetic shells, especially at the orbital distances from the sun. Radar echoes may help to establish their presence, in matter of minutes or hours.

X. Moon

A. the reason for repeated failures in directing projectiles with moon as target should be explored also as to the deflecting action of the magnetic fields (terrestrial and solar) with magnetopause and solar winds intervening.

B. laboratory experiments with terrestrial rocks as to splintering and erosion should be performed, duplicating the thermal conditions of the moon suddenly immersed, when hot, into coolness of space, as it happens during lunar eclipses; the sharp outlines of lunar formations should be subsequently evaluated as to their age.

XI. General Relativity Theory

A. the influence of the moon (lunar tides in the upper atmosphere) on the rectilinear propagation of stellar light as observed from the earth should be checked at different positions, especially when the moon is new and at lunar eclipses; in the solar eclipses investigated as to the bending of rays of light passing near the sun, the role of the moon and of atmospheric tides caused by it is neglected. The bending of the rays by even stronger solar tides in the atmosphere should be reduced to a minimum by balloon examination of solar eclipses.

B. the influence of Jupiter on the rectilinear propagation of stellar light should be investigated; if found, a reexamination of a possible bending of light by a strong magnetic field should be instituted, and laboratorial 100,-000 gauss strong fields applied.

C. bending of stellar light rays by solar plasma (in the corona) must be evaluated and taken into account.

XII. Special Relativity Theory

A. a direct comparison of velocity of light in relation to an observer in motion and in state of rest in relation to the source of light can be executed by comparing the velocity of light from a terrestrial source with that from the sun in the morning and in the afternoon. Details of the experiment upon request.

(signed) Im. Velikovsky

MARCH 14, 1967

Memorandum to the Space Board of the National Academy of Sciences. Submitted to H. H. Hess, Chairman. On Radioactivity Hazards on Moon and Mars.

In view of the fact that landing of astronauts on moon is planned for only a few years from now, I submit this memorandum to draw the attention of the Board and also of NASA to a special condition the astronauts most certainly will meet on the Moon that may to a great degree invalidate the effort and its usefulness, and endanger the lives of the astronauts even if they succeed in returning. The cosmic rays hitting the Moon, solar plasma, and other incoming radiation are thought of, but one more source of radioactive hazard needs to be met.

Because of the intensity and multiplicity of the interplanetary bolts to which the Moon was subjected only 27 and 35 centuries ago (as described in *Worlds in Collision*) radioactivity must still be present on the surface of the Moon in quantity damaging to unprotected man or animal and by far exceeding any exposure regarded as safe.

Although the heat in the Moon's subsurface is mostly a residue of the effects of disturbance in the Moon's motions that occurred in the same historical periods, some of the heat is also of radioactive origin. The half-mile of radium being 1580 years, enough radiation could be present on the Moon of this and other radioactive decays to prompt me to express this warning.

About four years ago, I drew the attention of Professor C. Pittendrigh to the danger of back-contamination, whereas then only the problem of micro-organic contamination of planetary bodies occupied the scientific advisers to space probes; not long thereafter the problem of back-contamination was discussed by Pittendrigh and others in committees and became a vital issue.

Everything that is said above of the radioactive perils to unprotected life on the Moon is applicable in the same degree to the future efforts to place man on Mars. Only on Mars, one should reckon with the probability of the presence of pathogenic, to man, micro-organisms, as well.

Of the many "craters" on the Moon, some—with raised rims and with no rills radiating from them—were in my understanding formed while, in cosmic disturbances, the surface of the Moon became molten and boiled (*Worlds in Collision*, p. 361). The subsequent discovery of domes or unburst bubbles confirms this understanding of the processes that created many of the craters.

"Craters" with rills radiating from them could be caused by infall of asteroids; granted that such a process also took place, I wish to stress that interplanetary discharges must have created a large number of such formations.

A landing of man on the Moon must be preceded well in advance by careful examination of the radioactivity on the Moon's surface. The source described here is of equal importance, or possibly even of greater, than the effect of cosmic or other incurrent radiations on unprotected organic life. The required measurements must be made, not from orbiting space probes but by landing vehicles with instrumentation designed to detect various forms of localized sources of radiation.

(signed) Im. Velikovsky

MAY 19, 1969

Memorandum Submitted to H. H. Hess, Chairman, Space Board, National Academy of Sciences, Washington, D.C., Concerning the Forthcoming Landings on the Moon the First of Which is Scheduled for the Summer of this Year.

The Moon was repeatedly heated and its entire surface melted less than 35 to 27 centuries ago. At the times the Moon's surface was molten in near approaches with other celestial bodies, it was enveloped in powerful magnetic fields; if the surface cooled down below the Curie point before the magnetic fields were weakened and removed, then it is to expect that lavas on the moon (most of its rock is lava) still possess a high magnetic remanence.

Of the lunar ringforming formations a larger number resulted from bubbling activity; but some of the craters (especially with rays extending) resulted from interplanetary electrical discharges. Near such craters a strong, decidedly harmful, radioactivity must still linger and magnetic anomaly could exist. Large meteorites caused a third group of craters. Rocks removed by astronauts should be marked as to their position in relation to cardinal points and not pulverized.

In the mid-second millennium before the present era, Earth was drenched in hydrocarbons of exogenous origin. The Moon may well have hydrocarbons in the form of dried naphtha, bituminous rocks, asphalt, or waxes.

"River beds" on the surface of the Moon resulted not from water streams but from local flows of lava after the crust cooled off to a semi-viscous consistency, following the last in the series of paroxysms (27 centuries ago).

(Signed) Immanuel Velikovsky

JULY 2, 1969

Dear Harry:

In April I read to you my short memo concerning the Moon; on May 19 I left a copy with Dr. Otalara, your scientific assistant; next you assured me that this time I would be proven mistaken. The future landings, not necessarily the first one, will bring the answers.

When I maintain (see the way I expressed myself in my memo) that the rocks on the moon may be magnetic though the moon possesses hardly any magnetic field of its own, I suggest something that is not expected. Yet should the rocks be found magnetic, the explanation will be immediately forthcoming that this proves their meteoric nature. Therefore I have urgently advised— and I repeat it here—that the orientation of the rocks before their removal should be noticed and marked.

Meteorites would fall at random and would not be all similarly oriented. You said to me that this simple task of marking the orientation is *not* included in the program; if it will be omitted you will have a question instead of an answer.

You expect ice under the upper layer of the crust. Some nine thousand years ago water was showered on Earth and Moon alike (deluge). But on the Moon all of it dissociated, hydrogen escaping; the rocks will be found rich in oxygen, chlorine, sulfur and iron.

Moon has no oceans and no marine life; water covered it only for a very limited time (following the deluge) counted in hundreds of years. Nevertheless I maintain bitumen and other hydrocarbon residues and derivatives will be discovered on the Moon, though not necessarily on the first landing; such discovery will be *followed* by the claim that rich marine life once existed on the moon. But my claim is based on the occurrence 34 centuries ago described in *Worlds in Collision*. Since the moon was heated and its surface became molten only a few thousand years ago, the temperature gradient under the surface crust will show, to some depth, a mounting curve.

In friendship,
(signed) Im. Velikovsky

AUGUST 7, 1969

Dear Harry:

Yesterday evening I called in connection with the long telephone conversation we had the day before, in the morning about 10 a.m., when I called you at your office. At that time I told you of my article in NY Times of July 21st and asked very insistently that thermoluminescence tests should be performed. You told me that age testing of the lunar rocks is scheduled; I asked by what methods, you answered, for instance, by the potassium-argon method; to this I replied that I definitely expect neon and argon as inclusions in lunar rocks but their origin is from near contacts with Mars in the eighth and beginning of the seventh century before the present era and I was concerned that the presence of argon next to neon in the rocks of the moon would cause wrong deductions as to the time when the lunar surface was molten for the last time. You told me that when a rock is molten an argon inclusion would escape; I asked in reply whether the softening of the rock would suffice for the escape of neon and argon or a higher heat would be required; you have considered the problem and it was left undecided in your mind whether the duration and the temperature of the process as I visualize in these catastrophic events would have sufficed for the inert gases to completely escape.

I also reminded you at that conversation in the morning of Aug. 5, that in Worlds in Collision (1950) I claimed that neon and argon are chief constituents of the Martian atmosphere; that already in 1945 or 1946 I registered a lecture copyright on "Neon and Argon in Mars' Atmosphere"; that I corresponded on the subject with H. Shapley and Walter S. Adams in 1946; in my book I also explained that Venus, earth, moon, and Mars had been at various times in near contacts; that Mars and the moon disturbed each other greatly, exchanged electrical discharges, and that Mars left some of its gases on earth and the moon.

When yesterday afternoon I read Wilford's dispatch from Houston in the morning NY Times concerning the find of neon and argon by Dr. Oliver A. Schaeffer who heated lunar dirt to 3,000° F and by this released radioactive neon and argon (besides helium, krypton, and xenon) I called you and reached you by phone at supper time at your home.

About twelve days ago I wrote to Prof. A. W. Burgstahler, Chemistry Department, University of Kansas, the same concern of what will be the verdict concerning the time the lunar rock was lastly molten because of the inclusions of argon and neon in lunar rocks, the gases being of Martian origin. Dr. Schaeffer ascribes them to solar wind but admits that their participation in solar wind was not expected.

Next, I expect that neon and argon will be found as

main ingredients of Martian atmosphere as I claimed for almost quarter of a century.*

Cordially,
(signed) Immanuel

* In March 1974, Soviet scientists reported that the Mars 6 spacecraft discovered "several tens of per cent of some inert gas," which they assumed was largely argon. This view has since gained acceptance among Western scientists. *Editor.*

PART II

A most remarkable aspect of the protracted debate over Velikovsky and his unsettling thesis of global catastrophes in historical times is the doggedness with which his critics insist on attacking his ideas with arguments based on assumptions that are entirely invalid in terms of his thesis. That such argumentation is both irrelevant and illogical seems never to occur to many of these critics, or at least they never publicly acknowledge that they recognize the fallacy of their approach. Nowhere is this strange effect more noticeable than in discussion of Velikovsky's claim that the Earth's "world order"—reflected in the observed motions of external bodies—changed repeatedly in the millennia before the present era. Again and again, astronomers have insisted that their retrospective calculations based on the *assumption* that the present order of things in the solar system was established billions of years ago, disprove Velikovsky's conclusions.

On the following pages are presented several papers in which Velikovsky returns to the defense of his position on changing world orders.

"The Orientation of the Pyramids" partially documents Velikovsky's case for changing world orders as based on the alignments and realignments of ancient structures built to reflect various astronomical phenomena.

The appearance in the mid-1960s of numerous writings by astronomer Gerald S. Hawkins on the subject of the possible purposes and alignments of various stages in the construction and reconstruction of Stonehenge, a megalithic monument in England, led to Velikovsky's writing

"On decoding Hawkins' *Stonehenge Decoded*." This paper first appeared as a part of "A Rejoinder to Burgstahler and Angino," in *Yale Scientific Magazine* for April 1967. In view of the growing interest in the entire field of archaeo-astronomy, or astroarchaeology, the timeliness of this paper has actually increased since it was written.

(In a more recent book, *Beyond Stonehenge* (New York: Harper & Row, 1973), Hawkins acknowledges (p. 267) Velikovsky's contentions regarding Stonehenge and the reasons for its many reconstructions. But he begs off being required to respond: ". . . the fitting of Stonehenge into the prehistoric chronology of western Europe [is] a specialized and difficult task, and in my own research I left it to the archaeo-experts. If he [Velikovsky] wished to take up his arguments with them . . . [sic]")

Writing of ancient "Babylonian Observations of Venus," Professor Lynn E. Rose backs up Velikovsky's argument with further documentation of changing world orders. Rose finds that "when you examine the content of those tablets [widely referred to as the 'Venus Tablets of Ammizaduga'], they turn out to support Velikovsky and not his critics . . . there is no way the tablets can be reconciled with the present motions of Venus, except by denying, in one way or another, that the Babylonians saw what they say they saw."

The final two entries in this section concern an ancient world order in which the Earth was companionless in space.

Velikovsky's "Earth Without a Moon" appears here exactly as it was written in the early 1940s.

"Giordano Bruno's View on the Earth Without a Moon" is part of a larger project involving the translation into English of Bruno's Latin works. Dr. A. M. Paterson, professor of philosophy at the State University of New York College at Buffalo, and author of *The Infinite Worlds of Giordano Bruno* (Springfield, Ill.: Charles C. Thomas, 1970), is editing translations prepared by Gail Paterson as an M.A. candidate at the State University of New York at Buffalo. The project is under the direction of Professor Rose.

THE ORIENTATION OF THE PYRAMIDS*

Immanuel Velikovsky

A little consideration reveals that, should the terrestrial axis be turned tomorrow into a new astronomical direction by *any* angle of inclination toward the ecliptic, the Great Pyramid would remain properly oriented to the north and south poles; there would be a new celestial pole and, if so positioned, a new polar star, but the pyramid would remain with two of its sides aligned with the geographical poles. Should the terrestrial axis be turned by anything like 180°, north and south would change places (a hieroglyphic text quoted in *Worlds in Collision,* p. 107: "The south becomes north, and the Earth turns over"), but the pyramid would not be disoriented. Actually, quite a number of authors of classical antiquity refer to earlier changes in the inclination of the terrestrial axis and to subsequent positions it took (*Worlds in Collision,* Part I, Ch. 5; Part II, Chs. 7 and 8).

Should the orbit undergo a change, and with it the length of the year, and besides, the relative length of the seasons, or should the rotational speed change, and with it the length of the day—the Great Pyramid would remain true to the terrestrial poles.

Only with the additional displacement of the *geographical* position of the axis (location of the poles), would the pyramid be disoriented (unless the poles should travel along the meridian of Gizeh). The present azimuth (orientation) of the sides of the Great Pyramid indicates that any disturbance in the geographical position of the poles

* Copyright 1967 by Immanuel Velikovsky. This first appeared in *Yale Scientific Magazine,* April 1967.

since it was built must have been of a temporary character, the Earth's equatorial bulge acting as a stabilizer. In such a case, wobbling would result—a residue of such wobbling is still present. For figures, see *Earth in Upheaval,* "Shifting Poles." In that book I also offer reasons why only the first kind of disturbance (shifting of the *celestial* pole) would be of stable nature.

In *Worlds in Collision* I described both kinds of change —in the direction of the axis and in the position of the poles; but in *Earth in Upheaval,* on the basis of geophysical facts, I ascribed lasting change only to the first kind of displacement, and changes of temporal character to the second.

An application of force (or force field) on the globe creating any such displacement would result in stress in the terrestrial strata and in great earthquakes, and the question can be asked: How is it that the pyramids still stand? Years ago, I wrote on the subject (in a debate with Professor J. Q. Stewart, Princeton astronomer, in *Harper's* for June 1951): "Their solid construction (one per cent free space inside) prevents the stones from being moved inward, and the angle of inclination of sides to horizon, from moving outward. The pyramid is the most stable of all forms. The king's chamber inside Cheops' pyramid has five ceilings of granite slabs, one above the other. Earthquakes have been 'extremely severe in wrenching, as all the deep beams of granite over the King's Chamber in the Great Pyramid are snapped through at the south end, or else dragged out. . . . The whole roof hangs now by merely catching contact' (Petrie, *Egyptian Architecture*)."

In a lecture delivered in April 1966 at Yale University on the subject "The Pyramids, Their Purpose and Orientation," I stressed that the entirety of Egyptian astronomy, as G. A. Wainwright brought out, was developed with the celestial position of the terrestrial axis playing the governing role. Chinese astronomy was so oriented, too (J. Needham). See also the section "Tao," in *Worlds in Collision.* The persisting order of the world and solar motions were watched with the help of the obelisks, for which we have the testimony of Pliny (*Worlds in Collision,* p. 320).

The Babylonian and Greek astronomies were oriented primarily toward east and west, or to the rising and setting points of the Sun at equinoxes and solstices; therefore the Babylonian stargazers, as a multitude of cuneiform texts witness, carefully watched whether the equinoctial days arrived on time and whether any change occurred in the horizon positions of sunrising points on the winter and summer solstice days. Should the equinox day retard or precede, or should the Sun rise too far or not far enough to the north or to the south on the solstices, the order of the world was no more the same. Actually, the very numerous cuneiform tablets found in the ruins of the Nineveh royal library, and if dating from before ca. —700, contain calendric and astronomical data that differ greatly from those of our times; that advanced mathematics was employed in preparing these tablets is readily admitted by specialists in Babylonian astronomy.

According to these tablets, the calendar was repeatedly altered, and at certain periods the vernal equinox was identified on dates far removed from March 21; the values for the longest and shortest days (daylight hours) of the year repeatedly and drastically changed, too.

Significantly, the very same changes in the calendar and in estimates of the longest and shortest days of the year can be traced in Egyptian texts.

Changes in the world order took place as late as the eighth century before the present era. With the recurrent alterations in the world order, the sunrising point on the summer solstice was inevitably displaced, and such displacement was observed and registered by the sages of all ancient civilizations; it can be traced in altered orientation of the foundations of Greek and Syrian temples— a subject discussed in *Worlds in Collision,* where works of J. N. Lockyer and F. G. Penrose, among others, are cited.

Only recently, the excavators of the Shechem temple (Jordan) found another such change in orientation: old foundations were not re-used when new foundations, less massive, were laid on the same site, differing in orientation by only five degrees. Professor Bull of Drew University commented that the change must have had to do with observations of the sunrising point (on the summer solstice) by worshipers.

ON DECODING HAWKINS'
STONEHENGE DECODED*

Immanuel Velikovsky

In 1963 and 1964, a young and talented astronomer, Professor Gerald S. Hawkins, published two papers in the British magazine *Nature* (October 26, 1963, and June 27, 1964). The subject of the papers was developed by him in articles (*Harper's* magazine, June 1964; *American Scientist,* December 1965; *Physics Today,* April 1966); in a book (Garden City, N.Y.: Doubleday & Company, 1965), *Stonehenge Decoded;* and in many lectures before scientific societies and the public.

In the 1963 article, Hawkins claimed that Stonehenge, a stone monument on Salisbury Plain, in England, was erected for astronomical observations (a view going back to Lockyer at the turn of the century and to earlier writers) and that the purpose was to watch the Sun rising on the summer solstices (also an often repeated view); but he claimed further that with certain four selected points as observational stations, the extent of the swing along the horizon between the rising and setting points of the Moon in summer and winter can also be followed up. Also, with some additional selected points, the movements of the Sun could be aligned with great precision for the winter solstice as well. Such a purpose is readily conceivable; the problem, then, is: if the ancient alignments are still valid, how could my reconstruction of past events of catastrophic nature with solsticial sunrising points repeatedly dislodged, be true? Not a small share of the public interest in Hawkins' theory can be attributed to this predicament.

Before we examine 1) whether the alignments are true today and 2) whether they were in the same in ancient times, I would like to present Hawkins' view on the motives that guided the ancients in erecting Stonehenge, a great monument that required very great efforts on the part of those who, as Hawkins says, "apparently did not know the wheel" (*Stonehenge Decoded*, p. 65) yet brought the huge monoliths from a great distance across plains on rollers and along rivers on rafts.

"They [the Stonehengers] had the means to confirm that the Sun was on course. They certainly had reasons to be vitally concerned with the observations. If the Sun ever failed to turn at the heelstone at midsummer and day after day rose further to the left, then intense heat and drought would surely follow. Today we have absolute confidence in the regular movement of the Earth around the Sun" (Hawkins, *American Scientist,* December 1965, 395).

This concern of the ancient Stonehengers is, of course, hardly understandable if past experience had given no reasons for such apprehension. This, however, Hawkins does not consider and thus he ascribes to the ancients, on the one hand, very advanced ideas like building an astronomical computer (his second article and thesis), and, on the other hand, an apparently unfounded fear that the Sun might go out of control.

In his second paper, in *Nature* (1964), titled "Stonehenge: A Neolithic Computer," Hawkins claimed that the Stonehengers dug out fifty-six holes in a circle (Aubrey holes, from the name of their seventeenth-century discoverer) around Stonehenge in order to predict lunar eclipses. Hawkins wrote in the preface to his book: "In retrospect it is a conservative hypothesis for it allows the Stonehenger to be equal to, but not better than, me. Many facts, for example the 56-year eclipse cycle, were not known to me and other astronomers, but were discovered (or rather rediscovered) from the decoding of Stonehenge."

A 56-year eclipse cycle was unknown to modern astronomers but known to the Stonehengers and learned from them by Hawkins, who, in order to find this secret of Stonehenge, used a modern computer.

How important was it for the Neolithic (late Stone Age) dwellers of Salisbury Plain to know in advance the times of lunar eclipses? Their computer was not built to predict solar eclipses.

"I could visualize Stonehenge being an instrument which was useful for giving some warning of the danger of an eclipse," says Hawkins in *American Scientist,* and in his book he details this warning system: "Not more than half of those eclipses were visible from Stonehenge, but the good chance that the inevitable eclipse might have been visible from England would have made it well worth while for the Stonehenge priests to use winter moonrise over the heel stone as a danger signal. Far better to call the people out for a false alarm—and then perhaps claim that skilled intercessions had averted the disaster—than to fail to call them out and have the eclipse come without warning!" (*Stonehenge Decoded,* pp. 139–40.)

The ancient computer could predict lunar eclipses only during one winter month, when "the full Moon nearest the winter solstice rose over the heel stone." Thus, the priests of Stonehenge could not spread the alarm during the entire year—lunar eclipses may occur in any of the twelve months of the year; but in order not to compromise themselves, they alarmed their congregation even of lunar eclipses that would be visible only in the Southern Hemisphere, because their computer was geared for such performance: Close to the time of the winter solstice, it was in working condition. The Stonehengers, apprehensive of the danger of lunar eclipses, were unconcerned about solar eclipses because their 56-hole digit computer was attuned only to the 56-year cycle of lunar eclipses, which Hawkins refers to "as those most frightening things" (*Stonehenge Decoded,* p. 147).

According to Hawkins, no other purpose of astronomical character will be discovered in Stonehenge since he has tried out every alignment: "I think there is little else in these areas that can be discovered at Stonehenge" (p. 147).

There are many more holes besides the Aubrey, or X, ring of fifty-six holes (closer to the sarsen monuments are thirty holes of a Y ring and twenty-nine holes of a Z ring, and inside the ring of the monoliths there are fifty-nine holes prepared for bluestones, from which those stones were removed) and many stones, large and small, as well. Hawkins subjected all possible alignments to a computer test to seek out their possible significance in observing celestial bodies.

"There are so many possible Stonehenge alignments —27,060 between 165 positions—that one could be found to point to practically anything in the sky, and, vice versa, there are so many objects in the sky—perhaps literally an infinite number—that hardly any line extended from earth could fail to hit at least one" (*Stonehenge Decoded,* p. 104).

With 27,060 alignments in a structure designed as an observatory, it is surprising to read that "stars and planets yielded no detectable correlation" (Hawkins in *Nature,* October 26, 1963). There was "no significant matching with planets or with the bigger stars, Sirius, Canopus, Arcturus, Betelgeuse, Spica, Vega . . ." (Hawkins in *Harper's,* June 1964). Not one planet, and not a single prominent star qualified, despite so many chances. The thought must occur that Stonehenge, if it was used for astronomical observations, must have been put together, let us say originally, under a different celestial order. I say "originally" because it will be shown that Stonehenge was repeatedly reordered.

Visiting Stonehenge in the summer of 1957, I, like other visitors, could not but be greatly impressed by the huge monoliths capped by lintels, all shaped by human hand: There is a circle of such rectangular stones, and inside the circle still larger stones capped to form trilithons. The larger of these "sarsen" stones weigh up to fifty tons each, and all the "sarsens" were brought south a distance of twenty miles to Stonehenge. Less spectacular features, not paid attention to by many a visitor, include a circular ditch with raised banks surrounding the area, in which, in concentric rings, the already mentioned X, Y, and Z holes surround the sarsen monoliths. Inside the ring of these monoliths, but outside the horseshoe-like formation of trilithons (originally five in number), there are fifty-nine or sixty holes, some of them still occupied by "bluestones," five or so feet high and weighing four to six tons each; inside the horseshoe, there is another horseshoe of bluestones. Outside the circular ditch, but actually in an "avenue" formed by two parallel extensions of the ditch, stands a roughly shaped (not trimmed by hand) stone with its apex leaning from the vertical—the so-called Heel Stone. It is not located centrally in the avenue, but closer to one of the side ditches. Several holes found in the avenue suggest that at various times other stones the size of the Heel Stone stood in them, or that the Heel Stone itself was moved from one to another of them and finally to its present position in the avenue. Between the Heel Stone and the sarsen stones lies the so-called Slaughter Stone.

It is generally believed that on the summer solstice (June 21) the sun, viewed from the central position through an aperture between two sarsen slabs, rises directly over the Heel Stone; this belief also served as the initial assumption of Hawkins' theories. However, the official guidebook on Stonehenge, written by Professor of Archaeology R. J. C. Atkinson and published by the British Government, states:

"It is commonly believed that on 21st June, when today large crowds gather to see the dawn, an observer at the center of Stonehenge will see the sun rise immediately over the Heel Stone, and that it will cast a shadow of the top of the Heel Stone on the Altar Stone. Neither of these widely held beliefs is correct. Today the midsummer sun rises appreciably to the left of the Heel Stone, and when Stonehenge was built it rose even further to the left; it will not rise *over* the Heel Stone for more than a thousand years." Atkinson is the recognized authority on Stonehenge.

When Hawkins published his theory, Atkinson came out with an annihilating criticism (*Nature,* 210 [1966],

1302; *The New York Review of Books,* June 23, 1966), and developed it in greater detail under the title "Moonshine on Stonehenge" in the September 1966 issue of *Antiquity,* a scholarly magazine published in England.

Atkinson accused Hawkins of being very inexact with figures and measurements. Instead of making measurements on the spot, Hawkins used two different maps, one of them by Atkinson, which, as the latter stressed, was never made for such a purpose, being intended only to show the approximate positions of the stones and holes, "wholly inappropriate as a basis for accurate measurement." The other map comes from "a now-obsolete" Ministry of Works plan from earlier editions of the official guide. Further, Atkinson stresses that even then Hawkins permits himself an inadmissible tolerance of two degrees of arc in accepting nonalignment as perfect alignment. He does this "in spite of the fact that 2° is equivalent to about four diameters of the sun or moon," whereas with a pair of sticks the rising or setting of the Sun can be fixed within "repeatable limits of 5 minutes of arc," or twenty-four times as accurately. "Translated into practical terms, it means, for instance, that the Heel Stone could be moved 12 feet to the northeast without affecting Hawkins' claim."

Hawkins says, "We have no record of what the ancients took to be the instant of sunrise. Was it the first gleam or the moment when the whole disk stands on the horizon?" (*Nature,* 1963). Feeling free to select either one or the other, he mostly chooses the complete emergence of the disk in fixing the rising point on the horizon, but occasionally half the disk, and then also (for 2000 B.C.) one full diameter *above* the horizon (*Stonehenge,* p. 18). This is hardly permissible: on the solar solstice the Sun rises obliquely, and when it is in full view its lower limb is not even approximately where its upper limb is when the first ray of sunshine appears; in one stance, incidentally, Hawkins refers to a 2° displacement of the Sun along the horizon during the time of emergence.

Contrary to that assumption that the ancients have not left any tradition for what they regarded as the rising moment of the Sun, we have records from many ancient

103

civilizations—Egyptian, Hebrew (Temple of Solomon*), Mexican—that the shining forth of the first ray of the sun was *the* moment. The heliacal rising of a star, important in the reckoning of the so-called Sothis period in Egypt, was defined by the moment the first ray of the Sun showed up.

Atkinson showed by a number of examples that Hawkins, in obtaining supposedly significant alignments for the Moon and the Sun, made "inadmissible" claims. Thus, of eight alignments claimed for Stonehenge III (one of the several periods during which the monument was taking its shape), "four of them fall outside Hawkins' own arbitrary limits of error; two more involve fallen stones; and one would almost certainly have been blocked by the Slaughter Stone when upright." Especially offended is Professor Atkinson by Hawkins' claims based on Bernoulli's law of statistical chance. "The probability quoted is wrong; the method of testing the hypothesis is wrong; and the restriction of the possible sightlines . . . is wholly inadmissible."

The final blow came when it was shown that the 56-year cycle of lunar eclipses, first allegedly discovered by the Stonehengers, does not exist in nature. Yet this was the only basis for identifying the fifty-six Aubrey holes and with them the entire Stonehenge complex as an ancient computer. "Such eclipses repeat every 65 years (in periods of 19, 19 and 27 years) and not every 56 years (19, 19 and 18 years) as claimed by Hawkins," write R. Colton and R. L. Martin in *Nature* for February 4, 1967, in a paper titled "Eclipse Cycles and Eclipses at Stonehenge." They also produce a table of eclipses for the past hundred years to demonstrate the true cycle. "The Aubrey holes at Stonehenge were not constructed to predict eclipses on a 56 year cycle."

Thus, of the entire theory not one thing is left. But this is significant in itself. Stonehenge emerges as an obsolete observatory, in the same state as the ancient sundials

(* *The Temple of Jerusalem was so built that on the two equinoctial days the first ray of the rising sun shone directly through the eastern gate."*—Worlds in Collision, *p. 318, with a reference to the* Tractate Erubin *of the* Jerusalem Talmud.)

and water clocks found in Egypt. These also do not work today; they disclose a ratio of the longest day in the year to the shortest day that is very different from what is valid at the latitudes of Egypt in the present arrangement of the world (cf. *Worlds in Collision,* "The Shadow Clock" and "The Water Clock"). However, Stonehenge could be rearranged to meet a new order, not so the water clocks and sundials.

That Stonehenge was actually and repeatedly rearranged is not given to question.

I will quote Hawkins as well as Atkinson, his own authority on the archaeology of Stonehenge. The history of this monument during construction is divided by Atkinson into periods I, II, IIIA, IIIB, and IIIC, all together some four hundred years. "As in many of our later cathedrals and churches, not all of the structures we see at Stonehenge today were built at the same time."

To Period I, according to Atkinson, belong the bank and ditch, the Heel Stone, and the Aubrey holes. "Nothing is known about the ceremonies for which they were used."

Period II. "About 150 years later," the monument "was radically remodeled. At least 80 bluestones, weighing up to four tons apiece, were brought from the Prescelly Mountains in Pembrokeshire," a place over 130 miles away (but as rollers roll and rafts float, 240 miles), and were set to form "a double circle in the center of the site." With an entrance on the northeast side, this double circle had a new axis: "On the opposite side was a large pit, which may have held a stone of exceptional size. . . . In order to make the entrance of the old earthwork fit this new axis, about 25 ft. of the bank on the east side of the entrance gap was thrown back into the ditch, to widen the original causeway." The builders of this period, at the end of the Neolithic age, "may possibly have introduced the idea of sky- or sun-worship." They "never completed their work."

Period IIIA. "The double circle of bluestones, still unfinished, was dismantled and its stones put on one side. In their place over 80 enormous blocks of sarsen stones were dragged from the Marlborough Downs"; they are what make the monument so impressive.

Period IIIB. Soon thereafter, "rather more than twenty of the dismantled bluestones were selected, carefully dressed to shape, and erected in an oval setting." The "exact plan is still uncertain."

"It seems clear that to complete the monument the builders intended to use the remaining 60 bluestones; and it is almost certainly to hold these that the two rings of Y and Z Holes were dug. But for some reason, perhaps an unforeseen catastrophe or an unlucky omen, the project was abandoned unfinished . . . the whole design was given up, and the oval setting of dressed bluestones in the center was demolished."

Period IIIC. "The final reconstruction of Stonehenge probably followed almost at once. The uprights of the dressed oval structure were re-set in the horse-shoe of bluestones we see today." Other changes were made and some stones were "battered down." "The rest of the circle was made up of the undressed bluestones which had earlier been intended for the Y and Z Holes. Originally the total number of stones in this circle must have been at least 60. . . . The largest bluestone of all, the Altar Stone, was probably set up as a tall pillar in front of the central sarsen trilithon and has since fallen down."

"The date of this final reconstruction is not known for certain; but it seems likely that all three stages of Period III followed closely on one another, and that Stonehenge as we see it today was already complete by 1400 B.C."

Hawkins, speaking of Stonehenge II and "a pattern of radiating spokes" of stones, says: "This was an unusual pattern. Could the spokes enclosing the sacred center have been meant to serve as sighting lines from or over that center? Were the stones only a ritual barrier? Or was the design a blunder?" Whatever it was, "for some reason the whole double bluestone circle structure was abandoned, apparently in a hurry."

An interesting detail. Just as the fifty-six holes in the Aubrey circle served Hawkins for his theory that Stonehenge was a computer, so four "stations," or points, rather symmetrically positioned along that circle served him for his initial theory about the extent of solar and lunar movements along the horizon. Atkinson claims that of these four points (none corresponds with any of the fifty-six holes) one is nothing but a hole left by a dead tree, and another of the four stations was simply postulated by Hawkins (no mark present) for the sake of symmetry. With the erection of the sarsen monoliths, the most important lines of sight were obstructed, and Hawkins readily admits this. The question then is: Why should the builders of the monument disregard the purpose of the whole and obstruct needed lines of vision?

Speaking of the sarsen circle of Stonehenge IIIA, Hawkins observes that its center did not coincide with that of the old, Stonehenge I circle of Aubrey holes. The Slaughter Stone was probably "tipped out of its hole . . . during the first centuries after the construction, perhaps because it interrupted the Heel Stone view."

In the IIIB period, ". . . the bluestones which had been taken down to make way for the sarsens were re-erected in an apparently oval formation within the sarsen horseshoe. Perhaps the 'Altar Stone' was erected. The Y and Z holes were dug. And then the bluestone oval was dismantled." "Like the Aubrey holes," the Y and Z holes were "filled soon after they were dug."

In the final stage—IIIC—"the builders re-erected the bluestones of the dismantled oval. They made the bluestone horseshoe whose remains still stand today. They also erected a circle of bluestones between the sarsen horseshoe and the sarsen circle."

Although in 1966 Professor Hawkins sent me a copy of *Worlds in Collision* with the request to inscribe it to him, I believe that at the time he wrote his *Stonehenge Decoded* he did not yet know the content of my book. Writing of the bluestone spoked wheel, "If the builders did design that bluestone wheel as a moon-follower, it may be that they abandoned it so suddenly because they found" that it did not work as it should—Hawkins was just one step from making a correct deduction.

One project after another was started by the ancient builders, then abandoned and replaced with another arrangement. The similar quotations from Atkinson and Hawkins bring close the idea that for purposes otherwise inexplicable, the structure was repeatedly remodeled to conform with the changed orders of the world. It seems to me that the work of decoding Stonehenge can advance if calendric and astronomical texts of literate peoples of antiquity are consulted. In the first place, the cuneiform texts with observations and calculations performed by the ancient sages should be brought into the picture—but first themselves processed by computers in order to find the direction of the terrestrial axis and the form of Earth's orbit in different periods of the second millennium before the present era. It is not an easy assignment, and all depends on the good will of specialists in cuneiform astronomy and calendarology. There exists, for instance, a cuneiform manual—*mul apin*—of before −700, using advanced methods, precise data, and proper mathematics, but in "complete disregard" of today's prevailing calendric and astronomical figures. The cuneiform material is the richest, but there are preserved ancient data from Egypt, India, and Mexico as well, and a comparative study of this material—a beginning made in *Worlds in Collision* —needs to be pursued as a major field of research.

The last change in the celestial order took place in the beginning of the seventh century, actually on March 23, −687 (*Worlds in Collision*, Part II, Ch. 2). It is easily conceivable that subsequent efforts were made to adjust once more the stone markers of Stonehenge, and it is quite probable that the Heel Stone was moved from its former position. Hawkins also speaks of a "hole in the avenue, large enough to hold a huge stone, from which the stone was removed."

The number fifty-six was sacred to Typhon, as Hawkins, advised by Professor G. de Santillana, found in Plutarch (*American Scientist,* December 1965). This author of the first century of the present era reports that in the Pythagorean secret teaching "the figure of 56 angles [is sacred] to Typhon," in whom they see "a demoniac power." In the same work of his (*Isis and Osiris*), Plutarch ascribes to Typhon "abnormal seasons," and in another essay, in *Morals,* he explains: "The sun was not fixed to an unwandering and certain course, so as to distinguish orient and occident, nor did he [the sun] bring back the seasons in order" (*Worlds in Collision,* p. 121).

Other ancient writers identified Typhon with Lucifer, the morning star, and also with Set (Satan). Late-Renaissance chronographers, on the basis of ancient texts, claimed that the comet Typhon shone at the same time the Israelites left Egypt (Abraham Rockenbach [1602] and other writers quoted in *Worlds in Collision,* pp. 82ff.). Thus fifty-six was connected by the Pythagoreans with the morning star; and the morning star by other early authorities with the Exodus. But care should be exercised not to make mathematical games out of Stonehenge.

Judging by the parallels in other civilizations and the repeated calendar changes in the next critical period, the eighth century and the beginning of the seventh, the late and massive Stonehenge III (A, B, and C) was, most probably, put together and repeatedly rearranged in that period of history to conform with the changes in the natural order. History also teaches that it took several centuries after the great devastations at the close of Middle Bronze IIB (Middle Kingdom of Egypt), in the mid-second millennium, before man could apply himself to the task of erecting massive temples and observatories.

A criterion was offered for determining the age of Stonehenge: an antler of a red deer was found under one of the stones and more antlers in the fill of the holes. But as the Lamont Geological Observatory of Columbia University answered (January 4, 1967) to an inquiry: "Antlers and bones are, in general, unreliable for radiocarbon dating." Also, the Radiocarbon Laboratory of the University of Pennsylvania, in answer to a similar inquiry, let it be known that experience in polar regions proves that antlers are easily contaminated and made to yield invalid dates.

The problem of the age of the various phases of construction of Stonehenge should not obscure the obvious fact that, whatever are the dates of various rearrangements, the ancient Stonehengers had true perils on their minds when they dragged huge monoliths from afar, when they made holes and filled them, when they watched that the Sun should not continue to rise past the foreordained point on the horizon; in this concern of the generations of the ancients, the modern Stonehengers should see a clue; it is in vain to search the motive for erecting Stonehenge in awe before "the perils" of lunar eclipses during the few weeks following Halloween.

BABYLONIAN OBSERVATIONS OF VENUS*

Lynn E. Rose

Ammizaduga was a relatively obscure king during what is
known as the first Babylonian dynasty; he is usually
thought to have reigned during the early or middle part
of the second millennium before the present era. One of
Ammizaduga's claims to fame is that various cuneiform
tablets describing conjunctions of the planet Venus with
the Sun are said by some to have derived from observations made during the twenty-one years of his reign.
Ammizaduga's other claims to fame are that he was the
great-great-grandson of Hammurabi, and that Ammizaduga (or perhaps it was his son) was the monarch who
lost the kingdom to foreign invaders and thus allowed the
dynasty of Hammurabi to come to an end.

One of the results of this paper will be the suggestion
that the so-called Venus tablets of Ammizaduga have
nothing to do either with Ammizaduga or with his times.
But the two major purposes of the paper are, first, to
examine some of the ways in which scholars have treated
these tablets over the past century or so, and, second, to
give you a progress report on the efforts that Raymond
Vaughan and I are making to try to determine just which
orbits of Venus and of Earth would have produced the
patterns of appearances and disappearances that the ancient Venus-viewers say they saw.

The first of these tablets that we are concerned with is
now in the British Museum, in whose catalogue it is called

* Copyright 1972 by Lynn E. Rose.

K. 160 because it came from Kuyunjik, the site of ancient Nineveh, where it was excavated from the library of Ashurbanipal by Layard about 1850. The text of this tablet was first published by Rawlinson and Smith, in 1870; the text was also published in 1874, by Sayce, this time with a transliteration and with a translation.

In 1880, Bosanquet and Sayce published a translation of K. 160, and offered a preliminary analysis of its contents. They recognized, for example, that K. 160 contains three distinct groups of "observations" of Venus: the first group consist of lines 1–29 on the obverse of the tablet, the second group consists of lines 31–45 on the obverse and lines 1–32 on the reverse, and the third group consists of lines 33–45 on the reverse. They also seem to have been the earliest to adopt with specific reference to the Venus tablets the attitude that might be called the "astronomers' dogma," which I will explain in a moment.

But before we consider any more of the literature on these tablets or the ways in which the astronomers' dogma has dominated that literature, it may be useful to look at the nature of the observations themselves. When Venus is to the east of the Sun, it can be seen in the western sky for a time after sunset and is then spoken of as the "evening star." As Venus moves directly between Earth and the Sun, it is said to be at inferior conjunction with the Sun, and for a brief time Venus cannot be seen because of the brightness of the Sun. But the "evening star" that vanishes from the western sky at inferior conjunction reappears in the eastern sky, west of the sun, as the "morning star," and can be seen for some months in the hours before sunrise. Then Venus approaches superior conjunction, where the Sun is directly between us and Venus, and Venus ceases to be visible from Earth. After this period of invisibility, however, Venus appears once more in the western sky as the "evening star" and the cycle continues.

K. 160 seems to be a record of these invisibilities at inferior and superior conjunction. Let me give some typical passages from the tablet:

In the month Sivan, on the twenty-fifth day, Ninsianna
   [that is, Venus] disappeared in the east;
she remained absent from the sky for two months six
   days; in the month Ulul, on the twenty-fourth day,
Ninsianna appeared in the west—the heart of the land
   is happy.
In the month Nisan, on the twenty-seventh day, Ninsianna disappeared in the west;
she remained absent from the sky for seven days; in
   the month Ayar, on the third day, Ninsianna
appeared in the east—hostilities occur in the land, the
   harvest of the land is successful.

The first invisibility mentioned in these lines involves
a disappearance in the east, an invisibility of two months
six days, and a reappearance in the west. This seems to
be a superior conjunction. The second invisibility involves
a disappearance in the west, an invisibility of seven days,
and a reappearance in the east. This seems to be an inferior conjunction. Most of the data in groups one and
three on the tablet are of this form. But the lengths
and spacings of these invisibilities have a certain irreg-
ularity about them, and they do not conform to the
manner in which Venus moves at present.

The data given in the second group on the tablet
do have regularity—even too much regularity to be be-
lievable—but they do not conform to the present state of
affairs either, and many have wondered if they are actual
observations at all. Actual observations would be marred
by adverse weather conditions, yet the data of this second
group seem to be almost perfect: the invisibility at superior conjunction is always three months, not a day more
and not a day less, and the invisibility at inferior conjunction is always seven days, not a day more and not a
day less. The visibility of the "morning star" lasts eight
months five days (just once, it is eight months four days),
and the visibility of the "evening star" also lasts eight
months five days (just twice, it is eight months four days).
This idealized regularity makes these "observations" very
suspicious-looking.

Another suspicious feature is that the initial appearances are on the first month, the second day; on
the second month, the third day; on the third month, the

fourth day; . . . and so on, up to the twelfth month, the thirteenth day. The idealized and somewhat numerological character of this group of data has led most readers, probably correctly, to suspect that this group of "observations" is not directly based on observation at all, and that if we are seeking actual astronomical observations and records, we should concentrate on the first and third groups on the tablet and not worry about the artificial insertion.

Unfortunately, nearly all treatments of groups one and three on K. 160, and of the genuinely observational material on the other Venus tablets that supplement K. 160, have been based upon what I will call the "astronomers' dogma." The "astronomers' dogma" is the uniformitarian attitude that the solar system has for untold years been just as it is now, and that Venus and Earth in particular have always been on the same orbits they are on now, except for certain very minor perturbations that are for most purposes entirely negligible. This means that we can look at the present motions of Earth and Venus and then judge on that basis how accurate the ancient observations were. If the ancient observations do not conform to what would be expected from the present state of affairs, then the ancient records were defective, and were either fictions or errors, but could not have been accurate observations of what was going on in the sky; accordingly, it is up to us to rewrite those ancient records so that they *will* conform to what we see in the sky today.

As I mentioned, Bosanquet and Sayce seem to have been the first to introduce this astronomers' dogma into the study of the Venus tablets. They did so very cautiously, not because they doubted the astronomers' dogma, but because they were afraid that the ancient records were so insufficient that even the astronomers' dogma would not permit the derivation of any definite conclusions. We shall see that others, such as Kugler, were not so cautious about this as were Bosanquet and Sayce.

We come next to Schiaparelli's 1906 paper in *Das Weltall.* This was an abridgment and updating of a long unpublished monograph on the same subject, the text of which was finally published in 1927, posthumously, in the collection of Schiaparelli's works on ancient astronomy

(*Scritti Sulla Storia Della Astronomia Antica* [Bologna: Nicola Zanichelli Editore, 3 vols.]). In that collection, the monograph on the Venus tablets is preceded by a long excerpt from one of Schiaparelli's letters that deals with further questions about the tablets.

In the literature on the Venus tablets, mention is usually made only of the *Das Weltall* paper; indeed, I have not yet seen any mention either of Schiaparelli's longer monograph or of his letter. So I take this occasion not only to recommend these neglected contributions of Schiaparelli's, which are important for anyone interested in the Venus tablets, but also to recommend in general the great work that Schiaparelli did on ancient astronomy. His reconstruction of the systems of Eudoxus and Kallippus would by itself rank him among the major historians of science. My admiration of his work is tempered by his unwavering loyalty to the astronomers' dogma, but even the astronomers' dogma did not prove an obstacle to his work on Eudoxus and Kallipus, since, after all, Eudoxus and Kallippus were dealing with a solar system not much different from our own.

But when Schiaparelli deals with other subjects—prior, let us say, to -687—it seems to me that his opinions are of less value, precisely because of his acceptance of the astronomers' dogma: Schiaparelli is one of those who feel free to ignore what the tablets actually say whenever they conflict with what modern retro-calculation indicates that they *should* say. But in spite of this weakness, enormous credit must be given to Schiaparelli for noticing what had escaped the attention of the philologists, that the tablet K. 2321 + K. 3032, which had been published in 1899 by Craig, was concerned with the same series of observations as was K. 160. K. 2321 + K. 3032 is referred to with two different numbers because the two pieces of what was later seen to be one tablet were originally numbered separately. Schiaparelli realized that the end of K. 2321 + K. 3032 overlapped the beginning of K. 160, and this gave him a larger sample of observations to work with.

Schiaparelli was also the first to recognize that the data on the reverse of K. 2321 + K. 3032 are actual observations. They are arranged, not chronologically, but in the order of the months of the disappearances of Venus. All the disappearances in the first month, or Nisan, are placed together at the beginning, all the disappearances in the second month, or Ayar, are placed next, and so on, down to all of the disappearances in the twelfth month, or Adar.

Another admirable feature of Schiaparelli's work is that he assigns the tablets to a period no earlier than the eighth century. Vaughan and I, unexpectedly, became inclined toward a similar dating, but for different reasons. Schiaparelli's reason was that the tablets refer to invading hordes of Manda, whom he believes not to have been on the scene in Mesopotamia prior to the eighth century. Some of the later criticisms of this account of the Manda are based on Hittite archives and Hittite chronology. Even in Schiaparelli's own day there were some similar efforts to place the Manda in Mesopotamia prior to the eighth century, but Schiaparelli held firm against this. (Velikovsky may feel that Schiaparelli was on the right track here, in his assignment of a relatively late date to the appearance of the Manda in Mesopotamia.)

The next important work was by Kugler in 1912. He had noted that some of the observations for the eighth year were missing, and that in their place there was a passage that had never yet been adequately understood. Kugler showed that this phrase meant "year of the golden throne," and that it was a year-formula that had been used to refer to the eighth year of the reign of Ammizaduga, the next-to-last king during the first Babylonian dynasty. And so it is at this point that the Venus tablets become linked to Ammizaduga. If the observations really do date from the time of Ammizaduga, then they are probably thirty-five hundred to four thousand years old.

Kugler tried to pin down the epoch more precisely. His method for doing this is, from my point of view, unsatisfactory. He realized that the observations as a whole have little similarity to anything we see Venus doing now, but he thought that if he could date one observation, regardless of its "impossible" context, that would be sufficient. So he picked out one date, from the sixth year of the observations, where Venus is said to have disappeared in the west on the twenty-eighth day of the eighth month. He then determined that if Venus has always moved in the way that it moves now, then there would have been a series of possible dates about four thousand years ago when Venus would have approached inferior conjunction at new moon and at about the right time of the year.

But even if this sort of backward calculation were sound, which it is not, Kugler's method would still be unsatisfactory in that it allows everything to rest on this one observational record. In the first place, the observation that Kugler selects is by no means one of our better-confirmed readings: for every one of the sources gives a slightly *different* report. One source says that Venus disappeared on the twenty-eighth and was invisible for five days. Another source says that Venus disappeared on the twentieth day of the month (or perhaps later—it isn't clear) and was invisible for three days—and here indeed the scribe adds a comment of his own that the text he is copying is defaced or damaged at this spot! A new tablet, discovered only *after* Kugler wrote, says that Venus disappeared on the eighteenth of the month and was invisible for three days. Obviously, this kind of textual evidence is not the sort on which one should be ready to stake one's whole case, and yet that is precisely what Kugler did.

In the second place, and more importantly, Kugler's use of just one observation is questionable in that if this one observation *is* ever placed in accord with modern expectations, then other observations on the tablets are automatically placed in conflict with modern expectations. If you are to reach back to the sixth year of the records by retro-calculation from the present behavior of Venus, you have to pass through all the tablet entries that come after the year six, and each of those later readings must likewise be in accord with your retro-calculation. This means that the five-month invisibility at superior conjunction in year twelve should have lasted only about two months, and that the nine-month invisibility at inferior conjunction in year nine should have lasted only a day or two! In spite of these difficulties, however, Kugler goes ahead with his calculations, and asserts that Ammizaduga's reign began in the year 1977.

In the next few years there were, as one might expect, a number of objections to Kugler's chronological conclusions, but no one seems to have gone so far as to challenge the astronomers' dogma, which was their real foundation.

In 1920, Hommel suggested that the reference to the "year of the golden throne" was inserted by a later copyist, perhaps during the reign of Ashurbanipal, in the seventh century. It does seem likely that the phrase is a later insertion, for it is located in the space that would originally have contained the rest of the observational material for the eighth year. As it is now, we have only the date of Venus' disappearance, not the interval of invisibility and not the date of reappearance. But Hommel thought that even if the insertion was late, the observations themselves still dated from the time of Ammizaduga. A little later I will question this, but at this point I will merely remark that Hommel's suggestion may also be vulnerable in that W. 1924. 802, which is a copy of K. 2321 + K. 3032, contains a scribal "signature" dated in an unreadable year of the reign of Sargon, which would put the insertion a number of decades, at least, prior to Ashurbanipal. Hommel, however, was not aware of W. 1924. 802, since, as the label implies, it was not discovered until four years after his 1920 paper.

The excavation of this new tablet, at Kish in 1924, was announced by Langdon in 1925, and was important in that only the right edge of W. 1924. 802 is unreadable, whereas its duplicate, K. 2321 + K. 3032, is readable on the right side but is broken off on the left. Thus, between them both, we have an excellent set of readings for the first six or seven years of the observations, with usually only very minor discrepancies.

In 1927, Sarton published his *Introduction to the History of Science,* where he made the later very influential pronouncement that: "As early as the close of the third millennium, Babylonian astronomers recorded heliacal risings and settings of the planet Venus." Sartan supports this claim with a footnote mentioning Kugler and Schiaparelli. As we have seen, however, Schiaparelli dated

117

these observations at about the eighth or seventh centuries, and Kugler dated them as covering the reign of Ammizaduga, from 1977–1956. Sarton's reference to "the third millennium" is quite an overstatement of the case, but if you think that's bad, consider what happened in 1950. In the rush to find evidence against Velikovsky, Sarton's sloppy use of "the third millennium" as a substitute for "1977–1956" was resurrected from the libraries and rephrased as "3000 B.C." by people like Kaempffert.* This whole comedy of errors is traceable back to Kugler. Why Schiaparelli was implicated in it escapes me.

The next major study of the Venus tablets was by Langdon and Fotheringham in 1928. Their book is important for the student of the tablets in that they bring together a great deal of material that is not available in any one other place; unfortunately, however, their book is dominated and severely handicapped by the astronomers' dogma, and they find it necessary to scoff at much of what the tablets say was seen, simply because such things are not seen today.

Further attempts to deal with the tablets along uniformitarian lines were made by Ungnad in 1940 and van der Waerden in 1946. Van der Waerden plays the uniformitarian game much better than some of his predecessors, but the main reason I want to mention him here is that he is the clearest example I have found of an unfortunate way of talking and thinking that is characteristic of uniformitarians. He says at one point, after either rejecting or radically rewriting about three out of four of the recorded observations, that: "All I have done is to remove inner contradictions from the text."

It must be admitted that there *are* several genuine "inner contradictions" in the texts; one of them occurs in the passage that I quoted earlier. When we are told that Venus disappeared on the twenty-fifth day of the third month, was absent from the sky for two months six days, and reappeared on the twenty-fourth day of the sixth month, something is wrong here, and it is fairly obvious

* Waldemar Kaempffert was science editor of the New York *Times*.

that we will have to reject at least one of those three items.

But to deal with textual errors of this sort and to rewrite radically the whole set of observations just in order to make them fit the present movements of Venus, as van der Waerden would do, are two entirely different things. And what van der Waerden and others have done is hardly a matter of correcting "inner contradictions." The fact that uniformitarians can think and speak of these things as "inner contradictions" is only symptomatic of how deeply ingrained the astronomers' dogma is. It just never occurs to its victims that they are making any assumptions at all. As far as they are concerned, if the historical record conflicts with modern retro-calculations, there must be some defect in the historical record, and it is perfectly all right to refer to this defect as an "inner contradiction."

The intransigence of this attitude is one of the barriers that Velikovsky ran into in 1950. *Worlds in Collision* devotes pages 198–200 to the Venus tablets. The approach is very cautious: Velikovsky does not claim to know when they originated, or even what orbits of Venus or of Earth could have produced such observations. But he does claim, quite correctly, that the present orbits of Venus and Earth could *not* have produced such observations, and that if the tablets have any reliability at all, then we must admit that Venus was *not* moving on its present orbit at the time the observations were made. Velikovsky thus became the first to propose a non-uniformitarian approach to the tablets.

The story from here on is probably familiar to most readers. You will recall that the Venus tablets came up in Payne-Gaposchkin's review, where she appealed to Sarton and to Langdon and Fotheringham. Payne-Gaposchkin's errors of several sorts were reworded by Kaempffert, with such improvements as the substitution of "3000 B.C." for "third millennium" (which had itself been a substitute for Kugler's "1977–1956"). Then Edmondson copied both the errors and the words of both Payne-Gaposchkin and Kaempffert.

The irony is that both Velikovsky and his critics were drawing upon exactly the same evidence, namely, the

Babylonian Venus tablets. But when you examine the content of those tablets, they turn out to support Velikovsky and not his critics. Those uniformitarians who do take the tablets seriously seem to be either unfamiliar with or oblivious to their contents. How else could Kaempffert say that the Babylonians "saw the planet exactly as we see it"? How else could Stephens say that: "As I consider the texts in their entirety I get quite the opposite impression [i.e., that Venus was *not* moving irregularly at the time these observations were made]"? How else could Neugebauer say that: "From the purely astronomical viewpoint these observations are not very remarkable"? Such statements fly in the face of the Venus tablets, for there is no way the tablets can be reconciled with the present motions of Venus, except by denying, in one way or another, that the Babylonians saw what they say they saw.

I would now like to conclude with a brief progress report concerning the efforts that Raymond Vaughan and I are making to try to find orbits of Earth and of Venus that will fit the recorded observations. Our first move, as you might suspect, was to ignore the astronomers' dogma, and to try to make no rash assumptions about what sorts of orbits we would find. Instead, we tried as far as possible to take the tablet reports as accurate descriptions of what was actually seen, even though they do seem to be marred by 1) a few serious textual inconsistencies of the sort discussed earlier; 2) a score or so minor discrepancies about dates, many of which amount to only a day or two; and 3) several contradictory readings about "east" and "west," none of which presents any major difficulty.

I pointed out to you a little earlier that the events on the tablets do follow a pattern of sorts—not the present pattern, but a pattern of sorts—in that an invisibility at superior conjunction is followed by an invisibility at inferior conjunction, then there is another invisibility at superior conjunction, and so on. In order for this kind of sequence to continue without an interruption, as it does, the orbits of the two planets must lie in nearly the same plane; otherwise, some conjunctions would not be accompanied by invisibility, or, if the inclination of the

120

orbital planes were great enough, the very concept of a "conjunction" with the Sun might lose much of its importance, as it does, for example, in the case of comets. At least for the time being, therefore, we decided to ignore any motions in latitude.

It should be recognized that a near-collision between Earth and another planet would likely have changed the length of the day, the length of the month, and the length of the year. So if the tablets refer to some state of affairs prior to such a near-collision, we cannot be certain what was meant by the words "day," "month," and "year." But in a *ratio* of quantities, the units are irrelevant, so we decided to work in terms of the ratio of the period of Earth to the period of Venus. For purposes of our constructions, we chose to work with denominators of 19. After investigating ratios of 2/19, 4/19, 6/19, and so on, up to 36/19, we found that the ratio at the time of the observations was just about 31/19, or about 1.63, a little higher than the present ratio of about 1.625.

Our lack of any definite units of time or distance was also a problem when we tried to deal with sightings of Venus made from Earth, where the nature of the sighting depends both upon the size and eccentricity of the orbit being followed by Venus and upon the size and eccentricity of the orbit being followed by Earth, and yet we were in no position to say anything about the actual sizes of the orbits. We found a way around this problem by working with changing heliocentric angular velocities, which provided a way of handling sightings and invisibilities without knowing the actual sizes of the orbits.

Proceeding in that way, we found that the observations recorded for years one through nine seem to make sense with an Earth eccentricity of about .1 and a Venus eccentricity of about .15. Years ten through seventeen also make sense with Earth .1 and Venus .15, but the perihelion of Earth's orbit appears to have been shifted from where it was during years one through nine, so that you do not have the same state of affairs as before. Years nineteen through twenty-one makes sense with Earth .0+ and Venus .15. These figures are tentative, and need to be tied down more precisely; and we also need to make sure that no better orbits for explaining the observations are available.

At present, there are still seven spots at which the fit between the pattern of invisibilities recorded on the tablets and the pattern of invisibilities that we constructed is less than satisfying. Six of these discrepancies vary from a few thousandths of a "year" to a few hundredths of a "year"; that is, from about a "day" or two to about ten "days" or so. I hope that we can eventually improve upon this by introducing slight changes and refinements into our model, for we still have considerable leeway for the further manipulation of the characteristics of the orbits.

The only discrepancy I really worry about is the seventh and most serious of those I mentioned. Even if we manage to save all of the remaining phenomena, I see little chance that anything can be done to save this one, which is the eastern disappearance on the twenty-fifth day of the twelfth month of the eighth year. Our model requires that the invisibility ought to have begun at least a month earlier than that. There is some consolation in the fact that this phenomenon belongs to the eighth year, the one that was partially missing and that now contains the year formula of Ammizaduga. There is further consolation in that no wholesale rewriting of the text is involved: if one word, the name of the month Adar, could be changed to Sabat, that would be enough to make things right. But perhaps we should not apologize at all for this one discordant reading, for in doing well by all but one of the phenomena we have already avoided the past practice of having to rewrite most or even nearly all of the recorded observations.

The ratio of the period of Earth to the period of Venus for years one through nine is very close to 31/19; and the ratio for years ten through seventeen is slightly less than 31/19; and the ratio for years nineteen through twenty-one is slightly greater than 31/19. Since there is no sign here of any definite change in the orbit of Venus, this change in the ratios would presumably be due to a change in Earth's orbit; and this suggests that Earth's orbit in years one through nine was slightly greater than in years ten through seventeen and slightly smaller than in years nineteen through twenty-one, *if* the

122

length of the day and the length of the month were not altered enough to distort the observers' estimate of the length of the year to such a degree that this inference about the sizes of Earth's successive orbits would be invalidated. That is a big "if."

In none of these three states of affairs do the orbits of Venus and Earth intersect; thus it seems clear that no collision between Earth and Venus was imminent at the time of these observations. Neither a very large Venus orbit, nor a highly eccentric one (say, .3 or greater), nor a Venus orbit that was highly inclined to the ecliptic, could have produced the observations recorded on the tablets. This does not mean, of course, that at some *other* point in time—presumably earlier—Venus could not have had a very large orbit, or a highly eccentric one, or one that was highly inclined to the ecliptic, but it does mean that such things were not going on at the time of *these* observations.

But what *was* the time of these observations? Since the ratio of the periods of Earth and Venus in each of the three situations is so close to what it is now, it seems unlikely that the observations date from very far before the present orbits of Earth and Venus were established. If we use Velikovsky's own theory as a guide in trying to date the observations, a favorable period would appear to be the eighth century, when Earth and Venus were perhaps not very far from their present orbits (compared, at least, to where they had been at earlier times) and yet were on orbits that were definitely *not* the same as their present orbits. If it was Mars that was the main threat during this period, it may be that the change in Earth's orbit at about year nine was due to a near-collision with Mars; the atmospheric opacity and the disruption of living conditions that would result from a near-collision might explain why Venus was not observed for a period of nine months and four days. A similar Earth-Mars perturbation might have been responsible for the transition from the year-ten-through-year-seventeen state of affairs to the year-nineteen-through-year-twenty-one state of affairs.

It seems clear, then, that our findings not only are consistent with Velikovsky's theory but also may be regarded as providing further confirmation of his theory.

123

It should be noted that if the Venus observations do indeed date from the eighth century, then they have nothing to do with Ammizaduga, and the later insertion of Ammizaduga's year-formula was an ancient error. Hommel suggests that this insertion was made by a scribe during the reign of Ashurbanipal (although we saw that the signature on W. 1924. 802 seems to preclude that late a date for the insertion). But whenever it was done, this error was presumably caused by the coincidence that the Venus observations and the reign of Ammizaduga both covered twenty-one years. If these observations do date from the eighth century, any attempt to connect them with Ammizaduga would involve an error of from seven to twelve centuries, depending upon just when it was that Ammizaduga actually reigned.

The catch-phrase "the Venus tablets of Ammizaduga" has a nice ring to it, but it may be time to give it up as obsolete.

In closing, I would emphasize that these results that Raymond Vaughan and I have reached so far are still tentative; our work is by no means completed, and there are numerous questions that remain to be investigated.

EARTH WITHOUT A MOON*

Immanuel Velikovsky

Democritus and Anaxagoras taught that there was a time when the Earth was without the Moon. Aristotle wrote that Arcadia in Greece, before being inhabited by the Hellenes, had a population of Pelasgians, and that these aborigines occupied the land already before there was a Moon in the sky above the Earth; for this reason, they were called Proselenes (1).

Apollonius Rhodius mentioned the time "when not all the orbs were yet in the heavens, before the Danai and Deukalion races came into existence, and only the Arcadians lived, of whom it is said that they dwelt on the mountains and fed on acorns, before there was a moon (2)."

Plutarch wrote in "The Roman Questions": "These were Arcadians of Evander's following, the so-called Pre-Lunar people (3)." Also Ovid: "The Arcadians are said to have possessed their land before the birth of Jove, and that folk is older than the Moon (4)." Lucian in his book on Astrology says that the Arcadians "affirm in their folly that they are older than the moon (5)."

Censorinus alludes to the time in the past when there was no Moon in the sky (6).

The Assyrians referred to the time of the Moon god as to the oldest period in the memory of the people: before other planetary gods came to dominate the world ages, the Moon was the Supreme Deity (7). Such references are found in the inscriptions of Sargon II (about —720): (8). "Since the far-off days of the Moon-god's time (era)."

Some allusions to the time before there was a Moon may be found also in the Scriptures. In Job 25:5 the grandeur of the Lord who "makes peace in the heights," is praised and the time is mentioned "before (there was) a moon and it did not shine." Also, in Psalm 72:5 it is said: "Thou wast feared since (the time of) the sun and before (the time of) the moon, a generation of generations." [See A.S.V., 1901, fn. 7.—Ed.]

A "generation of generations" means a very long time. Of course, it is of no use to counter this psalm with the myth of the first chapter of Genesis, a tale brought down from exotic and later sources.

It is probably the most remote remembrance of mankind: the time when there was no Moon.

The memory of a world without a Moon lives in oral tradition among the Indians. The Indians of the Bogota highland in the eastern Cordilleras of Colombia relate some of their tribal reminiscences to the time before there was a Moon. "In the earliest times, when the moon was not yet in the heavens," say the tribesmen of Chibchas (9).

The traditions of diverse people offer corroborative testimony to the effect that in a very early age, but still in the memory of mankind, no Moon accompanied the Earth. Since human beings already peopled the Earth, it is improbable that the Moon sprang from it: there must have existed a solid lithosphere, not a liquid earth. Thus it is more probable that the Moon was captured by the Earth.

REFERENCES

1. Aristotle, Fr. 591 (ed. V. Rose).
2. Apollonius Rhodius, IV, 264.
3. Plutarch's *Moralia,* tr. F. C. Babbit, Section 76.
4. Ovid, *Fasti,* tr. Sir James G. Frazer, II, 290.
5. Lucian, *Astrology,* tr. A. M. Harmon, 26 (p. 367).
6. Censorinus, *De die natal.* 19; also Scholium on Aristophanes, *Clouds,* 398.
7. "It is remarkable that at first the primacy was assigned to the moon." Fr. Cumont, *Astrology and Religion Among the Greeks and Romans* (1912), p. 124.
8. Luckenbill, *Ancient Records of Assyria,* Vol. II, 870.
9. A. Humboldt, *Vues des Cordilleras,* I, 87.

GIORDANO BRUNO'S VIEW ON THE EARTH WITHOUT A MOON

A. M. Paterson

Bruno (1548–1600) was a philosopher from the province of Nola, in southern Italy. He was well ahead of his times as he pushed the Copernican hypothesis to its fullest logical conclusion.

Bruno denied the physics of Aristotle. For Bruno, the Sun rotated on its own axis and had dark areas. He wrote that the Earth revolved around the Sun. There were an infinite number of suns, an infinite number of solar systems, and an infinite space. All of the planets (including the Sun and Moon) were made of the same substances as our Earth. All planets including the Sun and the Moon were of the same species and were subject to generation and decay. The Moon was no exception. Bruno wrote in *De Immenso* (Bk. IV, x 56–57):

"There are those who have believed that there was a certain time (as our Mythologian says) when the moon, which was believed to be younger than the sun, was not yet created. The Arcadians, who dwelt not far from the Po, are believed to have been in existence before it (the moon). Apollonius says in the fourth book of his *Argonautica* that the Danaan race had been heard of by no one; but at one time there were only the Arcadians dwelling in the Alps. Those Arcadians said that they were there before the moon, in time and years. They were dispersed throughout the high mountains and lived on acorns. Theodorus writes in his first book that the moon had appeared a little while before the war which was fought by Hercules against the giants. Aristochius, and Dionysius Chalcidensis, in the first of their works, confirm the same. Mnaseas says that Proselenus, son of Orchomenus, had ruled over the Arcadians; this Duris of Samos affirmed in the fifteenth book of his Macedonian deeds, when he said that he named the river Orchomenus after his father; and Mnaseas said that the Arcadians were born before the moon, and so they were called "proselenian"; meaning, "before the moon." There is nothing unfitting in nature adduced by these historians, nor is anything said here not most befitting nature (whatever may be said in peripatetic philosophy and the censure of the grammarians). For the earth, which is of the same species as the moon, is of creatable and destructible substance, and is truly animal and even mortal, although divine. Therefore, the planets (worlds) are able to be created and destroyed, and it is not possible that they have been eternal, since we have proved them to be alterable and consisting of changing parts. I shall not make interpretations of their matter and their spirit, since it requires a higher judgment. This, however, is certain, that all things, according to their whole being, come from God. But as to the beginning of the creation (according to its duration) there is much dispute. The vulgar herd cannot understand that the eternal, according to its whole being, can come from another."

Bruno points out here that planets, taken as members of a physical species, cannot be eternal. "Eternal" is not an object which has been created physically. "Eternal" is a characteristic of infinite power. This characteristic does not belong to created species or their members. Created species and their members are said to have *duration*. They have duration according to their whole being (species), which follows divine laws.

"Whole being comes from God," Bruno wrote. Whole being, in turn, belongs to its own species of God-given or divine laws. Man must understand that "eternal," a characteristic of God, or Origin, is a divine law which *governs* created physical species and their physical members. This divine law governs the physical generation and physical decay of physical things.

When a pilot governs a ship, *we do not take the ship to be the pilot,* even though the ship makes manifest the will and the power of that pilot. Bruno is saying here, very emphatically, that human experience cannot force the divine law of the universe to break its rules. In the *De l'Infinito,* Bruno writes that human reason must follow nature; nature does not follow human reason (p. 516 and p. 525). See, further, *The Infinite Worlds of Giordano Bruno* (Springfield, Ill.: Charles C. Thomas, 1970).

PART III

Velikovsky's research indicates that the order of the solar system was radically altered within the memory of man. This highly controversial conclusion was deemed unthinkable by many of Velikovsky's opponents even before official publication of *Worlds in Collision*.

As the crusade against Velikovsky gathered momentum, the author was accused not only of ignoring the record of success scored by conventional celestial mechanics (and the stability widely assumed to be inherent in its laws), but also of "inventing electromagnetic forces capable of doing precisely what he wants them to do." Such reactions so confused the public that the true challenge of *Worlds in Collision* remained obscure for almost a full generation.

Just how impossible are some of the dynamical effects Velikovsky had deduced from the historical record? In this section are assembled *Pensée* papers dealing with one or another aspect of this question.

"How Stable Is the Solar System?" asks C. J. Ransom in the first of these papers. The answer, it would appear, depends very much on the credentials of the one who would question the belief that the system lacks a recent history.

Dr. Ransom, who formerly taught at the University of Texas and is presently a plasma physicist in the Electro-optics and Reconnaissance Group of General Dynamics, Convair Aerospace Division, Fort Worth, cites numerous instances of solar-system alteration that have been advanced on theoretical as well as observational grounds by establishment scientists. He also presents findings in other fields that lend support to Velikovsky's reconstruction of solar-system history.

Since Velikovsky contends that a collision between Venus and Mars followed earlier encounters between Venus and Earth, Professor Lynn E. Rose asks: "Could Mars Have Been an Inner Planet?" Rose observes that such a possibility might account for the Mars-Earth scenario outlined in *Worlds in Collision*.

"The Orbits of Mars, Earth, and Venus," is a preliminary announcement by Professor Rose and his collaborator, Raymond C. Vaughan, of studies undertaken to determine the likely orbits of these three bodies during the intervals between major encounters, as described by Velikovsky.

Using the orbital parameters provided by Rose and Vaughan, C. J. Ransom and L. H. Hoffee report, in "The Orbits of Venus," on computer analyses of such planetary motions. They conclude that such a sequence of orbits is entirely consistent with the requirements of the laws of celestial mechanics.

Vaughan, who studied at Massachusetts Institute of Technology, works in the Research and Development Division, The Carborundum Company, Niagara Falls, New York. Hoffee is an optical engineer.

Rose and Vaughan report further progress in their studies of sequential planetary collisions in "Velikovsky and the Sequence of Planetary Orbits." They give several alternative sequences of Keplerian orbits that are consonant with Velikovsky's findings and discuss the relative merits of each sequence. They emphasize that formidable physical problems remain to be solved, but urge that such problems be viewed not as obstacles, but as opportunities for further discovery.

Chris S. Sherrerd, a statistical data analyst with a background in communications engineering and large-scale computer applications, contributes to the discussion with two papers. In the matter of "Venus' Circular Orbit," he suggests that the plasticity of the body of Venus might be such as to permit the conversion of energy of orbital motion into heat by tidal friction, and that by this mechanism an orbit initially of considerable eccentricity might be reduced to near-circularity in a brief period of time. He argues in "Gyroscopic Precession and Celestial Axis Displacement" that major shifts in the Earth's celestial poles caused by episodes of accelerated precession might best explain ancient accounts of prolonged daylight and darkness in various parts of the world.

In the concluding paper in this section, Ralph E. Juergens writes of "Plasma in Interplanetary Space: Reconciling Celestial Mechanics and Velikovskian Catastrophism." He offers a possible answer to the often-asked question: Why are the electromagnetic forces so prominent in Velikovsky's descriptions of near-collision events not evident today in the motions of solar-system bodies? He pursues the problem posed by the presence of interplanetary plasma—which he holds responsible for screening out electrical forces in the system—and suggests that a new theory of solar energy production is very much in order.

Juergens, a civil engineer living in Flagstaff, Arizona, contributed two essays on the scientific reception of Velikovsky's work to the 1966 book *The Velikovsky Affair* (edited by Alfred de Grazia).

HOW STABLE IS THE SOLAR SYSTEM?

C. J. Ransom

In his writings, Velikovsky contends that the solar system was not always stable, nor is it in the same state as that in which it originated. The Earth, as a member of this unstable system, has repeatedly been a participant in some discontinuous changes. A central feature of this theory is that these changes have occurred in many geological epochs, as well as several times in the historical past. The agents, external to the Earth, causing these most recent catastrophes can be identified by analysis of ancient scientific and literary writings. Although many of the events reconstructed by Velikovsky in 1950 were then highly controversial, a number of them might have been either confirmed or hypothesized in recent years by astronomers, geologists, geneticists, and other scientists, without drawing undue criticism.

A few of these "original ideas" are briefly surveyed in the following. They are mentioned to show that scientific thought, no longer restricted by an assumption that no changes have occurred in the solar system since very early in its history, is leading investigators to conclusions similar to Velikovsky's, which were deduced from analyzing data available in 1950.

Velikovsky contended that Venus originated as a proto-planet in a disruption of Jupiter. The origin of comets from or near Jupiter has been actively investigated by the Russians. In 1960, W. H. McCrea, then president of the Royal Astronomical Society, in an analysis of the nebular theory of the origin of the solar system, calculated that no planet could have originated inside the orbit of Jupiter (1). In the same year, R. A. Lyttleton claimed that at some time in its history Jupiter became unstable and could relieve this condition only by breaking into two very unequal parts (2). More recently, Mamedov has analyzed the orbits of hypothetical comets that originated from Jupiter (3). He also used computer calculations to modify and support Vsekhsvyatskiy's theory (4) of comet origin on or near the surface of Jupiter (5). Hills has recently suggested that the three outermost planets, Uranus, Neptune, and Pluto, were displaced into their present orbits by encounters with other planets (6): this is a consequence of his analysis of the solar nebula, which indicates that Jupiter and Saturn were initially the outermost planets to form in the nebula. It was theorized by Yamamoto, and later expanded by Lyttleton, that Pluto was an escaped satellite of Neptune (7). Recent evidence indicates that the Moon may have formed in another orbit and was later captured by the Earth (8). These papers demonstrate that discussion of changes occurring in the solar system are no longer prohibited.

According to Velikovsky, Venus at one time had an orbit intersecting the orbits of some of the other planets —Mars and Earth in particular. Venus nearly collided with Earth on two occasions and several times with Mars. These near-collisions resulted in changes in the orbits of Venus, Mars, and also of Earth. Lyttleton, in *The Comets* (9), diagramed orbital changes of bodies influenced when passing near Jupiter.

Velikovsky predicted that the ground-surface temperature of Venus would be found to be extremely high (whereas the accepted value in 1950 was only a few degrees above mean annual temperature of Earth). He reasoned that Venus' violent origin, and also its encounters with other planets, must have generated a large amount of internal heat, and that this heat could not have been completely radiated away, due to the planet's extreme youth. He explained the observation, known in 1950, that both the day and night sides of Venus' cloud surface have the same temperature, namely 25° C, by maintaining that the planet radiates much more heat than it absorbs from the sun (10). By 1962, there was no doubt that this was the case. This excess heat was not predicted by others and cannot be explained by the current concepts about the origin of the solar system. Since the presence of this excess heat has been confirmed, various authors have tried to explain it by the "greenhouse effect," but it was shown that this is not a viable explanation (11). One scientist proposed a collision of a hypothetical moon with Venus to explain the heat and anomalous spin (12).

Anomalous (retrograde) rotation and angular momentum would not be unlikely as a result of these encounters. In 1967, R. M. Goldstein wrote that it is necessary to consider twin anomalies of Venus' rotation: a retrograde direction, and resonance with Earth (13). Later, Colombo observed that although Mercury, the Moon, and several satellites of Jupiter and Saturn have odd angular momenta, the behaviors of Venus and Mars are much more difficult to explain (14).

In addition to the changed angular momentum of

Mars, recent radar studies and Mariner 9 photographs reveal that Mars has other unexpected features. Certain areas of the surface appear to be covered by recent lava flows crossed with wide faults. In *Worlds in Collision,* Velikovsky said that any "canals" on Mars were not constructed by intelligent beings but, rather, are ". . . a result of the play of geological forces that answered with rifts and cracks the outer forces acting in collisions" (Doubleday edition, p. 364). These external forces could also be effective mountain-builders. Although observations before 1962 were used by Slipher to "prove conclusively that there are no high mountains on Mars" (15), recent studies by Goldstein (16) indicate that thirteen-kilometer variations exist between peak and valley on Mars. Recently released photographs from Mariner 9 look down on a "super volcano," six miles high and 310 miles wide.

Collisions of the Earth with external bodies resulting in large-scale changes of the Earth, or collisions of other bodies within the solar system, are no longer considered unlikely. It has been postulated that the unexplained splitting of some comets may be accounted for by collisions between the comets and asteroids (17). In 1959, Ewing and Worzel of Columbia University found a layer of white ash in some ocean sediments and ascribed its deposition to a "fiery end of bodies of cosmic origin." This "cometary collision," they wrote, "could hardly be without some recorded consequences of global extent" (18). In 1965, Urey suggested that a collision of the Earth and an external body (a comet) produced violent events which caused rocky materials and water to leave the Earth and be captured by the Moon (19). Dachille (20) and Gallant (21) have presented calculations concerning axis-changes in the Earth resulting from large meteorite collisions. Thomas Gold showed that the terrestrial axis could be rather easily turned into a new direction by the application of a modest external force (22). This change and its possible effects on climate and tectonic movements are discussed.

The possibility of petroleum being deposited on the Earth as a result of encounters of this nature is claimed by Wilson (23). In 1966, Oro and Han (24) contended that aromatic hydrocarbons and other hydrocarbons could be produced from the collision of a comet and a planet. P. V. Smith (25) has shown that petroleum offshore and onshore in the Gulf of Mexico is found in recent sediments and can be carbon dated. This is a surprising result if all petroleum was formed millions of years ago. In *Worlds in Collision,* it is suggested that at least some of the Earth's oil deposits are the result of a recent Earth-comet collision (26).

In the past, the Earth's magnetic field has reversed its polarity a number of times. The geological data for this fact was referred to by Velikovsky in *Worlds in Collision* (1950) and *Earth in Upheaval* (1955). He suggested that the cause of this phenomenon was an interplanetary discharge. By 1971, physicists Durrani and Khan (27) had similarly suggested as a cause of magnetic reversal an interaction between the Earth and an external body. They claimed that tektites were deposited on portions of the Earth at the time of the last accepted reversal. Tektites, according to some authorities (28, 29), may have been the result of an Earth-comet encounter; G. Baker, the leading authority on Australian tektites (australites), maintained that, whatever their age, some lay on the ground no more than five thousand years (30). (Only recently, it was claimed that the last magnetic reversal occurred about 700,000 years ago; but even more recently, indications were found of a reversal 12,500 years ago (31), and other evidence from paleomagnetic study of ancient pottery (32), previously referenced by Velikovsky (33), indicates a reversal in the eighth century B.C.) Kennet and Watkins (34) have also drawn attention to the correlations between polarity changes, widespread faunal extinctions, climatic changes, and maxima of volcanic activity.

Velikovsky's original work was ridiculed, ignored, and then, as with all great work, it was copied, and its conclusions were often arrived at "independently" by other investigators without due credit being given to Velikovsky. Noted scientists have recently postulated interplanetary changes and collisions, collisions of the earth with external bodies, and the possibility of the very events, resulting from these collisions, that Velikovsky described in 1950.

REFERENCES

1. W. H. McCrea, *Proceedings,* Royal Astronomical Society, Series A, Vol. 256 (1960).
2. R. A. Lyttleton, *Monthly Notices,* Royal Astronomical Society, *121* (1960), #6; *Man's View of the Universe* (Boston: Little, Brown and Co., 1961), 36.
3. M. A. Mamedov, *Mathematicheskikh Nauk,* #3 (1969), 83–95.
4. S. K. Vsekhsvyatskiy, *Soviet Astronomy,* AJ 11, #3 (1967), 473.
5. M. A. Mamedov, *Dokl. Akad. Nauk Azerb,* SSR Vol. 26, #6 (1970), 15–18; in English (NASA-TT-F-13788) Avail: NTIS CSCL 03B.
6. J. G. Hills, "The Origin and Dynamical Evolution of the Solar System," Ph.D. thesis (Michigan University, Ann Arbor, 1969).
7. *Frontiers in Astronomy,* intro. by O. Gingerich (San Francisco: W. H. Freeman and Co., 1970).
8. S. F. Singel, L. W. Bandermann, *Science, 170* (1970), 438.
9. R. A. Lyttleton, *The Comets and Their Origin* (London: Cambridge University Press, 1953), 13.
10. I. Velikovsky, *Worlds in Collision* (Garden City, N.Y.: Doubleday & Company, 1950), 371.
11. M. B. McElroy, "Venus—A Mystery Still to Unfold," *Astronautics and Aeronautics* (January 1971), 19.
12. S. F. Singer, *Science, 170* (1970), 1196.
13. In A. Dollfus (ed.), *Moon and Planets* (Amsterdam: North-Holland Publishing Co., 1967), 126.
14. G. Colombo, *ESRO Planetary Space Missions,* Vol. 1: *Basic Data on Planets and Satellites* (November 1970), 29.
15. E. C. Slipher, *Photographic Story of Mars* (Cambridge, Mass.: Sky Publishing Corp., 1962), 67.
16. Downs *et al., Science, 174* (1971), 1324.
17. M. Harwit, *Astrophysical Journal, 151* (1968), 789.
18. *Proceedings,* National Academy of Science, *45,* #3.
19. H. C. Urey, *Science, 147* (1965), 1262–65.
20. F. Dachille, *Nature, 198* (1963), 176.
21. R. L. C. Gallant, *Nature, 197* (1963), 38.
22. T. Gold, *Nature, 175* (1955), 526; *Sky and Telescope* (April 1968).
23. A. T. Wilson, *Nature* (1962).
24. J. Oro and J. Han, *Science, 153* (1966), 1393.
25. P. V. Smith, *Science, 116* (1952), 437.
26. I. Velikovsky, *Worlds in Collision, supra,* 53.
27. S. A. Durrani and H. A. Khan, *Nature, 232* (1971), 320.
28. H. C. Urey, *Nature, 179* (1957), 556.

29. R. A. Lyttleton, *Proceedings,* Royal Astronomical Society, Series A, Vol. 272 (April 9, 1963), 457.

30. G. Baker, "The Present State of Knowledge of the 'Age-on-Earth' and the 'Age-of-Formation' of Australites," *Georgia Mineral Newsletter, 15,* No. 3–4 (Winter 1962), 68; *Nature* (1960).

31. *Nature, 234* (1971), 441.

32. G. Folgheraiter, *Rendi Conti dei Licei* (1896, 1889); *Archives des sciences physiques et naturelles* (Geneva, 1899); *Journal de physique* (1899); P. L. Mercanton, "La methode de Folgheraiter et son role en geophysique," *Archives des sciences physiques et naturelles* (1907).

33. I. Velikovsky, *Earth in Upheaval* (Garden City, N.Y.: Doubleday, 1955), 146.

34. J. P. Kennet and N. D. Watkins, *Nature, 227* (1970), 930.

COULD MARS HAVE BEEN AN INNER PLANET?

Lynn E. Rose

I will suggest a hypothesis concerning the orbit of Mars before its encounters with Venus and Earth. The hypothesis should be checked against both historical data and current theory and observation.

The historical material relating to the early status of Mars is summarized by Velikovsky (*Worlds in Collision,* p. 244) as follows:

> Mars did not arouse any fears in the hearts of the ancient astrologers, and its name was seldom mentioned in the second millennium. . . . But in the ninth or eighth century before this era, the situation changed radically. Mars became the dreaded planet.

Velikovsky does not attempt to describe the orbit of Mars three thousand years ago, before its near-collisions with Venus and the Earth. But the Martian orbit at that time probably did not cross the orbit of the Earth,

137

or even come close to crossing it, since such a Mars would have evoked periodic fear.

Nor is it likely that Mars was an outer planet, since it could then hardly have played a role in the final taming of Venus. Venus, between its near-collisions with the Earth and its near-collisions with Mars, was on an orbit of greatly reduced ellipticity that probably never took it much outside the orbit of the Earth. So there would have been no chance for Venus to collide with Mars if the Martian orbit already lay well outside the orbit of the Earth.

We are left with the hypothesis that Mars three thousand years ago was an inner planet.

Velikovsky has indicated several ways in which some of the angular momentum of Venus could have been dissipated without being transferred to Mars: some could have been transferred to Venus' trailing debris and gases that were separated off during these near-collisions, and some could have been transferred electrically or magnetically to the interplanetary medium. But the main recipient of any angular momentum lost by Venus during the ninth and eighth centuries was still probably Mars. Certain careless readers to the contrary notwithstanding, such a close encounter would not need to result in Mars' ejection from the solar system. Velikovsky did not say what Mars' orbit was before the eighth-century theomachy (battle of planetary gods). His own phrase is that Mars was "thrown out of the ring" in its contests with Venus: this might only entail that the Martian orbit was quite larger after the near-collisions with Venus than before.

If Mars was indeed an inner planet before its contact with Venus, its orbit was most likely elliptical after that contact: at aphelion, Mars would have been well outside the orbit of the Earth, and at perihelion, Mars would have been back inside the orbit of the Earth, near the site of its most recent encounter with Venus. There would suddenly be a danger of near-collision between the Earth and Mars, and Velikovsky has shown that such near-collisions did indeed occur some twenty-seven centuries ago and that they were a major factor in Mars' eventual arrival at its present orbit. If my own suggestion is correct, we should regard the Earth's principal role in this process as that of greatly reducing the eccentricity of the orbit pursued by Mars, so that Mars, like Venus before it, ceased to be a further threat to the Earth.

Several authors came to the conclusion, either on theoretical grounds or upon observation provided by Mars probes starting with Mariner 4, that Mars was disturbed on its path. Figuring the distribution of mass and angular momentum in the solar system, some researchers calculated an axial rotation of eight hours for Mars, whereas now Mars rotates in slightly over twenty-four hours. (Hartmann and Larson, *Icarus,* 7 [1967], 257–60.) "Mars . . . either must have lost considerable angular momentum or never possessed the initial angular momentum that would be inferred." "The means by which Mars could have decelerated presents a problem." (F. F. Fish, *Icarus,* 7 [1967], 251–56.) Fault patterns were observed on the surface of Mars. (Binder, *Science, 152* [1966], 1053–55. "A change of rotation may provide the stresses which produced them." (Hartmann and Larson, op. cit.)

Thus, through the disturbances that occurred, Mars seems to have lost much of its axial angular momentum, but to have gained much more in orbital angular momentum.

THE ORBITS OF MARS, EARTH, AND VENUS

Lynn E. Rose and Raymond C. Vaughan

The following orbits are generally consistent with Velikovsky's sequence of events following Venus' origination from Jupiter; they also satisfy conservation of angular momentum and do not violate (*per se*) conservation of energy. The orbits are given here by semimajor axis and eccentricity. The semimajor axis is the first figure in the parentheses; it is expressed in astronomical units. Other orbital parameters can be calculated in terms of these two.

Orbits during the period after Venus' origination from Jupiter and before Venus' encounters with Earth: Venus (3.0, 0.800); Earth (0.81, 0.067); Mars (0.55, 0.050).

Orbits during the period after Venus' encounters with Earth and before Venus' encounters with Mars: Venus (1.0, 0.500); Earth (1.1, 0.167); Mars (0.55, 0.050).

Orbits during the period after Venus' encounters with Mars and before Mars' encounters with Earth: Venus (0.72, 0.007); Earth (1.1, 0.167); Mars (1.0, 0.400).

Present orbits: Venus (0.72, 0.007); Earth (1.0, 0.017); Mars (1.52, 0.093).

The orbits may be regarded as approximate, within various limiting factors. A fuller discussion will be published as soon as possible.

THE ORBITS OF VENUS*

C. J. Ransom and L. H. Hoffee

In 1950, Immanuel Velikovsky suggested that several orbital changes had occurred among members of the solar system (1). These changes resulted in near-collisions between celestial bodies and a reordering of the solar system. In the following paragraphs, known changes in the orbits of comets, commonly considered not to be possible, will be discussed. In addition, calculations which provide approximate orbital parameters for the celestial bodies which Velikovsky contends were involved in these collisions are presented.

In *Worlds in Collision,* the term "comet" often arises with respect to Venus. This is a result of the ancient definition of a comet as a celestial object with an extended atmosphere, and in fact the word "comet" is derived from the Greek word for "hair." Therefore, such references to Venus as a comet are used in this context rather than according to the modern, although imprecise, definition of a comet. That the modern definition is little better than the ancient definition is seen from the following two statements: Roemer said that although Comet Arend-Rigaux had an orbit similar to a minor planet, it was designated as a comet because it, on occasion, showed some diffuseness. When Baade discovered Hidalgo, he was undecided whether to call it a minor planet or a comet, so he called it a minor planet because they were more popular at the time (2).

Although an exact definition of a comet may be in question, observation of the motions of accepted comets can be used to illustrate that some types of changes in the orbits of celestial bodies required as a result of Velikovsky's contentions are physically possible. For example, Brooks's Comet (1889V) went 313 degrees around Jupiter and changed its orbital period from twenty-nine years to seven years. Furthermore, in 1875, Comet Wolf had a close encounter with Jupiter, and as a result, its perihelion was changed from 2.5 A.U. to 1.5 A.U. In 1922, the same comet had a second encounter with Jupiter and reverted almost to its pre-1875 orbit. Its aphelion remained almost constant throughout these encounters (3). Fokin states that, during a near approach to Jupiter, the comet Oterma III, which before 1938 had an orbit entirely between the orbits of Jupiter and Saturn, changed its orbit so that it was entirely between Mars and Jupiter (4). After 1965, its orbit was again between Jupiter and Saturn (5).

A series of orbital configurations that is not inconsistent with either the events described by Velikovsky or the laws of physics is illustrated in Figure 1. (For convenience, orbits are drawn with perihelion to the right.)

141

Table 1 lists the orbital parameters for each of the four configurations.

A possible orbital configuration for the period after the ejection of Venus by Jupiter and prior to the encounter between Venus and Earth is illustrated in Figure 1a. The period of Venus in this configuration is 7.1 years, and the period of Mars is 0.56 year. A year is defined as the orbital period of the Earth at that time and is independent of the number of times the Earth revolved on its axis in one of its years. The 7.1-year period of Venus is in agreement with such literary references as the seven-year circle of sabbatical years as practiced by the Israelites (6).

A possible orbital configuration for the period between the time of the encounters between Venus and Earth and prior to the encounter between Venus and Mars is illustrated in Figure 1b.

A possible orbital configuration for the period between the time of the encounters between Venus and Earth and prior to the encounter between Mars and Earth is illustrated in Figure 1c.

The present configuration of the orbits of Mars, Earth, and Venus is illustrated in Figure 1d. The present near-circular orbit of Venus is often discussed as an orbital oddity. Sherrerd of Bell Laboratories has shown that an orbit of this nature would be expected were Venus in a near-plastic state while acquiring this orbit (7). Tidal friction would tend to keep the body hot and change the orbit, by the laws of Cassini, to one which would minimize energy loss by tidal friction.

In order to see whether the orbit of Venus given by Rose and Vaughan and shown in Figure 1a has more than a minute possibility of occurrence, a computer program was written and executed on a Hewlett-Packard Model 9810A calculator (8). The program assumes that an object is 1) placed at a specified distance from the Sun, and is 2) moving at a specified angle relative to a line drawn through the object and the Sun at 3) a specified velocity. The program operates on these three quantities and calculates orbital eccentricity (e) and semi-major axis (a). In practice, the initial distance is taken to be 4.4 A.U., the initial angle is zero degrees, and the

142

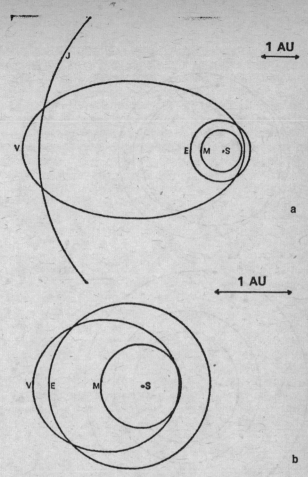

Figure 1

initial velocity is zero kilometers per second: and a solution for *a* and *e* is then calculated. The distance is increased by 0.01-A.U. increments until maximum of 5.4 A.U. is reached, the angle is increased by 0.5-degree increments until 180 degrees is reached, and the velocity is increased by 0.001 km/sec. A solution for *a* and *e* is calculated for each combination of distance, angle, and velocity.

143

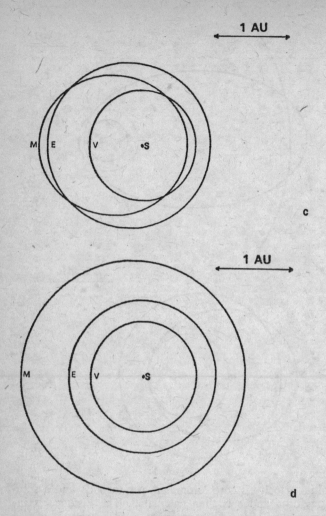

1 AU

M E   V   •S

c

1 AU

M   E V   •S

d

Figure 1

Figure 2 is a plot of the resulting calculations. Ejection angle is plotted as a function of velocity for an orbital eccentricity of 0.80 and distances of 4.4 A.U. and 5.4 A.U. The limits for the ejection angle are 40 degrees

144

TABLE 1
ORBITAL PARAMETERS

PLANET	a^*	e^*	PERIOD[1]	PERIOD[2]	SYNODIC PERIOD[1]	PERIHELION DISTANCE	APHELION DISTANCE
(1a)							
Jupiter	5.2	0.048	4335	16.28	1.07	4.95 AU	5.45 AU
Venus	3.0	0.80	1898	7.13	1.16	0.6	5.4
Earth	0.8	0.07	266.3	1.0	—	0.74	0.86
Mars	0.55	0.05	149	0.56	1.27	0.52	0.58
(1b)							
Jupiter	5.2	0.048	4335	10.29	1.11	4.95	5.45
Venus	1.0	0.5	365	1.15	6.51	0.5	1.5
Earth	1.1	0.17	421	1.0	—	0.92	1.28
Mars	0.55	0.05	149	0.35	0.55	0.52	0.58
(1c)							
Jupiter	5.2	0.048	4335	10.29	1.11	4.95	5.45
Venus	0.7	0.007	224.5	0.53	1.14	0.7	0.7
Earth	1.1	0.17	421.4	1.0	—	0.91	1.29
Mars	1.0	0.4	365	0.87	6.51	0.6	1.4
(1d)							
Jupiter	5.2	0.048	4335	11.87	1.09	4.95	5.45
Venus	0.7	0.007	224.5	0.62	1.6	0.69	0.71
Earth	1.0	0.017	365	1.0	—	0.98	1.02
Mars	1.52	0.093	687	1.88	2.14	1.38	1.66

(1) Expressed in present Earth days
(2) Expressed in Earth years

* Values for a and e for Venus, Earth, and Mars are those given by Rose and Vaughan (9).

and 140 degrees, with the angles above 90 degrees being read from the right-hand scale. Thus, all points lying between the lines labeled 4.4 A.U. and 5.4 A.U. result in orbits with an eccentricity of 0.80. Further, all points lying within the shaded area result in orbits with the added characteristic of possessing semimajor axes of between 2.95 A.U. and 3.05 A.U. It can be seen from the figure that the probability of an object achieving the required orbit is not minute, as is often assumed.

The equations used to arrive at the above conclusions can be found in references (9) through (11); the work of Rose and Vaughan was used to verify the results of independent calculations, and provided refined orbital

FIGURE 2

Angle, velocity, and distance requirements
for $e = 0.80$ and a between 2.95 AU and 3.05 AU.

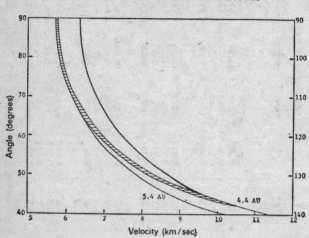

parameters for Mars, including the suggestion of the possibility of Mars having an interior orbit.

In summary, it can be stated that some objections to the contentions stated by Velikovsky in regard to orbital changes have been answered by the method of counterexample. It can also be stated that objections based on the contention that the probability of Venus acquiring the necessary orbital parameters is too small to even warrant consideration is shown to be unfounded. Granted, the probability is not unity; however, the point in question is not whether a celestial body will assume such an orbit either after being ejected by Jupiter or after its orbit is affected by Jupiter, but, rather, that the required orbit is theoretically possible.

REFERENCES

1. I. Velikovsky, *Worlds in Collision* (Garden City, N.Y.: Doubleday & Company, 1950).
2. E. Roemer, *Astronomical Journal*, 66 (1961), 368.
3. R. A. Lyttleton, *The Comets and Their Origin* (London: Cambridge University Press, 1953), p. 13.
4. A. V. Fokin, *Soviet Astro. AJ* 2 (1958), 628.
5. B. Middlehurst and G. Kuiper, *Moon, Meteorites and Comets* (Chicago: University of Chicago Press, 1963), p. 559.
6. I. Velikovsky, *Worlds in Collision, supra,* pp. 153–56.
7. C. Sherrerd, *Pensée, 2* (May 1972), 43.
8. The authors would like to thank Hewlett-Packard, 201 East Arapaho Road, Richardson, Texas, for the use of the 9810A calculator and plotter.
9. L. Rose and R. Vaughan, *Pensée, 2* (May 1972), 42.
10. A. G. Webster, *The Dynamics of Particles and of Rigid, Elastic, and Fluid Bodies* (New York: Hafner Publishing Company, 1949), p. 40.
11. F. R. Moulton, *An Introduction to Celestial Mechanics,* Second Edition (New York: The Macmillan Company, 1914), p. 150.

VELIKOVSKY AND THE SEQUENCE OF PLANETARY ORBITS

Lynn E. Rose and Raymond C. Vaughan

The orbits we proposed in 1972 (1) were intended to refute the claim that Velikovsky's theory was astronomically impossible. They demonstrate that Keplerian orbits can be proposed that not only cross each other—so that collisions or near-collisions will tend to occur—but also conserve total angular momentum and do not increase total orbital energy. Further investigation of these orbits was carried out by Ransom and Hoffee (2). In this article, we propose several alternative sequences of Keplerian orbits, accompanied by discussion of our methods, assumptions, and sources. All these orbits be-

147

long to the relatively calm intervals that were separated by the catastrophes; the interactions during the near-collisions have not been investigated in detail. We conclude with a discussion of two problems that are not yet satisfactorily resolved: eccentricity-damping and energy disposal.

It should be noted that the development of this article has relied greatly on an unpublished paper by Vaughan entitled "Orbits and Their Measurements" (3) The *map* of orbits presented there has been useful in several ways: as a slide-rule-like device for calculating orbital parameter values, as a graphical demonstration of the parameter interrelationships, and as a worksheet on which real and hypothetical orbits can be represented.

Our units of measurements are *geobasic units* (4): the unit of mass is *Earth's mass;* the unit of length is the *astronomical unit,* or present mean distance of Earth from the Sun; and the unit of time is Earth's present *sidereal year.* The traditional symbols are used for the planets: ♀ (Venus), ⊕ (Earth), ♂ (Mars), and ♃ (Jupiter).

Two examples showing how limits may be put on specific orbits will be presented before we discuss the sequences of orbits.

THE PRE-EXODUS ORBIT OF VENUS

Limits on Venus' orbit prior to its first encounter with Earth might be derived from the following assumptions: (A) Venus originated from Jupiter. (B) Venus later was involved in a near-collision with Earth. (C) The orbit of Venus was not changed substantially from the time of its last proximity to Jupiter to the time of its first encounter with Earth. (D) The orbit of Jupiter has not changed substantially since its last encounter with Venus. (E) The orbit of Earth was somewhat smaller than it is now, with its aphelion being perhaps eight-tenths of an astronomical unit.

It follows from assumptions A, B, and C that Venus' orbit extended at least as far from the Sun as the perihelion (r'_{min}) of Jupiter and at least as close to the Sun as the aphelion (r_{max}) of Earth. Incorporating assumption D, it follows that (r_{max}) ♀ $\geqq (r_{min})$ ♃ $= 4.95$, and, incorporating assumption E, it follows that (r_{min}) ♀ $\leqq (r_{max})$ ⊕ $= 0.8$. Using the map format presented by Vaughan (3), one can see that the orbit of Venus must lie above the $r_{max} = 4.95$ contour and below the $r_{min} = 0.8$ contour. These two contours are plotted on the map in Figure 1; the orbit must lie within the shaded area in the upper right-hand corner of the map. The lowest possible eccentricity for such an orbit is 0.722, requiring a semimajor axis of 2.875 A.U. The smallest possible semimajor axis is approximately 2.5 A.U., requiring an eccentricity between 0.95 and 1.0.

THE POST-BETH-HORON ORBITS OF EARTH

A second example will show how dynamical considerations might be used to set limits on the various orbits of Earth since its final encounter with Venus at the time of the battle of Beth-horon. Earth's present orbit is included in this period of time, as well as Earth's orbits before and during the Earth-Mars encounters; all would lie within these limits. The limits could be derived from the following assumptions: (A) The orbit of Earth was not changed substantially from the time of its final encounter with Venus to the time of its first encounter with Mars in the eighth century. (B) The orbit of Venus has not been changed substantially since its final encounter with Mars in the ninth or eighth century. (C) The present orbit of Venus has a semimajor axis $a = 0.72$ and an eccentricity $e = 0.007$. (D) The masses of Venus, Earth, and Mars have remained approximately the same since Venus' final encounter with Earth. (E) The total orbital energy of the three planets has either remained the same or decreased since Venus' final encounter with Mars (the present total is: $H = -43.61$). (F) The present total orbital angular momentum $(l = 11.54)$ of the three planets has remained the same since Venus' final encounter with Mars. (G) The orbits of all three planets lay more or less in the present ecliptic plane; none of the three was moving in a retrograde orbit.

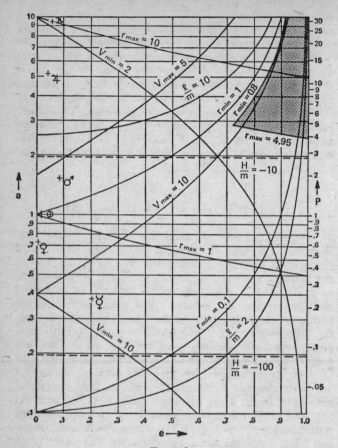

Figure 1

This derivation of limits applies to the period since the final Venus-Mars encounter, in the ninth or eighth century; all post-Beth-horon orbits of Earth are included in this period of time. Using assumptions B, C, and D, one can calculate that Venus has had an orbital energy $H = -22.24$ and an angular momentum $l = 4.36$ throughout this period of time. By subtracting Venus' values from the total values given in assumptions E and F, it follows that the sum of Earth's and Mars' orbital energies was greater than or equal to -21.37, while the sum of Earth's and Mars' orbital angular momenta was equal to 7.18.

The orbital energy of a planet must be less than zero, in the sense that a greater energy would cause the planet to escape from the Sun's gravitational field. Zero is thus the extreme limit for the greatest possible orbital energy of Mars. By subtracting this Mars limit of zero from the minimum Mars-Earth total of -21.37, it follows that the minimum value for Earth's orbital energy was -21.37. Since the mass of Earth (i.e., the Earth-Moon system) is 1.01, the minimum value for Earth's *orbital energy per unit mass* must have been -21.2. Thus, the location of Earth's orbit on the map of orbits must be above the orbital energy per unit mass contour $H/m = -21.2$. This contour is shown in Figure 2.

The smallest possible orbit for Mars would be an orbit whose *angular momentum per unit mass* is approximately 0.56, since a smaller orbit would pass within the Roche limit of the Sun, in which case Mars would tend to break up as the tidal force of the Sun exceeded the planet's own gravity and structural cohesion. (For Mars, the radius of the Sun's Roche limit is 0.0081 astronomical unit, so that the practical lower limit of orbits on the map of orbits would be the contour $r_{min} = 0.0081$, which coincides more or less with the contour $l/m = 0.56$.) The mass of Mars is 0.107; the smallest possible value for Mars' angular momentum would thus be $0.56 \times 0.107 = 0.06$. By subtracting this extreme minimum value for Mars from the Mars-Earth total of 7.18, it follows that the maximum value for Earth's orbital angular momentum was 7.12. Division by Earth's mass gives 7.05 as the maximum value for Earth's orbital angular momentum per unit mass. Thus, the location of Earth's orbit on the map of orbits must be below the angular momentum per unit mass contour $l/m = 7.05$. This contour and the contour derived in the preceding paragraph are plotted on Figure 2; these two contours are the extreme limits (according to our seven assumptions) on Earth's orbit since its last encounter with Venus.

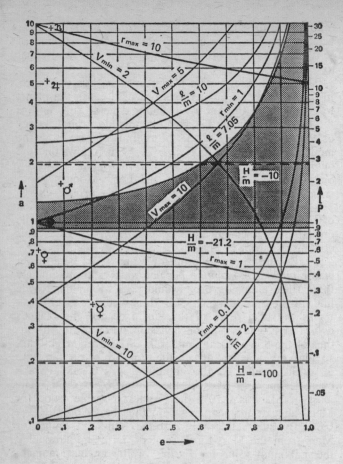

Figure 2

In these two examples, changes in our assumptions would have varying effects on our orbital conclusions. As an example of a quantitative change, it might be mentioned that a more realistic narrowing of the extreme limits used for Mars' orbit in the second example would result in a relatively slight narrowing of the limits derived for Earth, since Mars has only one-ninth the mass of Earth. One qualitative change affecting assumption E in the second example will be discussed in greater detail later; we have assumed that near-collisions could be either completely elastic (causing no change in orbital energy) or partially inelastic (causing a loss of orbital energy). The latter possibility may turn out to be severely limited.

Most of the other past orbits cannot be put within limits as close as in these two examples, so that there remains plenty of room for conjecture. As of now, there is just not enough information available, either from Velikovsky's theory or from independent ancient sources, for any further strict narrowing of this kind.

THE TABLES

We have tentatively worked out a more detailed sequence of events—indeed, three alternative sequences of events (Tables 1, 2, and 3)—that are to varying degrees consistent with Velikovsky's views as stated in *Worlds in Collision.* By making relatively minor adjustments in the various parameters, we have been able to incorporate into the models some Velikovskian features such as 50-"year" and 4-"year" cycles of Venus and 15-"year" cycles of Mars. (Words such as "year" will appear in quotation marks whenever they are not necessarily the same as our present units.)

In all three of the Tables, Stage 1 occurs before the first Venus-Earth contact at the time of the Exodus. Stage 2 is the interval of fifty to fifty-two "years" between the Exodus and the battle of Beth-horon, at which time Earth and Venus again came near each other. Stage 3 is the post-Beth-horon period, extending from the fifteenth through the eighth centuries. Stage 4 is after the first Earth-Mars contact and before the last Earth-Mars contact. Stage 5 is since −687. The numbering of the stages reflects the successive orbits of Earth; the lettered subdivisions of stages reflect those changes that did not affect Earth.

How Long Was 360 "Days"?

Velikovsky maintains that the post-Beth-horon "year"

153

contained 360 "days" (5), but he does not claim to know the exact length of the post-Beth-horon "day." Since the post-Beth-horon "year" had fewer "days" than the present year, it might seem probable that the post-Beth-horon "year" was slightly *shorter* than the present year and that the orbit was consequently smaller than the present orbit of Earth. This is not as easy as it sounds.

If the orbit of Earth at present is greater than during the fifteenth through eighth centuries (and if the present eccentricity of 0.017 is not greater than before), then Earth must have gained angular momentum at the expense of Mars. Thus we have some forbidding limits: the angular momentum of Mars on its former orbit must have been greater than that possessed by Mars today, and yet the perihelion of that orbit must have been quite near the present distance of Venus from the Sun. These conditions cannot be satisfied by any stable orbit, as can be shown either on the map of orbits or by algebraic calculation. On the assumptions that the perihelion of this elliptical orbit was 0.7 A.U. and that the angular momentum of this orbit was greater than Mars' present angular momentum of 0.826, we have

$$r_{min} = a(1-e) = 0.7$$

and

$$l = 2\pi m(a(1-e^2))^{1/2}$$
$$= (2\pi) \times (.107) \times (a(1-e^2))^{1/2} > 0.826,$$

from which it can be deduced that $e > 1.16$. But it is not possible for an elliptical orbit to have $e \geq 1.0$. And if the perihelion were any lower than 0.7, that would only serve to raise still *higher* the required eccentricity. Tables 1, 2, and 3 provide three different solutions to this angular-momentum obstacle.

Table 1

One way out of this difficulty is to make the "year" of 360 "days" longer than the present year of 365¼ days, as in Table 1, and to suppose that Mars *gained*

154

angular momentum from its cumulative contacts with Earth. Although we did not spell them out in our original proposal of orbits in *Pensée* (1), these were the considerations that lay behind our decision to have the present semimajor axis of Earth's orbit shorter than it was during the fifteenth through eighth centuries.

Table 1 is, for the most part, consistent with views expressed by Velikovsky. Thus, Table 1 incorporates a 7.144-"year" mean synodic period of Venus during the 50-"year" interval between the Exodus and the battle of Beth-horon: since $7 \times 7.144 = 50.01$, provision has been made for the possibility that Venus might collide with Earth again at the close of the seventh of these synodic periods. Note also the 4-"year" synodic period of Venus in Stage 3a (related to the olympiad?), the 1.6-"year" mean synodic periods in Stages 3b and 5 ($1.6 \times 5 = 8.0$), and the 1.333-"year" mean synodic period in Stage 4 ($1.333 \times 3 = 4.0$).

Table 1 also incorporates five different 15-"year" cycles for Mars: in Stages 3a, 3b, 3c, and 4, where fifteen "years" is very nearly equal to an integral number (41, 14, 8, and 8, respectively) of sidereal periods of Mars, and also to an integral number (26, 1, 7, and 7, respectively) of synodic periods of Mars; and in the present stage (Stage 5) of the solar system, where favorable oppositions of Mars occur about every fifteen years. Velikovsky suggests that this latter phenomenon might be regarded as a "vestige" of the approaches of Mars every fifteen "years" during the eighth and seventh centuries (6).

It may seem that we have been overzealous in our efforts to find opportunities to incorporate cycles of fifteen "years" into the model. But we do not claim that all the 15-"year" cycles in our model actually occurred, nor do we claim that those cycles that did occur were of *exactly* fifteen "years." Our only intention has been to illustrate the relative ease with which several different sets of orbits could have involved Martian cycles of approximately fifteen "years." The other cycles that we have introduced are subject to similar qualifications.

Stage 1 and Stages 3a, 3b, and 3c also incorporate the ratio of 210:400 that is reported in the *Shitah Mekub-*

bezet (7): the sidereal period of 0.593 is 210/400 of the later sidereal period of 1.1295. (This source is discussed in greater detail in a separate article in this issue, in relation to the vital statistics of persons in the Bible.) Velikovsky mentions this Midrash from the *Shitah Mekubbezet,* but he is reluctant to accept the exact ratio of 210:400 (8). Velikovsky's caution is justified, but it should be stressed that such a ratio is not at all incompatible with Velikovsky's general sequence of events.

Table 2

Another solution to the angular-momentum limitations on the orbit of Mars involves abandoning the tacit but crucial assumption that the last Mars-Venus contact preceded the first Earth-Mars contact. If we abandon that assumption, and have the first Earth-Mars contact *precede* the last Mars-Venus contact, it then becomes possible for Mars to obtain angular momentum at the expense of Venus, lose it to Earth, gain more from Venus, regain most of what it had previously surrendered to Earth, and then proceed eventually to its present orbit. This sequence of events is illustrated quantitatively in Table 2.

Table 2, like Table 1, contains a number of Velikovskian features. There is a 7.144-"year" mean synodic period of Venus in Stage 2, and there are mean synodic periods of 51.618 "years," 4.003 "years," and 1.599 years in Stages 3a, 3b, and 5, respectively. Table 2 also incorporates five different 15-"year" cycles for Mars: in Stages 3a, 3b, 4a, and 4b, where fifteen "years" is very nearly equal to an integral number (34, 11, 37, and 14, respectively) of sidereal periods of Mars, and also to an integral number (19, 4, 22, and 1, respectively) of synodic periods of Mars; and in Stage 5, where favorable oppositions occur every fifteen years or so.

Table 3

There is still a third—and extremely speculative—way to resolve this question. If we allow Venus to move spontaneously from right to left along its *l/m* contour on the map of orbits—conserving angular momentum but losing both eccentricity and orbital energy—we would make it possible for the energy loss over the past four

TABLE 1

	Semi-major Axis	Eccentricity	Mass	Sidereal Period	Mean Synodic Period*	Perihelion	Aphelion	Minimum Velocity	Maximum Velocity	Energy	Angular Momentum
Stage 1											
Earth	.706	.070	1.012	.593		.656	.755	6.972	8.022	-28.307	5.330
Mars	.555	.075	.107	.413	2.299	.513	.596	7.825	9.094	-3.807	.499
Venus	3.000	.794	.870	5.196	1.129	.618	5.382	1.229	10.705	-6.724	5.756
										-37.839	11.585
Stage 2											
Earth	.985	.260	1.012	.978		.729	1.241	4.852	8.261	-20.285	6.095
Mars	.555	.075	.107	.413	.732	.513	.596	7.825	9.094	-3.807	.499
Venus	1.089	.450	.850	1.137	7.144	.599	1.579	3.708	9.775	-15.405	4.978
										-39.497	11.572
Stage 3a											
Earth	1.085	.090	1.012	1.1295		.987	1.182	5.513	6.603	-18.422	6.597
Mars	.555	.075	.107	.413	.577	.513	.596	7.825	9.094	-3.807	.499
Venus	.935	.472	.835	.904	4.000	.494	1.376	3.892	10.851	-17.634	4.472
										-39.863	11.568
Stage 3b											
Earth	1.085	.090	1.012	1.1295		.987	1.182	5.513	6.603	-18.422	6.597
Mars	1.136	.570	.107	1.210	15.038	.488	1.783	3.086	11.267	-1.860	.589
Venus	.785	.305	.825	.695	1.600	.545	1.024	5.176	9.719	-20.753	4.373
										-41.036	11.558
Stage 3c											
Earth	1.085	.090	1.012	1.1295		.987	1.182	5.513	6.603	-18.422	6.597
Mars	1.649	.725	.107	2.118	2.143	.454	2.845	1.954	12.254	-1.281	.595
Venus	.723	.007	.815	.615	1.196	.718	.728	7.338	7.438	-22.241	4.355
										-41.944	11.546
Stage 4											
Earth	1.050	.200	1.012	1.077		.840	1.261	5.005	7.508	-19.020	6.387
Mars	1.597	.340	.107	2.019	2.143	1.054	2.140	3.489	7.084	-1.322	.799
Venus	.723	.007	.815	.615	1.333	.718	.728	7.338	7.438	-22.241	4.355
										-42.584	11.541
Stage 5											
Earth	1.000	.017	1.012	1.000		.983	1.017	6.179	6.389	-19.981	6.359
Mars	1.524	.093	.107	1.881	2.135	1.381	1.666	4.635	5.590	-1.386	.826
Venus	.723	.007	.815	.615	1.599	.718	.728	7.338	7.438	-22.241	4.355
										-43.608	11.540

*The mean synodic periods are expressed in terms of the "year" that obtained at that time; all other values are expressed in geobasic units.

TABLE 2

	Semi-major Axis	Eccentricity	Mass	Sidereal Period	Mean Synodic Period*	Perihelion	Aphelion	Minimum Velocity	Maximum Velocity	Energy	Angular Momentum
Stage 1											
Earth	.706	.070	1.012	.593		.656	.755	6.972	8.022	-28.307	5.330
Mars	.574	.080	.107	.435	2.748	.528	.620	7.655	8.986	-3.680	.508
Venus	3.000	.794	.870	5.196	1.129	.618	5.382	1.229	10.705	-6.724	5.756
										-37.712	11.594
Stage 2											
Earth	.985	.260	1.012	.978		.729	1.241	4.852	8.261	-20.285	6.095
Mars	.574	.080	.107	.435	.801	.528	.620	7.655	8.986	-3.680	.508
Venus	1.089	.450	.850	1.137	7.144	.599	1.579	3.708	9.775	-39.370	4.978
										-39.370	11.580
Stage 3a											
Earth	.990	.090	1.012	.985		.901	1.079	5.769	6.910	-20.176	6.303
Mars	.574	.080	.107	.435	.789	.528	.620	7.655	8.986	-3.680	.508
Venus	1.003	.424	.835	1.005	51.618	.577	1.429	3.987	9.869	-16.428	4.758
										-40.285	11.569
Stage 3b											
Earth	.990	.090	1.012	.985		.901	1.079	5.769	6.910	-20.176	6.303
Mars	1.218	.510	.107	1.344	3.750	.597	1.839	3.243	9.995	-1.734	.638
Venus	.854	.275	.825	.789	4.003	.619	1.088	5.129	9.019	-40.991	4.604
										-40.991	11.546
Stage 4a											
Earth	1.077	.070	1.012	1.118		1.002	1.152	5.645	6.494	-18.552	6.584
Mars	.590	.723	.107	.453	.682	.163	1.016	3.280	20.402	-3.580	.357
Venus	.854	.275	.825	.789	2.396	.619	1.088	5.129	9.019	-19.080	4.604
										-41.213	11.545
Stage 4b											
Earth	1.077	.070	1.012	1.118		1.002	1.152	5.645	-6.494	-18.552	6.584
Mars	1.128	.535	.107	1.197	15.006	.524	1.731	3.257	10.750	-1.873	.603
Venus	.723	.007	.815	.615	1.224	.718	.728	7.338	7.438	-22.241	4.355
										-42.666	11.542
Stage 5											
Earth	1.000	.017	1.012	1.000		.983	1.017	6.179	6.389	-19.981	6.359
Mars	1.524	.093	.107	1.881	2.135	1.381	1.666	4.635	5.590	-1.386	.826
Venus	.723	.007	.815	.615	1.599	.718	.728	7.338	7.438	-22.241	4.355
										-43.608	11.540

*The mean synodic periods are expressed in terms of the "year" that obtained at that time; all other values are expressed in geobasic units.

or five thousand years to occur gradually, rather than only at those times when near-collisions were in progress. It should be noted, however, that we would still not be in a position to identify the form or the mechanism or the destination of this lost energy.

With this effect operative on a sufficiently large scale, Earth's orbit during the post-Beth-horon period could be smaller than the present orbit of Earth, *without* requiring the first Earth-Mars collision to precede the last Mars-Venus collision. For this effect might allow Venus to emerge from the last Mars-Venus contact with an aphelion substantially farther from the Sun than Venus' present aphelion, and might allow Venus gradually to circularize its orbit, that is, to reduce its semimajor axis slightly and to reduce its eccentricity greatly. It then

TABLE 3

	Semi-major Axis	Eccentricity	Mass	Sidereal Period	Mean Synodic Period*	Perihelion	Aphelion	Minimum Velocity	Maximum Velocity	Energy	Angular Momentum
Stage 1a											
Earth	.706	.070	1.012	.593		.656	.755	6.972	8.022	-28.307	5.330
Mars	.574	.080	.107	.435	2.748	.528	.620	7.655	8.986	-3.680	.508
Venus	3.000	.794	.870	5.196	1.129	.618	5.382	1.229	10.705	-5.724	5.756
										-37.712	11.594
Stage 1b											
Earth	.706	.070	1.012	.593		.656	.755	6.972	8.022	-28.307	5.330
Mars	.574	.080	.107	.435	2.748	.528	.620	7.655	8.986	-3.680	.508
Venus	2.100	.687	.870	3.043	1.242	.657	3.543	1.867	10.067	-8.178	5.756
										-40.165	11.594
Stage 2											
Earth	.962	.225	1.012	.943		.745	1.178	5.096	8.055	-20.776	6.077
Mars	.574	.080	.107	.435	.855	.528	.620	7.655	8.986	-3.680	.508
Venus	1.063	.417	.850	1.097	7.144	.620	1.507	3.908	9.499	-15.778	5.006
										-40.234	11.590
Stage 3a											
Earth	.990	.090	1.012	.985		.901	1.079	5.769	6.910	-20.176	6.303
Mars	.574	.080	.107	.435	.789	.528	.620	7.655	8.986	-3.680	.508
Venus	1.003	.424	.838	1.005	52.171	.577	1.429	3.988	9.869	-16.499	4.778
										-40.356	11.589
Stage 3b											
Earth	.990	.090	1.012	.985		.901	1.079	5.769	6.910	-20.176	6.303
Mars	.574	.080	.107	.435	.789	.528	.620	7.655	8.986	-3.680	.508
Venus	.969	.389	.838	.954	30.164	.592	1.346	4.234	9.623	-17.081	4.778
										-40.937	11.589
Stage 3c											
Earth	.990	.090	1.012	.985		.901	1.079	5.769	6.910	-20.176	6.303
Mars	1.037	.428	.107	1.056	15.034	.593	1.481	3.905	9.750	-2.037	.619
Venus	.877	.315	.832	.822	5.023	.601	1.154	4.841	9.294	-18.727	4.650
										-40.940	11.572
Stage 3d											
Earth	.990	.090	1.012	.985		.901	1.079	5.769	6.910	-20.176	6.303
Mars	1.218	.490	.107	1.344	3.750	.621	1.814	3.331	9.372	-1.734	.647
Venus	.853	.280	.825	.788	4.000	.614	1.092	5.101	9.069	-19.082	4.597
										-40.993	11.547
Stage 3e											
Earth	.990	.090	1.012	.985		.901	1.079	5.769	6.910	-20.176	6.303
Mars	6.023	.843	.107	14.782	1.071	.946	11.101	.747	8.772	-.351	.888
Venus	.784	.278	.815	.694	2.383	.566	1.002	5.332	9.444	-20.520	4.355
										-41.047	11.546
Stage 4											
Earth	1.039	.166	1.012	1.059		.866	1.211	5.213	7.289	-19.232	6.393
Mars	1.580	.340	.107	1.986	2.143	1.043	2.117	3.508	7.123	-1.337	.795
Venus	.780	.270	.815	.689	1.861	.570	.990	5.396	9.380	-20.625	4.355
										-41.194	11.542
Stage 5a											
Earth	1.000	.017	1.012	1.000		.983	1.017	6.179	6.389	-19.981	6.359
Mars	1.524	.093	.107	1.881	2.135	1.381	1.666	4.635	5.590	-1.386	.826
Venus	.776	.261	.815	.684	2.160	.574	.978	5.463	9.313	-20.731	4.355
										-42.098	11.540
Stage 5b											
Earth	1.000	.017	1.012	1.000		.983	1.017	6.179	6.389	-19.981	6.359
Mars	1.524	.093	.107	1.881	2.135	1.381	1.666	4.635	5.590	-1.386	.826
Venus	.723	.007	.815	.615	1.599	.718	.728	7.338	7.438	-22.241	4.355
										-43.608	11.540

The mean synodic periods are expressed in terms of the "year" that obtained at that time; all other values are expressed in geobasic units.

becomes possible for Mars, with a very high eccentricity and a rather long period, to *lose* angular momentum in its collisions with Earth and for Earth to *gain* a very slight amount of angular momentum, just enough for the transition from a "year" of 360 "days" to a year of 365¼ days to represent a genuine lengthening.

Thus we have prepared Table 3, which incorporates certain Velikovskian features such as a 7.144-"year" mean synodic period of Venus, with the seventh such period ending about fifty "years" after the beginning of the first such period; a 52.171-"year" mean synodic period of Venus; a 4-"year" synodic period of Venus (that may be associated with the olympiad); and a number of 15-"year" cycles of Mars (the situations in Stages 3a, 3b, 3c, 3d, 3e, and 4, where fifteen "years" is very nearly equal to an integral number (34, 34, 14, 11, 1, and 8, respectively) of sidereal periods of Mars, and also to an integral number (19, 19, 1, 4, 14, and 7, respectively) of synodic periods of Mars; and the 15-year cycle of favorable oppositions in Stages 5a and 5b).

"Days," "Months," and Eclipses

According to Velikovsky, the post-Beth-horon "year" (Stage 3) contained 360 "days" and 12 "months." If, as Table 1 indicates, the post-Beth-horon "year" was equal to 1.1295 of our present years, some important consequences follow: The length of the post-Beth-horon "day" would have been 27.5 modern hours. The length of the post-Beth-horon "month"—that is, the synodic period of the Moon—would have been 34.38 modern days; thus the sidereal period of the Moon would have been 31.74 modern days (which is 1.1615 times its present value), and the semimajor axis of the Moon's orbit would have been $(1.1615)^{2/3} = 1.105$ times its present value. The semimajor axis of Earth's orbit would have been $(1.1295)^{2/3} = 1.085$ times its present value. While both the Sun and the Moon would have been at greater distances from Earth than at present, the Moon's distance was greater by 1.105 times and the Sun's distance was greater by only 1.085 times. This means that it would have been slightly more difficult (but by no means impossible, given appropriate eccentricities) for the Moon to cover the Sun completely.

Both in Table 2 and in Table 3 the post-Beth-horon "day" would have been almost exactly twenty-four present hours. The "month" would have been almost exactly thirty present days. The sidereal period of the Moon would have been 27.69 days; hence, the semimajor axis of the Moon's orbit would have been 1.009 times its present value. Both in Table 2 and in Table 3, the Sun would have been slightly closer to Earth than at present, while the Moon would have been slightly farther from Earth than at present. The relative distances of the Sun and the Moon would again suggest that total solar eclipses were less frequent in the post-Beth horon period than now.

ECCENTRICITY AND ENERGY

In constructing each of the tables, we have followed this guideline: If the transition from one stage to another is marked by a near-collision of planets A and B, then the presumed point of that near-collision, expressed in terms of its distance from the Sun, should be greater than the perihelions of A and B in both the earlier and later stages, and less than the aphelions of A and B in both the earlier and later stages. The presumed "point" of such a near-collision is of course not a precise point, because the planets are not only some distance apart during their near-collision, but also may both be moving in the same general direction for some time, so that the "point" where the planets "are colliding" may actually move over some distance. The guideline also needs to be qualified insofar as it is quite possible for a larger planet to "capture" a smaller planet at one distance from the Sun and "release" it at another distance from the Sun, so that the earlier and the later orbits of the smaller planet need not overlap at all.

But this guideline cannot be followed in the transition from Stage 4 to the present Stage 5. The present orbits of Earth and Mars do not intersect, and it is obvious that the two planets did not leave the sector of their near-collision on the same Keplerian orbits that they have followed to this day. As Juergens describes this problem, ". . . the final encounter must necessarily leave at least one participant traveling on a highly eccentric orbit —one that must return the body again and again to at least one point of possible collision with its late antagonist" (9). Yet neither Mars nor Earth is presently on an orbit eccentric enough to carry it to a point on the orbit of the other.

There are two major problems here. First, there is the problem of identifying a process capable of reducing orbital eccentricity following the last encounter. Second, there is apparently an energy-disposal problem that accompanies this final eccentricity-reduction and may also accompany the entire sequence proposed by Velikovsky. The following discussion involving Venus, although it puts off the question of the final eccentricity-reduction involving Earth and Mars, will illustrate the nature of these two problems.

Reduction of Eccentricity

The planets continuously undergo deformation by the tidal force of the Sun. Tidal friction occurs insofar as the movement of a tidal deformation (either its rotation around the planet due to the planetary rotation, or variation in its magnitude caused by the orbital eccentricity) is opposed by internal friction within the planet; the effect is to convert rotational and/or orbital energy to thermal energy. Such a process was suggested by Sherrerd (10) to explain the last stages of the reduction of Venus' orbital eccentricity. Sherrerd's proposal is attractive, but is apparently not sufficient for our more general purposes here. Even if we assume an unlimited ability for conversion of orbital energy to heat, it is difficult to explain the destination of this heat. How much heat can Venus have absorbed and retained, and how much can have been lost as thermal radiation? Since we know that the present surface temperature of Venus is approximately $750°$ K, we can make some educated guesses. It would appear that Venus cannot have absorbed and retained much tidal-friction heat (especially since a high initial temperature is postulated for the tidal-friction process), and it would appear that the surface temperature of Venus has not been great enough to radiate a significant amount of energy in terms of our orbital requirements, even if we assume Venus to be a perfect black-body (which is certainly not true now, since its clouds and atmosphere are opaque to many parts of the electromagnetic spectrum).

According to Stefan's law, the rate of radiation from a black-body is proportional to the area and to the fourth power of the temperature. A black-body the size of Venus would have a surface area of 4.83×10^{18} cm². At a surface temperature of $1000°$ K, the rate of radiation would be 2.75×10^{26} ergs/second or 6.5×10^{-6} geobasic energy unit/year; at $2000°$ K, the rate would be 4.4×10^{27} ergs/second or 1.0×10^{-4} geobasic energy unit/year (4). A Venus surface temperature as high as $2000°$ K within the historical past is surely hypothetical; such an extreme temperature seems to require an unacceptably high rate of cooling, and is more than is needed for the incandescence claimed by Velikovsky (the approximate relationship between observed incandescence and temperature is: dark-red heat, 925 to $1025°$ K; bright-red heat, 1125 to $1225°$ K; yellowish-red heat, 1325 to $1425°$ K; white heat, $1725°$ K and up (11)). Nevertheless, as an extreme example, how much energy could be radiated during two thousand years at $2000°$ K? The amount would be 2.8×10^{38} ergs, or 0.21 geobasic energy unit.

The present orbital energy of Venus is -22.24 geobasic energy units (see tables). Venus' orbital energy thus would have been $-22.24 + 0.21 = 22.03$ geobasic energy units prior to this hypothetical energy dissipation. Expressed as a percentage, Venus' loss of orbital energy would have been 0.95 per cent, or just under one per cent.

An orbital change due to planetary tidal friction would presumably involve a loss of orbital energy accompanied by either a loss of, or no change in, angular momentum. The decrease of eccentricity per unit decrease of energy is greater when the angular momentum remains unchanged; this would be the most favorable case from our viewpoint. Such an orbital change can be visualized on the map of orbits as movement (of the point representing the orbit) toward the left along an l/m contour. Changes of eccentricity along the contour can be readily correlated with changes of energy, although direct measurement on the map is impractical for determining relative changes along the contour near the left-hand edge of the map (eccentricities between zero and one-tenth). In this zone, where the l/m contour is practically horizontal, the per cent change of energy is very nearly equal to $100(e_2{}^2 - e_1{}^2)$ as the eccentricity changes from e_1 to e_2. Our example falls in this zone; thus, since the per cent change of energy was $-0.95 = 100(0.000049 - e_1{}^2)$, the former eccentricity would have been $e_1 = (0.009549)^{1/2} = 0.098$. A *greater* loss of eccentricity due to tidal friction would not seem possible; even this value, being based on some seemingly unrealistic assumptions, appears too high. Earth and Mars, of course, have much lower surface temperatures than Venus, so that tidal friction seems quite useless in explaining the transition from their final encounter to their present orbits.

The General Problem of Energy

There is a still more general problem of energy disposal. Consider the present orbits of Venus, Earth, and Mars in comparison with their orbits prior to the initial encounter between Earth and Venus some thirty-five centuries ago. No definite orbits are known for the pre-Exodus period; however, certain limits follow from Velikovsky's hypotheses, especially for Venus, as was shown in Figure 1. The Table 1 orbits for the pre-Exodus period can be used as an example: the total orbital energy for Stage 1 of Table 1 is -37.84 geobasic energy units. The total for the present orbits (shown as Stage 5) is -43.61 geobasic energy units. This implies that 5.77 geobasic units (i.e., approximately 10^{40} ergs) have somehow been disposed of within the past thirty-five centuries.

This amount of energy presents a formidable problem. An interesting book by Lane (12) gives a scale of energy magnitudes that is useful for reference. A letter to *Nature* by Urey (13) is concerned with a similar situation, but on a smaller scale: the disposal of 10^{31} ergs and its terrestrial effects. We are talking about the disposal of *one billion* (i.e., 10^9) *times* as much energy. While this energy would not all have resulted from a single encounter, but from several encounters occurring over a span of nearly one thousand years, it nevertheless seems unlikely that this amount of energy could be absorbed and stored by Venus, Earth, and Mars, or that it could be dissipated into space by the three planets during the time available.

The Energy Problem: Alternatives

Dissipation into space would normally occur by means of electromagnetic radiation. The limitations according to Stefan's law have already been discussed; however, that discussion did not consider the possibility that the radiation was emitted from an excited plasma surrounding the particular planet, rather than from the planet's surface. If this were the case, a much higher temperature would be available, resulting in a higher rate of energy emission, but this emission would seemingly consist of a greater proportion of short-wavelength (ultraviolet, X-ray) radiation—more than enough, perhaps, to produce the mutations described by Velikovsky.

Likewise, it seems questionable whether substantial amounts of energy were absorbed and stored by Venus, Earth, and Mars. The total mass of the three planets is approximately 1.2×10^{28} grams; if 5×10^{39} ergs were absorbed, the average energy storage requirement would be 4×10^{11} ergs, or ten thousand calories, *per gram* of planetary material. Current theories do not leave any room for such a possibility, but it should perhaps be mentioned that our knowledge of the planetary interiors and their histories is composed from a great deal of circumstantial and indirect evidence. Suppose, hypothetically, that 10^{39} or 10^{40} ergs were suddenly delivered to Earth's core: how long would it take for the effects to become manifest at the surface? How hot are the interiors of Earth and the other planets, and what latent energies reside there (i.e., what is the energy difference between the present state of Earth and a uniformly cold Earth)? Cook considers the deep interior of all celestial bodies to be high-density plasma, or pressure-induced metallic states, which are characterized by a deep "energy well" (14). It remains to be seen whether this sort of energy capacity is available to satisfy a significant part of our requirements.

Can different pre-Exodus orbits be selected that would eliminate the energy problem? We have been using a pre-Exodus orbit near ($a=3.0$, $e=0.8$) for Venus; a smaller, less eccentric orbit would be ideal. But our reasons for fixing Venus' orbit within the limits shown in Figure 1 have already been described; unless these reasons are invalidated, we can only vary the orbits of Earth and Mars. There do exist two sets of pairs of orbits for Earth and Mars that (in combination with the Venus orbit) exactly conserve both total orbital energy and total orbital angular momentum at their present levels, but none of these orbital pairs seems satisfactory, since none of the pairs will tend to produce a Velikovskian sequence of encounters, while, at the same time, one or the other planet is required to be too close to the Sun. The best possible (i.e., least objectionable) pairs occur when both orbital eccentricities are zero: the semimajor axes of Earth and Mars are, respectively, 0.87 and 0.14 A.U. for the best pair in one set and 0.53 and 5.1 A.U. for the best pair in the other set (15). Thus, there is no apparent solution to this energy problem by choosing different pre-Exodus orbits. The energy problem could be resolved, with a variety of possible orbits for Earth and Mars, by assuming that total angular momentum was not conserved, but this seems to raise even more difficult questions than the energy-disposal problem.

The participation of at least one other body besides Venus, Earth, and Mars in the encounters that have occurred since Venus' final departure from the vicinity of Jupiter could provide an easy solution to this energy-disposal problem (16). Although such a proposal might be described as *deus ex machina,* the possibility should not be completely overlooked. To provide the desired effect, the additional body would have gained orbital energy from Venus, Earth, or Mars. For example, it is possible that a small planet or planetoid was on a relatively small ($a<3.0$) orbit around the Sun, and that various near-collisions either have propelled it right out of the solar system or else have placed it on a highly eccentric orbit with such a large semimajor axis that it is noticeable now only at its perihelion passages, which may be separated by many centuries. (This type of occurrence might explain why deities major enough to be "planetary" no longer have planets to which we may assign them.)

The involvement of an additional body of this sort would permit the Velikovskian sequence of events to occur *with a strict balancing both of energy and of angular momentum;* if we permit this "other body" to interact with Mars after −687, then *the problem of eccentricity-damping will evaporate* as well. It should be emphasized, however, that Velikovsky has never endorsed such an approach, and has preferred instead to explain the final stages of his sequence of events in terms of electromagnetic processes.

It is also possible that a once-separate body, on a relatively small orbit, collided directly and thereby merged with the original Venus, or that a former part or parts of Venus (or Mars) was split off in an encounter and is now one or more separate bodies following relatively large orbits around the Sun. In the latter case, it is possible that the original mass of Venus was substantially greater than its present mass and that the debris of Venus' stormy career carried off substantial amounts of orbital energy.

There are a number of seemingly unlikely ideas that might lead to a solution of the energy problem. Much attention has been given recently to the possible existence of black holes in the universe; it would be worth investigating the effects of a black hole passing through the solar system—or even passing directly through Jupiter. It is interesting to note that the energy needed for the original escape of Venus from Jupiter is roughly comparable to the energy that Venus must thereafter lose to reach its present orbit; no energy need ultimately be gained or lost if it could somehow be "borrowed." Perhaps there have been fields of force acting in the solar system whose effects, including potential energy, we do not fully appreciate.

In looking for possible answers to the energy problem, we are speculating freely, but with a definite purpose in mind. We believe that it will ultimately be possible to assemble enough numerical historical data to settle the question of orbital changes; so far, the question has seldom been asked, much less answered. If there turns out to be consistent evidence for currently unexplained orbital changes within the historical past, science will need to seek hypotheses that fit the historical record, rather than demand that history conform to the expectations of present-day science.

Earth and Mars

The energy-disposal alternatives in the preceding discussion also apply to the final reduction of the orbital eccentricity of Earth or Mars or both. There are no orbits for Earth and Mars that cross each other and that also have values of orbital energy and angular momentum that add up to the present Earth-Mars totals. There do exist two sets of pairs of orbits for Earth and Mars that exactly conserve both total orbital energy and total orbital angular momentum at their present levels, but none of these paired orbits will cross each other. Conversely, there exist various paired orbits that cross each other while conserving the total orbital angular momentum at its present level, but, for every pair, the total orbital energy is at least 0.3 geobasic energy unit, or 4×10^{38} ergs, higher than the present level. While this excess energy is less than the 10^{40} ergs in the preceding problem, it nevertheless remains difficult to explain, especially since the energy disposal must have occurred within a relatively short time following the last encounter.

In summary, the two major energy-disposal problems can be put in the form of questions: Has there been an overall loss of orbital energy since the first Earth-Venus encounter? Has there been an overall loss of orbital energy since the final Earth-Mars encounter? Both these questions imply others: if so, by what process was the orbital energy lost, and where has it gone? If not, how could the various orbits have resulted from or led to a Velikovskian sequence of encounters? The resolution of these questions is crucial to Velikovsky's theory.

We have suggested several alternative models for Velikovsky's sequence of planetary orbits. At this point, we are inclined to think that any well-founded establishment of one model rather than another will await the discovery, or the recognition, of further historical information. Ancient reports are usually of isolated events, but the determination of orbits requires a *series* of observations. As far as we know, the only dated sequence of observations from before −687 is on the so-called "Venus Tablets of Ammizaduga." We have given preliminary accounts of our work on those tablets (17, 18); our investigations are continuing, but we do not yet have any final results to report. Additional historical data of the sort found on these tablets will be needed for the development of more definitive models. But not *all* of the information that we need would have to be precise or sophisticated; even casual reports could conceivably be quite important. Thus a report that something happened at night rather than during the day could be decisive in the choice between one model and another.

It should be pointed out that even if we could choose one model rather than another, the models that we have been considering are in a sense only outlines of the possible orbital sequences: the precise description of a planetary orbit would involve six different elements. Our approach has been to treat all planetary orbits as lying in the ecliptic plane and to focus our consideration on two elements, the semimajor axis and the eccentricity, and on various other parameters that are functions of those two elements. There is much that can be accomplished using this restricted approach, but a fully detailed model would of course have to treat all six orbital elements. Such a fully detailed model does not seem imminent—mainly because of a lack of clues about precise longitudes.

We close with a cautionary note regarding energy disposal, eccentricity-damping, and electromagnetic processes in astronomy. These may indeed be consequences or ramifications of Velikovsky's theory, but at this point it is largely a matter of attitude whether one sees these as vulnerable points of the theory or as strong opportunities for discovery. An analogy could be drawn to the Copernican theory, which entailed that either there was a measurable stellar parallax or the stars were fantastically farther away than anyone had guessed. Since there was at that time no measurable parallax, some saw this "problem" as an insuperable barrier to the Copernican theory and rejected the theory as absurd. Others, like Giordano Bruno, saw clearly that the Copernican theory entailed an enormous universe, and Bruno concluded that the stars were so far away that they must be *suns*. The parallax "problem," which some saw as a reason for rejecting the Copernican theory, Bruno saw as the key to his own discoveries that the stars are suns and that those suns are probably centers of planetary systems of their own.

Let us not suppose that our relative ignorance, at present, of the processes that damp eccentricities or dissipate energy or produce electromagnetic effects in the solar system shows that Velikovsky is wrong. Instead, let us study the consequences of Velikovsky's theory and engage in serious and systematic search for the information and the understanding that will enable us to evaluate the role of those processes toward which Velikovsky points. We do not stand before a wall: we stand before a door.

NOTES AND REFERENCES

1. Lynn Rose and Raymond Vaughan, "The Orbits of Mars, Earth, and Venus," *Pensée*, 2 (May 1972), 43.
2. C. J. Ransom and L. H. Hoffee, "The Orbits of Venus," *Pensée*, 3 (Winter 1973), 22.
3. Raymond C. Vaughan, "Orbits and Their Measurements." Unpublished. ABSTRACT: *A diagram or "map" is developed that shows the values (±1 per cent) of various orbital parameters for a given orbit, or establishes the orbit when parameter values are given. The map shows graphically the interdependence of parameters and thereby illustrates the limitations on orbital change. First, a brief description is given of orbital parameters, Kepler's laws, and ellipses. Elliptical orbits are then classified and represented as points on a semi-log grid, using coordinates*

a *and* e, *in order to form the basic map. Other kinematic parameters are introduced that are functions of* a *and* e, *and a network of parameter contours is superimposed on the map, allowing parameter values to be read from the map by direct measurement. Conservation of energy and of angular momentum are discussed insofar as they define the limitations on orbital change.*

4. See (3) regarding geobasic units and cgs-mks-geobasic conversion factors.

5. Immanuel Velikovsky, *Worlds in Collision* (New York: The Macmillan Company, 1950), pp. 330–42.

6. Velikovsky, *Worlds in Collision*, p. 363.

7. [Bezalel ben Abraham Ashkenazi?], *Shitah Mekubbezet. Nedarin* (Berlin: Kornegg, 1860).

8. Velikovsky, *Worlds in Collision*, p. 124.

9. Ralph Juergens, "Reconciling Celestial Mechanics and Velikovskian Catastrophism," *Pensée*, 2 (Fall 1972), 6.

10. Chris Sherrerd, "Venus' Circular Orbit," *Pensée*, 2 (May 1972), 43.

11. "Color Scale of Temperature," in *Handbook of Chemistry and Physics*, 43rd ed. (Cleveland, Ohio: The Chemical Rubber Publishing Co., 1961), p. 2321.

12. Frank W. Lane, *The Elements Rage* (Philadelphia: Chilton Company, 1965).

13. Harold C. Urey, "Cometary Collisions and Geological Periods," *Nature*, 242 (March 2, 1973), 32.

14. Melvin A. Cook, untitled remarks, Number V in "Special Supplement: On Celestial Mechanics," *Pensée*, 3 (Winter 1973), 55.

15. We assume that neither Earth nor Mars was moving in a retrograde orbit.

16. One candidate to play the role of this other body would be Jupiter: although it seems unlikely, it is possible that ordinary gravitational perturbations by Jupiter would be sufficient to accomplish this.

17. Lynn E. Rose, "Babylonian Observations of Venus," *Pensée*, 3 (Winter 1973), 18.

18. Lynn E. Rose and Raymond C. Vaughan, "Analysis of the Babylonian Observations of Venus." Unpublished. Presented at the symposium "Velikovsky and the Recent History of the Solar System," McMaster University, Hamilton, Ont., June 19, 1974.

VENUS' CIRCULAR ORBIT

Chris S. Sherrerd

I do not see that the high degree of circularity of Venus'
orbit presents a difficulty for Dr. Immanuel Velikovsky's
view that Venus once traveled a highly elliptical path.
The ascertainment that the surface temperature of Venus
is so great that the body is incandescent indicates a high
degree of plasticity (if not an actually molten state until
very recently) for the planet's body. If such a body approaches the intense gravitational field near the Sun on
an elliptical orbit, considerable energy of motion will
be converted by tidal friction into heat. This will: a) tend
to keep the body plastic or molten; and b) change the
orbit to that, by the laws of Cassini, which minimizes
energy loss by tidal friction. That is, the effects of tidal
friction tend to decrease the magnitude of the velocity
at nearest passages, which in turn reduces the ellipticity
of the orbit. If the spin rate is high (short day), such an
orbit will be still elliptical, with a shifting perihelion and
slowly decreasing major axis; if in addition the initial
orbit and equator are severely non-coplanar, strong librations will also result. If the spin rate is very slow, on
the other hand, that orbit will be nearly circular. It
seems very credible, not only by virtue of Velikovsky's
theories, but also by the physics of tidal energy dissipation and the current knowledge of the surface temperature of Venus and its Earth-synchronous spin, that this
indeed has happened over the past three thousand years.
Also, if there exist strong electromagnetic forces, attractive or repulsive, between Venus and the Sun, the orbit
of Venus would tend to reach circular orbit in less time

than expected by gravitational and tidal-dissipation considerations alone.

To Sherrerd's concluding remark concerning the additional ease with which Venus could achieve a circular orbit in an electromagnetic solar system, I would refer the reader to a 1970 paper by D. K. Sarvajna, in Astrophysics and Space Science, 6, 258, and to a 1971 paper by I. P. Williams on "Planetary Formation from Charged Bodies," in the same publication (Vol. 12, 165–71), showing how "a charged body ejected from the Sun can be captured in orbit because of electromagnetic effects." (Williams' model requires a much smaller charge than Sarvajna's.) But to these things I also referred over twenty years earlier in the only italicized sentence in Worlds in Collision (p. 387). I would also assume that Venus' orbit slowly continues to approach a true circle.

Immanuel Velikovsky

GYROSCOPIC PRECESSION AND CELESTIAL AXIS DISPLACEMENT

Chris S. Sherrerd

Many readers of Velikovsky's writings and associated papers perhaps find it very difficult to accept the historical reports of prolonged periods of daylight or darkness, as if "the Sun stood still," or as if temporary but very severe perturbations occurred in the rotation of the Earth about its polar axis. One would think intuitively, at first glance, that such occurrences would require impossibly large angular decelerating and accelerating forces, which in turn would so totally disrupt the Earth's crust as to make impossible any human survival.

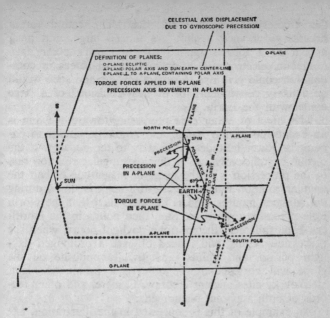

CELESTIAL AXIS DISPLACEMENT
DUE TO GYROSCOPIC PRECESSION

DEFINITION OF PLANES:
O-PLANE: ECLIPTIC
A-PLANE: POLAR AXIS AND SUN-EARTH CENTER-LINE
E-PLANE: ⊥ TO A-PLANE, CONTAINING POLAR AXIS
TORQUE FORCES APPLIED IN E-PLANE
PRECESSION AXIS MOVEMENT IN A-PLANE

Sudden and major displacements in the *geographical* position of the Earth's polar axis would most likely require such unthinkable circumstances. Those geographical shifts which have occurred during historical time involved at most a few degrees of arc distance on the surface of the globe, and were indeed tectonically quite disruptive at that.

However, unusual changes in the Sun's apparent position in the sky would also result from major shifts in the *celestial* position of the poles, i.e., the direction of the Earth's spin axis in the celestial sphere. These could occur without large angular decelerating and accelerating forces and without major tectonic disruptions, by the phenomenon of gyroscopic precession. Since gyroscopic precession involves a temporary transfer of angular momentum from spin to precession, when beginning and terminating it moderately affects the rate of rotation of a spinning object and introduces small horizontal forces on points on its surface; but it significantly shifts the absolute orientation of the spin axis in space as long as

173

the precession continues in effect. The causal forces necessary for such a shift are indeed large, and must appear as a torque applied to the Earth's polar axis. Magnetic, electrostatic, and gravitational forces in combination could give rise to such a torque, and such would be a likely consequence of a "near-collision" of a large comet with the Earth.

The effect of either pole precessing toward the Sun is an expansion of the Arctic and Antarctic circles to encompass lower latitudes, ultimately to the equator. If the torque is sufficiently strong that the angular rotation rate of the precession is of the order of magnitude of half the angular rotation rate of the Earth's spin, is timed during the summer months, and is directed such that the North Pole precesses toward the Sun, then points in the Northern Hemisphere in the morning daylight hours, when the precession begins, will indeed observe a prolonged daylight period, and points diametrically opposite on the globe will correspondingly observe a prolonged night. Velikovsky cites ancient Hebrew, Chinese, and other records of both apparent phenomena.

An example of this is suggested in the illustration. Let (O) be the plane of the Earth's orbit about the Sun (i.e., the ecliptic), (S) be a reference direction vector perpendicular to (O) through the center of the Sun, (A) be a plane defined by the Earth's polar (spin) axis and the Sun-Earth center line, and (E) be a plane containing the Earth's polar axis and perpendicular to (A). (Except for the exact moments of winter and summer solstices, the Earth's orbital velocity will not be coplanar with (E).) Then, if a torque represented by a force moment or couplet lying entirely within (E) is applied in the direction illustrated, the polar axis will precess entirely within (A) and directed such that the North Pole shifts toward the Sun.

From the theory of gyroscopic precession of a rigid body, it is a simple matter of estimating the force moment or torque required. Using $s = 7.29211 \times 10^{-5}$ sec^{-1} as the Earth's spin velocity and $I = 8.11992 \times 10^{44}$ gm-cm^2 as the Earth's moment of inertia, the torque required to give a precessional spin velocity s' equal to $s/2$ is given by $t = Iss' = 2.15888 \times 10^{29}$ newton-meters.

It has been suggested that perhaps an extraterrestrial magnetic field acting upon the earth's magnetic field could give rise to a precession of the Earth's celestial axis. But if the present value of the Earth's magnetic dipole moment of $u = 6.4 \times 10^{21}$ amperemeters^2 is assumed, the strength of the external magnetic field required to exert a torque of this magnitude on the Earth is $B = t/u = 3.368 \times 10^{11}$ gauss. Even if the Earth's magnetic dipole moment were several orders of magnitude greater in the past than it is now, it appears that the required magnetic field strength is well beyond that which is reasonably conceivable as the sole source of this torque.

However, gravitational and electrostatic forces could conceivably give rise to torques of this magnitude. If a large comet were momentarily "captured" in a local suborbit about the Earth with perigee slightly beyond the Roche limit and in a suborbital plane tilted with respect to the Earth's equatorial plane (for example, in the illustration, in a suborbital plane which is approximately perpendicular to the (E) plane but neither perpendicular to nor coplanar with the (A) plane), then a fluctuating torque would be exerted with two maxima during each suborbit in such a way as to cause a positive cumulative precession effect of considerable magnitude. Such gravitational/electrostatic forces would also somewhat affect the Earth's orbit about the Sun, the spin rate (length of the day), and the *geographical* position of the Earth's spin (polar) axis, undoubtedly also with accompanying major tectonic disruptions.

Historical records establish that such phenomena *have* occurred. This simple model of course can only suggest orders of magnitude, since many unknown orbital and rotational characteristics of the Earth and other celestial effects pertaining at the historical times of interest have been ignored. Furthermore, it is most likely that magnetic, gravitational, and electrostatic forces were *all* involved in concert. Nevertheless, such phenomena are quite plausible within the present knowledge of astrophysics. It is intellectual dishonesty to dismiss the historical records on the basis of alleged astrophysical impossibility. A more fruitful endeavor would, rather, be to explore what quantitative models are consistent with the historical records and what other logical conclusions can be drawn from such models.

PLASMA IN INTERPLANETARY SPACE: RECONCILING CELESTIAL MECHANICS AND VELIKOVSKIAN CATASTROPHISM*

Ralph E. Juergens

I

Physical scientists were outraged in 1950 when Immanuel Velikovsky (1) published historical evidence from around the world suggesting that the order and even the number of planets in the solar system had changed within the memory of man. Ideas in nearly every field of scholarship were challenged, but most seriously challenged of all were certain dogmas in the field of astronomy, which had only in recent centuries succeeded in convincing mankind that Spaceship Earth was a haven of safety.

The emotional outburst from the community of astronomers that so blackened the name Velikovsky and so successfully—if only temporarily—discredited *Worlds in Collision* has been laid to many causes, from the psychological and the political to simple resentment against invasion of the field by an outsider. Whatever the nature of such intensifying factors, however, I believe it is only fair to acknowledge an underlying and totally sincere scientific disbelief in the historical record.

Perfectly valid dynamical theories—valid in the sense of having met and passed every conceivable kind of test —simply could not be reconciled with the story told by

Velikovsky. In short, conventional celestial mechanics, which had proved time and again its ability to describe and predict planetary motions in today's solar system, could in no way accommodate a disordering and rearrangement of the planets as recently as three or four thousand years ago.

In terms of celestial mechanics, a system of bodies whose motions are governed entirely by gravitational forces and the inertia of masses could not conceivably restabilize itself within mere millennia—let alone within the few decades or centuries allowed by the historical record—following disruptions of the kind described in *Worlds in Collision*.

Even were each near-collision in such a series so providentially contrived as to leave one or the other participant moving along a near-circular orbit close to the ecliptic plane, the final encounter must necessarily leave at least one participant traveling on a highly eccentric orbit—one that must return the body again and again to at least one point of possible collision with its late antagonist. Yet today's solar system—with one possible exception involving Neptune and Pluto—seems ordered in such a way that further planetary collisions are out of the question.

Velikovsky was quite aware of the discord between his findings and current ideas as to what constitutes propriety in celestial mechanics. He insisted, however, that the fault must lie in dynamical theory, not in the evidence of history. He suggested that the Sun and the planets must be electrically charged, and that electromagnetic and electrostatic forces—which could quite easily be capable of cushioning collisions, altering rotational motions, tilting axes, and perhaps even damping eccentricities over relatively short spans of time—must play unrecognized roles in celestial affairs.

As we shall note presently, there is compelling evidence to indicate that the Sun, the Earth, and the Moon, to name only a few major bodies in the solar system, are electrically charged. Yet the very precision with which gravitational theory accounts for the planetary motions seems to belie this evidence. Perturbations due to repulsive electrical forces, for example, are nowhere in evidence today—not even, I hasten to suggest, in the strange behavior of comet tails, about which I shall have more to say later.

This impasse between celestial mechanics and the notion of cosmic electrical interactions was recognized long ago. A reconciliation seemed so unlikely that physical scientists of half a dozen successive generations felt compelled to devise all sorts of exotic theories to explain away the most obvious evidence for electric charge on the Earth.

An important clue to the vanity of all such *ad hoc* theorizing was radioed back to earth in 1962 by Mariner 2.

Man's first successful Venus probe established once and for all that the interplanetary medium is not a near-vacuum, as most astronomers had always supposed, but is actually a plasma—a gas of dissociated positive ions and electrons. This disclosure instantly invalidated the argument that the planets, if electrically charged, would perturb one another in most obvious ways.

According to the physics of electricity, a charged body isolated in a vacuum, which is a dielectric medium, surrounds itself with an electric field that reaches to infinity, with strength diminishing as the square of the distance. Thus, in a vacuous interplanetary medium, or even in a medium of neutral atomic or molecular gases, planetary charges must give rise to electric fields detectable by their influences upon planetary motions.

In an interplanetary medium consisting of ionized gas, however, things are radically different.

One of the primary characteristics of a plasma has up to now received little or no attention from astronomers. This is its ability to shield itself from the electric field of any body in contact with it, or contained within it, and charged to an electric potential different from that of the plasma itself. The mechanism by which such shielding is accomplished was named the space-charge sheath by those who first studied the phenomenon.

In a space-charge sheath, positive and negative charges collect and arrange themselves in such a way that the electric field of a body with alien potential is contained within a limited region surrounding the body. This does not mean that the total electric charge of the isolated body must be compensated by equal and opposite charge in the sheath; rather, it means only that enough charge must be assembled in the sheath to increase or decrease the potential of the outer sheath boundary to match the potential of the surrounding plasma.

As a laboratory phenomenon, the space-charge sheath was described, studied, and given a measure of quantitative theoretical explanation half a century ago. The most lucid accounts of this work are probably those to be found in the papers of Irving Langmuir (2), the physicist who coined the term "plasma" in reference to fully ionized gases.

Up to this point, I have neglected to mention two most important facts about space-charge sheaths and plasmas:

1. An isolated body whose alien potential is not continually renewed by means of electric currents will quickly acquire a potential practically equal to that of the surrounding plasma, and its sheath will all but disappear; and

2. A plasma does not necessarily possess an intrinsic electric potential. Where plasmas form in electrical discharges, however—and this is the connection in which Langmuir studied them—they do acquire non-zero potentials.

These are clearly matters of immense importance. I will return to them later.

For now, we can say that in a solar system pervaded by plasma, each charged planet with a potential unlike that of the local plasma must have its electric field bound up in a space-charge sheath of limited volume. When no orbital conflict exists, the system operates serenely under the direction of forces accounted for in conventional celestial mechanics.

But let us imagine what might occur should two electrically charged major bodies in this system find themselves on intersecting orbits. Inevitably, as the two bodies pursued their separate paths on separate time tables, the stage would be set eventually for a rendezvous at one or another point of orbital contact. Since the space-charge sheaths of the bodies would occupy greater volumes than

179

the bodies themselves, a collision between sheaths would actually be more likely to take place than a direct, bodily collision, and in any case it would occur first.

When the moment arrived for the inevitable encounter, sheaths would make contact. Unleashed electric fields would clash. Almost instantly, forces immeasurably greater than gravitation would be brought to bear on the charged bodies. Cosmic thunderbolts would flash between the bodies in an effort to equalize their electric potentials.

The list of unthinkably disastrous effects that would result could go on and on. The point to be made, however, is that *Worlds in Collision*—at least in my opinion —documents historical evidence to indicate that phenomena associated with space-charge-sheath destruction were actually suffered and survived by peoples of antiquity.

II

Let us now consider the problem posed by the seeming fact that the Sun and the planets, all immersed in the interplanetary plasma, ought to acquire the electric potential—zero, one would guess—of that plasma.

Some might claim that the problem itself is spurious, and that dispensing with it is as simple as chucking *Worlds in Collision* into the trash heap. I contend, nevertheless, that the problem is real, and that observational evidence from many parts of the solar system can be marshalled to resolve it.

This problem is real because we have ample evidence that the Sun, the Earth, and the Moon are electrically charged bodies. Only one of the three—the Moon— seems to have an electric potential equal to that of its environment, but from this we can only conclude that the environment itself has a potential as high as that of the Moon.

A quick review of just a few points of evidence will serve here to establish the reality of our problem.

The Sun is known to have a magnetic field of great complexity. Observations of coronal streamers at the poles of the Sun during total eclipse suggest that at least a portion of this field has a dipole configuration, similar to that of the Earth's field. Other observations suggest that in the Sun's lower atmosphere the field is in a state of continual torment. The existence of the field, however, and even the existence of the complexities of that field in the lower atmosphere, can only be laid to electric currents. No matter how much theorists might like to minimize or even deny it, the fact remains that only electric currents give rise to magnetic fields.

It is misleading to state simply that "moving charges" generate magnetic fields. Any body of ionized gas, for example, might be described as a collection of moving charges, since its charged particles are indeed in motion. For that matter, each charged particle moving about in such a gas can be said to constitute an elementary electric current. But so long as there is no net differential motion between positive and negative charges, the net electric current will be zero, and the body of gas will generate no magnetic field regardless of how violently it may be agitated. (However, if charges of one sign predominate over charges of the opposite sign, so that the body of gas indeed has a net electric charge, the effect of bulk gas motion will be quite different.)

The fact that magnetic fields and effects attend motions in the Sun's ionized gases—prime examples being the strong fields evident in connection with rotary motions in sunspots—is explainable most simply and satisfactorily by the conclusion that the solar gases are electrically charged (they contain an excess of particles of one kind) either positive or negative, but almost surely negative.

The dipole component of the solar magnetic field can only be attributed to the rotation of the charged Sun as a whole, as Dr. Velikovsky pointed out more than two decades ago (3).

The Earth's magnetic field was tentatively ascribed to electric charge on the Earth nearly a hundred years ago. In 1878, H. A. Rowland attempted to calculate the electric potential the Earth would have to sustain to produce its observed magnetic field. His result—more than 4×10^{16} volts, negative—seemed to him so ridiculous that he rejected it immediately. An electric charge of the necessary magnitude to give the Earth such a potential, wrote Rowland, "would undoubtedly tear the earth to pieces and distribute its fragments to the uttermost parts of the universe (4)."

Such arguments have convinced geophysicists ever since Rowland's time that an electric charge on the Earth cannot be held responsible for terrestrial magnetism.

Most recently, it has been fashionable to rest content with the so-called dynamo theory as an explanation for the Earth's magnetic field. It is supposed that the field is generated by motions in the molten core of the Earth. No one, however, has yet been able to show how electric currents might be produced by such motions.

Professor James Warwick, of the University of Colorado, recently pointed out that the "dynamo theory has not yet successfully predicted any cosmical [magnetic] fields. Its use today rests on the *assumption* that no alternative theory corresponds more closely to observations (5)." (Warwick's italics)

Even stronger objection to the dynamo theory is implied in this remark by Palmer Dyal and Curtis W. Parkin of NASA's Ames Research Center: "No rigorous theory has evolved that satisfactorily explains the earth's permanent magnetic field (6)."

"Satisfactorily," of course, means without acknowledging the electric charge of the Earth.

Before proceeding, let us consider Rowland's notion that an enormous electric charge must blow the Earth to smithereens. This is the same idea advanced by Donald Menzel in 1952 to add zest to his "quantitative refutation of Velikovsky's wild hypothesis" that the Sun is electrically charged (7).

In the first place, as Professor Fernando Sanford pointed out forty years ago, "[Such] conclusions are all based upon the assumption that electric charges are held to conductors by [gravity]. . . . If this assumption were correct, it would be impossible to give a negative charge to any small conductor while in the gravitation field of the earth (8)."

Sanford also pointed out that "a soap bubble and a platinum sphere of the same diameter, if joined by a connecting wire and charged from the same source, will take equal charges. This shows conclusively that whatever the force may be which holds electrons to a charged

182

conductor it is not a force which acts between the electrons and the atoms of the conductor. This being the case, the outward pressure of the charge upon a conductor will have no tendency to pull the conductor apart."

The Earth's atmospheric electric field has been the subject of controversy ever since it was discovered, about two hundred years ago. At issue is the question of where resides the electric charge responsible for it—negative charge on the Earth itself, or positive charge high in the atmosphere?

In 1803 Professor Erman, of Berlin, demonstrated the negative charge of the Earth by a simple experiment. He found that a gold-leaf electroscope fitted with a short, pointed collecting rod showed positive electrification when he first grounded it and then raised it a few feet in the air. When he discharged it to the ground while holding it in the upper position and then lowered it, it showed negative electrification. After he placed a ball over the collecting rod—even after he placed the entire apparatus inside a sealed glass tube—and found the same results, he concluded, correctly, that the effects observed were due to electrical induction from a negatively charged Earth (9).

Erman's findings were derided, then promptly forgotten, even though only one year later two balloonists were mystified when their collector and electroscope gathered only negative charge from high-level air, instead of the positive charge they expected (10).

In 1836, Peltier, on the basis of experiments similar to but rather more elegant than Erman's, came to the same conclusion: the Earth is negatively charged, and this charge gives rise to the atmospheric electric field (11).

Through all the years since, no one has come up with a more plausible theory of atmospheric electricity than that of Erman and Peltier. Time after time, scientists have tried by one means or another to detect an excess of positive charge high in the atmosphere, but always in vain. (In *Scientific American* for March 1972, Professor A. D. Moore, writing on the subject of "Electrostatics," states: "The atmosphere of the earth is somehow supplied with a positive charge that sets up a downward electric field

183

amounting to between 100 and 500 volts per meter on a clear day." One might question the efficacy of "somehow" as an explanation; but perhaps it suffices for a phenomenon whose existence no one has been able to demonstrate.)

In the closing years of the nineteenth century, the electrical genius Nikola Tesla built and operated an electrical observatory in the Colorado mountains. Very early in his researches, he proved that the Earth harbors enormous numbers of free electrons. One of his obsessions at the time was to transmit electric waves through the ground. He reasoned that if the Earth were not negatively charged, it would act as a vast sink into which enormous amounts of electricity would have to be injected to bring it to a state where it would vibrate electrically. He discovered that the necessary electrification was already present in great abundance (12).

Tesla's finding was recently—and quite inadvertently—repeated for the Moon. In *Nature* for November 12, 1971, Winfield Salisbury and Darrell Fernald, of the Smithsonian Astrophysical Observatory, reported that they had received signals from the command module of the Apollo 15 flight at a time when it was behind the Moon. The signals had been carried around the curvature of the supposedly radio-opaque moon by electric waves in the Moon's surface layers (13).

If, then, the Sun, the Moon, and the Earth are electrified bodies, how may we square this fact with the ubiquitous presence of plasma in the solar system?

One is nagged by the suspicion that F. A. Lindemann was not entirely mistaken concerning free (excess) charges on the Sun when he wrote as follows, in 1919: "It is easy to show that appreciable electrostatic forces cannot exist on the sun. The outer layers . . . must certainly be highly ionized . . . so that any charges on the sun as a whole would rapidly be neutralized by the emissions of ions (14)." In other words, the mutual electrical repulsions among excess like charges must drive them outward and away from the Sun.

Lindemann went on to assume that the electric forces must be balanced by gravitational forces—the concept later shown to be invalid by Sanford. But if we neglect gravity, the argument seems to lead to the conclusion that the Sun's potential can only be zero, instead of the few thousand volts calculated by Lindemann.

Furthermore, Lindemann's case seems to gain from our present knowledge of the interplanetary medium. Surely a conducting plasma pervading space can only facilitate the dissipation of excess charge by the Sun.

But Lindemann's argument is sound only if two unstated assumptions are valid:

1. The interplanetary medium is devoid of electrical strain—the plasma harbors no electric potential of its own—and can therefore serve as a sink for excess solar charges; and

2. The Sun's electric charge is not continually renewed via electric currents.

I propose to challenge both these assumptions. However, as the reader may already surmise, this can be done only at the cost of challenging astrophysical dogmas more precious than that which denies the Sun and the planets electrostatic charge.

I offer what follows merely as a very brief summary of my own notions as to how and why the solar system is electrified in spite of all arguments that it can't be.

III

I can find no way to state this diplomatically, so let me be blunt: *The modern astrophysical concept that ascribes the Sun's energy to thermonuclear reactions deep in the solar interior is contradicted by nearly every observable aspect of the Sun.*

It seems astonishing that in the course of half a century of studies of the Sun in context with thermonuclear theory, very few professional astrophysicists have ever expressed the slightest discomfort over discrepancies between observation and theory, or even over the fact that an *ad hoc* extra theory has had to be devised to explain practically every individual feature of the solar atmosphere.

Apparently with a steady hand, Fred Hoyle wrote some years ago: "We should expect on the basis of a straightforward calculation that the Sun would 'end' itself

185

in a simple and rather prosaic way; that with increasing height above the photosphere the density of the solar material would decrease quite rapidly, until it became pretty well negligible only two or three kilometres up. . . . Instead, the atmosphere is a huge bloated envelope (15)." And today we know that this "bloated envelope" extends out among the planets.

Even the photosphere, where theory would suggest the Sun ought to "end," fails miserably to conform with expectations. Its opacity almost conspires to prevent the Sun from radiating away its internal energy, if that is indeed where the energy comes from. The granular structure of the photosphere is still attributed to "nonstationary convection," even though Minnaert pointed out decades ago that the Reynolds number of the photospheric gas exceeds the critical value by eight powers of ten—which is to say, by a factor of 100 million—and therefore convection currents in the photosphere should be completely turbulent (16).

(The convection currents themselves are postulated to explain how all that internal radiant energy is brought to the surface in spite of photospheric opacity.)

In the solar atmosphere at intermediate altitudes, astronomers observe an amazing variety of phenomena, none of which can be shown to have any business there if the Sun's prime purpose is to shed energy liberated deep in its interior, as the thermonuclear theory would have it.

Essential to the received theory is the conviction that inside the Sun is a steep temperature gradient, falling toward the photosphere, along which the internal energy flows outward. If we stack this internal temperature gradient against the observed temperature gradient in the solar atmosphere, which falls steeply *inward,* toward the photosphere, we find we have diagrammed a physical absurdity: The two gradients produce a trough at the photosphere, which implies that thermal energy should collect and become stuck there until it raises the temperature and eliminates the trough. That this does not occur seems to bother no one.

But suppose we remove the hypothetical internal temperature gradient. What then? Why, then we see that the Sun's bloated atmosphere and the "wrong-way" temperature gradient in that atmosphere point strongly to an external source of solar energy.

Professor Melvin Cook dared to call attention to this matter in the 1950s (17). However, since he was not a professional astrophysicist, his comment was as unnoted as it was unsolicited.

The phenomena of the photosphere, the phenomena of the chromosphere, the phenomena of the corona, and the known characteristics of the interplanetary medium all fit so nicely into a unifying hypothesis based on energy supplied to the Sun from the outside that I cannot resist mentioning it here: I believe that the Sun behaves as an anode collecting electric current from its environment, and that the energy it radiates is delivered entirely by way of this postulated electrical discharge.

C. E. R. Bruce identified an impressive number of solar atmospheric phenomena as electrical-discharge effects as long ago as 1944 (18), and since then he has compiled an impressive record of prediction in the field of astrophysics with a comprehensive theory of cosmic electrical discharges (19). Apparently, however—and puzzlingly, too, in view of some of his conclusions concerning the nature of our galaxy—he does not question the idea that the Sun and the stars are thermonuclear engines that live and die totally oblivious of their surroundings.

For reasons I can only touch upon here, I would urge Bruce to modify his grand scheme to embrace the idea that stellar energy is electrical in origin. This, to my way of thinking, would finally justify his vision that "it is the breakdown of electric fields . . . which has shaped and lit the universe from the beginning (20)."

The kind of electric discharge I conceive to be responsible for solar radiation must necessarily be driven by an electric potential in interstellar space—a condition to be expected in a galaxy electrified by the separation of charges on a truly magnificent scale. Just such a situation is postulated by Bruce, who explains the spiral arms of our galaxy as electrical discharges initiated by the breakdown of a radial electric field extending through the entirety of galactic space. And just such a situation could provide the enormously high space potential (negative) that the discharge hypothesis requires.

As I see it, then, the Sun, already negatively charged to an extremely high electric potential, behaves as an anode and collects more negative charge because its interstellar environment has a potential that is even higher in the negative sense. It is a matter of relative potentials.

By analogy with electrical discharges studied in the laboratory, we can predict certain conditions that should prevail in interplanetary space if the Sun is indeed fueled electrically. For now, I would mention only this: The interplanetary medium near the Earth seems to be characterized by approximately equal numbers of protons and electrons, which fact identifies it as a true plasma. Farther out—say, near the orbit of Jupiter—the protons should be traveling away from the Sun with considerably increased velocities, and the electrons should be present in lesser numbers than the protons.

Hopefully, the Grand Tour space probe of the outer planets, which is projected by NASA for the late 1970s, will be instrumented to sample the interplanetary medium, and thus will be able to furnish evidence in support or in refutation of the discharge hypothesis. The presence of thermal electrons from the solar corona as far out as Jupiter would put the idea on very shaky ground, it seems to me. But if protons alone are still being accelerated away from the Sun at that distance, no other conclusion could be drawn but that an electric current flows through interplanetary space.

Even in the Earth's neighborhood, by the way, solar-wind theorists have been experiencing great difficulty in reconciling observations of particle densities and temperatures with Eugene Parker's hypothesis (21) that the solar wind represents material unavoidably boiled off by the Sun's hot corona (whose millions-of-degrees temperature, so predictable on the basis of a discharge hypothesis, is unexplained in terms of the conventional theory of stellar energy). Positive ions in the solar wind cross the orbit of the Earth with velocities and in numbers close to those predicted by Parker. Solar-wind electrons, on the other hand, seem unacquainted with the rules of the game. In numbers they match the protons pretty well, but they travel rather too slowly and tend to become sidetracked along magnetic field lines (22).

Interestingly enough, a solar-wind model that claims better than average success in squaring predictions with observations is that of two Belgian scientists, J. Lemaire and M. Scherer (23). An unusual feature of this model is that it calls for an electric field high in the solar corona to slow electrons and accelerate protons to observed speeds.

Even more interesting is a recent summary of solar-wind-speed observations covering a nine-year period. Published in 1971 by J. T. Gosling et al. (24), this study shows that "the yearly distributions of solar wind bulk speeds during the years 1962–1970 . . . are found to be remarkably constant from year to year. There is no tendency for the solar wind speed to increase with increasing solar activity."

This suggests to me that the solar wind is more nearly related to the Sun's energy supply, which is also remarkably constant, than to the sunspot cycle. If solar energy actually derived from processes going on inside the Sun, one could expect disturbances of the types characteristic of the most active phase of the sunspot cycle to affect the outward flow of the energy; if, however, solar energy did arrive from outside the Sun, events upon the solar surface would be much less likely to affect the dissipation of that energy back into space in the form of visible and invisible radiation.

The interplanetary medium, considered as a current-carrying channel in an electrical discharge, offers an explanation of the fact that Jupiter radiates several times as much energy as it receives from the Sun (25). If Jupiter and its space-charge sheath (magnetosphere) are intercepting energetic primary electrons headed for the Sun, the source of the giant planet's excess energy is no longer a mystery.

In cosmic rays we have a mystery that has never been solved: where and how are these subatomic particles accelerated to the tremendous kinetic energies they exhibit when they reach the Earth? But in the fact that they do reach the Earth we find one more important bit of evidence that the Earth is negatively charged. And the electric-discharge hypothesis suggests a possible answer to the mystery of cosmic-ray energies.

Edward O. Hulburt, writing in *The Scientific Monthly* (Feb. 1954), noted that the primary cosmic rays deliver a very considerable amount of positive electric charge to the Earth. By his calculation, an aggregate positive charge of 7×10^6 coulombs, sufficient to prevent the arrival on Earth of any more cosmic-ray protons with energies of 10^{10} electron volts or less, would accumulate in only 16½ years. Annually, then, the positive charge collected by the Earth from this source amounts to more than 4×10^5 coulombs.

Hulburt brought out these facts before electrons—negative charges—were discovered in the flux of cosmic rays. Electrons are now detected with more sensitive and more sophisticated devices than were available in the early 1950s, but they have proved to be only about 1 per cent as numerous as protons in the total cosmic-ray population. So, for all practical purposes, Hulburt's calculation is still valid.

Cosmic rays, in spite of the fact that they deliver 4×10^5 coulombs of positive charge to the Earth each year, continue to arrive in undiminished numbers year after year. Presumably they have "always" done so. If we assume, then, that "always" is a matter of billions of years, we can only conclude either that the Earth started out with a negative charge in excess of, say, 10^{16} coulombs, so that in all those years the cosmic-ray protons haven't yet been able to cancel that negative charge, or the Earth picks up at least an equal amount of negative charge each year by some other means. In any case, the Earth can be neither electrically neutral nor positively charged; only a negatively charged Earth fits the evidence provided by the cosmic rays.

At first glance, the solar-discharge idea might seem confounded by the fact that cosmic-ray protons reach the inner parts of the solar system. After all, the hypothesis requires that protons from the Sun be accelerated out of the system, and indeed that these protons carry practically all of the discharge current as far as the local disturbance extends into interstellar space. Should not the cosmic rays—the 99 per cent of them that are posi-

190

tively charged particles—be turned around and driven out of the system in the same way?

But suppose that the Sun's driving potential—the drop in potential between the Sun and the boundary of its discharge—is of the order of 10 billion volts. Then solar protons reaching the boundary would be launched into interstellar space with energies of 10 billion electron volts. They would be cosmic rays in their own right.

Astrophysicists tell us that the Sun is a rather mediocre star, as far as radiating energy goes. If it is electrically powered, it would seem reasonable to conclude, at least tentatively, that its mediocrity is attributable in some measure to a relatively unimpressive driving potential. This would mean that hotter, more luminous stars should have driving potentials greater than that of the Sun and should consequently expel cosmic rays of greater energies than solar cosmic rays.

A star with a driving potential—cathode drop is a more appropriate term—of only 20 billion volts would expel protons energetic enough to reach the Sun, arriving with 10 billion electron volts of energy to spare. Such would be merely average cosmic rays, as we know them here on Earth. Actually, particles with energies up to 100 billion billion electrons volts reach the Earth from galactic space; to such cosmic rays, the adverse electric field in the Sun's postulated 10-billion-volt cathode drop would be less than negligible.

What all this suggests to me is that cosmic-ray protons and other atomic nuclei reaching the Earth are nothing more or less than the spent current carriers of stars other than the Sun. In this connection, it is interesting to note that the calculated energy density of cosmic rays in our galaxy is comparable to the total energy density of electromagnetic radiation, including starlight. This is what one would expect to be the case if electric stars were responsible.

IV

All this has seemingly led us far astray from the subject matter of *Worlds in Collision*. Nevertheless, I am convinced that an excursion like this into astrophysical problems in regions of space as far removed as distant stars and the outer reaches of the galaxy is necessary to make some kind of sense out of problems inside the solar system. If the galaxy is electrified, as Bruce supposes, that fact cannot help but have major implications for the solar system. If the galaxy is not electrified, it would seem to me that prospects will ever remain poor for reconciling evidence of electrification within the solar system and celestial motions that seem to deny that evidence.

Back toward the beginning of this paper I promised to return to the subjects of space-charge sheaths and comet tails. Actually, in terms of the postulated electrical discharge centered on the Sun, these would appear to be not two subjects, but merely two aspects of a single subject.

A comet on an extremely eccentric orbit spends by far the greater part of its time in the uttermost parts of the solar system. This is because, according to Kepler's laws, orbital speeds near aphelion are so much less than near perihelion. Supposing, then, that space potentials in such regions are vastly greater, in the negative sense, than they are close to the Sun, as the discharge hypothesis requires, any long-period comet could be expected to acquire local space potential quite readily during its long sojourn far from the Sun. Quite possibly, too, its body materials would become electrically polarized in response to the buildup of charge on its surface.

Consider next what would happen to this charged, electrically polarized body as its orbit brings it with ever increasing speed back toward the Sun. By the time it reaches the orbit of Jupiter, solar-wind protons will have stripped away its superficial blanket of negative charge. No longer does its surface potential match that of its surroundings, yet its internal (radial) polarization produces an external electric field, just as polarization in an electret made of wax exhibits an external field here on Earth. A space-charge sheath will begin to form to shield the interplanetary plasma from the comet's alien field.

As the comet races toward the Sun, its sheath takes the form of a long tail stretching away from the Sun. This happens not because the electrified Sun repels the tail material, but because voltage differences between the comet and the interplanetary plasma vary sharply with direction and because sheath thicknesses are dictated not only by voltage differences, but by gas pressure as well. The potential difference between the head of the comet and the plasma in the direction of the Sun might be substantial. But in any case, the potential difference between the comet and plasma farther out from the Sun will be greater still. Also, the plasma density is greater nearer the Sun than farther from the Sun. Hence the sheath remains close to the comet on the sunward side, and it reaches perhaps millions of miles into space on the antisolar side.

This rather sketchy qualitative explanation for comet tails is not advanced here as any sort of final answer to the comet-tail mystery. I include it only as an example of the kind of explanation that can at least be discussed in the light of the discharge hypothesis. I hope, too, that it offers a measure of solace to those who might feel cheated by the fact that the interplanetary plasma knocks down the idea that comet-tail gases might be repelled by the Sun's electric charge.

By the same sort of analysis, I would conclude that the Earth has a potential not quite in keeping with its space environment, and that it therefore is surrounded by a space-charge sheath. For the same reasons that a comet's sheath is elongated away from the Sun, I would suppose that the Earth's sheath has a tail; in other words, I would equate the terrestrial sheath with the Earth's so-called magnetosphere.

It seems to be pretty well established that the Earth's "magneto-tail" does not reach as far as Mars, and thus the two planets no longer perturb one another electrically. (The Moon, however, sweeping in and out of the Earth's sheath every month, does appear to be perturbed by non-gravitational forces—a point emphasized by Dr. Velikovsky on many occasions.) But it seems conceivable that the long reach of the Earth's space-charge sheath may have played an important role in settling Mars on an orbit at a safe distance from the Earth.

A century ago, James Clerk Maxwell, in his monumental *Treatise on Electricity and Magnetism,* wrote these prophetic words: "The phenomena of electrical discharge are exceedingly important, and when they are better understood they will probably throw great light on the nature of electricity as well as on the nature of gases and of the medium pervading space."

For the next fifty years, studies of the electrical discharge were pursued with considerable vigor, and the world was led into the age of electronics. After that, however, as Professor Hannes Alfvén reminded us when he accepted the 1970 Nobel Prize in Physics (26), "most theoretical physicists looked down on this field, which was complicated and awkward . . . not at all suited for mathematically elegant theories." The theorists, says Alfvén, preferred to approach plasma physics by way of the kinetic theory of gases, which led to "mathematically elegant" theories.

In Alfvén's estimation, "the cosmical plasma physics of today . . . is to some extent the playground of theoreticians who have never seen a plasma in a laboratory. Many of them still believe in formulas which we know from laboratory experiments to be wrong . . . several of the basic concepts on which theories of cosmical plasmas are founded are not applicable to the condition prevailing in the cosmos. They are 'generally accepted' by most theoreticians, they are developed with the most sophisticated mathematical methods; and it is only the plasma itself which does not 'understand' how beautiful the theories are and absolutely refuses to obey them. . . ."

The implication of Alfvén's remarks is clear enough: astrophysicists must bone up on the neglected field of electrical discharge phenomena. I, for one, believe that when they do so the new lines of inquiry will rather quickly lead to the rejection of the idea that stars are thermonuclearly powered.

REFERENCES

1. I. Velikovsky, *Worlds in Collision* (New York: Doubleday & Company, 1950).
2. I. Langmuir, *Collected Works* (Oxford, England: Pergamon Press, 1961), Vols. 3 & 4.
3. Velikovsky, *Cosmos Without Gravitation* (New York: Scripta Academica Hierosolymitana, 1946), p. 18.

4. H. A. Rowland, *American Journal of Science*, (3)*15* (1878), 30–38; cited by F. Sanford, *Terrestrial Electricity* (Stanford University, Calif.: Stanford University Press, 1931), p. 79.

5. J. W. Warwick, *Phys. Earth Planet. Interiors, 4* (North-Holland, 1971), p. 229.

6. P. Dyal and C. W. Parkin, *Scientific American*, August 1971, 66.

7. D. Menzel, *Proceedings of the American Philosophical Society*, 96 (1952), 525.

8. F. Sanford, *Terrestrial Electricity, supra*, 80.

9. *Gilbert's Annalen, 15* (1803), 386; cited by Sanford, op. cit., p. 106.

10. F. Sanford, op. cit., p. 107.

11. Ibid, p. 107.

12. J. O'Neill, *Prodigal Genius—The Life of Nikola Tesla* (New York: Ives Washburn, 1944), p. 178.

13. *Science News* (November 20, 1971).

14. F. A. Lindemann, *Philosophical Magazine*, Series 6, Vol. 38, No. 228 (December 1919), 674

15. F. Hoyle, *Frontiers of Astronomy* (New York: Mentor Books, 1957), p. 103.

16. M. Minnaert, Chapter 3 in *The Sun*, G. P. Kuiper, ed. (Chicago: University of Chicago Press, 1953), pp. 171–72.

17. M. A. Cook, *Bulletin of the University of Utah*, Vol. 46, No. 16 (November 30, 1955).

18. C. E. R. Bruce, *A New Approach in Astrophysics and Cosmogony* (London: Unwin Brothers, Ltd., 1944).

19. C. E. R. Bruce, in *Problems of Atmospheric and Space Electricity*, S. C. Coroniti, ed. (Amsterdam: Elsevier, 1965), pp. 577–86.

20. Private communication, September 21, 1965.

21. E. Parker, *Astrophysical Journal, 128* (1958), 664–67.

22. See, for example, M. D. Montgomery et al., *EOS Transactions of the American Geophysical Union*, Vol. 52, No. 4 (April 1971), 336; and K. W. Ogilvie et al., *Journal of Geophysical Research*, Vol. 76, No. 34 (December 1, 1971), 8165ff. See also J. V. Hollweg, *Journal of Geophysical Research*, Vol. 76, No. 31 (November 1, 1971), 7491ff.

23. J. Lemaire and M. Scherer, *Journal of Geophysical Research*, Vol. 76, No. 31 (November 1, 1971), 7479ff.

24. J. T. Gosling, R. T. Hansen, and S. J. Bame, *Journal of Geophysical Research*, Vol. 76, No. 7 (March 1, 1971), 1811ff.

25. *Science News* (June 13, 1970).

26. Lecture published in *Science, 172* (June 4, 1971), 991–94.

PART IV

A still-unsettled question posed by Velikovsky in *Worlds in Collision* concerns the composition of the atmosphere and clouds of the planet Venus. In his words, "The brilliant envelope of Venus is the remnant of its tail of the days when, three thousand years ago, it was a comet. . . . On the basis of this research, I assume that Venus must be rich in petroleum gases. If and as long as Venus is too hot for the liquefaction of petroleum, the hydrocarbons will circulate in gaseous form. The absorption lines of the petroleum spectrum lie far in the infrared where usual photographs do not reach. When the technique of photography in the infrared is perfected so that hydrocarbon bands can be differentiated, the spectrogram of Venus may disclose the presence of hydrocarbon gases in its atmosphere, if these gases lie in the upper part of the atmosphere where the rays of the sun penetrate."

It may well be that in the near future direct analysis of the gases present at all levels in the dense atmosphere of Venus will render debate on this subject unnecessary. For now, however, such debate remains in the forefront of nearly every discussion of *Worlds in Collision.* The *Pensée* papers collected here provide a thorough sampling of the arguments that have been advanced on both sides of the issue.

William T. Plummer opens the discussion with "Venus Clouds: Test for Hydrocarbons." This paper originally appeared as a research report in *Science* (Vol. 163 (1969), No. 3872, pp. 1191–92) and is reprinted with the permission of the author and of *Science*. Plummer, a member of the physics and astronomy faculty at the University of Massachusetts, Amherst, when this paper was prepared, is now Senior Scientist with Polaroid Corporation.

Dr. Plummer compares the infrared spectrum of Venus with laboratory spectra obtained by simulating solar illumination of "several representative hydrocarbons" in both liquid (cloud) and solid (frost) forms. He concludes that Velikovsky's prediction is not supported by the evidence in such reflection spectra, and he suggests that the Venus clouds consist primarily of ice particles.

Velikovsky prepared "Venus and Hydrocarbons," the reply to Plummer that appears here, in the spring of 1969 and submitted it to *Science*. It was returned to him with the request that he revise it as suggested by several referees, which he chose not to do. Therefore it never made print until it appeared in *Pensée* almost five years later.

Valikovsky takes exception to several assumptions adopted by Plummer and points out that various investigators whose results Plummer cites were much less certain than he that their findings excluded hydrocarbons. Velikovsky also indicates a number of counts on which ice particles fail to conform with observational facts about the clouds of Venus.

"The Nature of the Cytherean Atmosphere" is discussed in a comprehensive review article by Albert W. Burgstahler, professor of chemistry at the University of Kansas (Lawrence). Dr. Burgstahler notes a number of problems still to be solved concerning the atmosphere of Venus before its composition can be said to be "known," and he concludes that Velikovsky's advance claim cannot yet be confirmed or denied.

In reply to Burgstahler, Velikovsky prepared "Venus' Atmosphere," a paper in which he reviews the entire controversy in considerable detail and suggests, by way of tabulation of Burgstahler's remarks, that the available evidence actually does support his claim in preference to alternative hypotheses.

Peter R. Ballinger, a researcher in organic chemistry, comes to Velikovsky's support with a letter pointing out that the sulfuric-acid-cloud hypothesis is not without problems of its own and that the spectroscopic evidence now at hand does not exclude the possibility that hydrocarbons may be present in gaseous or liquid form even in the upper atmosphere of Venus.

VENUS CLOUDS: TEST FOR HYDROCARBONS*

William T. Plummer

Abstract. *Infrared reflection spectra of hydrocarbon clouds and frosts now give a critical test of Velikovsky's prediction that Venus is surrounded by a dense envelope of hydrocarbon clouds and dusts. Venus does not exhibit an absorption feature near 2.4 microns, although such a feature is prominent in every hydrocarbon spectrum observed.*

Some of the least expected discoveries made by planetary astronomers in recent years were correctly predicted by Velikovsky (1). He argued that Jupiter should be a strong source of radio waves, that the earth should have a magnetosphere, that the surface of Venus should be hot, that Venus might exhibit an anomalous rotation, and that Venus should be surrounded by a blanket of petroleum hydrocarbons (2). All except the last of these predictions have been verified, most of them by accident (3).

New data on hydrocarbon clouds and frosts, together with infrared observations of Venus, now permit a test of the remaining prediction. Each hydrocarbon (from methane through the hydrocarbon waxes and tars) ab-

* Copyright 1969 by the American Association for the Advancement of Science. Reprinted by permission of the author and *Science* from *Science*, Vol. 163 (March 14, 1969), pp. 1191–92.

sorbs infrared radiation in a band of wavelengths centered between 2.3 and 2.5μ , the position varying somewhat with the molecular structure (4). This band is weaker than several other hydrocarbon absorption bands at longer wavelengths, but it lies conveniently in a spectral region for which the terrestrial atmosphere is rather transparent.

Reflection spectra of Venus in this wavelength region have been obtained by Kuiper (5), Sinton (6), Moroz (7), and Bottema *et al.* (8) (Figure 1). Kuiper's spectrum is a ratio of the Venus reflectivity to that of a block of MgO in sunlight. The reflectivity of MgO falls off somewhat at longer wavelengths, at a rate which is dependent upon its moisture content; thus, if Kuiper's curve were corrected for this, it would be in better agreement with the other curves. The spectrum recorded by

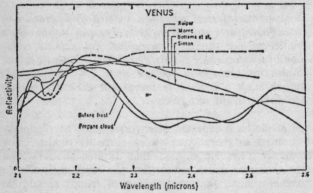

Figure 1. Infrared reflectives of propane cloud and butane frost contrasted with the reflection spectrum of Venus as measured by four observers.

Bottema *et al.* was measured at a lower resolving power than that of the others (0.08 μ), and therefore the CO_2 absorption feature at 2.15 microns on Venus is smoothed out; a greater range of wavelengths was covered because the spectrum was recorded from a high-altitude balloon.

Reflection spectra of several representative hydrocarbons were recorded (9). Some hydrocarbons were formed into clouds by refrigeration in a copper box cooled with dry ice, following the procedure of Zander (10). Other hydrocarbons were formed into white frost on a blackened copper block partially immersed in liquid nitrogen. A few hydrocarbons of higher molecular weight, such as the waxes, were granulated and supported on black paper. Zander discovered that the spectral properties of clouds are quite similar to those of frosts; our results confirm his finding.

A 625-watt quartz-tungsten lamp illuminated the cloud, frost, or powder directly. Radiation scattered by each sample at an angle of $60°$ from the direction of incidence was reflected to a spectrophotometer (Perkin-Elmer model 12C) equipped with a LiF prism and an InAs detector. A layer of powder sulfur was used as a reflectance standard (11), and all hydrocarbon spectra were compared with the sulfur reflection measurements in order to eliminate instrumental properties.

All hydrocarbons studied exhibited a substantial drop in reflectivity in a band near 2.4μ. From the close similarity of the transmission spectra of all hydrocarbons in this region, it appears that a substantial loss in reflectivity near 2.4μ should be a common property of clouds composed of hydrocarbon droplets or dust. Figure 1 shows the reflection characteristics of a cloud of liquid propane droplets in the refrigerated box and also of a frost of solid butane particles on a cold surface. For both, reflectivity between 2.3 and 2.5μ is reduced below the continuum by a factor of about two. This spectral feature, as well as a few others exhibited by hydrocarbon clouds at shorter wavelengths, is absent from the reflection spectrum of Venus.

The presence of condensed hydrocarbons in the clouds of Venus, a prediction regarded by Velikovsky as a crucial test of his concept of the development of the solar system, is not supported by the spectrophotometric evidence. On the other hand, Venus observations in this wavelength range and at other wavelengths are entirely compatible with the reflection spectrum of a non-infinite cloud layer composed of very small or slender ice particles (12).

REFERENCES

1. I. Velikovsky, *Worlds in Collision* (Garden City, N.Y.: Double-

day & Company, 1950); *Ages in Chaos* (Garden City, N.Y.: Doubleday & Company, 1952); *Earth in Upheaval* (Garden City, N.Y.: Doubleday & Company, 1955).

2. F. Hoyle later predicted a hydrocarbon cloud layer for different reasons (*Frontiers of Astronomy,* New York: Harper & Row, 1956).

3. V. Bargmann and L. Motz, *Science,* 138, 1350 (1962); I. I. Shapiro, *Science,* 157, 423 (1967).

4. W. W. Coblentz, *Investigations of Infrared Spectra* (Carnegie Institution of Washington, Washington, D.C., 1905), republished by the Coblentz Society, Norwalk, Connecticut, 1962; R. N. Pierson, A. N. Fletcher, E. StC. Gaintree, *Anal. Chem.,* 28, 1218 (1956).

5. G. P. Kuiper, *Commun. Lunar Planet. Lab.,* 1, 83 (1962).

6. W. M Sinton, *Mem. Soc. Roy. Sci. Liege,* 7, 300 (1962).

7. V. I. Moroz, *Astron. Zh.,* 41, 711 (1964); *Soviet Astron. AJ Engl. Transl.,* 8, 566 (1965).

8. M. Bottema, W. Plummer, J. Strong, R. Zander, *Astrophys. J.,* 140, 1640 (1964).

9. Specifically: acetylene, anthracene, benzene, biphenyl, butane, cumene, cymene, cyclohexane, diphenylmethane, hexane, paraffin wax, pinene, polyethylene, polystyrene, propane, toluene, and xylene.

10. R. Zander, *J. Geophys. Res.,* 71, 375 (1966).

11. M. Kronstein and R. J. Kraushaar, *J. Opt. Soc. Amer.,* 53, 458 (1963).

12. J. E. Hansen and H. Cheyney, *J. Atmos. Sci.,* 25, 629 (1968); W. T. Plummer, *J. Geophys. Res.,* in press.

13. Supported in part by NASA grants NGR 22-010-023 and NGR 22-010-025. Contribution No. 22 of the Four College Observatories.

VENUS AND HYDROCARBONS*

Immanuel Velikovsky

In 1950, I offered the thesis that Venus joined the

planetary family less than thirty-five hundred years ago, and that it is still a protoplanet. In doing so, I claimed that Venus possesses a massive atmosphere, a high surface heat, abnormal (disturbed) rotation, and hydrocarbon gases in its atmosphere (1).

Plummer's Test

In the March 14, 1969, issue of *Science,* W. T. Plummer undertook to examine the last of these claims. He compared the reflection spectrum of Venus with those of a cloud of pure propane droplets and a frost of pure solid butane particles, selecting these compounds from a number of representative hydrocarbons. He chose the 2.1–2.5-micron range in the infrared as best suited for the analysis. He concluded that, whereas a certain feature of reduced reflectivity apparent in the hydrocarbons tested is regularly found between 2.3 and 2.5 microns, its position varying with molecular structure, a similar feature is not present or, more correctly, not present in the same degree, in the infrared spectra of Venus obtained by Sinton (1962), Moroz (1964), and Bottema *et al.* (1964). "The presence of condensed hydrocarbons in the clouds of Venus, a prediction regarded by Velikovsky as a crucial test of his concept of the development of the solar system, is not supported by the spectrophotometric evidence. On the other hand, Venus observations in this wavelength range and at other wavelengths are entirely compatible with the reflection spectrum of a non-infinite cloud layer composed of very small or slender ice particles."

Plummer's verdict is not conclusive, however. First, it is based upon three incorrect assumptions: (a) that I stipulated that hydrocarbons are present in *condensed* form (producing a reflection spectrum); (b) that I located them in the upper (*reflecting*) layer of the clouds; and (c), following from Plummer's comparison, that I maintained that they are the sole constituent of the clouds. In my original statement (2), however, I made it clear that polymerized and therefore heavy molecules of petroleum hydrocarbons are not necessarily present in the upper layer of the dense atmosphere; that in the lower levels, because of heat, they must circulate in gaseous form; and that they are not the only components of the clouds. Second, Plummer's conclusion neglects some important considerations: (a) Depressions in the reflectivity of Venus near 2.4 microns have been detected. Both Sinton and Moroz identified a depression in the reflectivity of Venus at 2.35 microns, but ascribed it to CO. Of another depression feature at 2.28 microns, Moroz wrote: "Its nature is not clear yet" (3). Connes *et al.* confirmed the band at 2.35 microns and identified one at 2.48 microns as due to HF. (b) The general depression in reflectivity between 2.3 and 2.5 microns in the spectra of Venus obtained by Sinton, by Moroz, and by Bottema *et al.* permits a conclusion only as to the upper limit for hydrocarbons' concentration in Venus' atmosphere (4).

In a composite atmosphere of CO_2 and H_2O, hydrocarbon gases would not show well in the 2.1–2.5-micron range. Pollack and Sagan wrote (1968): "We no longer consider the region between 1 and 3 microns sufficiently well defined to permit a definite compositional analysis" of Venus' atmosphere (5). (c) The 1.0 atmosphere of pressure in the laboratory equipment and the 0.3 atmosphere inside the absorbing layer for the 1–2.5-micron wavelength on Venus (J. and P. Connes) represent different conditions. (d) Kuiper observed that in the 1–2.5-micron range, strong bands are stronger in the laboratory than in Venus' spectrum, while the reverse is true for the weaker bands (6). Finally, (e) it should be borne in mind that bright lines of emission from molecules in the hot low atmosphere of Venus could mask some of the loss in brightness due to the presence of similar molecules in the reflecting layer of the clouds.

Plummer's conclusion regarding the possible presence of ice crystals in the atmosphere of Venus is unsound. (a) It contradicts the refractive index of the clouds, which is definitely higher than that of ice or water (1.33) (7), whereas quite a few hydrocarbons exhibit the observed refractive index; (b) it does not explain the yellowish color of the clouds, whereas organic substances of the benzenoid or olefinic type absorb in violet and thus have a yellowish tint; and (c) it is incompatible with the very small amount of water vapor in the region above the clouds—the mixing ratio H_2O/CO_2 being fifteen parts per million (Belton and Hunter) or only one part per million (Kuiper) (8).

Evidence of Hydrocarbons Lies Deep in Infrared

As I clearly stated in 1950, the evidence of the presence of hydrocarbons and their derivatives in the atmosphere of Venus should be sought deeper in the infrared. The infrared absorption of hydrocarbons is pronounced in the 3.4–3.5-micron range and in several other ranges of longer wavelengths. The 8–12-micron region is especially suited for tracing hydrocarbons and their derivatives, for between eight and thirteen microns carbon dioxide absorbs only slightly and water vapor absorbs not at all (9). Actually, wide and strongly expressed bands were observed in the infrared spectrum of Venus in the 3.5-micron range (starting at 2.8 and continuing past 3.8) and again in the 8–13-micron region. "The substance responsible for this absorption—it is not H_2O —has not been identified so far, but its importance in the physics of Venus is enormous" (Moroz, 1963) (3). Gillett, Low, and Stein also observed these sharply expressed bands in Venus' atmosphere and wrote (1968): "We do not attempt an interpretation of the spectra at this time. However, it should be noted that two fundamental problems are now apparent: 1) What mechanism accounts for the strong absorption of sunlight in the 3 to 5 micron region? 2) What property of the clouds causes the low brightness temperature between 8 and 10 microns?" (10).

The solution to the problem of the strongly expressed bands at 3.5 microns and 8 to 13 microns in the infrared spectrum of Venus should be sought in the presence of organic molecules. "It is well known that organic molecules containing C—H bands give characteristic spectra in the wavelength region of 3.4 to 3.5 microns," wrote Glasstone (concerning Mars) (11). "The infrared spectrum should receive more attention, particularly the region from 8 to 14 microns where some of these substances (benzene and several other substituted hydrocarbons as well as some purines and pyrimidines) and their derivatives exhibit absorptions," wrote Owen and

Greenspan (concerning Jupiter) (12). "In the 8 to 14 micron spectral interval carbon dioxide appears to contribute about 20–35% of the opacity and a particulate medium presumably contributes the remainder."

Processes Occurring on Venus Which Must Be Taken into Account

In the hot and oxidizing atmosphere of Venus, chemical reactions must be occurring. Mueller, writing on the "Origin of the Atmosphere of Venus," referred to the "instabilities of the hydrocarbon compounds in an anhydrous, oxidizing hot environment" (13). I assume that (a) in the lower, high-pressure layers, a cracking of most hydrocarbons to hydrogen and smaller CH units is occurring, which may be polymerizing to give aromatic hydrocarbons of higher and higher molecular weight; (b) in the middle layers, hydrocarbons are being converted into CO_2 and H_2O ("If there is oxygen on Venus, petroleum fires must be burning there") (1); and (c) in the higher layers, water is being dissociated by the ultraviolet rays of the sun, with H escaping—actually hydrogen has been observed in Venus' upper atmosphere. Whereas Venus' atmosphere is oxidizing, its upper atmosphere is reducing—a fact which, when first discovered, seemed surprising (14). This also explains why only a small quantity of water is present in transition between the two reactions.

Another process possibly occurring on Venus is a bacterial transformation of hydrocarbons into carbohydrates and proteins (previously discussed by me in 1951, prior to the conversion of asphalt into food products by a similar action). (a) In the ultraviolet wavelength of 2600 angstroms, a narrow band attributed to organic material was identified on Jupiter by Stecher (1965) (15) and confirmed by Evans (1966) (16). It was surmised to be aromatic hydrocarbons by Owen and Greenspan (12). (b) At the same wavelength a similar feature was detected on Venus by Evans and confirmed by Jenkins *et al.* (1967).

In 1950, I suggested that polymerized hydrocarbons could be created by electrical discharges in an atmosphere of methane and ammonia (known ingredients of Jupiter's atmosphere) (1). In 1960, A. T. Wilson successfully conducted such an experiment (17). This process may have occurred on Venus.

Finally, the envelope of Venus may well contain some ferruginous particles and ash. The "small dust like ashes of the furnace" which fell "in all the land of Egypt" (Exodus 9:8) and throughout the globe is, I surmise, still preserved at the bottom of the ocean. Called Worzel Ash after its discoverer, its even distribution was attributed by him to a "fiery end of bodies of cosmic origin" and by Ewing "to a cometary collision." "It could hardly be without some recorded consequences of global extent" (Ewing) (18). A reflection spectrum of Worzel Ash should be compared with the reflection spectrum of Venus' clouds.

Original Thesis Is Consistent with Evidence

Although my claim regarding the presence of organic molecules in the atmosphere of Venus awaits future testing, my thesis concerning the recent origin and history of Venus is consistent with the discovered data.

(a) Venus is very hot (about 1000° F).

(b) Its heat comes from the subsurface (there being no phase effect at various wavelengths) (19).

(c) It has a massive atmosphere (contrary to theoretical expectations) (20).

(d) It rotates anomalously (retrogradely).

(e) In rotating, it turns the same face to the Earth at every inferior conjunction. This "resonance effect" could indicate that Venus passed near the Earth at some point in the past.

(f) Its axis of rotation is perpendicular to the ecliptic, not to the plane of its own revolution (21).

(g) Its atmosphere rotates at many times the rotational velocity of the planet (22). (In my opinion, the protoplanet's trailing part, upon being absorbed, preserved some of its rotational momentum.)

(h) Its orbit is nearly circular. (Venus is hot enough now to have many metals on its surface in a molten state; in my opinion, its body was all molten or plastic not so long ago. Approaching the sun on an elliptical orbit, as I have claimed that it did as a protoplanet, it had some of its energy of motion converted by tidal friction into heat. This tended 1) to keep the body plastic or molten and 2) to decrease the elongation of its orbit with each passage around the Sun, thereby minimizing the energy loss from tidal friction and resulting in an almost circular orbit (23).

(i) Even on a near-circular orbit, Venus may possess ground tides in its molten crust. The claim by Soviet scientists, based upon data obtained by Venera 5 and 6, that there are high mountains on Venus was met with disbelief by American scientists, who could not visualize how plastic rock could sustain mountains. Would ground tides explain 1) the difference in altitude measurements of the two Venera probes, which reached the planet's atmosphere 185 miles apart? 2) the observed precession and lateness of the optical dichotomy—the terminator does not bisect the planetary disk at exactly eastern and western elongations?

Lastly, (j) it must be noticeably cooling. In 1967, I offered this additional crucial test of my thesis: Venus' heat being of recent origin, the planet must be cooling off (24). This loss could be determined by taking repeated measurements of the cloud-surface temperature with a bolometer or thermocouples and would be observable from one synodic period of Venus to the next —"even if in only fractions of a degree." Since then, Gillett, Low, and Stein compared their 1968 absolute spectrum of Venus with earlier spectral work of Sinton and Strong (1960) "which gave somewhat higher surface brightness." They added, "the reasons for this disagreement are not understood at present" (10). It appears that in eight years (five synodical periods), the cloud-surface temperature of Venus dropped by several degrees.

REFERENCES
1. I. Velikovsky, "Gases of Venus" and "Thermal Balance of Venus," in *Worlds in Collision* (New York: Macmillan, 1950; Doubleday, 1950).
2. Ibid. "Carbon dioxide is an ingredient of Venus' atmosphere. . . . On the basis of this research, I assume that Venus must be rich in petroleum gases. If and as long as Venus is too hot for the liquefaction of petroleum, the hydrocarbons will circulate

in gaseous form. The absorption lines of the petroleum spectrum lie far in the infrared where usual photographs do not reach. When the technique of photography in the infrared is perfected so that hydrocarbon bands can be differentiated, the spectrogram of Venus may disclose the presence of hydrocarbon gases in its atmosphere, if these gases lie in the upper part of the atmosphere where the rays of the sun penetrate."

3. V. I. Moroz, "The Infrared Spectra of Mars and Venus," in *Life Science and Space Research,* vol. 2, 4th International Space Science Symposium, 1963 (Amsterdam: North-Holland Publishing Company, 1964), pp. 230–37.

4. W. T. Plummer, "Venus Clouds: Test for Hydrocarbons," *Science,* 163 (14 March 1969), 1191–92.

5. J. B. Pollack and C. Sagan, *Journal of Geophysical Research,* 73, 5945.

6. P. Swings, "Venus Through a Spectroscope," *Proceedings of the American Philosophical Society,* vol. 113, no. 3 (June 1969), 229–46.

7. A. Arking and J. Potter, "The Phase Curve of Venus and the Nature of Its Clouds," *Journal of Atmospheric Research,* vol. 25, no. 4, pp. 617–28.

8. G. Kuiper, *Communications of the Lunar and Planetary Laboratory,* University of Arizona, 1968.

9. H. M. Randall, R. G. Fowler, N. Fuson, and J. R. Dangle, *Infrared Determination of Organic Structure* (New York: D. Van Nostrand Company, 1949), pp. 46–65 and chart following p. 20; F. F. Bentley, L. D. Smithson, A. L. Rozek, *Infrared Spectra and Characteristic Frequencies 700–300cm⁻¹* (New York: Interscience Publishers, 1968), pp. 21–28, 65–71.

10. F. C. Gillett, F. J. Low, and W. A. Stein, "Absolute Spectrum of Venus from 2.8 to 14 Microns," *Journal of Atmospheric Sciences,* vol. 25, no. 4 (July 1968), 594–95.

11. S. Glasstone, *The Book of Mars* (NASA, 1968), p. 220.

12. T. Owen and J. A. Greenspan, *Science,* 156 (1967), 1489.

13. R. F. Mueller, *Science,* 163 (21 March 1969), 3873.

14. T. M. Donahue, "Upper Atmosphere of Venus," *Journal of the Atmospheric Sciences,* July 1968.

15. T. P. Stecher, *Ap. J.,* 142 (1965), 1186.

16. D. C. Evans, *NASA Goddard Space Flight Center Report,* X-613-66-172.

17. A. T. Wilson, *Nature,* 6 October 1962.

18. J. L. Worzel, *Proceedings, National Academy of Science,* 45 (15 March 1959); M. Ewing, ibid.

19. At 2-cm wavelength: D. Morrison, *Science,* 163 (1969), 3869; at 4.5 cm: J. R. Dickel, W. J. Medd, W. W. Warnock, *Nature,* 220 (1968), 1183; at 11 cm: K. I. Kellerman, *Icarus,* September 1966.

20. H. Spencer Jones, *Life on Other Worlds* (London: English

Universities Press, 1952), p. 167; V. A. Firsoff, *The Interior Planets* (Edinburgh: Oliver & Boyd, 1968), p. 102.
21. P. Goldreich and S. T. Peale, *Nature,* 209 (1966), 1117; I. I. Shapiro, *Science,* 157 (1967), 423–25; R. B. Dyce *et al., Astronomical Journal,* 72 (1967), 351.
22. B. A. Smith, *Science,* 158 (1967), 114–16.
23. From a private communication by C. Sherrerd, Clinton, N.J.
24. *Yale Scientific Magazine,* 41 (April 1967).

THE NATURE OF THE CYTHEREAN ATMOSPHERE

SEARCHING FOR HYDROCARBONS ON VENUS

Albert W. Burgstahler

INTRODUCTION

Despite being completely covered by a thick envelope of slightly yellowish clouds, the planet Venus, because of its similarity to the Earth in size and mass and the amount of energy it absorbs from the Sun (Table I), was long believed to possess atmospheric and other properties not too unlike those of the Earth. For example, a typical view prevailing well into the present century stated: "There can therefore be no doubt that the atmosphere of Venus exerts an absorption similar to our own, and hence the nature of the two atmospheres must be similar. . . . condensed vapors would be naturally supposed to be situated at a considerable altitude in the atmosphere. . . . we may safely assume that the clouds of Venus consist of condensed aqueous vapor, thus again resembling those of the Earth"(1).

Subsequently, more-refined spectral investigations revealed the presence of carbon dioxide on Venus, but not even traces of water or oxygen could be detected (2).

Until about 1960, the depth and density of the Cytherean atmosphere were generally considered to be about

Table I. Physical Properties of Earth and Venus [a]

Property	Earth	Venus
Average cloud cover (percent)	ca. 50	100
Average albedo (reflectance)	0.35	0.77±0.07
Mean distance from Sun (miles)	92,957,000	67,200,000
Mean solar constant (ergs/cm-sec²)	1.4×10^6	2.7×10^6
Equatorial diameter at surface (miles)	7,927	7,520
Equatorial radius at surface (kilometers)	6,378	6,050±5
Oblateness (departure from sphericity)	0.003	0.000
Volume relative to Earth	1	0.855
Total mass (kilograms) [b]	5.976×10^{24}	4.86594×10^{24}
Mass relative to Earth	1	0.8149
Mean density (grams/cm³) [c]	5.52	5.23
Gravity at surface (feet/sec²)	32.2	28.9
Escape velocity (miles/sec)	7.0	6.4
Sidereal orbital period (Earth days)	365.256	224.701
Mean synodical period (Earth days)	·············	583.92
Mean orbital velocity (miles/sec)	18.5	21.8
Orbital eccentricity	0.0167	0.0068
Inclination of orbit to ecliptic	0°	3.393°
Axial rotational period (sidereal)	23h 56m 04s	243.0±0.1 Earth days
Duration of solar day	24h 00m 00s	116.8 Earth days
Direction of rotation	Direct	Retrograde
Inclination of axis to orbit	23.5°	2.2°

[a] Derived mainly from refs. 3 and 7.
[b] Includes atmosphere.
[c] Computed from volume of solid planetary body.

the same as on Earth (3). Moreover, except for a few "high" estimates, such as R. Wildt's proposal of 93° to 135° C (4), the temperature at the surface was widely thought—before the advent of radiometric data in the late 1950s—to be about that of tropical or even temperate regions on Earth (5). On the other hand, there was no agreement on how smooth or rough the surface might be (5). Likewise, proposals for the axial rotational period varied widely, with many centering around an Earth- or Mars-like day of twenty-four hours, others around fifteen to thirty days, and still others favoring the planetary sideareal orbital period of 224.7 terrestrial days (6).

Thus at the time Immanuel Velikovsky's *Worlds in Collision* first made its appearance, in 1950, few persons other than Velikovsky had strong reason to believe that Venus would prove to have an extraordinarily hot and comparatively flat surface, an extremely dense lower atmosphere, a peculiarly perturbed axial rotation, and hydrocarbon gases (or polymers) deep in its lower-lying atmosphere. Although the last of these four predictions remains in dispute and still awaits adequate testing, the

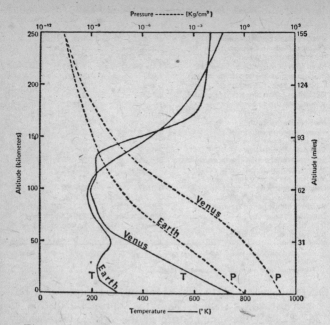

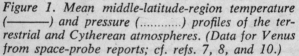

*Figure 1. Mean middle-latitude-region temperature
(————) and pressure (............) profiles of the terrestrial and Cytherean atmospheres. (Data for Venus
from space-probe reports; cf. refs. 7, 8, and 10.)*

first three have been amply vindicated, evidently—at least
in part—to the surprise of many astronomers who had
long entertained contrary views (3, 7).

CONFIRMATORY FINDINGS

In recent years, Earth-based studies of the microwave
emission spectra of Venus, which indicate an intensely
hot surface and suggest a rather dense lower atmosphere,
have been fully corroborated by interplanetary space
probes. The latter show that although the temperature
and pressure at the upper boundary of the main cloud
layer are only about 240 to 250° K (−33° to −23° C)
and 0.2 atmosphere, respectively, on both the sunlit and

dark sides of the slowly rotating planet (7, 8), they soar to the neighborhood of 750° K (477° C or 890° F) and about 90 atmospheres at the surface (Figure 1). Venera 7, which soft-landed on the nocturnal side of Venus on December 15, 1970, recorded a surface temperature of 747±20° K and a pressure of 90±15 kilograms per square centimeter (9). Venera 8, which successfully landed on the illuminated limb on July 22,

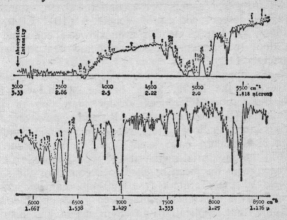

Figure 2. Near-infrared ratio spectrum, Venus/ Moon. (Adapted from ref. 31, p. 98. Copyright 1971 by D. Reidel Publishing Company, Dordrecht, Netherlands.)

1972, relayed a similar temperature of 743±8° K and a pressure of 90±1.5 kg/cm² (10).

Mariner occultation experiments (8) and other evidence (7) also suggest that the brightly reflecting cloud envelope, with an albedo of 0.77±0.07 according to Irvine (11), is probably multilayered, and that its opaque portion extends to an altitude of sixty-five to seventy kilometers (ca. forty to forty-three miles). An additional overlying aerosol or haze of optically thin clouds detectable by ultraviolet photography evidently reaches to an altitude of eighty to ninety kilometers (7, 8).

In the upper part of the visible cloud layer, a fair amount of turbulence appears to be present, but at the height of the thin ultraviolet clouds a rapid four-to-five-day equatorial planetary circulation or wave motion seems to predominate (7, 12). This movement is retrograde (i.e., east to west) and if real, corresponds to wind velocities in excess of one hundred meters per second (ca. 230 miles per hour). Deeper in the atmosphere, as would be expected, wind movement is definitely less. At a height of forty-five kilometers a lateral wind velocity of ca. forty-five meters per second has been estimated from the descent pattern of Venera 8 (10). At lower altitudes, wind movement is even slower, decreasing to less than two meters per second below ten to twelve kilometers (10).

Radar imaging (13) reveals Venus to be generally flatter than the Earth, Mars, or the Moon, with few surface-elevation differences greater than one or two kilometers (0.6 to 1.2 miles). Recently, however, numerous large, shallow craters, twenty-one to one hundred miles in diameter, have been shown to be present, at least in the equatorial region at 40° west longitude (14). No agreement has been reached to account for the shallowness of these craters (the 100-mile-diameter crater being "only a quarter of a mile deep"), which obviously has important implications for their origin and history.

Other radar studies (15) indicate that Venus turns on its axis in a retrograde (east-to-west) sense with a sidereal rotational period of 243.0 ± 0.1 (Earth) days. This corresponds closely, but apparently not quite, to an Earth-locked "resonance" period of 243.16 days. With the latter, exactly the same point on the Cytherean surface would be turned toward the Earth at each inferior conjunction, when Venus passes directly between the Earth and the Sun (mean synodical period occurring every 583.92 days).

EXPLANATION STILL SOUGHT

Not surprisingly, the basis on which Velikovsky anticipated properties of this nature—namely, his belief that Venus is a comparatively young planet, originating from Jupiter only a few thousand years ago, and that, within the span of recorded human history, it has had a series of enormously destructive encounters with the Earth, Mars, and the Moon as an incandescent, hydrocarbon-rich protoplanet—has not been received with much favor among professional astronomers. In general, they have preferred to consider Venus to be about the same age as the Earth and to attribute its high surface temperature not to residual natal heat, as Velikovsky proposes, but instead to an extremely efficient greenhouse effect and/or a deep-circulation, convective solar heating mechanism (7).

Venera 8 photometric measurements indicate, however, that the dense clouds allow only a small fraction of heat-producing visible and near-infrared solar radiation to penetrate to the Cytherean surface (10). Moreover, calculations show that an atmosphere such as that of Venus, consisting essentially of carbon dioxide (see below), cannot provide enough infrared opacity to maintain the observed high surface temperature (7, 16). Water would provide much of the required extra opacity, if present in sufficient amount. However, a recent microwave study (17) of the 1.35-centimeter water absorption resonance has set an upper limit of only 0.2 per cent water at almost any level in the lower atmosphere. This amount, it was concluded, is insufficient to produce dense water or ice clouds within the main cloud deck, "and it is doubtful that it may contribute significantly to a greenhouse effect," to quote the authors of the report (17).

With an opaque, highly reflecting cloud envelope (regardless of composition) insulating the surface from direct solar heating and also no doubt preventing much heat from escaping, several deep-circulation, convective heat-transfer mechanisms have been proposed to account for the high surface temperature (7,18). A fundamental feature of these mechanisms is that "a lateral temperature gradient is created at the surface with higher temperature on the dayside" then on the nightside (18). It is suggested that "the deposition of solar energy at the top of the atmosphere could drive a dynamical system in which the energy is conveyed downward in a narrow region . . . with rising motion at the sub[s]olar and sinking motion at the antisolar point" (19).

Owing to its enormous mass, the atmosphere of Venus

has a large thermal inertia. Hence these regions of energy transfer required by convective circulation mechanisms would probably be quite difficult to detect. According to Marov (7), "during the Cytherean night . . . only 0.25% of the energy store" in the atmosphere is lost. "Thus the temperature difference between the night and day sides is expected to be quite small: maximum diurnal variation at the surface should be . . . $\leqq 1°$ K" (7). Obviously, this small a difference will be very difficult, if not impossible, to measure reliably. The close agreement of the Venera 7 nightside (9) and Venera 8 dayside (10) surface-temperature readings has already been noted. Disk-brightness measurements by Earth-based spectroscopy also show that "diurnal temperature variations are practically absent" (7).

Without regions of suitable temperature difference, a convective circulation mechanism to heat the surface cannot operate. As Velikovsky has observed (20), it violates the second law of thermodynamics to have heat transferred from uniformly colder parts of an atmosphere to portions that are uniformly hotter.

An alternative explanation for the high surface temperature of Venus has been offered by Hansen and Matsushima (21). These authors postulate that an internal heat source (of unspecified origin) comparable to, or up to ten times, that of the Earth can maintain the high surface temperature through the powerful insulating effect of micron-sized dust particles held aloft by turbulence. As they point out, "the most crucial question for the dust insulation model is whether sufficient wind speeds may exist near the planetary surface" to raise the required amounts of dust to the required altitudes. With the evidence from the Venera probes indicating a fairly calm atmosphere below ten to twelve kilometers (10, 12), it would appear that this mechanism is also rather questionable.

Undoubtedly, other models and explanations will be proposed to account for the apparently uniform high surface temperature of Venus. However, if the planet is, in fact, of comparatively recent origin, then, as Velikovsky has suggested (22), it is probably not yet in thermal equilibrium with its environment, and it should still be cooling off. Under these circumstances, with reliable techniques, a gradual decrease in the temperature at the surface and at various altitudes in the atmosphere might be detectable. The rate of cooling will depend, of course, on how effectively the cloud cover insulates against such heat loss, but it would not seem unreasonable to expect to find a small decrease in temperature over the course of several synodical periods (23).

ATMOSPHERIC CONSTITUENTS

Before considering the question of whether hydrocarbons are to be found on Venus, it will be useful to review briefly some of the information that is available about the composition of the Cytherean atmosphere and the nature of the clouds. As would be expected, the high reflectivity of the clouds makes spectral determination of atmospheric constituents difficult and complicated. Indeed, early spectral observations failed to disclose any absorption band not present in the solar spectrum, and it was not until 1932, shortly after the development of high-resolution near-infrared photographic spectroscopy, that the major constituent, carbon dioxide, was tentatively identified through three nonsolar bands at 0.7820, 0.7883, and 0.8689 micron (10^{-4} centimeter) in the Cytherean spectrum (2). Later investigations have fully confirmed this identification and have uncovered many additional CO_2 absorption features (Figure 2). At present, over 185 near-infrared absorption bands corresponding to various vibrational states of the different isotopic forms of carbon dioxide are known (24).

Unfortunately, it has not proved feasible to determine with certainty from spectral data alone the total or absolute amount of CO_2 in the atmosphere of Venus. However, the ^{12}C-to-^{13}C abundance ratio in the CO_2 has been estimated by such means to be ca. 100:1, or about the same as on the Earth (25). With direct chemical sampling of the lower atmosphere by Venera probes 4, 5, and 6, CO_2 has been found to be present to the extent of about 97 per cent, at least in the 0.6-atmosphere region (26). This result is based on absorption by potassium hydroxide, which measures other acidic substances besides CO_2. The Soviet investigators were of course aware of this fact and noted that trace amounts of hydrogen chloride and hydrogen fluoride (Table II), which have been estimated from spectral evidence (see below), would also be absorbed but would not interfere. However, should substantial amounts of some other acidic substance(s) be present, the CO_2 results would be spuriously high. No chemical analyses below the 10-atmosphere level have been made, but densimeter readings and other Venera data indicate that the proportion of CO_2 probably remains essentially unchanged down to the surface (7, 9, 10, 26).

Among other constituents of the atmosphere, carbon monoxide was originally detected by its first overtone band near 2.35 microns (27). Its volume-mixing ratio relative to the CO_2 content is estimated to be about 5×10^{-5} (fifty parts per million) and is apparently fairly uniform throughout the atmosphere (24). In addition, there are three other substances positively identified by near-infrared absorption bands, with possible higher concentrations in and below the clouds. These are water vapor (0.6 to 1.0 ppm), hydrogen chloride (0.4 to 0.6 ppm), and hydrogen fluoride (0.005 to 0.01 ppm) (24, 28, 29). Upper limits for other possible components of the spectroscopically accessible region of the atmosphere have been established (Table II), but such information does not in any way imply the presence of these substances in these limiting concentrations. In this connection, it should be noted that the accurate determination of the amount of water vapor in the atmosphere of Venus has been especially complicated by telluric (Earth-atmosphere) water (7, 24, 28).

Venera probe analyses of the lower atmosphere indicate the presence of less than 2 per cent elementary nitrogen (and other inert gases), no more than 0.1 per cent free oxygen, and between 1.1 per cent water at the 0.6-atmosphere level and 0.007 per cent water at the 10-atmosphere level. Spectroscopically, the upper limit for oxygen above the cloud layer is 10 ppm (0.001 per cent) (30), and for water, as mentioned above, only 0.6 to 1.0 ppm.

In contrast to the Venera findings, recent microwave

studies cited earlier (17) suggest a maximum of 0.2 per cent water in the same altitude region in which the Venera probes recorded up to 1.1 per cent water (ca. forty-five to fifty-five kilometers). As already indicated, these microwave results are interpreted (17) as excluding the possibility of water or ice clouds in the lower atmosphere, in agreement with a similar conclusion based on near-infrared evidence (24, 28).

TABLE II. SPECTROSCOPIC UPPER
LIMITS ON MINOR CONSTITUENTS IN
THE CYTHEREAN ATMOSPHERE[a]

Substance (Formula)	Maximum Concentration[b]
Acetaldehyde (CH_3CHO)	1.0
Acetone (CH_3COCH_3)	1.0
Acetylene (C_2H_2)	1.0
Ammonia (NH_3)	0.03
Carbon monoxide (CO)[c]	50
Carbon oxysulfide (COS)	0.1
Carbon suboxide (C_3O_2)	0.1
Ethane (C_2H_6)	20
Ethylene (C_2H_4)	30
Formaldehyde CH_2O)	1.0
Hydrogen chloride (HCl)[c]	0.4–0.6
Hydrogen cyanide (HCN)	1.0

219

Substance (Formula)	Maximum Concentration[b]
Hydrogen fluoride (HF)[c]	0.005–0.01
Hydrogen sulfide (H_2S)	0.1
Methane (CH_4)	1.0
Methyl chloride (CH_3Cl)	1.0
Methyl fluoride (CH_3F)	1.0
Nitric oxide (NO)	1.0
Nitrogen dioxide (NO_2)	0.01
Nitrogen tetroxide (N_2O_4)	0.04
Nitrous oxide (N_2O)	20
Oxygen (O_2)	10
Ozone (O_3)	0.005
Sulfur dioxide (SO_2)	0.01
Water (H_2O)[c, d]	0.6–1.0

[a] Compiled from refs. 7, 24, 28, 29, 31, and T. Owen and C. Sagan, *Icarus,* 16 (1972), 557. Up to 2% (20,000 ppm) nitrogen and other inert gases may also be present.
[b] In parts per million, if present.
[c] The presence of this substance appears to be definitely confirmed (see ref. 24).
[d] The figures represent the water in the atmosphere above the clouds (ref. 28). Microwave data (ref. 17) place an upper limit of 2,000 ppm water in the 0.6–10-atmosphere region below the visible cloud tops.

Although spectral data reveal an upper limit of 0.03 ppm ammonia relative to CO_2 in the atmosphere above the clouds (31), photo-resistance measurements of color-change indicators on board Venera 8 are reported (10) to have recorded between 0.01 and 0.1 per cent (100 to

1000 ppm) free ammonia during the descent of the spacecraft through the 46–33-kilometer altitude region. In view of the fact that larger amounts of HCl than ammonia are present above the clouds, these findings, if valid, suggest that the clouds may act as a barrier to the movement of ammonia to higher altitudes (see further discussion below). In any event, ammonia (and certain of its compounds) would be expected to interfere with the methods employed in previous Venera missions to determine the water content of the Cytherean atmosphere (7, 26) and thus might account in part for the differing results of the Venera and microwave analyses for water.

SULFURIC ACID CLOUDS?

Many different substances have been proposed for the visible clouds of Venus (31, 32), but none of them quite meets all the requirements of the currently available data. In addition to specific spectral requirements in the visible, ultraviolet, and infrared, optical polarization measurements show that the cloud particles are spherical with a narrow distribution of radii near one micron. Moreover, in the region of maximum albedo at a wavelength of 0.55 micron, they exhibit a refractive index of 1.45 ± 0.02 (33), revised recently to 1.44 ± 0.015 (34). This is much too high to be compatible with that of pure water (1.33) or ice (1.31) at $0°$ C. Actually, any deviation greater than ±0.01 from 1.44 introduces marked disparity between the calculated and found polarization. Sphericity of course strongly implies that the particles are liquid droplets. However, considering that the temperature of the upper regions of the clouds is uniformly ca. $-23°$ C (34), only a very limited number of possible candidates would appear to meet this requirement.

Solutions of HCl in water, for example, as proposed by J. S. Lewis (35), either have too low a refractive index and too high a vapor pressure of water or else, if highly concentrated, have too high a vapor pressure of HCl to be compatible with observed cloud-region values (24, 28, 34). In addition, although they exhibit some of the spectral features of Venus (35), aqueous HCl solutions particularly lack the absorption bands found in the 9.5-and 11.2-micron regions of the Cytherean spectrum (34, 36).

The same spectral shortcomings apply to most other candidates, including ammonium bicarbonate (37) and the related carbamate, which obviously are logical entities for consideration in view of the Venera 8 data indicating the presence of ammonia in the 46–33-kilometer region. The high thermal lability of these substances provides a plausible mechanism for keeping them aloft by dissociation and recombination at lower and higher altitudes, respectively. On the other hand, because they are solids at the temperature of the upper surface of the clouds, these materials would not appear able to match the polarization data nearly so well as would a liquid condensate, even assuming satisfactory agreement with the observed refractive index (37).

Various organic compounds, including certain types of unsaturated hydrocarbons, have refractive indexes and volatility properties that are reasonably consistent with those of the cloud particles. Some of them also possess at least part of the ultraviolet absorption displayed by Venus. However, none have been found which do not appear to be excluded by the absence of requisite bands in the near infrared (see next section).

In apparent contradiction to the Venera 8 report concerning the presence of ammonia in the lower Cytherean atmosphere, a proposal has been advanced by G. T. Sill and developed recently by A. T. Young (34) that the cloud particles consist mainly of 75 per cent sulfuric acid (by weight) in water. At the temperature of the upper part of the clouds (ca. $-23°$ C), 75 per cent H_2SO_4 has a refractive index of 1.44, the very same value observed for the clouds. As a liquid at this temperature, it can be expected to exist as spherical droplets. Its equilibrium water-vapor pressure is only one hundredth that of pure water or ice, thereby accounting for the relatively small quantity of water found in the region of the clouds.

Equally striking is the fact that 75 per cent H_2SO_4 exhibits an infrared spectrum that is remarkably similar to that of Venus (Figure 3), with prominent absorption bands at 9.5 and 11.2 microns as well as in the 3–4-micron region (34). In the lower regions of the atmosphere, where high temperatures prevail, the dissociation of H_2SO_4 into water and sulfur trioxide would serve as a mechanism to recirculate its components back to cooler, higher altitudes for recombination as a dense mist and re-formation of liquid droplets.

Only the short-wavelength absorption of Venus in the near ultraviolet, which produces the light yellowish color, is not accounted for by strong solutions of sulfuric acid in water. Unless some additional substances are present, such solutions are transparent in this region. One possibility that is considered attractive (34) is iron(II) sulfate monohydrate, since its short-wavelength reflection spectrum is similar to that of Venus (38). Iron(III) chloride, along with photodissociation of HCl in the upper atmosphere to produce chlorine and HOCl (by reaction of chlorine with water), has also been proposed to account for the yellowish color resulting from the increased absorption at shorter wavelengths (35, 39). The nature of the high, optically thin "clouds" or haze above the visible deck is still obscure (34).

Although it is argued (34) that there is no overriding chemical incompatibility between sulfuric acid and the other known constituents of the Cytherean atmosphere, the coexistence of free ammonia with an excess of sulfuric acid, as already noted, would appear to be contraindicated. Moreover, the view has been expressed (28) that sulfuric acid clouds must "most certainly be rejected, due to the other chemical complications this model would create." On the other hand, the cosmic abundance of sulfur in relation to the small amounts apparently needed to produce the observed cloud opacity does seem to be compatible, since a mixing ratio of H_2SO_4 to CO_2 ranging from only 3 to 3000 ppm is held to be required (34).

One other implication of sulfuric-acid clouds which should be mentioned is the fact that in the hot, lower regions of the atmosphere, sulfuric acid and its dissociation product, sulfur trioxide, would be expected to behave as strong oxidizing and sulfonating agents. They would therefore be incompatible with the sustained presence of any readily oxidizable substances, such as hydrocarbons and their derivatives. A related argument has been advanced previously in connection with the relatively small amount of carbon monoxide in the Cytherean atmosphere (40). Under high-temperature conditions, the amount of CO present presumably would be much larger if reducing agents such as hydrocarbons were available to enter into equilibrium reactions with CO_2.

HYDROCARBONS PRESENT?

On the basis of the considerations just mentioned, it would appear that there is not much likelihood of finding any significant amount of hydrocarbons on Venus at the present time. Of course, this does not mean that hydrocarbons could not have been present at some time in the past. It has been argued, for instance, that photodissociation of water in the upper atmosphere of Venus, followed by escape of hydrogen from the planet, might even today be generating oxygen for the conversion of hydrocarbons to CO_2 and water (40, 41).

In any event, if the Venera 8 analysis of ammonia in the lower atmosphere is essentially valid, then the fact that only traces of ammonia can be detected spectroscopically in the region above the clouds is no proof that more substantial amounts are not present at lower altitudes. Hence it is legitimate to ask: are other substances possibly present in the clouds or lower regions of the atmosphere that are not yet recognized through Earth-based spectroscopic observations? Assuming for the moment that Velikovsky's proposal for its origin by cleavage from the planet Jupiter is basically sound, then Venus might well be expected to have not only ammonia in its atmosphere, as found on Jupiter, but also hydrocarbons, such as methane (or derivatives thereof), which are also present in the Jovian atmosphere.

As indicated in Table II, at most only trace amounts of low-molecular-weight hydrocarbons appear to be present in the Cytherean atmosphere above the clouds. This conclusion is based largely on the absence of various C—H stretching overtones and combination bands (Figure 4) in the high-resolution near-infrared spectrum of Venus

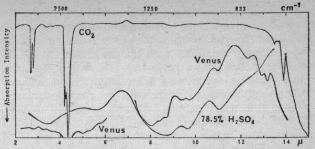

Figure 3. Infrared spectra of carbon dioxide (gas), Venus, and 78.5% aqueous sulfuric acid. (CO$_2$ spectrum adapted from Sadtler Standard Infrared Spectra No. 1924. Copyright 1962 by Sadtler Research Laboratories. Permission for the publication of Sadtler Standard Spectra has been granted, and all rights are reserved by Sadtler Research Laboratories, Inc. Spectra of Venus and 78.5% H$_2$CO$_4$ adapted and redrawn from ref. 34, copyright 1973 by Academic Press.)

(Figure 2). Unfortunately, the many intense CO$_2$ lines in this spectral region make detection of the generally weak C—H (and related N—H and O—H) overtone and combination bands extremely difficult and uncertain. Such bands often coincide with positions of CO$_2$ bands or at best can be expected to occur as poorly resolved shoulders on them. At the present time, however, virtually all previously unidentified bands (42) in the near-infrared spectrum of Venus have been shown to belong to CO$_2$ (43).

In the infrared proper (2.5–15 microns), hydrocarbons and their derivatives display much stronger C—H absorption bands than in the near infrared. In particular, the strong fundamental C—H stretching modes in the 3.2–3.5-micron region (3125–2850 cm^{-1}) are especially useful. This portion of the Cytherean spectrum (Figure 3) shows intense, poorly resolved absorption, only a small portion of which can be due to CO$_2$ (weak band at 3.4 microns). Certain types of compounds entirely lacking in C—H bonds, such as weak and strong acids (H$_3$O$^+$ ion), ammonium salts, bicarbonates, and certain metal ion hydrates (e.g., Fe^{++}), also exhibit strong absorption in this region. Hence, although the origin of these bands in the spectrum of Venus is still uncertain, they are not inconsistent with an assignment to C—H stretching modes.

The intense absorption of 4.3 microns in the infrared spectrum of Venus is clearly due to the fundamental C=O asymmetric stretching vibration of carbon dioxide. Additional CO_2 bands occur at 2.7, 2.8, 13.9, and 15 microns, with weaker bands at 12.6, 13.5, and 13.7 microns. The strong band at 15 microns is due to the principal scissoring (bending) vibrations. Broad absorption in the 8–10-micron region may in part be due to hydrated CO_2, but it would also result from C—O and C—N bond stretching that would be expected of various

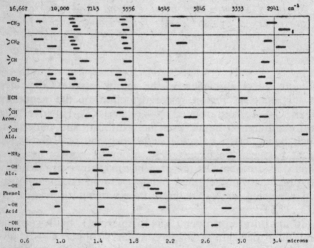

Figure 4. Chart of characterizing near-infrared bands. (Adapted and redrawn from W. Kaye, "Near-Infrared Spectroscopy," Spectrochimica Acta, 6 (1954), 281. Copyright 1954 by Pergamon Press, Ltd. Reprinted with the permission of Microform International Marketing Corporation, exclusive copyright licensee of Pergamon Press Journal back files.)

derivatives of hydrocarbons such as alcohols, ethers, esters, amines, etc.

Although the refractive-index data would appear to exclude most types of aromatic (benzenoid and/or heterocyclic) compounds from the cloud layer, olefinic substances, if present in this region of the atmosphere, could have the observed refractive index and might also exhibit some of the ultraviolet absorption properties. They would also be expected to display fairly strong C—H out-of-plane deformation vibrations in the 10–14 micron region as well as double-bond stretching and other types of C—H absorption in the 6–8-micron region of the infrared spectrum.

As seen in Figure 3, the infrared spectrum of Venus exhibits a significant amount of absorption in the regions just mentioned—absorption that is not due to CO_2, sulfuric acid, or other known constituents of the atmosphere (34). Assignment of at least a portion of this absorption to olefinic and/or other organic compounds is not unreasonable (if sulfuric acid is *not* present!). But without confirmatory evidence in the near infrared, no firm conclusion along such lines can be drawn.

In an attempt to demonstrate the presence or absence of hydrocarbons in the upper levels of the clouds, W. T. Plummer (44) measured the reflectance/absorption spectra of various paraffinic hydrocarbon frosts. He reported a marked depression in reflectivity in the 2.3–2.5-micron region which is not observed, or rather, observed less strongly, in the near-infrared spectrum of Venus.

The infrared evidence for hydrocarbons in the spectroscopically accessible regions of the Cytherean atmosphere is therefore tenuous at best. Nevertheless, the possibility of finding hydrocarbons in the lower parts of the atmosphere beneath the clouds cannot be dismissed. As L. D. Kaplan has pointed out (45), the microwave-emission spectra of Venus show a double maximum in rotational temperature distribution that "implies a stratified cloud layer at a level corresponding to a temperature of about 400° K" (127° C). In his view, "All molecules that are likely candidates for condensation or polymerization at this temperature have CH bonds, and therefore absorb strongly around 3.5μ. . . . The problem now is to account quantitatively for the very great opacity of the lower atmosphere by identifying the absorbing gases. . . ."

Future space-probe investigations of Venus will obviously be called upon to achieve this goal.

QUESTIONS AND CONCLUSIONS

Today, much is known about our nearest planetary neighbor that was not known or widely recognized just a few years ago. At a time when quite contrary views prevailed, Velikovsky made the bold claim that Venus would prove to be extremely hot and that it has a massive atmosphere which in times past gave evidence of being rich in hydrocarbons. The first two parts of this claim have been remarkably vindicated, and at least an enormous quantity of oxidized carbon (CO_2) has been demonstrated to be present in the Cytherean atmosphere.

However, many important questions remain. We still do not know for certain whether the deep, lower-lying atmosphere contains hydrocarbons besides carbon dioxide. Not only is it most urgent that this question be resolved, but also whether the ammonia reported by Venera 8 is really present and whether the clouds do, in fact, consist of sulfuric acid droplets, as has been proposed recently.

In addition, we are still uncertain about the origin and constancy of the high surface temperature, the evolution of the large, shallow craters, the intimate workings of the atmospheric circulation, the reason for the essentially Earth-locked, retrograde axial rotation, and the cause of the constantly recurring, planet-wide variations in the height of the cloud cover that have been verified recently (46).

Finally, with reference to Velikovsky's postulate of the origin of Venus from Jupiter—which, as we have seen, has obviously scored some very impressive successes in predicting recent discoveries about Venus—how does it happen that at present the planet is so rich in carbon dioxide but apparently not in hydrocarbons, at least in the region of the cloud tops? Moreover, why is there so little water in the Cytherean atmosphere?

Various answers to these questions have been proposed.

If the CO_2 (and also the HCl and HF) came mostly from volcanic activity, then substantial amounts of water should likewise be present. But if the atmosphere originally contained or later acquired relatively large amounts of water, what has become of it? One view is that the water has undergone photodissociation in the upper atmosphere at a rate sufficient for loss of most of the hydrogen from the planet into outer space. But, then, what became of the resulting oxygen? (It is too heavy compared to hydrogen to escape easily.) Were reduced forms of carbon present that were then oxidized to CO_2, as has been suggested (40, 41)?

In his partial reconstruction of its history in *Worlds in Collision,* Velikovsky proposed that Venus had a number of atmosphere-interaction-and-exchange contacts with other celestial bodies during the centuries before it was brought into its present, nearly circular orbit around the Sun. These encounters could thus account for the acquisition of water (or oxygen) needed to convert the original Jovian mantle of hydrocarbons on Venus into carbon dioxide.

However, the proposed loss of large amounts of hydrogen to space by photodissociation of water in the upper atmosphere suggests that the ratio of deuterium to hydrogen in the lower atmosphere should be significantly higher on Venus than on Earth, since the latter has retained such a large quantity of water on its surface. In fact, the search for DCl and HOD in the near-infrared spectra of Venus has not yet disclosed the presence of even the detection limit of a 1:10 ratio of deuterium to hydrogen in the lower atmosphere (47). Likewise, a reinvestigation of the far-ultraviolet spectrum of the upper atmosphere of Venus by means of an Aerobee 150 rocket (48) has not confirmed the deuterium enrichment that was derived earlier from the Mariner 5 data (47, 49).

Thus the interrelated problems of the origin of the carbon dioxide, the possible presence of the hydrocarbons —now and/or in the past—and the comparative lack of water in the atmosphere of Venus do not appear to have been adequately resolved. However, judging by the rapidity with which major advances in our knowledge about the planets have been occurring in recent years, it seems more than likely that satisfactory solutions will soon be forthcoming.

ACKNOWLEDGMENTS

I am deeply grateful to various colleagues for their many valuable suggestions and to Dr. L. D. G. Young for her most helpful comments on an earlier draft of the manuscript.

REFERENCES

1. J. Scheiner, *A Treatise on Astronomical Spectroscopy*, trans. E. B. Frost (Boston: Ginn and Co., 1894), pp. 197–98.
2. W. S. Adams and T. Dunham, Jr., *Publications of the Astronomical Society of the Pacific*, 44 (1932), 243; cf. C. E. St. John and S. B. Nicholson, *Astrophysical Journal*, 56 (1922), 380 (also printed in *Contributions from the Mount Wilson Observatory*, Vol. 11, No. 249 [1921–22], pp. 377–96).
3. P. Moore, *The New Guide to the Planets* (New York: W. W. Norton & Co., 1971), p. 63.
4. R. Wildt, *Astrophys. J.*, 91 (1940), 266.
5. Cf. P. Moore, *A Guide to the Planets,* rev. ed. (New York: W. W. Norton & Co., 1960), chap. 5 and app. V; also pp. 125–26 of ref. 6 below.
6. For summary, see P. Moore, *The Planet Venus*, 3rd ed. (New York: The Macmillan Co., 1960), chap. IX and app. 2; also pp. 63–64 of ref. 3 above.
7. M. Ya. Marov, *Icarus*, 16 (1972), 415; cf. V. I. Moroz, *Uspekhi Fizicheskikh Nauk*, 104 (1971), 225 (*Soviet Physics Uspekhi*, 14 [1971], 317).
8. G. Fjeldbo, A. J. Kliore, and V. R. Eshleman, *Astronomical Journal*, 76 (1971), 123; cf. S. I. Rasool and R. W. Stewart, *Journal of the Atmospheric Sciences*, 28 (1971), 869.
9. V. S. Avduevsky *et al.*, *J. Atmos. Sci.*, 28 (1971), 263.
10. *Pravda,* 10 September 1972; cf. *Nature*, 239 (1972), 125; also *Sky and Telescope*, 44 (1972), 303.
11. W. M. Irvine, *J. Atmos. Sci.*, 25 (1968), 610.
12. V. V. Kerzhanovich, M. Ya. Marov, and M. K. Rozhdestvensky, *Icarus*, 17 (1972), 659; cf. A. H. Scott and E. J. Reese, *Icarus*, 17 (1972), 589; also T. Gold and S. Soter, *Icarus*, 14 (1971), 16.
13. W. B. Smith *et. al.*, *Radio Science*, 5 (1969), 411; cf. R. P. Ingalls and J. V. Evans, *Astron. J.*, 74 (1969), 258; also, R. M. Goldstein and H. C. Rumsey, *Icarus*, 17 (1972), 699. See also ref. 15 below.
14. E. Driscoll, *Science News*, 4, August 1973, p. 72.

15. R. L. Carpenter, *Astron. J.*, 75 (1970), 61; R. F. Juergens, *Radio Science*, 5 (1970), 435.

16. J. B. Pollack, *Icarus*, 10 (1969), 314; idem, *Icarus*, 14 (1971), 295; G. Ohring, *Icarus* 11 (1969), 171.

17. M. A. Janssen *et al.*, *Science*, 179 (1973), 994.

18. R. M. Goody and A. R. Robinson, *Astrophys. J.*, 146 (1966), 339; R. E. Samuelson, *J. Atmos. Sci.*, 25 (1968), 634; P. H. Stone, *J. Atmos. Sci.* 25 (1968), 644; R. Goody, *Annual Review of Astronomy and Astrophysics*, 7 (1969), 303; and P. J. Gierasch, *Icarus*, 13 (1970), 25.

19. G. E. Hunt and J. T. Bartlett, *Endeavour*, 32 (1973), 39.

20. I. Velikovsky, *Yale Scientific Magazine*, 41 (April 1967), 20–21.

21. J. E. Hansen and S. Matsushima, *Astrophys. J.*, 150 (1967), 1139.

22. I. Velikovsky, *Celestial Observer*, December 1966 (reprinted in *Pensée*, 2 [May 1972], 51).

23. I. Velikovsky, *Yale Scientific Magazine*, 41 (April 1967), 32.

24. L. D. G. Young, *Icarus*, 17 (1972), 632.

25. V. I. Moroz, *Astronomicheskii Zhurnal*, 40 (1963), 144 (*Soviet Astronomy*-AJ, 7 [1963], 109).

26. A. P. Vinogradov *et al.*, "The Chemical Composition of the Atmosphere of Venus." In *Planetary Atmospheres*, ed. C. Sagan, T. C. Owen, and H. J. Smith, International Astronomical Union Symposium No. 40 (Dordrecht, Netherlands: D. Reidel Publishing Company, 1971), pp. 3–16.

27. W. M. Sinton, *Transactions of the International Astronomical Union*, XIB (New York: Academic Press, 1962), p. 246; cf. refs. 29 and 42 below.

28. U. Fink *et al.*, *Icarus*, 17 (1972), 617.

29. P. Connes *et al.*, *Astrophys. J.*, 147 (1967), 1230.

30. M. J. S. Belton and D. M. Hunten, *Astrophys. J.*, 153 (1968), 963; also T. Owen, *J. Atmos. Sci.*, 25 (1968), 583.

31. G. P. Kuiper, "On the Nature of the Venus Clouds." In *Planetary Atmospheres*, ed. C. Sagan, T. C. Owen, and H. J. Smith, International Astronomical Union Symposium No. 40 (Dordrecht, Netherlands: D. Reidel Publishing Company, 1971), pp. 91–109.

32. For partial listing, see J. S. Lewis, *American Scientist*, 59 (1971), 557; also C. Sagan, *Science*, 133 (1961), 849.

33. J. E. Hansen and A. Arking, *Science*, 171 (1971), 669.

34. A. T. Young, *Icarus*, 18 (1973), 564.

35. J. S. Lewis, *Astrophys. J.*, 171 (1972), L75, and earlier papers cited therein. See also B. Hapke, *Science*, 175 (1972), 748.

36. F. C. Gillett, F. J. Low, and W. A. Stein, *J. Atmos. Sci.*, 25 (1968), 594; cf. W. M. Sinton and J. Strong, *Astrophys. J.*, 131 (1960), 470.

37. R. Beer, R. H. Norton, and J. V. Martonchik, *Astrophys. J.*, 168 (1971), L121.

38. G. P. Kuiper, *Comm. Lunar Planet. Lab.*, 6 (1969), 229; cf. D. P. Cruikshank and A. B. Thomson, *Icarus*, 15 (1971), 497; idem, *Icarus*, 15 (1971), 504.

39. R. G. Prinn, *J. Atmos. Sci.*, 28 (1971), 1058.

40. M. O. Dayhoff *et al.*, *Science*, 155 (1967), 556.

41. S. I. Rasool, *J. Atmos. Sci.*, 25 (1968), 663.

42. V. I. Moroz, *Astron. Zh.*, 41 (1964), 711 (*Soviet Astron.-AJ*, 8 [1965], 566).

43. J. Connes, P. Connes, and J. P. Maillard, *Near Infrared Spectra of Venus, Mars, Jupiter and Saturn* (Paris: Editions du Centre National de la Recherche Scientifique, 1969).

44. W. T. Plummer, *Science*, 163 (1969), 1191.

45. L. D. Kaplan, *Journal of Quantitative Spectroscopy and Radiative Transfer*, 3 (1963), 537.

46. L. G. Young *et. al.*, *Astrophys. J.*, 181 (1973), L5.

47. M. B. McElroy and D. M. Hunten, *Journal of Geophysical Research*, 74 (1969), 1720.

48. L. Wallace *et al.*, *Astrophys. J.*, 168 (1971), L29.

49. L. Wallace, *J. Geophys. Res.*, 74 (1969), 115; T. M. Donahue, *J. Geophys. Res.*, 74 (1969), 1128; *J. Atmos. Sci.*, 25 (1968), 568.

VENUS' ATMOSPHERE*

Immanuel Velikovsky

I have claimed a massive atmosphere around Venus—while my 1951 reviewer and opponent, the Royal Astronomer Sir H. Spencer Jones, maintained that Venus has less atmosphere than the earth (1). After a bitter experience with Venera 4, crushed while descending in the Venus atmosphere, the Russians learned that near the ground it is in excess of ninety atmospheric pressures. I also claimed that in historical times the trailing part of the protoplanet Venus became partly absorbed into the atmosphere and cloud covering of Venus and that quite probably till today there are hydrocarbons present or, instead, quite possibly organic molecules.† Venus, according to many ancient sources, poured naphtha on Earth; the Mayan sources, for instance, are so insistent in their connecting the planet with "fire water" that a modern author, L. Sejourne, wrote an entire book on the subject, *Burning Water* (1956), without, however, a reference to the outpouring of naphtha on Earth. Again, according to a number of ancient sources as far apart as Scandinavia, Greece, India, and Judea, during a number of years that followed the great outpouring and conflagration— the years that carry the appellative "Shadow of Death" or "Götterdämmerung"—ambrosia (Greeks), manna (Israelites), madhu (Hindus), or morning sweet dew (Scandinavians), fell on Earth. I drew the conclusion that there must have been occurring a process of conversion of hydrocarbons, in the cloud envelope that enshrouded the Earth, into edible (carbohydrate or protein-like) substance. In an article printed in *Harper's* magazine for June 1951, "Answer to My Critics," I speculated that through prolonged bacterial action, hydrocarbons could have been converted into edible products. In this I followed the suggestion offered me by the late Vasili I. Komarewsky (Illinois Institute of Technology), my classmate and close friend through the eight years of gymnasium in Moscow, and in this country a leading authority on petroleum and catalysis. This was an answer to a critic, Cecilia Payne-Gaposchkin, who wrote that if a conversion of petroleum products (hydrocarbons) into edible products were feasible, the problem of feeding the growing population of the hungry in the world would have been solved—but it is unsolvable. But some years later, through the study of premature destruction of asphalt roads, it was learned that certain bacilli convert asphalt (petroleum products) into edible products; since then, the Food and Agriculture Organization of the United Nations erected in southern France a factory for converting asphalt into edible products, exactly for the

†Hydrocarbons of petroleum products consist of only two elements—carbon and hydrogen; carbohydrates, besides carbon and hydrogen, contain also oxygen.

233

purpose of helping to solve the nutrition problems of the growing population of the world. Hydrocarbons can be changed into nutrition products, and not only by bacterial action, but also by some other, modern methods.

My other assumption, namely, concerning the origin of hydrocarbons in Venus' trailing part, was all my own. In *Worlds in Collision* (1950), in the section "The Gases of Venus," I have assumed that by electrical discharges in the atmosphere of methane and ammonia (known ingredients of the Jovian atmosphere), hydrocarbons of heavy molecular weight could have been created. Of electrical discharges in the short and stormy history of Venus, as witnessed by the peoples of the world, there was no dearth. In 1952, not long after the publication of *Worlds in Collision,* H. C. Urey suggested that in a mixture of methane, ammonia, and hydrogen, electrical discharges would produce amino acids; the following year, S. L. Miller succeeded in verifying this by an experiment (2). In 1960, A. T. Wilson of Australia published in *Nature* a report of a successful experiment: by electrical discharges in a mixture of gaseous methane and ammonia, he produced heavy molecules of hydrocarbons, exactly as I had suggested. Two years later, Wilson published another article in *Nature* and again, without referring to my work and my claims, suggested that the atmosphere of Venus abounds in hydrocarbons (3).

In the meantime, meteorites were observed possessing organic material, and around this claim, by Nagy and his collaborators, grew a large and impassioned scientific literature in the beginning denying the find as self-deception of the finders, but as time passed, the scale of the debate startd slowly to incline toward an acceptance of the claims of Nagy and his colleagues as true and not built on self-deception.

There were also numerous spectroscopic observations made of the tails of comets that disclosed the presence, even abundant presence, of hydrocarbons. In my understanding, those comets originated in the disturbances that accompanied the near-collisions of Venus with other celestial bodies; thus the evidence appears to be still present.

In *Worlds in Collision,* toward the end of the book, I put two sections concerning Venus' physical properties.

One deals with its atmosphere ("The Gases of Venus"), the other with its thermal state ("The Thermal Balance of Venus"). Since I claimed that Venus is extremely hot, I also maintained that any hydrocarbons present in its lower atmosphere must be in a gaseous state, though some of the hydrocarbons, such as paraffins, require high temperatures in order to convert to gases. I also wrote: "Moreover, if there is oxygen present on Venus, petroleum fires must be burning there" (*Worlds in Collision*, "The Thermal Balance of Venus").

With these considerations in mind, and in order to trace the possible fate of Venus' hydrocarbons, I envisaged two processes, the first a transformation into other organic products concentrating in the cloud cover of Venus, either through microbial activity or through electrical discharges, this last possibly having been in the process that went on for decades thirty-four centuries ago. The second manner of conversion of hydrocarbons into other products in the lower atmosphere, in the high temperature prevailing there, would be in combustion—in case oxygen is or was present there. When hydrocarbons burn, two products result—carbon dioxide (CO_2) and water (H_2O). But if oxygen is not present, or not present in sufficient quantity, in the great heat and pressure a cracking of naphtha, a process familiar in the petroleum industry, must take place. As Burgstahler [article beginning on page 210] correctly notices, oxygen of the terrestrial atmosphere, or water acquired from the Earth in the exchange that took place, could provide the necessary oxygen to start the process. (One could be reminded that Harold Urey, my severe critic since a few years after the publication of *Worlds in Collision*, claims that a comet hit the Earth and splashed the water of the ocean onto the Moon, 240,000 miles away.)

If the process of conversion of hydrocarbons into other organic molecules took or still takes place, the product, "ambrosia" of the Greeks ("the ambrosial robe of Athene"), would be most probably one of the main ingredients of the clouds; yet if microbial activity did not develop in Venus' atmosphere, then hydrocarbons would be present. As to the oxidizing of hydrocarbons, or combustion, the reaction would follow this pattern: upon hydrocarbons converting into carbon dioxide and water, the latter as steam would rise to higher strata until in a photodissociation process it fell apart to hydrogen and oxygen, the former escaping into, first, the upper atmosphere and then into space, but the oxygen returning to continue the burning of the remaining hydrocarbons. And since only a few thousand years have passed since the process started, hydrocarbons, even in the case of presence of initial oxygen or initial water, would still be present. Actually, at some time past, Burgstahler advised me that by the quantity of the remaining hydrocarbons the lapse of time since the start of the process can be made known, if the rate of conversion can be evaluated.

Before continuing on the theme, I wish to return to 1946. In advance of approaching any publisher with the manuscript of *Worlds in Collision,* I approached Harlow Shapley of the Harvard College Observatory with the request (letter of April 1946) to perform the spectroscopic tests on the presence of hydrocarbons on Venus. I will not enter here the sordid story, partly described by Horace M. Kallen. Shapley subsequently wrote to Kallen that the Harvard College Observatory has no facilities to perform the test and that the best facilities are in the hands of Walter S. Adams, Director of Mount Wilson and Mount Palomar observatories. I wrote Adams and on September 9, 1946, he replied most courteously and assured me that "The absorption bands of the petroleum gases are in the infrared, far below where photographic plates can be used. It is true that the spectrum of some of the hydrocarbon compounds do occur in the photographic region, but these would necessarily arise from the gases and not from hydrocarbon dust. There is no evidence of the presence of hydrocarbon gas in the atmosphere of Venus." But he also stipulated that "The work which we have done at Mount Wilson on the spectrum of Venus is necessarily limited to the spectral region which can be photographed."

Thus I was warned. Nevertheless, I preferred to adhere to the conclusions I reached and, when, in 1950, *Worlds in Collision* was published, to express myself in the following way: "If and as long as Venus is too hot for the liquefaction of petroleum, the hydrocarbons will circulate in gaseous form" ("The Gases of Venus"). Since the envisaged hydrocarbons would be mostly heavy molecules, just by physical laws they would not be expected at the top of the atmosphere. Further, acknowledging that "the absorption lines of the petroleum spectrum lie far in the infrared where usual photographs do not reach," I made my assumption:

"When the technique of photography in the infrared is perfected so that hydrocarbon bands can be differentiated, the spectrogram of Venus may disclose the presence of hydrocarbon gases in its atmosphere, if these gases lie in the upper part of the atmosphere where the rays of the sun penetrate" (*Worlds in Collision*, "The Gases of Venus").

In this form I presented my views to the reader, undaunted by the warnings of the man at that time best authorized to give an answer.

My correspondence with Adams continued also past the publication of *Worlds in Collision,* and by his attitude, in my opinion, he redeemed the honor of his profession that in its behavior reached low ethical standards never before attained. On July 28, 1950, he advised me that the "oil companies use special types of spectroscopes to analyze some of the components of petroleum," advice good today as it was over twenty-three years ago.

In 1955, five years after the publication of *Worlds in Collision*, Fred Hoyle, in his book *Frontiers of Astronomy,* expressed the view that the clouds of Venus "might consist of drops of oil" and that "the oceans of Venus may well be oceans of oil." He did not consider that Venus is very hot and therefore he spoke of oil oceans on it. His line of thought brought him to very similar conclusions as to the atmosphere of Venus. "Carbon was much more likely to be initially present in combination with hydrogen, not with oxygen. . . . If all the carbon was initially locked away in the higher hydrocarbons, an oxidation process was necessary in order to produce the carbon dioxide that we now observe. It is possible that the oxygen derived from the dissociation of the water was all absorbed in the oxidation of hydrocarbons" (pp.

68–72). Also, several other scientists theorized about the presence of hydrocarbons (petroleum) in Venus' atmosphere.

In the meantime, deeper-infrared spectra became accessible for spectral analysis. The upper and lower atmospheres of Venus are separated by a cloud layer over fifteen kilometers thick. Thus, when we speak of the atmosphere of Venus and its composition, we need to define one of the three areas as the subject of discussion: the upper atmosphere, the dense cloud layer, or the lower atmosphere. By means of spectral analysis we cannot reach the lower atmosphere—unless we deal with the *emission spectrum* of the light that glows through the cloud. Of the cloud layer, we can know by means of a spectral analysis only the constituents of its top layer, because we have only the *reflection* spectrum, which, as Burgstahler stated, is not as clear in revealing the composition of the layer as an *emission* spectrum (only from hot substances) or *absorption* spectrum (of light going through gases). The upper atmosphere reveals itself through an absorption spectrum, but this atmosphere is very rarefied and the absorption spectrum is "engulfed" by the reflection spectrum from the top of the cloud; the albedo, or the reflection power, of this cloud is close to the albedo of freshly fallen snow.

The rich presence of carbon dioxide (CO_2) on Venus was assumed at least since the work of C. E. St. John and J. B. Nicholson (1922). In *Worlds in Collision,* before speculating on the presence of hydrocarbons, I stated that "carbon dioxide is an ingredient of Venus' atmosphere" and referred to the work by St. John and Nicholson, before introducing my hypothesis: "On the basis of this research, I assume that Venus must be rich in petroleum gases."

The confirmation of the very large amounts of carbon dioxide came also with the Russian attempts to place a miniature laboratory on the surface of the planet and to analyze various layers of the atmosphere through which the laboratory was descending. In the first probes, only eleven various analyses could be made—in search for oxygen, nitrogen, hydrogen, a few other gaseous elements, and water, carbon dioxide (CO_2), and carbon monoxide (CO). Also, only a few selected layers were explored. The probes indicated at some altitude as much as 95 per cent carbon dioxide, but no atomic nitrogen; nitrogen was generally expected to compose up to 90 per cent of Venus' atmosphere (L. D. Kaplan), this by assuming that Venus and Earth must have had a similar origin and history. But I did not share this expectation concerning atomic nitrogen. The problem of the origin of huge quantities of carbon dioxide on Venus was perplexing, and several authors expressed themselves as baffled by it.

From where could the massive amount of carbon dioxide have come? If volcanism on Venus is much stronger than on Earth, not only carbon dioxide but some other ingredients as well—such as water vapor in rich quantities—needed to be produced. Besides, the radiometrically obtained topographical picture of Venus' ground surface did not reveal volcanoes resembling terrestrial volcanoes, but only immense circular formations some hundred miles across and with walls as low as a quarter of a mile at most—appearing more like effects of bubbling on a grandiose scale. Then, what is the possible origin of carbon dioxide on Venus?

Hydrocarbons in combustion produce carbon dioxide. In the process I described a little earlier, the dissociation of water by photoelectric or any other process would cause the lower atmosphere to be oxidizing, whereas the upper atmosphere, with the escaping hydrogen, would be reducing. This situation is also detected—to the surprise, even disbelief, of many researchers.

Are, then, any hydrocarbons or other organic molecules still present on Venus?

After the first American fly-by probe, Mariner 2, passed its rendezvous point with Venus in December 1962, the results were first made public in February 1963, and it was claimed by the NASA spokesman, Dr. Homer Newell, that the clouds on Venus are rich in hydrocarbons. I have repeatedly read in the polemic surrounding my work that this statement at the press conference was a mistake seized upon by the followers of my concepts. It was not a press-conference "mistake." The conclusion was based upon very careful consideration of the physical characteristics of the cloud layer that was found homogeneous at the top and the bottom, at temperatures of ca. $-35°$ F on the top and over $+200°$ F ($400°$ K) at the bottom. Professor L. D. Kaplan, the researcher on the staff of the Jet Propulsion Laboratory responsible for the statement, discussed the phenomenon in several papers and memoranda, and his conclusion was that only the multiple radical CH (hydrogen and carbon bound) has the same physical characteristics at the two ends of the range of temperature as discovered. It is also untrue that JPL revoked the statement made; contrariwise, in *Mission to Venus* (Mariner 2), published in 1963, the statement is repeated in this form: "At their base, the clouds are about 200 degrees F and probably are comprised of condensed hydrocarbons."

Although the question is not about what was said and what was not, but of the veritable content of the clouds, I found it necessary to tarry here on this issue because of the sociological aspect that intervened, unfortunately, in a scientific problem: I read quite a few vitriolic comments and heard of a few college lecture tapes about a "crucial test" for my entire work. (I introduced the sentence on hydrocarbons with the words "I assume," and also said that if there is oxygen present, petroleum fires must be burning. Therefore, the presence in our time of hydrocarbons, even in lower strata, could not be construed as a crucial test. Moreover, I discussed also the conversion of hydrocarbons into other organic molecules by catalysis. The high, near-incandescent heat of Venus —which I claimed at a time when scientific opinion favored a near-ground-surface temperature only a few degrees higher than the mean annual temperature of Earth—constitutes a crucial test). But it seems that, if anything, the subsequent work only increased the probability (today I am inclined to say the "near-certainty") of the presence of organic material in the Venus clouds. Since the episode in the sociology of science is of interest, so also is a sentence in a letter by L. D. Kaplan (dated April 1963)—not yet realizing why his findings were engendering a storm of protest—to a friend, a member of the Institute for Advanced Study in Princeton.

Kaplan wrote that his having identified hydrocarbons caused a violent reaction among astronomers. The word hydrocarbon "was used only to avoid the use of 'organic compounds' for obvious reasons. The reaction to even 'hydrocarbons' was much too violent." In a copy of a published report that he sent to his friend, he struck out by pencil the word "hydrocarbons," changing it to "organic compounds."

In 1969, W. T. Plummer, at that time with the University of Massachusetts, undertook to investigate whether the reflection spectrum of Venus' clouds at the near infrared, at the range of 2.1 to 2.5 microns, duplicates the reflection spectra of the solid butane particles and of liquid propane droplets. He selected these two hydrocarbon compounds out of a group of seventeen—there are in nature or can be constructed practically tens of thousands of hydrocarbon combinations. (Professor W. C. Harris of Furman University wrote me very recently: "These [organic compounds] may, in fact, be specific molecules synthesized in this environment—containing carbon, hydrogen and other elements—that simply are not common to our laboratory models.") The logic actually demanded an approach reversed from that pursued by Plummer. He needed not to look for hydrocarbons that may give a reflection spectrum different from that of Venus in the waverange he selected, but for hydrocarbons and other organic molecules that may produce a reflection spectrum similar to that of Venus. He reproduced the reflection spectra of Venus in that range (2.1 to 2.4 microns) as observed by four different researchers —and they differ among themselves. Plummer claimed that the cloud of Venus does not show the same darkening in spectrum (absorption) as the frost of butane and the mist of propane, both, as I stressed in my reply, used at a different atmospheric pressure (0.2 against 1.0) and at different concentrations. And then, I stipulated in *Worlds in Collision,* "if the gases lie in the upper path of the atmosphere where the rays of the sun penetrate . . . ," whereas Plummer was looking at the top of the cloud only. Yet I pointed out that the spectrum of Venus, especially as found by Sinton (1962) and by Bottema *et al.* (1964) (4), produces a *definite* absorption of light in this wave range, pronounced as lacking by Plummer.

In my answer to Plummer, I stressed also an important point, namely, that the glow ("ashen light") that shimmers on the dark side of Venus must produce bright spectral lines of emission, and upon traversing the cloud layer would definitely much erase the effect of the absorption spectrum created by the upper atmosphere or the reflection bands from the top of the cloud layer.

I opposed Plummer's assertion that the reflection spectrum at the wavelength he investigated proves the abundant presence of water in the form of ice crystals in the clouds, to which he ascribed the spectral absorption: My main argument was that the refractive index (1.44) is definitely higher than the refractive index of ice or water (1.33). By the way, today Plummer's view has hardly any adherents, and one of the main counterarguments against the view of water or ice in the clouds is the same that I offered, namely that "The results for the index of refraction eliminate the possibility that the visible clouds are composed of pure water or ice" (J. E. Hansen and A. Arking, *Science,* vol. 71, 19 Feb. 71, pp. 669ff).

In the meantime, Plummer's article in *Science* caused some reverberations; thus, the London *Times* printed an article under a title suggesting my theory was disproved; but despite the title and the case of ice against hydrocarbons on Venus, the article was rather sympathetic to my other claims and their · verification, as was also Plummer's paper: he has the distinction of being the first in his profession to undertake tests to check on one of my propositions, even if only with a claim of disproving a particular proposition. As I learned at a later date, he had to persevere and not submit to the insistent demand of the reviewers of his article for *Science* before publication that my name should be omitted from his article—he agreed only that it should not appear in its title.

My answer, submitted to *Science*'s editors, was returned for rewriting after one or two reviewers took issue with my statement that the lower atmosphere of Venus is oxidizing. I had an easy answer to make: actually, in the issue of *Science* which a week later followed Plummer's article, written on March 21, 1969, R. F. Mueller, discussing the content of the Venusian atmosphere, referred to the "instabilities of the hydrocarbon compounds in an anhydrous, oxidizing, hot environment."

But I grew tired of the prospect of negotiating and rewriting and have satisfied myself by having sent an early version of my reply to Professor Plummer.

By 1971, Kuiper concluded that it is *not* known of what the clouds of Venus consist, and hydrocarbons and carbohydrates were mentioned as possible candidates among several others.

At the symposium at Lewis and Clark College, Oregon, in August 1972, Burgstahler read a paper on the positive indications of the presence of hydrocarbons in Venus' atmosphere. By the time he presented his paper for printing in *Pensée,* the perusal of the literature (he did not make any tests) made him take a more cautious stand, and it may even appear that he tends toward regarding sulfuric acid as having the better chance of proving itself as the main constituent of the cloud cover of Venus. If I have not lost the ability of logical deduction and conclusion, Burgstahler's paper is nothing but a strong supporting evidence for the presence of hydrocarbons (or other organic material) on Venus, and this despite the way he presents the case and draws his conclusions. Good chemistry needs to be matched by equally good dialectics.

First, Burgstahler presents the new data of Venus' midinfrared spectrum of absorption—at 3.5 microns, and in deeper infrared—8 to 13 microns. It follows that, in these ranges, Venus and many hydrocarbons alike—as I also assumed when writing the article offered to *Science*—produce strong bands of absorption, whereas the sulfuric acid does not produce all such bands. But Venus has them. Also in the ultraviolet, the absorption bands (lines) are what hydrocarbons would produce and what Venus' spectrum shows, but not sulfuric acid. And when on both ends of the spectrum the finds are for hydrocarbons, Burgstahler bends the scale by sending the entire question back to the near infrared, already discussed by Plummer (who claimed water) and answered by myself (at that time, not without repeated counsel from Burgstahler). But, earlier in the present article, he made, himself, a very clear statement that the 2.1–2.4-micron range is *not* well suited for defining any presence of hydrocarbons or other organic molecules, because, as he says, carbon dioxide present on Venus overwhelms at this wave range the spectrum picture and smears any absorption features that could be the effect of the presence of hydrocarbons or other organic molecules. "Unfortunately, the many intense CO_2 lines in this spectral region make detection of the generally weak C—H (and related N—H and O—H) overtone and combination bands extremely difficult and uncertain," wrote Burgstahler, who stresses the preference of the deeper-infrared range, and Plummer in his article before Burgstahler also admitted that a much better area for investigation would be in the deeper infrared that by now is available.

I have composed a table for a better evaluation of Burgstahler's findings made through his perusal of literature (see following page).

All statements in this table are from Burgstahler's article. It is immediately seen that the presence of organic molecules on Venus is well supported by the spectral features in the ultraviolet, infrared, and deep infrared, and by the physical characteristics of the cloud particles (refractive index, volatility).

The sulfuric acid, on the other hand, needs to be dissolved in 25 per cent of water to meet the refractive index. It does not account for the ultraviolet features and can account for only single features in the deep infrared, but for no feature whatsoever in the near infrared.

In the near infrared a few hydrocarbons tested by Plummer (out of tens of thousands of hydrocarbon and other organic molecules possible) produced reflection-spectrum features which are "not observed, or rather, observed less strongly in the near-infrared spectrum of Venus" (Burgstahler) and this despite the admitted fact that C—H bands would be obscured in this range by CO_2 bands, this therefore being an inferior range for the identification of hydrocarbons on Venus (Burgstahler).

	Refractive Index	Volatility and Chemical Compatibility	Ultraviolet Spectrum And Color	Near Infrared 2.1-2.5 Microns	Infrared 3.2-3.5 Microns	Deep Infrared 8-15 Microns
Hydrocarbons	"Various organic compounds, including certain types of unsaturated hydrocarbons, have refractive indices and volatility properties that are reasonably consistent with those of the cloud particles." "Olefinic substances [hydrocarbons] ... could have the observed refractive index."		"Some [organic compounds, including unsaturated hydrocarbons] possess at least part of the ultraviolet absorption displayed by Venus."	"The many intense CO_2 lines [of Venus] make detection of the generally weak C-H (and related N-H and O-H) overtone and combination bands extremely difficult and uncertain. Such bands often coincide with positions of CO_2 bands."	"In particular, the strong fundamental C-H [bands] in the 3.2-3.5 microns region are especially useful [for identification]. This portion of the [Venus] spectrum shows intense absorption, only a small portion of which can be due to CO_2." "Although the origin of these bands in the spectrum of Venus is still uncertain, they are not inconsistent with an assignment to C-H [bands]."	"In the infrared proper (2.5 to 15 microns), hydrocarbons and their derivatives display much stronger C-H absorption bands than in the near infra-red."
Sulfuric Acid	"In apparent contradiction to the Venera 8 report concerning the presence of ammonia in the lower Cytherian atmosphere, a proposal has been advanced by G. T. Sill and developed recently by A. T. Young that the cloud particles consist mainly of 75 percent sulfuric acid (oil of vitriol) in water. At the temperature of the upper part of the clouds (ca. -23°C) 75 percent [sulphuric acid] has a refractive index of 1.44."	"As a liquid at [-23°C] it can be expected to exist as spherical droplets." "Co-existence of free ammonia with ... sulphuric acid ... would appear to be contraindicated. Moreover, the view has been expressed [by Kuiper et al.] that sulphuric acid clouds must 'most certainly be rejected due to other complications this model would create.'"	"The short-wave length absorption of Venus in the near-ultraviolet, which produces the light yellowish color is *not* accounted for by strong solutions of sulphuric acid."		"The infrared spectrum of Venus exhibits a significant amount of absorption in [the 6-8 and 10-14 micron] regions ... absorption that is not due to CO_2, sulphuric acid, or other known constituents of the atmosphere. Assignment of at least a portion of this absorption to olefinic and/or other organic compounds is not unreasonable."	"75 percent sulfuric acid [exhibits] prominent absorption bands at 9.5 and 11.2 microns."

Then, how fair is it to state that "none [no hydrocarbons] have been found which do not appear to be excluded [from Venus' clouds] by the absence of requisite bands in the near infrared" (Burgstahler)? Or how proper is it to assess the entire range of the "infrared evidence in the spectroscopically accessible regions" of the Venus atmosphere as "tenuous at best"? And this independent of the question as to what is in deeper layers of the cloud, or what was the content of the atmosphere in the past.

The recent (1973) claim by A. T. Young and L. D. G. Young, favored (5) by Burgstahler, has the spectral bands of Venus' cloud, where they cannot be accounted by carbon dioxide, as due to sulfuric acid, or oil of vitriol (H_2SO_4). It is true that sulfuric acid (used in the petroleum industry and for many other caustic purposes) produces certain bands found in Venus' spectrum, but, then, it does not produce other bands observed in the infrared, whereas organic molecules can account for almost all of them. In the near infrared (2.1 to 2.5 microns) the Youngs do not even attempt to make sulfuric acid accountable for the bands of absorption. Sulfuric acid cannot produce the observed features in the ultraviolet and cannot be held responsible for the yellowish color of Venus. Further, Kuiper and his colleagues have argued that sulfuric acid is incompatible with various chemical conditions on Venus. As Burgstahler mentioned, its presence is incompatible with ammonia detected by the Russians deeper in the atmosphere in direct chemical analysis in a search for this compound.

As to the color of Venus, Burgstahler borrows from the Youngs that an iron compound of sulfur could have been the cause of the absorption in the ultraviolet; certain other spectral features could have also been attributed to an iron compound of sulfur. This seems to be a better surmise.

Now, is the idea of the presence of sulfur and iron, or their compounds, on Venus new? As to the iron, I described from ancient sources the world turning red because of particles "of ferruginous or other soluble pigment" (*Worlds in Collision,* "Red World"); it gave a red hue to the rivers and caused death and decomposition to the animal population of the rivers. The pigment was followed in a few days by "small dust," like "ashes of the furnace," and then by the outpouring of bituminous stuff, followed in turn by large meteorites. Actually, if we believe numerous testimonies bequeathed to us by ancient sources, the ancients had already what we intend some day to obtain from Venus—samples of its dust, ash, atmosphere, and rocks. Studying the spectra of comets with hydrocarbons in their self-illuminating tails, and bituminous material in some meteorites, we have, most probably, another indirect way to study Venus' composition.

Whether the pigment that fell on Earth was a compound of iron and sulfur, as it appears to have been, or not, it caused death of the aqueous fauna. But of the presence of sulfur on Venus, in addition to iron and organic material, I was conscious some twenty years in advance of the Youngs.

On January 28, 1945, I registered a lecture copyright titled "Transmutation of Oxygen into Sulfur." This was over six months before the fission (atom) bomb was dropped on Hiroshima and years before a fusion (thermonuclear) process was worked out. In my understanding, the phenomenon of brimstone (sulfur) falling from the sky (or filling the air) in the course of great discharges, as narrated in ancient sources (Old Testament and Homer among them), resulted from smashing two oxygen atoms into one atom of sulfur. I assumed that, on Jupiter and on Venus, sulfur must be present; on Jupiter because it acquired much of the water of Saturn after Saturn exploded, and in great thunderbolts converted the oxygen of the water into sulfur; and on Venus because it brought sulfur from its parental body, Jupiter, and also because in violent discharges it would fuse oxygen snatched from Earth's atmosphere or hydrosphere into sulfur. In July 1955, I wrote to Professor Walter S. Adams, by then retired from the directorship of Mount Palomar and Mount Wilson observatories, but heading the solar observatory in Pasadena affiliated with the Mount Wilson Observatory. The pertinent passage in my letter is this:

"I assume on the basis of my theory that Saturn has chlorine, or possibly sodium chloride, and also water. Is anything known in this matter? I would also like to know whether the spectral analysis gives reason to assume that Jupiter and Venus, alike, have iron and sulfur in ionized state?"

Adams answered my questions in a hand-written letter dated July 25, 1955. After discussing the principles of spectroscopy (the spectrum of reflection was not yet worked out), he wrote:

"Now to apply these facts and considerations to your questions. 1) The presence of chlorine in Saturn is improbable. It is not an abundant gas, shows great affinity for chemical combinations, and so far as I know has never been identified with certainty even in the sun or stars. 2) Water or water vapor might be present in the atmosphere of Saturn, but would be completely frozen at the temperaure, and hence unobservable. 3) Ionized iron and sulfur could not possibly be present in the atmosphere of Jupiter and Venus, because their spectra are atomic and would require very high temperatures for their production."

Eight years later, in 1963, on September 11, in a memorandum submitted to H. H. Hess in his capacity as Chairman of the Space Science Board of the National Academy of Sciences, I repeated my assumptions concerning Saturn, Jupiter, and Venus. The memo was reproduced in the Fall 1972 issue of *Pensée*.

By then it had already been known that Saturn has water, actually almost consists of water or ice, and that chlorine is one of the very few elements discovered on Saturn by spectral analysis. At another occasion I will discuss some details of how I came to these conclusions.

It is also known by now that Jupiter has sulfur and there appears to be spectral evidence for a compound of iron and sulfur on Venus. I firmly believe that iron will be found on Jupiter unless most of it was smashed into heavier elements by the Jovian bolts, and in the mentioned memo I suggested a search for it in atomic or molecular form in and above the Red Spot.

In a most recent publication on the subject of Venus'

spectrum that appeared after Burgstahler wrote his paper, R. O. Prinn of M.I.T. examined the idea of sulfuric acid and observed that "a surprising aspect of spectroscopic studies of Venus has been the apparent failure to detect any sulfur-bearing gases in the visible atmosphere" (6). He arrived at the conclusion that sulfuric acid could reasonably be only at the very *deck* (upper surface) of the cloud. Then Prinn pointed out that Young and Young "did not suggest any feasible source for the sulfuric acid," and he argued: "Even if Venus received very little FeS during accretion from the primitive solar nebula, or if a considerable amount of FeS lies in the core, only extremely small quantities of sulfur are required to saturate the atmosphere [of cloud's deck?]. The element is of sufficiently high cosmic abundance that cometary impact alone could provide all that is necessary." Thus Prinn leaves unanswered what constitutes the main body of the clouds.

With hydrogen liberated by photodissociation as one of the final products of burning hydrocarbons and entering into reaction with sulfur, the possibility of the presence of small quantities of sulphuric acid in the uppermost layer of the cloud cannot be entirely negated; but some sulfur and iron compounds should be present. The main body of the clouds, however, seems to be of organic nature, converted from the original hydrocarbons.

REFERENCES

1. H. Spencer Jones, *Life on Other Worlds* (1952), p. 167.
2. Harold C. Urey, *Proceedings, National Academy of Sciences*, 38 (1952), 351; S. L. Miller, *Science*, 117 (1953), 528; *Journal of the American Chemical Society*, 77 (1955), 2351.
3. A. T. Wilson, *Nature*, 17 Dec. 60; ibid., 6 Oct. 62.
4. W. M. Sinton, *Mem. Soc. Roy. Sci. Liege*, (1962), 300; M. Bottema *et al.*, *Astrophysical Journal*, 140 (1964), 1640.
5. L. D. G. Young and A. T. Young, *Astrophysical Journal*, 179 (1973), L39; also, A. T. Young, *Icarus*, 18 (1973), 564.
6. R. O. Prinn, *Science*, 182 (14 Dec. 73), 1132ff.

A CONCLUDING NOTE FROM PROFESSOR BURGSTAHLER

I appreciate Dr. Velikovsky's lucid discussion of my article, and especially the provocative tabular presentation of spectral comments drawn from it. I wish also to take this opportunity to express my deep appreciation to him for the valuable suggestions and various reprints he kindly provided me at the time I began writing my article on the nature of the atmosphere of Venus.

Through my reading of Dr. Velikovsky's publications and my correspondence with him, I have of course been well aware of his arguments for the presence of iron and sulfur in the clouds of Venus. His priority in the matter should have been noted in my discussion of proposals for the origin of the yellowish appearance of the planet, and I offer my sincere apologies to him and to readers of *Pensée* for not having done so. At some future date I hope he will present a more detailed discussion of the nature of the powerful discharges he proposes can transmute oxygen into sulfur.

According to Prinn, the clouds of Venus are composed of an extensive haze of sulfuric-acid droplets formed from above as a result of a "very rapid photo-oxidation of carbonyl sulfide [COS] in the upper atmosphere." This he views as a continuing cyclic process fully compatible with the ammonia detected by Venera 8 in the lower atmosphere.

The compatibility of sulfuric-acid clouds with the sustained presence of appreciable amounts of hydrocarbons, especially in the lower regions of the atmosphere, would therefore also appear to be possible but for the present I would like to defer further comment.

Albert W. Burgstahler

At several points in the course of his otherwise excellent review, Burgstahler makes a choice between hydrocarbons and other chemical species in the atmosphere of Venus. Nearly always, he rules (somewhat arbitrarily, considering the paucity of data) against the hydrocarbons. At one point he describes the evidence for their presence "tenuous at best." In fairness it should be pointed out that, for example, the experiments of Plummer do not necessarily rule out the possibility of gaseous or even liquid hydrocarbons in the upper atmosphere. In the lower regions, not only are there insufficient data to exclude the presence of hydrocarbons, but the infrared spectrum (Figure 3 in Burgstahler's review) has several features consistent with hydrocarbons, and compounds with $C-C$ and $C=C$ bonds (e.g. hydrocarbons) as well as those with $C-N$ and $C-O$ bonds, should have been included by him among the species absorbing in the 8–12-micron region.

The hypothesis that the outer layers of cloud consist of an aerosol of sulfuric acid dihydrate is an interesting one, although one would expect that compounds of iron, adduced, *inter alia,* to account for the yellowish tinge of the clouds, would be oxidized to the Fe^{III} rather than the Fe^{II} state. Another explanation for the yellowish color might be the presence of unsaturated hydrocarbons in solution in sulfuric acid as carbonium ions. It is likely that sulfuric acid would be gradually decomposed by solar radiation of ultraviolet and shorter wavelength, particularly in the presence of iron compounds (F. S. Dainton and F. T. Jones, *Transactions of the Faraday Society,* 61 [1965], 1681) to give hydrogen and oxygen. This process would also be expected to result in the preferential retention of deuterium, as discussed in another context in Burgstahler's review. Because of this and other chemical reactions, sulfuric acid might well have a relatively short lifetime, consistent with a recent installation of the planet in its present orbit.

The presence of sulfuric acid in the clouds of Venus is

still only hypothetical. The ratio of water to acid is chosen so as to agree with the observed refractive index, and the infrared spectrum of this mixture, while consistent with that of the atmosphere, does not completely account for it. Nor does the spectrum of the acid exclude contributions by other substances, such as hydrocarbons. But Burgstahler proceeds to the assumption that if sulfuric acid is present, it eliminates the possibility of coexistent hydrocarbons. This appears to be too hasty a judgment. Although most unsaturated hydrocarbons are attacked by (concentrated) sulfuric acid, they are not necessarily destroyed by it. Olefins may be polymerized to higher-molecular-weight olefins, or reacted with paraffins to give other paraffins, a process widely used in the manufacture of iso-octane. Paraffins are inert toward sulfuric acid. In the hotter regions of the atmosphere, where Burgstahler assumes the sulfuric acid to be decomposed to water and sulfur trioxide, sulfonation of paraffins could occur. The resulting sulfonic acids, descending to regions of still higher temperature, would then decompose regenerating olefins. In the virtual absence of oxygen, a steady state is conceivable in which the acid species and hydrocarbons could coexist, just as free ammonia coexists with sulfuric acid, if the data and the hypothesis are to be believed.

Until further direct observations are made to decide the issue, the data cited by Burgstahler can be interpreted in *support* of the hypothesis of hydrocarbons in the atmosphere of Venus.

Peter R. Ballinger
Albany, California

PART V

The extreme youth of the present order of the solar system and the catastrophic events that led to its establishment, as proposed by Velikovsky, permit no other conclusion than that many physical aspects of the bodies in the inner solar system must reflect this recent, violent history. Venus, Mars, the Moon, and the Earth have major roles in Velikovsky's scenario of cosmic events that took place between thirty-five hundred and twenty-seven hundred years ago; if this reconstruction of history is correct, the scars must still be fresh.

Velikovsky himself asks, "Are the Moon's Scars Only Three Thousand Years Old?"—and answers, definitely, yes. This article was written in response to a request from the editor of the New York *Times* for an essay outlining Velikovsky's antipications on the eve of man's first landing on the Moon. It was published in the *Times*'s early, City Edition for July 21, 1969. (The material in brackets was acknowledged by the *Times* to have fallen out of the piece during the production process.)

Opposition to Velikovsky's conclusions comes from Professor Derek York of the geophysics division at the University of Toronto, a Foreign Principal Investigator for the Apollo Project (1971–72). York discusses "Lunar Rocks and Velikovsky's Claims" from the standpoint of the conventional consensus on the history of the Moon, concluding that Velikovsky's claims are refuted by the Apollo evidence.

Responding to York, Velikovsky asks, "When Was the Lunar Surface Last Molten?" He assembles evidence from the Apollo and other programs in support of recent catastrophes on the Moon and challenges the dating methods applied to the lunar samples.

Robert C. Wright, Senior Development Engineer with the Princeton Applied Research Corporation, considers "Effects of Volatility on Rubidium-Strontium Dating." He argues that lunar surface conditions promote the preferential loss of rubidium over strontium from lunar rocks, with the result that age determination based on the rubidium-strontium dating method are unreliable.

"Magnetic Remanence in Lunar Rocks," a quality that surprised most investigators when the first Apollo samples were returned, is discussed in the light of Velikovsky's advance claim on this score by Robert Treash. This paper also emphasizes the strange behavior of Nobel laureate Harold Urey when he was confronted on several occasions with the fact of Velikovsky's prediction of lunar remanent magnetism.

Looking beyond the Moon, Velikovsky considers a seeming trend in reports of Venus' temperatures measured in the course of several decades and asks, "Is Venus' Heat Decreasing?" Such an effect would be entirely in keeping with the thesis of *Worlds in Collision,* and he suggests that a program to investigate this possibility would be of great value for our understanding of the solar system's cosmology.

ARE THE MOON'S SCARS ONLY THREE THOUSAND YEARS OLD?

Immanuel Velikovsky

Man, free from the bonds tying him to the rock of his birth, is about to make his first steps on the lunar landscape. It is an amazing achievement of man's technological genius, and with it the first stage of the space age (1957–69) will be concluded.

These twelve years have been unkind to many accredited scientific theories of the solar system. Some of the most fundamental concepts are being summoned for revision.

In celestial mechanics, all new evidence has conjured against the concept—basic in science until very recently —that gravitation and inertia are the only forces in action in the celestial sphere.

The new discoveries are the interplanetary magnetic fields centered on the sun and rotating with it; the solar plasma; the terrestrial magnetosphere that caused the moon to rock when entering and leaving the magnetic funnel; the enormously powerful magnetic envelope around Jupiter through which the Galilean satellites plow, themselves influencing the Jovian radio signals.

Who is the physicist that would insist that Jupiter, traveling with its powerful magnetosphere through the interplanetary magnetic field, is not affected by it? Or that the Jovian satellites are not influenced in their motions by the magnetic field of their primary?

And in cosmology the puzzling discoveries have been Venus' incandescent heat; its massive atmosphere (140 atmospheric pressures!); its retrograde rotation controlled by the earth (it turns the very same face to us when in inferior conjunctions); its mountain-high ground tides (this is my understanding of the paradoxical altitude readings of the recent Venera 5 and 6), which also have caused it in the past to acquire a nearly circular orbit; Mars's moon-like surface and its apparent loss of a large part of its rotational momentum (Mariner 4); and the moon's active state—it is not a dead body cold to its core.

All these discoveries unite to defend the thesis that the present order of the solar system is of recent date.

In divergence from accepted views, I maintain that less than three thousand years ago the moon's surface was repeatedly molten and its surface bubbled. Since the nineteen fifties, many unburst bubbles—domes—have been observed on the moon and gases have been found escaping from several orifices.

The moon has hundreds of hot spots, and even its light is not all reflected solar light; researchers have come up with calculations that fluorescence would not account for the rest.

In thermoluminescence tests, it should be possible to establish the recentness of the last heating (melting) of the lunar surface. For that purpose, astronauts need to take samples from about three feet below the surface, to where the long lunar day hardly transmits any solar heat. Such tests could establish the time when the lunar surface was molten.

The moon has a very weak magnetic field; yet its rocks and lavas could conceivably be rich in remanent magnetism resulting from strong currents when in the embrace of exogenous magnetic fields.

Before their removal from the ground, the specimens should be marked as to their orientation *in situ*. Meteorites could not fall all similarly aligned. This simple performance of marking the orientation of samples, I was told, is not in the program of the first landing.

Despite the fact that there are no oceans on the moon and no marine life to give origin to petroleum hydrocarbons, I would not be surprised if bitumens (asphalts, tar or waxes) or carbides or carbonates are found in the composition of the rocks, although not necessarily in the first few samples.

A visitor to the earth would not detect deposits of petroleum in the first few hours, either. I have claimed an extraterrestrial origin for some of the deposits of petroleum on earth; the moon did not escape the same shower. Only, in a subsequent melting of the ground such deposits would most probably convert into carbides or carbonates.

It is quite probable that chlorine, sulfur, and iron in various compounds, possibly [oxidized, will be found richly presented in lunar formations. In my understanding, less than ten thousand years ago, together with the Earth, the Moon went through a cosmic cloud of water] (the Deluge) and subsequently was covered for several centuries by water, which dissociated under the ultraviolet rays of the sun with hydrogen escaping into space.

I maintain that—although not already at the first landing—an excessively strong radioactivity will be detected in localized areas, in those among the crater formations that resulted, I contend, from interplanetary discharges.

I also maintain that Moonquakes must be so numerous that there is a bit of a chance that during their few hours on the Moon the astronauts may experience a quake.

Some authorities (Harold Urey among them) claim that the scars on the face of the moon are older than four and a half billion years. The lunar landings will provide the answer: Was the face of the moon as we see it carved over four and a half billion years ago, or, as I believe, less than three thousand years ago?

If this unorthodox view is substantiated, it will bear greatly not only on many fields of science but also on the phenomenon of repression of racial memories, with all the implications as to man's irrational behavior.

LUNAR ROCKS AND
VELIKOVSKY'S CLAIMS

Derek York

In 1896, a 44-year-old French professor, Henri Becquerel, discovered that uranium compounds emitted rays which penetrated glass and paper and blackened photographic plates. Becquerel had discovered what we call radioactivity. Uranium atoms are unstable, and a group of them will very slowly (that is, over hundreds of millions of years), spontaneously change into the stable element lead. This transformation is accompanied by the emission of the rays which Becquerel detected. The important thing about uranium radioactivity from our point of view is that it goes on at a rate characteristic of uranium, and this rate cannot be altered by heating the uranium, hitting it with a hammer, or exposing it to a vacuum. Radioactivity, ticking steadily away, therefore provides us with a nature clock.

All rocks contain at least traces of uranium and can therefore be dated using the uranium clock. Suppose we had a piece of terrestrial rock whose age we wished to calculate. We would firstly measure the number of uranium and lead atoms it now contains. Imagine that we found in this rock seven million atoms of uranium and three million atoms of lead. Then we would argue that all these three million lead atoms were originally uranium atoms and that when this rock originally solidified (say from molten lava) it contained ten million uranium atoms and no lead. By the time we reach the present, three million (that is, 30 per cent) of the uranium atoms have changed into three million lead atoms. We would, therefore, conclude that since this rock is old enough for 30 per cent of its original uranium content to have decayed to lead, it must be about two billion years old. This is because we know from the results of nuclear physics that it always takes about two billion years for 30 per cent of a set of uranium (U-238) atoms to decay into lead. Thus in general by measuring what fraction of the uranium originally trapped in a rock at solidification has changed to lead, we can say how long ago that rock did in fact solidify.

Apart from the uranium-lead clock, we can also use the potassium-argon and rubidium-strontium clocks. For potassium slowly changes radioactively into argon, as does rubidium into strontium. So by measuring what fraction of the original potassium in a rock has changed into argon (or what fraction of the original rubidium has decayed to strontium) we can again calculate its age. In the past twenty years, these three radioactive clocks have been studied intensively for terrestrial rocks and meteorites in laboratories in many countries. These studies have revealed that the oldest rocks formed on the Earth are about four billion years old and are found in southwestern Greenland. The oldest rocks so far analyzed in North America are in Minnesota and were formed about three and a half billion years ago. Most terrestrial rocks, however, are younger than this. The Columbia River volcanics in Oregon, for example, were mainly erupted a mere fifteen million years ago. The meteorites, in contrast, almost all date at about 4.5 billion years. These are chunks of rock and iron-nickel alloy which bombard the Earth-Moon system.

The general conclusion from these thousands of age analyses is that the meteorites formed somewhere in the solar system about 4.5 billion years ago and that the Earth formed essentially at the same time.

When the Apollo 11 astronauts returned to earth in 1969, the lunar samples were immediately examined for the reading on their uranium-lead, potassium-argon and rubidium-strontium clocks. The potassium-argon and rubidium-strontium results were in essential agreement that the rocks analyzed were last molten on the Moon approximately 3.6 billion years ago. Because of the low concentrations of uranium and lead found, the uranium-lead technique was less definitive, but it also agreed that the rocks were formed somewhere between three billion and five billion years ago.

Succeeding missions have yielded fairly similar results. The Apollo 12 rocks were last molten about 3.3 billion years ago; the Apollo 14 rocks formed about 3.9 billion years ago; most of the Apollo 15 rocks crystallized at about the same time as the Apollo 12 samples, about 3.3 billion years ago.

Obviously, the four lunar sites so far visited on Apollo missions are all characterized by very old rocks, that is, rocks which evidently last solidified from a fluid state over three billion years ago. If these sites are not atypical, we may therefore conclude that the Moon was a very active place geologically between three billion and four billion years ago, undergoing severe meteoritic bombardment and internally generated volcanic activity. Since then, it has been a remarkably quiet body suffering only the occasional large meteorite impact. Subsequent modification of the surface features has been mainly erosion due to the impact of small meteorites, cosmic rays, and particles from the Sun. This is in great contrast with the

Earth's history, which has been one of continued volcanic and mountain-building activity up to the present day.

The fine-grained soils (as distinct from the rocks) returned from the Moon are probably the nearest we will come to having an average Moon sample. These date by the rubidium-strontium and uranium-lead techniques at 4.4 to 4.6 billion years old and probably indicate that the Moon as a whole formed at about the same time as the Earth and the meteorites. Potassium-argon dating of the soils is complicated by the presence in the soils of large volumes of all the rare gases (helium, neon, argon, krypton, and xenon), whose presence remains to be finally explained.

In his book *Worlds in Collision* Dr. I. Velikovsky suggested that significant areas of the Moon's surface were melted during close approaches by Mars within the last few thousand years. As may be seen from this article, no evidence of this has been found in studies of the uranium-lead, potassium-argon, and rubidium-strontium clocks. We therefore appear to be faced with the following possibilities: (a) this part of Velikovsky's thesis is wrong; (b) Velikovsky is right, but the four Apollo landings and the Soviet Luna 16 landing were in areas which escaped the "catastrophes" referred to by Velikovsky; (c) there is something seriously wrong with the radioactive clocks or our readings of them. There seems to be no good reason for choosing possibility (c), and the evidence favors (a) over (b).

WHEN WAS THE LUNAR SURFACE LAST MOLTEN?*

Immanuel Velikovsky

I appreciate the challenge concerning the last time the lunar surface was heated and became also partly molten. I intend to show that of the three possibilities in Professor Derek York's discourse, the evidence is for (c)— "there is something seriously wrong with the radioactive clocks or our readings of them."

First I will cite the impression the physical appearance of the lunar rocks made on qualified observers.

The Lunar Sample Preliminary Examination Team ("Preliminary Examination of Lunar Samples from Apollo 11") recorded "the extremely fresh appearance of the interior of all crystalline rocks, in spite of their microfractures and high potassium-argon age."

As to the exterior of the lunar material, T. Gold, writing in *Science,* discussed "Apollo 11 Observations of a Remarkable Glazing Phenomenon on the Lunar Surface." Gold, looking for a cause of the glazing, assumed "a giant solar outburst in geologically recent times" that sprayed the surface of all lunar rocks with metallic glaze. How recent? "The glazing occurred less than 30,000 years ago: otherwise the glaze would have been eroded and dusted over by slow bombardment of the moon by cosmic dust. On the other hand, the event must have taken place some thousands of years ago, not only because it was not observed historically, but also to allow enough time for the metal-plating process to coat the glass."

The event *was* observed historically; however, it was not due to the Sun becoming a nova for a second or so, but to the repeated disturbance in the Moon's motion and the near-encounters in the celestial sphere described in *Worlds in Collision,* Part II, "Mars."

With the knowledge attained in attempting to reconstruct the cosmic events of the eighth century and the beginning of the seventh before the present era (in which the Earth, but mainly the Moon and the planet Mars, were involved at 15-year intervals), I made the following claims concerning the Moon:

a. The lunar surface rocks must show the effects of their melting and bubbling. Actually the rocks were found to be of igneous nature, containing pyrogenic mineral assemblages and cavities created by bubbles of gas.

b. There must exist a steep thermal gradient toward the surface: "Since the moon was heated and its surface became molten only a few thousand years ago, the temperature gradient under the surface crust will show, to some depth, a mounting curve" (my communiqué to Professor H. H. Hess, Guyot Hall, Princeton University, dated July 2, 1969). Such a gradient was detected over two years later by the Apollo 15 team and startled the theorists: the outflow of heat was almost three times more than expected by those who hold to the hot origin of the Moon; those who hold to the cold origin of the Moon are baffled even more.

c. The hydrocarbons that have been deposited on the Moon in an earlier cosmic event (*Worlds in Collision,* Part I, "Venus") must have "in a subsequent melting of the ground" converted "into carbides or carbonates."

Small quantities of hydrocarbons and organic carbon were found in lunar material (and surprised the researchers); and substantial quantities of carbides have been found, too, and created a problem.

d. Radioactivity of the lunar material and especially localized areas of excessive radioactivity (where interplanetary bolts have fallen or emerged) would be found. Radioactive elements were first found in the rocks and fines brought by the Apollo 11 team. Localized thermal spots of high radioactivity were detected by the circling Apollo 15 craft, and large amounts of highly radioactive

KREEP were discovered in samples brought by the astronauts.

e. Excessive quantities of argon and neon would be found captured in the lunar rocks, having originated in an external source (Martian atmosphere); further, the abundance in which these noble gases would be found would lead to wrong, even bizarre, conclusions about the age of the lunar rocks.

Actually, rich inclusions of both argon and neon were found in lunar material. Ages of 7 billion and even 20 billion years were deduced, estimates that exceed the accepted age of the universe. Then it was claimed that much of the argon 40 arrived in the solar wind, though previously only atoms of hydrogen and helium were thought to be present in the wind (plasma). It was retorted that the solar wind *cannot* possibly contain argon 40; and it was found that the smaller the lunar grains are, the larger is the proportion of argon (and neon) to the grain's mass—it means that much of the argon must have come from the outside—therefore its presence is proportional to the surface, not to the volume of a rock or a fine.

Since argon 40 could not have arrived from the Sun and most of it could not have been formed *in situ* by the decay of potassium 40 (because such an origin would have required a Moon several times older than the accepted age of the universe), a rather far-fetched theory was offered and, in the absence of anything better, also accepted: namely, argon 40 was formed at the usual rate from the decay of potassium 40 and accumulated in the deeper strata of the Moon; then, because of heating from some unidentified origin, the argon succeeded in coming to the outside and forming a lunar atmosphere, but then it was *pushed* back into the surface rocks and grains by the solar wind acting purely mechanically. This, furthermore, requires that the rocks and grains opened themselves to permit an inclusion of argon and neon.

Is this not a most artificial explanation, especially in view of my advance claim of rich invasions of argon *and* neon of extralunar origin?

The conclusion is inescapable that the potassium-argon method of measuring the age of the lunar rocks needs to be discounted. And Professor York concedes this in the present short paper (and also conceded this to me following my lectures at the University of Toronto in October 1971).

Before we proceed, I wish to make it clear that the question is not *when* the rocks have been *formed* or for the *first* time crystallized, but when they were heated and partly molten for the last time. The *age* of the *rocks* is not in dispute, only the time of the "carving" of the lunar surface. The rocks could be billions of years old. And let me repeat Professor York's words: the transformation rate of radioactive elements cannot be altered by "heating" or "hitting" or "exposure in vacuum." Since heating by itself cannot influence the radioactive decay, a melting in the past cannot be detected by the resulting ratio between the quantities of the radioactive element found and the element product of the decay. However, one of the two may escape because of volatility in the process of heating. This is the case with lead—the end product of radioactive uranium or thorium.

It was found (and it caused one of the surprises in which the lunar exploration was rich) that the lunar rocks are greatly depleted of all volatile elements: lead, bismuth, cadmium, thallium, indium, and others. Actually, the lunar rocks contain only 10 per cent, and down to as little as one per cent, as much of these elements as corresponding terrestrial rocks. Thus, the uranium-lead and thorium-lead methods for estimating the age of lunar rocks are as inapplicable as the potassium-argon method. One method is undermined by the bountiful addition of the final product and the other method by the depletion of the final product.

Then, how good is the third method for measuring the age of lunar rocks, by rubidium decaying to strontium (with a half of the rubidium 87 converting into strontium 87 in 50 billion years)?

I have asked Robert C. Wright, Senior Development Engineer with Princeton Applied Research Corporation, to tackle this method for its validity in measuring the time since the lunar rocks were last molten. His remarks follow my discourse.

At the Third Lunar Conference, held at Houston in

January 1972, Leon T. Silver of the Division of Geological and Planetary Sciences, California Institute of Technology, challenged the age estimates of the lunar rocks. Lead and rubidium can become heated sufficiently to move freely over the Moon as gases. Silver gave no estimate of how much the lunar "boil-off" might have affected the estimates of the Moon's age and by how much the "ages" need to be revised.

Already at the First Lunar Conference (1970), Silver had drawn attention to the volatile transfer of lead "as a major lunar geological process" and referred to "an early high temperature episode in lunar history" which "produced an apparent depletion in volatile elements, including lead, as indicated by the extraordinarily high uranium-238 to lead-204 ratios of lunar material from Tranquillity Base, compared to terrestrial and chondritic materials." This and other observations made him conclude his paper with these words: "Continuous examination of basic assumptions provides some of the greatest harvests in Science."

Upon observation and detection of more "parentless lead" in subsequently obtained lunar material, Silver, reporting to the 1972 Lunar Conference, gave the figures arrived at in laboratory experiments. He concluded that at some time in the past the lunar surface became heated to volatilize the lead; at 475° to 600° C, a major release of lead would take place; and at 1000° C, from 70 to 80 per cent of the total lead would be volatilized. The heating of the surface is reflected in vitrification; some "drastic" lunar event converted at least half of the lunar soil (sample 14163) to various glasses. "One can reasonably expect some moon-wide volatile transfer effects from very large surface thermal events on the moon." This has "major implications and remarkable potential for understanding and explaining lunar surface history."

Thermal events must have enveloped the lunar surface to affect the transfer of lead. In such events, the rock needed to be heated to something like 800° C, but did not need to be molten and recrystallized.

Rubidium evaporates at much lower temperatures than lead. As Wright shows in his paper, the heat of one long lunar day is amply sufficient for the transfer of rubidium. Thus the third method is most unreliable for dating even at normal conditions prevailing on the Moon. Now we can ask how it is that it is claimed that concordant results have been obtained by the three methods unless a preconceived idea of the age of lunar rocks guides the researchers. In the meantime, we learned once more that the lunar surface was subjected to heating or several heatings after it was already cooled off.

In my article in the New York *Times,* written at the invitation of the editors for the "Man Walks on Moon" issue, I suggested that the thermoluminescence level of the rocks and glasses is the proper criterion for establishing the time when the last melting of the surface took place. This method is applied on inorganic material like pottery, glass, lava, rocks; the longer the time that has passed since the last heating to above ca. 150° C, the more luminescence must be stored for another heating or firing, which is then done in a laboratory. To exclude the effect of the solar heat during the two-week-long lunar day, I suggested the extraction of a core from a three-foot depth.

The thermoluminescence study by R. Walker and his collaborators at Washington University, St. Louis, was made on Apollo 12 cores. They reported tersely: "The TL (thermoluminescence) emitted above 225° C by samples between 4 and 13 cm show *anomalies resulting from disturbances* $\geq$ *10,000 years ago.*" The "disturbances" referred to were of a thermal nature.

Upon more consideration, I think that the increased radioactivity in lunar material must increase the thermoluminescence effect and thus let it appear that the last heating occurred earlier than historically true. Therefore it is necessary to extract material from sites which are the least radioactive.

The "extremely fresh" appearance of the interior of all crystalline lunar rocks, the vitrification of a large proportion of the lunar soil, the volatilization and transfer of lead, the glazing of the rocks (which must be of recent date), the thermoluminescence studies indicating thermal disturbances in historical times, and the steep thermal gradient that bewilders the researchers—all point to the fact that the thermal history of the Moon is not what it was thought to be only a few years ago.

Concluding, I wish to raise a fundamental question. When we measure the age of the universe, why do we assume that at creation the heavy elements like uranium predominated and not the simplest ones, hydrogen and helium?

It is philosophically simpler to assume that all started —if there ever was a start—with the most elementary elements. A catastrophic event or many such events were necessary to build uranium from hydrogen. Although the radioactive clock cannot be disturbed by heating or hitting, it can be disturbed by discharges of interplanetary potentials. This is what made me also claim localized areas of high radioactivity on the Moon and Mars alike.

EFFECTS OF VOLATILITY ON RUBIDIUM-STRONTIUM DATING

Robert C. Wright

Some estimates of the age of Moon-rock specimens have been based on the ratio between rubidium and strontium. It should be pointed out that under the conditions of temperature and pressure known to exist at the surface of the Moon, unequal migration of these two elements must result.

Examination of the vapor-pressure curves for the elements shows that pressure of rubidium is more than 10^7 and up to 10^8 times that of strontium at a temperature of the lunar surface reached during the long lunar day ($+150°$ C), and the vapor of rubidium at this temperature reaches a value of .01 Torr; the inevitable result would be for a substantial amount of rubidium to vaporize and migrate freely. Even if the rubidium were to be chemically combined in the form of less volatile compounds, the constant bombardment of the surface by hydrogen ions in the solar wind would reduce the compounds to free the metallic rubidium.

The metal vapor would tend to migrate to locations of lower temperature, where it would recondense unless it were to achieve sufficient thermal energy to reach velocity and leave the lunar scene completely. Recondensed rubidium might be found concentrated in clefts of shadowed areas, and there might be a systematic gradient in concentration with significant enrichment in the polar regions and accompanying depletion in the equatorial regions.

Strontium, having a vapor pressure more than ten million times lower than that of rubidium, would be far less affected by this mechanism. The result might be that the estimate of age based on the ratio of these elements would be strongly affected by their local origin on the lunar surface. Vapor migration is a mechanism that may cast doubt on the elemental ratio dating, at least when pairs with widely different volatility are employed.

MAGNETIC REMANENCE IN LUNAR ROCKS

Robert Treash

Prior to the first Apollo Moon landing, July 21, 1969, Dr. Immanuel Velikovsky on three occasions successfully predicted the scientifically unexpected—that remanent magnetism would be discovered in the lunar rocks. Outlining his ideas in a memorandum submitted to H. H.

Hess, Chairman of the Space Science Board, National Academy of Sciences, on May 19, 1969, Velikovsky wrote:

"The moon was repeatedly heated and its entire surface melted less than thirty-five and twenty-seven centuries ago. At the times the Moon's surface was molten in near approaches with other celestial bodies, it was enveloped in powerful magnetic fields; if the surface cooled below the Curie point before the magnetic fields were weakened and removed, then it is to be expected that lavas on the Moon (most of its rocks are lava) still possess a high magnetic remanence."

Again, on July 2, 1969, Velikovsky wrote to H. H. Hess, Guyot Hall, Princeton University: "When I maintain (see the way I expressed myself in my memo) that the rocks on the Moon may be magnetic though the Moon possesses hardly any magnetic field of its own, I suggest something that is not expected. I have urgently advised—and I repeat it here—that the orientation of the rocks before their removal should be noticed and marked. . . . You said to me that this simple task of marking the orientation is *not* included in the program; if it will be omitted, you will have a question instead of an answer."

Again, on July 21, 1969, on the eve of man's first landing on the Moon, Velikovsky wrote in the New York *Times* early, City Edition: "The moon has a very weak magnetic field; yet its rocks and lavas could conceivably be rich in remanent magnetism resulting from strong currents when in the embrace of exogenous magnetic fields.

"Before their removal from the ground, the specimens should be marked as to their orientation *in situ*. . . . This simple performance, I was told, is not in the program of the first landing."

On September 19, 1969, confirmation of this prediction was published: "Natural remanent magnetization has been found in the crystalline rocks and breccias . . . the result of processes not yet understood" (1).

After the discovery of remanent magnetism in the rocks brought by Apollo 11 astronauts, it was ruefully stated in a NASA relsease that "there was no attempt, in Apollo

11, to document individual samples photographically" (2).

NASA also announced that the prime task of the next, Apollo 12 mission would be to register the orientation of the rocks before their removal by photographing them while on the ground. (Apollo flights cost a few billion dollars each.)

The remanent (or "fossil") magnetism of the lunar surface was confirmed on the rocks brought back from the sites of all subsequent Apollo missions.

"The magnetic people immediately started to look for magnetic effects on the moon. The idea of the magnetic effect in the lunar samples occurred to everybody."

> *Dr. Harold C. Urey, in a letter (October 4, 1971) to Dr. D. Carlyle disputing the significance of Velikovsky's prediction that remanent magnetism would be found in lunar rocks.*

"When we received the Apollo landing sample, as with the other groups who had been studying the magnetic properties, we were all surprised to find remanent magnetization."

> *Dr. S. K. Runcorn, in a speech (December 29, 1971) to an AAAS gathering. Urey, who was present at the meeting, offered no challenge to the statement.*

"The Apollo XVI astronauts will return a moon rock to the lunar surface next month to prove that the moon has its own magnetic field. . . . The discovery of a magnetic field on the moon has been one of the biggest surprises of the Apollo program. . . . These findings did as much as anything to upset prevailing theories about the origin and formation of the moon, especially the theories that held that the moon has always been cold and lifeless. The discovery of fossil magnetism in the moon rocks tells scientists that the moon once was hot. . . ."

> *Los Angeles Times (March 5, 1972).*

Scientific deliberations grew in intensity after the third (Apollo 14) and the fourth (Apollo 15) missions testified to the bewilderment among astrophysicists. It transpired that sometime in the past the Moon must have been heated in the presence of a strong magnetic field. The best guess was: "It is a thermoremanent magnetism acquired when the specimen cooled in the presence of a magnetic field." Other possibilities were weighed (3). Was the inducing field due to a close approach of the Moon to the Earth? "In this model the hard remanence suggests a distance of closest approach of 2 to 3 earth radii." But this is "an uncomfortable proximity to the Roche limit . . ." (4). The Moon would have been broken into pieces if it ever approached the Earth so closely. Another team of scientists found that the magnetization "shows a well defined Curie temperature at 775° C" (5): the lunar surface must have been heated above this temperature in the presence of a magnetic field and must have cooled off thereafter (To melt the rock, a temperature over 1200° C is needed.)

Hess died on August 25, 1969, barely five weeks after the Apollo 11 flight, leaving vacant his position as chairman of the Space Science Board of the National Academy of Sciences. With him passed the only prominent geophysicist who demanded a hearing for Velikovsky's proposals. Twelve years earlier, on the eve of the International Geophysical Year, he wrote to Velikovsky (January 2, 1957): "Scientific discoveries and ideas are produced by the intuition, creativeness and genius of a man. Dollars of themselves don't produce this any more than they could be expected to produce another Mona Lisa. This is something which I believe you can readily understand."

MISEDUCATED GENERATION

Twenty years of systematic barring of Velikovsky from publishing in the scientific journals has left its cruel mark, primarily on those scientists and their following public whose silence and incomprehension indicates a helpless ignorance in dealing with certain larger problems. During a score of years spent climbing to academic and professional success, constantly bombarded by harsh, anti-Velikovsky words, a whole generation has grown up miseducated by the very scientific educators themselves, with notably few exceptions.

I have witnessed at least four local events bearing this fact out. In an interview in a local magazine (6), Dr. Harald Urey, Nobel prizewinning chemist and "cold-moon"-ologist, took advantage of his platform by interjecting an irrelevant jab at Velikovsky: ". . . the mass of material we get is so consistent that no one fails to recognize that it is true except crazy folks. There are always fringe people—people who still talk about a flat Earth. And there are men in science like Emanuel [sic] Velikovsky, author of *Worlds in Collision,* who can toss out all the excellent work of centuries and assume that Venus moves in some curious and funny orbit that suits him."

Like most scientists, Urey here assumes what he must prove, namely, that the orbit of Venus (a highly atypical planet) has always been as stable as at present. Investigation will indicate, however, that Velikovsky's supposed "curious and funny orbit" of Venus is not his own fantasizing but the verdict based on the surviving documents from all ancient civilizations, too many to enumerate here: ancient Rome's most celebrated man of science, Varro, wrote of what happened at an earlier age: "To the brilliant star Venus . . . there occurred so strange a prodigy, that it changed its color, size, form, course, which never happened before nor since" (7). Velikovsky's "crime" has been precisely not to "toss out all the excellent work of centuries." Instead, he has preserved and sifted and explained the thoughts of great men since antiquity, retaining also from early religious and mythical traditions those scientific facts which are now so needed and usable.

How could he have *successfully* predicted remanent magnetism on the Moon if he had discarded the sound evidence that Venus drastically shattered the old Earth-Moon system in historical times, as witnessed by all the Earth's survivors?

Again, on January 25, 1971, I attended a meeting at UCSD at La Jolla to hear a report by famous scientists just back from the Houston 2nd Lunar Science Conference. Urey, Hannes Alfvén (Nobel-prizewinning astro-physicist), cosmo-chemist J. R. Arnold, English geophysicist S. K. Runcorn, and other professors and students listened to Professor G. Arrhenius, one of the principal investigators of the Moon rocks, reporting on the Houston deliberations. His report was followed by a discussion among these luminaries.

Arrhenius reported the baffling new discovery that the Moon had apparently at one time entered an ancient magnetic field, from which it had picked up a remanent magnetism. At Houston no general agreement as to the source of this astounding remanent magnetism could be reached. Five theories had been put forth: 1) shock from meteorite impact; 2) solar or galactic magnetic field; 3) solar flare; 4) internal Moon magnetic field; 5) Earth's magnetic field.

Each of these theories was outlined and discussed, ending with no agreement. A gloomy attitude prevailed that more evidence is needed. At one point, someone from the floor asked how much remanent magnetism (RM) the Moon was thought to have had prior to Apollo. The answer was none at all, or extremely little. No one disputed the fact that previous theory had provided no clue. No one disputed the stated assumption that the RM had been acquired, astronomically speaking, very early.

ENORMOUS BURDEN OF DOUBT

Again, on November 10, 1971, I attended a Physics Colloquium at UCSD where Urey reviewed "Evidence Relating to the Origin of the Moon." He opened with the statement: "I do not know the origin of the moon, I'm not sure of my own or any other's models, I'd lay odds against any of the models proposed being correct." The impression thereafter was that an enormous burden of doubt obviously underlies the thinking of all these scientists. (I recalled hearing J. R. Arnold refer ironically and modestly to the earlier certitude with which he himself used to make speeches only a few years ago.) Urey made no reference to RM but did manage to state that his own well-known, long-time thesis of a cold Moon "proved not to be true."

Yet when the Physical Sciences Division of *Cosmos and Chronos* (initiated in 1965 by Hess) published a bulletin, "Lunar Probes and Velikovsky's Advance Claims," Urey wrote a letter of depreciation to each of the sponsoring groups at three universities in Texas. He claimed that everyone expected what was later discovered on the moon, remanent magnetism included. Yet, soon thereafter, in the last week of December 1971, Runcorn spoke at the annual meeting of AAAS and stated that nobody in the scientific world anticipated remanent magnetism on the moon. Urey, in the audience, kept silent.

Finally, on January 24, 1972, I heard Prof. Arrhenius report again, this time on the recently concluded Houston 3rd Lunar Science Conference. The principal new point concerning RM was that magnetic concentrations (magcons) exist within the impacted meteorite mascons (mass concentrations) below the surface. Urey thinks many such have soft-landed on the Moon, preserving their magnetism, thereby throwing off existing RM figures. Alfvén claims magcons vaporize on hitting the surface at high speeds. (Otherwise, this meeting was enlivened by a running dispute between Urey and Alfvén/Arrhenius, the former leaving the room finally, protesting: "No use trying to discuss this subject if you call in miracles." Alfvén countered: "It's regrettable if people take part in a discussion completely ignorant of six papers [on the subject].")

SCHOLASTIC FARCE

Now it is planned in all earnest to send a lunar rock back to the Moon with Apollo 16 to exclude the possibility that somehow it acquired its remanent magnetism on its voyage to the Earth.

What can one make of these events adduced as illustrative symptoms from the heart of science? The following points seem obvious to me:

1. In spite of the crying need for "more evidence" to account for the Moon's unsuspected RM, no scientist at La Jolla (and presumably Houston) has ever listed, much less discussed, Velikovsky's *successful* prediction as a possible clue.

2. Whatever the cause of this default (ignorance, forgetfulness, willful spite, etc.), it must be adjudged as reckless incompetence.

3. High incompetence in scientific strategy (great technical competence being granted) denotes a dangerous departure from reality, making further errors highly likely and very costly. One or more Apollo missions could have been spared were Velikovsky's books and memoranda considered.

4. Immense theoretical and practical labors to make credible some "proof of the Moon's origin" hidden in swirling gases for billions of years are a scholastic farce *in a context* where science refuses to recognize or even consider the drastic upheavals involving both Earth and Moon within the historical memory of man.

5. To reap the full benefits of the space program, the shutout of Velikovsky's views from scientific discussion must be ended.

6. The American taxpaying public will, if given the chance, support the space program better when it is presented as a means of learning about humanity's past experience with disasters involving Earth, Moon, Venus, and Mars. Perhaps only through such enlightenment can mankind rise to the intellectual and emotional levels needed for continued progress into the space age.

REFERENCES

1. Lunar Sample Preliminary Examination Team (LSPET), *Science,* September 19, 1969.
2. Release by Sutton and Shafer of the U. S. Geological Survey.
3. D. W. Strangway *et al., Science, 167* (January 30, 1970), 691.
4. P. Dyal *et al., Science, 169* (August 21, 1970), 762.
5. R. R. Doell *et al., Science, 167* (1970), 695.
6. M. H. Hall, "Harold Urey on the Moon," *San Diego Magazine,* August 1969, p. 69.
7. I. Velikovsky, *Worlds in Collision* (Garden City, N.Y.: Doubleday & Company, 1950), 158.

IS VENUS' HEAT DECREASING?*

Immanuel Velikovsky

Not quite six years ago, on a summer day in 1966, I had an unannounced visit by two young men, in their teens. They brought me the news that I was selected the first honorary member of the Celestial Observer Society, composed of high school and college amateur astronomer-observers of New York City, with quarters at the Brooklyn Technological Institute. The society publishes a mimeographed monthly magazine. The two delegates made their way from Brooklyn to Princeton, New Jersey, on bicycles—a distance of sixty miles. It was my first (and still my only)† honorary distinction; I reciprocated by publishing in the December 1966 issue of Celestial Observer *the paper reprinted here.*

The purpose of this paper is to suggest repeated measurements of the infrared radiation emitted by the cloud surface of Venus. It is expected by the author of this communication that a slow drop in the temperature will be detected; it is suggested that the measurements should be made at synodical intervals. It should be possible to determine the phenomenon in about five synodical periods of Venus, or eight terrestrial years at the most. The measurements need to be taken of the night and day sides of the planetary envelope and also of the terminator.

The basis for this expected detection is in my maintaining that Venus is a newcomer to the solar system

---

* Copyright 1966 by Immanuel Velikovsky
† In 1974 Velikovsky received an honorary doctorate from the University of Lethbridge, Alberta. *Editor.*

(which is what the Romans also intended to indicate by giving it its name). I argued (*Worlds in Collision,* 1950) that, under its massive envelope, Venus, with a short but stormy history, must be very hot, even incandescent, owing to the presence of natal heat and to the disturbance in motion with "a thermal effect caused by conversion of momentum into heat" (*Worlds in Collision,* p. 371). I made this statement when Venus was thought, due to the strong, reflecting power of its clouds, to have a ground-surface temperature of only a little above that of the Earth.

I offer the new proposition as another crucial test of my theory. Since "Venus gives off heat" (*Worlds in Collision,* p. 371), the drop in the temperature of the ground surface must be reflected in a smaller drop in the temperature of the cloud surface. In the 1920s, E. Pettit and S. B. Nicholson measured the cloud-surface temperature and obtained ca. $-25°$ C for both sides, illuminated and shadowed, which seemed paradoxical. But almost thirty years later they recalculated their original finds and gave $-38°$ C for the day side and $-33°$ C for the night side, which is even more paradoxical (1). In the 19mm wavelength, Mariner 2 also found that the ground surface is warmer on the night side, but hottest on the terminator (2).

In 1956, Strong and Sinton made known their measurements (1953–54) of the cloud surface of Venus, indicating "approximately $40°$ C." on both sides of the planet, but found a gradient of $5°$, which they ascribed to the heating effect of the sun, on the assumption that Venus rotates directly (3), but since it rotates retrogradely, the phenomenon is again in conformity with the Pettit-Nicholson observations.

Bolometric measurements can be made to detect even a small fraction of a degree centigrade. Were it possible to take the Pettit-Nicholson and the Strong-Sinton figures as a basis for comparison, the drop of circa $1°$ C per eight years would already be attested. But in view of the implications of the test, also for the cosmology of the solar system, an exact series of measurements needs to be organized, possible by more than one team of observers. If Venus has revolved on its orbit for billions of years, there should be no measurable drop in the temperature of the planet that could be detected from its cloud surface. But if Venus' history is measured in thousands of years only, there will be found a detectable drop in the temperature from the top of the cloud envelope.

REFERENCES

Thus, I maintained that should subsequent measurements show a falling of the cloud-surface temperature, if only in fractions of degree per year, it would reflect a substantial loss of heat at the ground surface of the planet and thus document its youth. I repeated this claim in *Yale Scientific Magazine, 41* (April 1967).

In the July 1968 issue of the *Journal of Atmospheric Sciences,* Gillett, Low, and Stein published a short paper ("Absolute Spectrum of Venus from 2.8 to 14 Microns"). They obtained a definitely lower figure for the cloud-surface temperature than had Sinton and Strong eight years earlier. Gillett and his co-workers wrote: "The reasons for the disagreement are not understood at present."

1. E. Pettit, *Astronomical Society of the Pacific, 67* (1955), 293ff.
2. F. T. Bareth *et al.,* "Microwave Radiometers in Mariner 2 Preliminary Report," *Science, 139* (March 8, 1963).
3. J. Strong and W. S. Sinton, *Science, 123* (April 20, 1956), 676.

PART VI

The debate over Velikovsky and his work goes on in every field of science or scholarship touched by his thesis, and it is likely to continue so for years to come. But Professor William Mullen, in his essay "The Center Holds," reminds us that it is not too soon to look beyond the debate. "Some corner of the mind has to be reserved in which one can act as though the struggle has been won and begin surveying the new domain."

When this paper was written, Dr. Mullen taught in the departments of classics and comparative literature and in the division of interdisciplinary general studies at the University of California at Berkeley. He left Berkeley to spend a year at Princeton University working on a new translation of the ancient Egyptian Pyramid Text of Unas. At present, he is a member of the classics-department faculty at Boston University.

THE CENTER HOLDS

William Mullen

During any revolution, it is wise to keep thinking ahead to the new order that will emerge once victory is secure. Velikovsky's work may well catalyze a scientific revolution for which not even the familiar cases—Copernicus, Newton, Darwin—are adequate precedents. His reconstruction of the history of the solar system will not be accepted widely unless articulate readers who have found it sound persist in demanding objective consideration from the scientific community. Yet it would be wrong for them to devote energy exclusively to debating. Some corner of the mind has to be reserved in which one can act as though the struggle has been won and begin surveying the new domain. There is a growing literature on the phenomenon of Velikovsky's rejection and on the ceaseless confirmations of his advance claims, but the body of work which simply assumes him correct and proceeds to further research is still insignificant.

Velikovsky himself has been aware that research is not best carried forward amid vituperative debate. He has followed his numerous confirmations closely and at all times been open to debate scientifically conducted, but most of his energy has gone to further study, lucid and patient. Like Confucius, he eschews rancor, preferring to extend his knowledge of particulars. Over twenty years ago, in the epilogue to *Worlds in Collision,* he succinctly surveyed the major problems still unsolved. I would like here to elaborate a little on them in each of the disciplines he takes up.

These disciplines can be seen as a spectrum of which physics and history form the extremes, the one dealing with general laws for living and non-living phenomena alike, the other with specific records left by the most complex single form of life, man. It is not surprising that, in 1950, physicists felt absolved from considering Velikovsky's historical evidence, because it contradicted their "known laws." He foresaw conflict from the beginning, and in the original preface defended his procedure explicitly: "If, occasionally, historical evidence does not square with formulated laws, it should be remembered that a law is but a deduction from experience and experiment, and therefore laws must conform with historical facts, not facts with laws" (1).

Methodologically, this is unassailable. Still, tactically speaking, sooner or later it is necessary to meet the physicists on their own ground. From the historical facts established in *Worlds in Collision*, more-adequate physical laws still wait to be formulated in detail. The specific laws the book was thought to contradict are those of the celestial mechanics which assumes the solar system to be electrically sterile and on that assumption successfully calculates planetary positions. It should be well known that, since the early fifties, radiology and space probes have rendered such an assumption false many times over. However, the accusation is still heard that if Velikovsky dethrones Laplacian celestial mechanics, he must offer something better in its place; until then, he has not approached the problem "quantitatively" and therefore physicists are still absolved from considering it. The less generous among them even assume that he was not aware of the problems involved.

It is not so well known that in his correspondence and discussions with Einstein, which grew in complexity till the latter's death in 1955, the relationship between electromagnetic and gravitational forces was the principal subject. That was only as it should have been, since Einstein's own work in his last years was toward a unified field theory explaining the two orders of phenomena in common terms. It makes sense that Einstein should have chosen this undertaking, since, if successful, it would have satisfied in the highest degree the requisite of generality which makes any scientific theory valuable. He was involved in a search for first principles. As he once put it himself, "The idea that there are two structures of space independent of each other, the metric-gravitational and the electromagnetic, is intolerable to the theoretical spirit" (2). Is it fair that a synthesis which Einstein after decades of work was not able to conclude satisfactorily be demanded of Velikovsky before his evidence from other disciplines is even considered? The space probes have only shown that a more comprehensive celestial mechanics, based on a physics in which electromagnetism and gravitation are explained by common laws, would have been necessary even if Velikovsky had never raised the issue. It should also be obvious that if gravitation can in fact be cogently described in terms of some more-fundamental forces, this does not mean that Newtonian physics need be "thrown out"; Velikovsky never suggested that it should be.

What remains is a major task. It is to carry forward study of celestial mechanics to the point where the behavior of a magnetized solar system in hypothetical catastrophic conditions can be quantitatively described. Only then will the possibility of the actual behavior Velikovsky reconstructs seem to physicists a subject verifiable by their own discipline. Obviously, specific paths of the planets in catastrophic events of the past can never be calculated with the same precision that their present stability allows. Such precision would in any case be pointless. But a very satisfactory proof of the physical possibility of such events can be made through approximation. Assume certain masses, charges, and paths for certain planets such that they cannot help disturbing each other's motions, then calculate in precisely what ways these motions would be disturbed. If the same effects which Velikovsky presents descriptively can be deduced to many decimal places, then the exact science of physics will be contributing its share. And in so doing it will be impelled to broaden its theoretical understanding of a problem which Einstein singled out as crucial, the co-operation of electromagnetism and gravitation in the same domain.

GEOLOGY

The second relevant discipline dealing with inorganic materials is geology. Velikovsky considered its problems the most imperative and turned to them after finishing *Worlds in Collision. Earth in Upheaval* has left no doubt that the house of geology needs to be rebuilt from the cellar up. At no point, however, does this book claim to be a textbook—it only collates a certain kind of evidence as proof that certain events occurred. In fact, it devotes only limited space to chronology of catastrophes described in *Worlds in Collision;* much of the material is meant only as decisive evidence for catastrophism in general. The geologists therefore are left with the enormous labor of distinguishing, to the limited extent possible, among effects of a series of catastrophes extending indefinitely back in time. No longer free to appeal to the uniformitarian notion that the record is incomplete, they will have to pay more serious attention to the fact that alterations between strata are abrupt.

It is, of course, impossible to reconstruct celestial events from the geological record alone. Confronted with evidence from times before the memory of man, the geologist can only describe the nature of the change the Earth underwent. Nevertheless, his position is unique, because no other discipline has any access at all to these earlier catastrophes. Celestial mechanics can go only a very little way back through approximate retrograde calculations, while human mythology and history obviously cannot be expected to contain accounts of events in prehuman times. The geologist, left with a framework of epochs (Cretaceous, Jurassic, Triassic, etc.) which has been given new meaning, will have the last word. However, it must be added that this last word has no chance of making sense in his current terminology. *Earth in Upheaval* exposes a number of terms as simply *ad hoc* inventions to describe phenomena they do not explain.

"Erratics," "moraine," "till," "upthrust," "faulting," "vulcanism," "igneous," "sedimentary," not to mention "ice ages"—these and many other terms will be useful to a revised geology only if their present associations are purged away.

PALEONTOLOGY AND BIOLOGY

Inseparable from the geological record is the paleontological and biological. This touches a part of Velikovsky's work which can legitimately be called a theory—that of catastrophic mutation. The bulk of his effort has been toward a reconstruction of specific events, while the term "theory" is better applied to a general account (verifiable by experimentation). Darwinian evolution lays claim to the status of a theory not because it can be experimentally verified, but only because it claims that processes that occurred in the past are also occurring unnoticeably in the present. Velikovsky's theory of mutations on the other hand, is supported by experiments already performed (cf. Muller's subjection of vinegar flies to X rays) (3). Here, future possibilities are endless. It is even a bit frightening to speculate how techniques of inducing mutation might be sophisticated through experiments. From the point of view of historical reconstruction, however, knowledge thus gained will be invaluable. Like the geologist, the biologist will have to face more seriously the fact that, between strata, many new species appear abruptly. His task is to devise laws of mutation refined enough to explain how a given species came from one preceding it and why it took the form it did. The early-nineteenth-century evolutionist Etienne Geoffroy Saint-Hilaire speculated that birds might have been generated directly from fish through sudden mutation in catastrophic circumstances, but he was not prepared to explain the mechanics.

A second large subject for biological experimentation is the old Lamarckian theory of inheritance of acquired characteristics. It has never been decisively disproved. If anything, increased experimental sophistication has only revealed greater complexity in genetic structures, leaving the possibility of the subtlest kinds of transmission wide open. Inheritance of behavior patterns laid down in catastrophic circumstances might explain a number of biological enigmas: bird migration; swarming; acute sensitivity of many species to the subtlest earth tremors, solar eclipses, etc. The inheritance of memory has already been suggested by experiments on rats and worms.

PSYCHOLOGY

Here, without any perceptible break between disciplines, one touches a major premise of Velikovsky's psychology, barely adumbrated in the epilogue to *Worlds in Collision*. Referring to Freud's idea of an archaic heritage of traumatic memories transmitted from generation to generation, and also to Jung's concept of a collective unconscious, he wrote: "In the light of these theories, we may well wonder to what extent the terrifying experiences of world catastrophes have become part of the human soul and how much, if any, of it can be traced in our beliefs, emotions, and behavior as directed from the unconscious or subconscious strata of the mind" (4). If biological experimentation offers concrete proof that instincts acquired under catastrophic circumstances might be transmitted genetically, then the whole psychology implicit in this sentence is objectively grounded. Whatever their accounts of the content of the unconscious, Freud and Jung agreed that one of its principal compulsions was to act out what has been repressed. If the collective unconscious of man contains memory of catastrophic experiences which his collective consciousness represses, then in a sense he may be doomed to act those experiences out. Many irrational rituals—war and religion chief among them—would thus be grimly explained. Resistance to such an etiology will naturally be intense. The more comprehensively a theory relates past events to present behavior the more readily is it denounced as deterministic. There are already enough schools of psychology at each other's throats, and none more beleaguered than Freudians who hold to an original orthodoxy or Jungians who champion their apostate.

But this is not the place either to expound or defend Velikovsky's psychological hypotheses. I wish only to make two points about them. First, his deductions are less problematical than those of his predecessors, because his first principles are not in themselves psychological: he does not have to fabricate a primal psychic complex, like Freud's father-murder, nor an innate psychic content, like Jung's archetypes. His psychology accepts data objectively established by other disciplines. At most, he borrows a psychological mechanism, the so-called "repetition-compulsion," and any theory explaining wars will hardly be able to deny that, for whatever reason, they are being compulsively repeated. Second, if these hypotheses contain any correctness at all, then they constitute the most urgent aspect of his work. There is a paradox here: before one can accept his diagnosis, one must be satisfied with his conclusions in all the other disciplines, but none of these others claim nearly the same immediacy to our present situation. One cannot resolve this paradox, one can only seek a mean. Velikovsky himself, in recent lectures, has often given the psychological aspect prominence and has mentioned that it is the subject of a separate, as yet unfinished, book.

MYTHOLOGY

Psychology studies a specific realm of organic behavior —man's—in its least rational manifestation. The subject closest to it might well be mythology, one of man's earliest manifestations of a rational impulse. As Hermann Broch wrote, "Myth is the archetype of every phenomenal cognition of which the human mind is capable" (5). The popularity of Lévi-Strauss's structuralist school indicates the respect accorded nowadays to primitive thinking. Followers of Velikovsky need have no quarrel with the structuralists. Their approaches are complementary and await synthesis. Lévi-Strauss has shown that the logic of many myths is as rigorous as that of science; Velikovsky, that the subjects of many myths are as real as those of science. Their subjects are events, and "the event is the unit of things real" (Whitehead). Primitive cultures grow enormously in stature once it is realized that the bizarre cosmological myths central to their traditions in fact describe the major events in the history of the earth. And they do more than describe; in their own way, they attempt to explain and master what would otherwise have paralyzed by its terror. Isak Dinesen remarked that there is no event too terrible to bear so long as men can make a story about it (6).

But just as *Earth in Upheaval* does not set out to be a geology textbook, so *Worlds in Collision* is not concerned to analyze the mechanisms of mythmaking or systematically describe any particular body of myths. These enterprises remain. Anyone who has ever entered the labyrinth of an archaic culture's mythical compendia (the Pyramid Texts, the Vedas, the *Theogony*) can testify to a desperate suspicion that there is no thread of objective reality. Velikovsky has provided the common thread; it remains for the labyrinths to be explored one by one. This not just for the sake of completeness. Only when we have grasped relations of the specifically catastrophic to the rest of a given culture's myths can we appreciate its full intellectual and ethical achievement. (Velikovsky's remarks on the emergence of Judaic monotheism are a case in point) (7). And only someone who has grasped the unity of mythical thought in a number of cultures will be in a position to formulate general laws for its mechanisms. Of course, such synthetic efforts have been made already, ever since classical times. What is extraordinary is that never, before Velikovsky, have so many disciplines been united to illuminate those major events which myths were first to describe.

HISTORY

The final discipline dealt with in the epilogue to *Worlds in Collision* is history. Velikovsky has described himself as a psychiatrist by vocation and a historian by avocation. It might be added that, if any single disciplinary method took precedence in the researching of *Worlds in Collision,* it was the historical. There is a certain logic in the fact that, of all the problems mentioned in the epilogue, Velikovsky has himself given the most energy to revising ancient chronology: the first volume of *Ages in Chaos* appeared shortly after *Worlds in Collision,* and several more are now in preparation. Insofar as his task there has been to align records left by the ancients, he has been engaged in an activity, historiography, which is in itself a mode of behavior—organic, human, rational —that forms its own subject. While the conventional material out of which "history" is made—battles, usurpations, conquests—often show human behavior at its most irrational, the art of historiography, by contrast, is a highly civilized manifestation. And in *Ages in Chaos* the historiography of the ancients is always given first place as evidence by which to reconstruct the sequence of events.

Massive as it is, however, *Ages in Chaos* covers only one major area of the ancient world, stretching from the Middle East to the central Mediterranean, and has one, circumscribed purpose, to correct Egyptian chronology and all others based on it. Two assumptions from *Worlds in Collision* are taken as fundamental: first, that no chronology using retrograde calculations of the positions of heavenly bodies is reliable earlier than −687; second, that the principal clue for synchronizing histories of ancient nations should be the breaks caused in all of them by catastrophic events. Both assumptions are equally valid for a number of other civilizations which *Ages in Chaos* does not touch, China and India chief among them. Of these, China has the more developed historiography, with a list of dynasties, kings, and hypothetical dates reaching roughly as far back as the Egyptian. Like the Egyptian, some of the more ancient dates have been arrived at through retrograde calculations of the position of constellations (cf. the Canon of Yao in the *Shu King*) (8) and are therefore baseless. Many later dates, on the other hand, synchronize to the day with biblical and Egyptian records, and there is no single ancient document which dates each episode in the most recent series of catastrophes more meticulously than the *Spring and Autumn Annals,* beginning with the year −776. Again like the Egyptian, Chinese remote antiquity is divided into three major phases, the Hsia, Shang, and Chou dynasties. Whether the breaks between them are in each case to be co-ordinated with global catastrophes is a problem which the stratigraphist and the historian should together be able to solve. India has no such detailed historiography, but the combination of myth and history in her epic and other literary traditions should yield richly to a similar effort. The total destruction of the Indus Valley civilization, in −1500, like that of the Middle Kingdom in Egypt, gives a firm starting point.

THE INTERDISCIPLINARY APPROACH

Having traversed the range of disciplines between physics and history, I would now like briefly to consider it as a whole. Just as all the colors in a spectrum united make a white light, so all the disciplines in science united make one mode of knowledge. Not the least effect of a Velikovskian revolution should be to make scientists unable to forget that certain problems can be solved only if data from the most widely divergent fields are considered together. Interdisciplinary research will have to be regarded not as a luxury, but as an essential. A case in point is the problem which Velikovsky sets first in his epilogue (9), that of the great catastrophe preceding those described in *Worlds in Collision* but still part of human memory, the Deluge. An ideal researcher trying to reconstruct this event would have to consult in detail both the latest findings of the space probes and the pyramid inscriptions of Old Kingdom Egypt. Obviously, not every young scientist should be educated toward multidisciplinary mastery. Nevertheless, certain options should be left open to a few. It would not be unthinkable to institute an interdisciplinary program in which an undergraduate would give four or more years to mastering rudiments of each of the disciplines I have dealt with—physics, geology, biology, psychology, mythology, history —and only at the graduate skills needed to research a specific problem related to catastrophism.

Inevitably, each will be tempted to plead that he cannot pass judgment on any novel thesis beyond his own field. This can lead to obscurantism but is tolerable so long as he is ready to admit that a solution to a problem within his own field might still be reached by someone working in other fields. The physicist or geologist must consider the possibility that an ancient myth or document might require a reconsideration of physical laws or geological doctrine; the anthropologist or historian must admit the importance of celestial mechanics or paleontology for his own discipline.

Ultimately, the interdisciplinary synthesis Velikovsky's work calls for should have more than academic reverberations. The better we comprehend how celestial mechanics and ancient mythology meet in the same nexus, the closer we come to bridging the abyss between material and spiritual realities. It is paradoxical that rediscovery of the facts of chaos in the solar system should lead to new principles of order for the human intellect. One must simply learn to look at the matter from two opposite points of view until they become the same. Awesome as catastrophic events may be, they remain subject to comprehensible laws. Comprehensible as their laws may be, the events of the past remain awesome. In the poet Rilke's words, "Beauty's only the beginning of terror we're still able to bear (10)." Such thoughts seem to lie at the center of man's earliest metaphysical speculations, and scientific revolutions may be only a means of returning to them.

REFERENCES

1. I. Velikovsky, *Worlds in Collision* (Garden City, N.Y.: Doubleday & Company, 1950), vii.
2. Cited by Lincoln Barnett, *The Universe and Dr. Einstein* (Time Inc., 1962; originally published by Wm. Sloane Assoc., 1948), 102.
3. I. Velikovsky, *Earth in Upheaval* (Garden City, N.Y.: Doubleday & Company, 1955), 253.
4. I. Velikovsky, *Worlds in Collision*, p. 383.
5. Hermann Broch, "The Style of the Mythical Age," introduction to Rachel Bespaloff's *On the Iliad* (New York: Harper Torchbook, 1962, originally published by the Bollingen Foundation, 1947), 15.
6. Cited by Hannah Arendt in *Between Past and Future* (New York: Viking Press, 1961), 262.

7. I. Velikovsky, *Worlds in Collision*, pp. 382–83.
8. *The Shu King*, trans. James Legge, *The Chinese Classics* (Hong Kong: Hong Kong University Press), p. 19; cf. I. Velikovsky, *Worlds in Collision*, p. 103.
9. I. Velikovsky, *Worlds in Collision*, pp. 381–82.
10. R. M. Rilke, *Duino Elegies* I, 4–5.

EDITORS' POSTSCRIPT

The papers collected in this volume are drawn from issues in *Pensée*'s series, Immanuel Velikovsky Reconsidered (IVR), as follows:

IVR-I, May 1972: "The Scientific Mafia," by David Stove; "The Censorship of Velikovsky's Interdisciplinary Synthesis," by Lynn E. Rose; "Shapley, Velikovsky, and the Scientific Spirit," by Horace M. Kallen; "On Decoding Hawkins' *Stonehenge Decoded*," by Immanuel Velikovsky; "How Stable Is the Solar System?" by C. J. Ransom; "Could Mars Have Been an Inner Planet?" by Lynn E. Rose; "The Orbits of Mars, Earth, and Venus," by Lynn E. Rose and Raymond C. Vaughan; "Venus' Circular Orbit," by Chris S. Sherrerd; "Are the Moon's Scars Only Three Thousand Years Old?" by Immanuel Velikovsky; "Lunar Rocks and Velikovsky's Claims," by Derek York; "When Was the Lunar Surface Last Molten?" by Immanuel Velikovsky; "Effects of Volatility on Rubidium-Strontium Dating," by Robert C. Wright; "Magnetic Remanence in Lunar Rocks," by Robert Treash; "Is Venus' Heat Decreasing?" by Immanuel Velikovsky; and "The Center Holds," by William Mullen.

IVR-II, Fall 1972: "H. H. Hess and My Memoranda," by Immanuel Velikovsky; and "Plasma in Interplanetary Space: Reconciling Celestial Mechanics and Velikovskian Catastrophism," by Ralph E. Juergens.

IVR-III, Winter 1973: "The Orientation of the Pyramids," by Immanuel Velikovsky; "Babylonian Observations of Venus," by Lynn E. Rose; "Earth Without a Moon," by Immanuel Velikovsky; "Giordano Bruno's View on the Earth Without a Moon," by A.M. Paterson;

and "The Orbits of Venus," by C. J. Ransom and L. H. Hoffee.

IVR-V, Fall 1973: "Gyroscopic Precession and Celestial Axis Displacement," by Chris S. Sherrerd.

IVR-VI, Winter 1973–74: "Venus Clouds: Test for Hydrocarbons," by William T. Plummer; "Venus and Hydrocarbons," by Immanuel Velikovsky; "The Nature of the Cytherean Atmosphere," by Albert W. Burgstahler; and "Venus Atmosphere," by Immanuel Velikovsky.

IVR-VIII, Spring 1974: Letter from Peter R. Ballinger on the atmosphere of Venus.

IVR-VIII, Summer 1974: "Velikovsky and the Sequence of Planetary Orbits," by Lynn E. Rose and Raymond C. Vaughan.

INDEX